The Lion and the White Rose

Richard de

First published by White Boar Publishing Ltd 2007

Re-issued by White Boar Publishing Enterprises 2011

www.whiteboarpublishing.com

© Richard de Methley

Richard de Methley has asserted his right under the Copyright, Designs and Patents Act 1988 to be identified as the author of this book.

A CIP record for this book is available from the British Library.

ISBN 978-0-9557480-1-1

Cover design by Debbie Kelsey and Richard Lyne-Pirkis

Cover photograph of Bodiam castle by Anthony McCallum, WyrdLight.com

Prepared and Printed by

MPG Biddles Ltd, Kings Lynn, Norfolk. PE30 4LS. Tel : 01553.764728

www.mpg-biddles.co.uk

Dedication

This book is dedicated, not least, to Diana L-P in whose company I first wrote it, and who typed the original manuscript, Bless her! Since then it has gone through many transformations, been published once, November 2007, and has now been revised and reissued.

But also to Andrea Atkinson without whose persistence, kindness and constant, warm encouragement I would **never** have written the next three books, let alone have revised this one. She has been such a star in every way.

And another is Simon Carpenter, my 'Admiral Red-Pen'! He has read every single chapter, paragraph by paragraph; checked my Botany, Herbology, and my Medical skills and Anatomy. He is also a deep water sailor, and his advice on wind and sea was masterly. He has corrected my language and punctuation, suggested fantastic changes to the text where I had got myself in a dreadful muddle...and forced me to re-think and re-work many parts that he thought were simply not good enough! Just terrific!

Finally I could not have written these books without the amazing richness of the Google website: 'Nicky's Seeds'...and of the superb knowledge of Nicola herself who gave me terrific personal help with streamside plants and wayside flowers, especially with waterside plants around Narbonne in the 12th Century. Her help was just invaluable.

And the warmest of thanks also go to my Graphic Artist, Debbie Kelsey, whose support and encouragement has been enormous...who has done amazing 'things' with the cover, and with the fine photograph of Bodiam Castle by Anthony McCallum of WyrdLight.com.

Thank you all so much.

Richard de Methley: October 2011.

3

About the Author

Richard de Methley lives in Nailsworth with his ginger cat, Paddypus, and his Baby Clio, called 'Ruth'! He is named after the town of Methley in West Yorkshire where a branch of his family settled at the time of the Norman Conquest, and now follows in the footsteps of his cousin, Violet M. Methley, who was famous between the wars for her children's novels of Dragons, Vampires and the Supernatural.

He is a Medieval and Tudor Specialist of Worcester College, now the University of Worcester, has fought in armour on horse and foot alongside The Knights of Arkley; trained and flown hawks and falcons; is an expert on Castles, especially those in the Welsh Borders, and has been a teacher for forty years, fourteen of those as Head. He is also noted for his workshops on Creative Writing and his History Seminars on the Murder of Thomas Becket, the Hastings Campaign, the Wars of Edward Ist and the Fall of Wales.

He wears a cloak and carries a sword!

PART ONE: AND SO OUR STORY BEGINS.

Chapter 1...First Attack: Siege of Cahors, Henry II's Toulouse Campaign. July, 1159.

Daybreak...and the mists off the river were opaque, cloudlike, filling the dips and vales around it so the great city seemed to float upon them like some vast stone vessel on a sea of steam; its fortress towers and battlements rising up out of the mists wraithlike, ethereal, their sharp outlines etched black against the lightening sky, itself pale as a wild mallard's egg, just flushing pink and saffron with the dawn. And at that time of early morning beauty all was breathless, silent...until with a roar of fury a host of armoured men rushed howling out of the shrouded Western darkness towards the city ditch, and the peace of all was shattered.

Bridged at that point with huge stones, rubble and tight bundles of faggots, now topped with doors torn from house and stable by the King's sappers, cast over them that very night, the ditch was still a formidable defence, and as the first attackers reached it...they checked briefly, til urged on by the fierce shouts and curses of their officers they poured across in a wild torrent of steel and armoured leather.

And as the sun thrust its first spears of gold and crimson light across the eastern sky so, armed with sword, shield and gavelock, they reached the breach itself and hurled themselves onto the steep glacis of shattered masonry and coarse rubble that had spilled out of it like an avalanche. But swiftly as King Henry's men began to climb the huge pile of scree and scrambled ashlar that now reared up out of the mists before them, scrabbling on hands and knees for purchase...so did the defenders leap in a rage of towering defiance to meet their fierce assault.

In moments all order vanished as huge bales of burning straw were hurled down upon their heads, together with myriad pots of sulphur, pitch and oil, each with a faint trail that sullied the morning sky with a lattice of smoky vapours before bursting amongst the attackers in violent explosions and great gouts of oily smoke and flame. Many on whom they fell were swiftly encased in fire and rushed screaming off the glacis to plummet like flaming meteors to the great ditch below; others flung themselves to the ground wreathed in flames and writhed and howled and were consumed. And with the fire-pots came spears, arrows and sharp edged stones; great baulks of timber studded with nails and sharpened iron, and huge chunks of jagged masonry that shattered amongst the enemy host struggling on the glacis, to scatter a deadly hail of bitter shards that ripped into Henry's men and tore their flesh to shreds.

Yet still amidst the roiling smoke and flames, the flicker of arrows and the shrieks and screams of the wounded, the attackers continued to fight their way upwards towards the breach horizon beyond which the city lay open to their lusts. Baying and roaring out their challenge, faces twisted with wild rage and feral hatred they stormed upwards, their dead and wounded strewn in bloodied heaps behind them...until two thirds up that brutal slope their whole charge stalled, checked by an appalling obstacle that lay stretched out across the whole of their assault...

A great Chevaux de Frise.

A vast tree trunk into which a terrifying hedge of huge iron spikes had been hammered into three sides and then fiercely re-sharpened, together with a multitude of piercing glaives of steel, like mighty sword blades, each honed to a razor's edge, the whole monstrous thing lowered down the slope and held in place by ships' anchor chains. There was no way round it, the breach was too narrow; nor in that violent press was there any way of burrowing beneath it. The only way was over it, and in moments, as their officers and sergeants bawled abuse and encouragement at their men, it claimed the lives of hundreds more of King Henry's soldiers as they hurled themselves at it again and again in a frenzied effort to move it...or to make of their bodies a pathway over which their comrades could still make good their fierce attack. But those who did so were swiftly assailed by the defenders, who hacked and battered at them with every weapon in their armoury: thrusting them through with swords and spears in a violent spray of blood and torn intestines; or hooking them aside with gisarmes and bursting them apart with the axe blade on the reverse of every wicked bill, so that limbless, headless bodies soon littered the slope with crushed skulls, shattered bone and shredded tissue everywhere.

And always above them, in the smoke and screaming fury of that dreadful morning, with men being slain on every side by fire, rock and sharpened steel, the defenders were hallooed forwards and encouraged by the roaring voice of a single mighty warrior.

Tall and broad of stature, clad from head to toe in shimmering mail, his great fighting helm of shining steel masking his face, the man stood at the very top of the breach like a giant of old and shook his great sword in a rage of battle fury at the enemy toiling below him, while above his armoured head a vast curling green banner with a huge black Boar's Head, eyes, teeth and wicked tushes red as blood all deeply stitched upon it, snapped and shivered in the breeze. The Boar's Head erased Sable, armed Gules on a field Vert...the House Flag of the Lord Baron Sir Thibault de Brocas, known to all as 'The Cruel', Lord of Montauban, Narbonne and Gruissan whose enormous frame seemed to fill the breach, and whose spirit of contempt and hatred for his enemies drove the defenders onwards and finally forced King Henry's assault troops to a shameful, desperate retreat.

Terrified and demoralised, Henry Plantagenet's men fled away from the horrors of the breach and its appalling glacis, leaving hundreds of bodies scattered all across it, butchered, crushed, and burned, their blood drenching the stones on which they lay. And ever immoveable, the great Chevaux de Frise that had broken them, draped all over with a multitude of torn and rendered corpses, remained to mock their efforts. Mired in brains and offal it was as much a testimony to the courage of all those who had attacked there...as to the ferocious ingenuity of the Lord Baron de Brocas to deny them access to the great fortress city of Cahors.

As King Henry's attack force straggled back to their camp, dragging their wounded with them, so with a thumping crash and whistle, the three great trebuchets the King had built for his assault burst into action again. Their huge counterweights falling to bring their throwing arms sweeping upwards, each one the length and breadth of a mighty tree, the great slings at each end whipping over as they passed their apogee to hurl their three hundred pound stone balls high into the air to fall with an enormous, rending *crash*! onto the already broken walls of Cahors.

If the breach had been too narrow for that morning's attack...it would not be so in three day's time!

Chapter 2...*King Henry's siege camp, Cahors, after the failed attack.*

Sprawled in a vast tented city that stretched right across the Northern end of the great curving meander of the river Lot in which Cahors was securely nestled, as well as on the other side of the river, King Henry Plantagenet's great armed host was drawn from all over his new empire that stretched from Scotland to the Pyrenees and even to the great Circle Sea of the Mediterranean. Fighting men, priests, varlets, cooks and drudges; Kings, barons, knights and squires; butchers, bakers, candlestick makers; serving girls, camp followers, doxies and whores...all packed in together, the morning sky smirched by their cooking fires, vats and ovens, as well as by the dense twisting columns of smoke still boiling up from the failed attack that dawn.

The whole huge encampment hummed like a giant swarm of bees, punctured by the dink and clatter of field forges and by the sobbing howls and cries of the wounded, their screams ululating like the shrieks of peacocks through the smoky air, itself thick with the stench of blood and vomit from sick and wounded alike, and from the piles of dung from man and beast, soiled straw and rotting scraps that lay in great heaps everywhere.

Amidst which rose all the multitude of other scents that accompany a vast army stalled and waiting: sweat, horses, leather, cooking, hot steel, wine, beer and urine and the sickly perfume from the many night moths who flitted amongst the soldiery as they roistered, boozed and fornicated their time away. Reviews, inspections, foraging for food and booty...all had their part to play for the soldiers in King Henry's army that summer...as well as mounting horrifying attacks upon their enemies within the great fortress city that blocked the army's route towards Toulouse, and which King Henry Plantagenet of England had sworn to capture.

★

With a grunt of rage Sir Yvo de Malwood stumped into his tent and hurled his helmet from him in disgust so that it bounced off his camp bed and clattered into a far corner amongst a pile of spare armour, sending his Squire, young Jonathan Romsey, leaping off to rescue it.

"Bad day then, My Lord?"

"God's Throat, it was a bloody shambles, Jonathan!" The burly knight swore as he lifted his heavy mail hood back onto his shoulders and fratched his sweaty head. "For God's sake, boy," he growled, thrusting his laden baldric into his hands. "Give me a drink. I need it!"

Of more than medium height, with black hair and piercing blue eyes, Sir Yvo de Malwood was a master in the saddle with sword, lance and battle axe: and a terror on the ground. At twenty five, just two years younger than the King himself, he had enormous upper body strength as you would expect of a man who had carried his harness for a dozen years in all weathers, and was a classic product of his age: a brutal fighter in a brutal time, yet mild mannered and courteous when at rest, and a born leader to all who fought under his banner of the Scarlet Lion Rampant.

To those who worked his lands around Castle Malwood in the old Conqueror's New Forest, or who served his family in any way, he was a good master, and his lands prospered under his hand. He was known to be firm but fair, with a voice that could be heard across a raging field of battle...when all around him knew it was time to jump, and jump quickly!... and he had a thumping fist to beware of. But he also had a kind heart, preferring to find good in people wherever possible, not evil. Yet God help those who mistook his kindness for weakness, because he could be ruthless where necessary or where his honour, or the safety of his people, was concerned - and he was a determined and pitiless enemy. Fiercely loyal to his King, Henry II, and to the whole Plantagenet family; he was the King's Leal man for the vast royal estates and messuages that made up the King's New Forest, and was well trusted by the King's Council, which was why he was now in southern Toulouse fighting for Henry II of England against King Louis VII of France, in this the first major war of Henry's reign.

Sweeping away all that stood in his path since the raising of a glittering host in Poitiers on Midsummer's Day, it was Henry's aim to seize control of Toulouse, the greatest county in the Kingdom of the Franks, promised to him through his marriage to Eleanor of Aquitaine his gorgeous, clever wife...yet denied him by King Louis, her former husband, and his allies And now that swift advance was stalled outside the great fortress city of Cahors due to the stupidity and ignorance of his Lord Chancellor's chief engineer who had declared the breach in its mighty walls practicable.

Only it needed a bigger breach to seize Cahors, than Vernaille's Trebuchets had so far provided. Not the fucking whore's crack Henry had sent them off to assault that very morning in a dawn attack! Sod de Vernaille and his bloody 'engines'! And sod the King who should have known better than to send brave men to face certain death in an assault on a breach he had left to his sodding engineers! So...*sod all fucking engineers as well!* And he hurled his sweat soaked woollen arming cap after his helmet.

9

"A complete, bloody shambles!" The big armoured knight swore again as he ripped off his mailed mittens, the blood off his arms running over his hands as he shook them steel-free at last, before seizing the silver-gilt goblet that his squire handed him and emptying it in a few huge swallows. "The bastards were waiting for us of course, but whoever told the King that de Vernaille's breach was practicable needs his fucking brains examining...and after this morning I feel just the man to do it too! Practicable? The thing was a bloody nightmare. Sodding engineers! Once let them in on a siege, young Jonathan, and you can be stuck outside for months!"

And holding out his large goblet for a refill of fine Bordeaux off a nearby chest, he kicked an innocent, unoffending wooden bucket with such sudden violence that it soared clear out of the tent making a distant camp varlet shout out in sudden alarm as it shattered into a dozen pieces on the rock-hard ground

"Clarence Wigmore, My Lord. One of the Lord Chancellor's men," his young squire replied, watching with a grin as the bucket soared past him.

"*What?*"

"Clarence Wigmore, Sir Yvo," he said again, laughing as the bucket crashed to the ground and burst into pieces making a servant carrying a tray of wine cups throw them all up in the air with a wild shout. "The Engineer who advises the Chancellor, Lord Thomas Becket, who advised the King. About the breach, My Lord," the young man added...still chuckling over the camp varlet now being furiously berated with shouts and curses by the men he had been about to serve...while steering Sir Yvo outside his tent so he could be completely disarmed without pools of blood and muck forming on the tent floor any longer. "The King did not examine the wall himself, My Lord. He trusted others to do that for him."

"So I gather, silly ass! Well he won't do that again, that's for certain! Despite this morning's fuck-up the King's no fool, but we lost hundreds up there this morning, Jonathan. Bloody hundreds, and not once did we get to the top. Have you seen Sir Henry?"

"Sir Henry de Burley, My lord?"

"Yes, Jonathan. My long suffering and well beloved friend, Sir Henry!"

"Yes, Sir Yvo. He was on his way to the horse lines with some carrots to see his charger, Alexander."

"*Carrots?* I swear he loves that bloody horse more than his latest lady-love! And 'Alexander'?..."

"Named after the Greek Emperor, My Lord."

"Yes, I know that, Jonathan," he answered swiftly, batting the lad's cheeky face at the same time. "But really! Here, boy. Give me a hand to pull off these damned boots," he said collapsing onto a stout wooden bench closeby. "They're killing me! And what about our Spanish Hidalgo, Don Mateo..."

"...de Silva de Pampalona from Navarre!" came a merry voice as a tall, black-haired man with deep brown eyes in a face with fine cheekbones and a high domed forehead, sauntered up. Lightly dressed in scarlet suede leather chausses, with a fine Egyptian cotton shirt, striped blue and green, open to the waist and soft purple leather half boots on his feet he was encumbered with neither armour nor his beloved twin swords that he nearly always carried strapped to his back, and paused with a look of mock horror at Sir Yvo.

Red-faced and sweating in gambeson and link mailed armour, off which blood was still dripping, Sir Yvo de Malwood was not a pretty sight. His long white cyclas with its great rearing scarlet lion armed in blue, was drenched in it and his chest was thick with the filth and human mucous of battle: torn flesh, brains, human faeces and shards of bone, that wrinkled the tall Spaniard's hawk-like nose as he sniffed at him disgustingly.

"My dear, Yvo!" he exclaimed in his soft musical Spanish lilt, eyes sparkling with sudden mischief, while he bent to flick stray gobs of flesh and hair off his friend's chest with long delicate fingers: "Whatever have you been doing? You look as if you have been...fighting?"

"Don't you start, Matthew!" The big knight growled, offering the man his campaign chair. "Some ignorant, fucking bastard of an engineer told Henry that de Vernaille's breach was practicable! One of Becket's men I gather from Jonathan, here: Clarence Wigmore. Fucking lunatic! Told Becket it was practicable, and Henry, trusting his Chancellor had got it right, ordered us to assault it at dawn."

"I heard you all go in! Not good, I see," he said indicating his friend's bloodied state and lack of good humour.

"No. Matthew. Not good, a huge Chevaux de Frise stopped us in our tracks. It was bloody Hell up there...we lost hundreds! And guess who was roaring down at us from the top of that cunt's crack of a breach? Our good and noble friend the Lord Baron Thibault de Brocas! That double dyed treacherous, lying bastard...and Sir Henry's vastly unloved Uncle. That man's family has been the bane of both mine and Henry's lives since they drove our ancestors out of France a hundred years ago. Before my father's grave I swore to have that bastard's head after the Malwood Emerald disappeared when Henry's mother died. She was that murderer's aunt, one of the most beautiful women of her age and a lovely lady too, the Lady Philippa, Henry's dear Mama: a bit

11

wild at times and quite capable of making old Ralf de Burley blench with her antics. But wholly different from her brother, Thibault, and Sir Ralf adored her.

So did Sir Alun, my own dear Papa as much as he adored old Ralf himself. Everyone loved the Lady Philippa, and so on their wedding day he gifted her our family's greatest heirloom, the Malwood Emerald. A magnificent jewel of great size and beauty, in an ancient and intricate golden setting that my ancestor, old Gui de Valance, had found when Castle Malwood was being built. Roman I always understood...but for her lifetime only! And when she died...it mysteriously disappeared! Vanished and has never been seen since. But that bastard up there had a hand in it, I swear. And when my father died four years ago, I swore on his grave that I would sort out de Brocas once and for all and restore the Malwood Emerald and our family's honour with it."

"I know the story, Yvo," the tall Spaniard said in his soft, lilting English. "Have heard it many times, my friend. But this time that man has finally overreached himself. When King Henry heard who had defended the breach so boldly, and what his men had suffered through Thibault's actions he has declared the man a proven traitor. Remember, Yvo, he holds his lands around Montauban under Henry's favour...Yes? He was supposed to be fighting for us, not against us...Yes? But all these lands are disputed, and King Louis promised Thibault the earth if he would defend Cahors for him and not surrender it to us as he was supposed to do. That's what I have come over to tell you...I had it from Chancellor Becket himself not half an hour ago. That Man-of-Blood and Treachery is doomed! So, my friend, let's get you out of this disgusting armour, washed and properly fed, and Henry and I can tell you what plans we have formed for dealing with the Chevaux de Frise that so halted your assault this morning.

Jonathan!" He shouted out to Sir Yvo's squire. "Come and give me a hand with this great lump of armoured humanity, then take his filthy clothes away and burn them. He cannot wear those again...they offend me! And then go swiftly and find Sir Henry de Burley. I last saw him near the horse-lines talking to that great beast of his he loves so well. Bring him to us here and tell my man, Hererra Alcazar, to join me here also and collect Sir Henry's young squire, Andrew Redlynch, as you return.

Once our fine Horatio here has bathed and changed, we will all eat here tonight, and you idle varlets can serve us as if we were all at home, and not out here in this appalling camp! Now, my friend," he laughed at Sir Yvo in his musical Spanish lilt. "Come on, on your feet my brave Caballero, and bend forward, and let Jonathan and me get all this stuff off you at last

Chapter 3...How the conquest of the breach was planned: Sir Yvo de Malwood's campaign tent.

That night, as the sun sank to its rest in a blaze of glory that filled the Western sky with great flotillas of scarlet and crimson cloud touched with amethyst amidst a shimmering sea of gold Sir Yvo, Don Mateo and Sir Henry de Burley sat at ease amidst the cheerful ruins of their alfresco supper. Laid outside their tent on stout trestles beneath spotless damask napery by their squires who had then served their knights as if they had indeed been at home. Small chickens barbecued on long wooden spits, collops of beef from a steer freshly slain for the men that morning; smoked meats and pickled vegetables, some in ginger, some in turmeric; crisp lettuce and scallions; butter, fresh fruit and wine drawn from their own supplies, with new baked bread from the field ovens set up by order of the King for all those serving with his field forces while on campaign...it had been a cheerful meal.

Sir Yvo and his companions mopped their mouths with their knee cloths, sighed with pleasure and sat back in their chairs, while their squires came round with steaming bowls of hot scented water for them to wash their hands, each youth with a clean towel over his arm on which his master could dry his wetted fingers. Meanwhile a handful of other varlets cleared the meal, brushing the fragments off the white tablecloth onto the ground before leaving the three knights to mull over the day with refreshed goblets of wine and small bowls of goats cheese and olives, beneath a cluster of flambeaux thrust into the ground beside them, their resin flames flickering and flaring in the warm night airs.

By then the moon had risen into a star dazed sky, her silver light casting long shadows across the vast encampment, still watchful, wakeful and alive with a multitude of flickering camp fires, the soft night breezes full of its noise and bustle: raucous bursts of laughter from the thousands of men bivouacked all about them, the ring of hammer on anvil, the stamp and whicker from horses and mules, the bray of a donkey, the scream from a girl, or from one of the many wounded, the cry of a child.

"So, Henry," Sir Yvo said at last, stretching his great shoulders as he spoke. "Tell me what you and Mateo have cooked up between you about that bastard tree trunk with all its spikes and blades. The thing is enormous, and deadly. It stopped the whole assault this morning. That and the fact that the breach was impossible anyway! We couldn't shift it; far too heavy for one thing and it was held in place by bloody great ships' anchor chains for another. I had thought that Vernaille's fresh bombardment might scupper it once and for all. But they were already drawing it up the glacis as we were scuttling back down it. So next time it will be back out there again sure as sure: maybe two of them if Vernaille's engines can bring down a really decent stretch of their curtain wall? To conquer that breach we have to be able to overcome those obstacles!"

Sir Henry de Burley, unlike his great friend, was not so heavily built, being both taller and more willowy, moving always with a grace that his bigger, more solid friend could not manage. But both men had the same great upper body strength needed to wield their weapons and hold their place in the battle line if required and, like Sir Yvo, Henry de Burley was a bruising rider. Always his charge hit an enemy like a thunderbolt, and his sword could split a man from crutch to navel, spilling his guts steaming onto the bloodied ground and then take his head off with the returning blow as sweetly as you could ever wish to see.

On his cyclas he wore a great red stag's head with golden antlers on an ermine background...Stag's Head erased Gules, attired d'Or on a field Ermine...in recognition of his own forest lands for Burley, like Malwood, was within the New Forest, though several miles apart, where their ancestors had settled on great estates gifted to them by the Conqueror. The first of all his knights to be so honoured, William had given them their lands the very night of that desperate battle for saving his life at the height of the fighting, when his horse had been gutted out beneath him and the whole of his Allied-Norman army believed he had been slain.

Since that moment, as much as from before, the two families had been inseparable. The sons of each doing all things together, as much 'Roland and Oliver' as it was possible for two great friends to be in their day and age, so it was that night that Yvo listened to all his friend had to say with real interest not just because he was his friend, but because Henry was by far the better strategist.

"Well, Yvo, the thing is a real bastard and no mistake. And we have to find a way to deal with it if we are to gain the city as the King wishes us to do. Firstly, we cannot move it while it is anchored. Secondly, you can't climb over it without being cut to pieces; your lot tried that this morning and it was hopeless. Thirdly, as for burrowing under it - forget it!"

"So?" Yvo asked sharply. "We know all that, Henry. Have you two come up with a solution?"

"Yes, Yvo, if you'd just be a little patient. God's Bones but you are impulsive! Just shut up and listen you blighter! Yes? Good! We have to do what the Romans used to do in these situations..."

14

"…The *Romans?*" Sir Yvo interrupted with a howl of derision, and a thump on the campaign table that made every thing jump about. "God's Blood, Henry! The fucking Romans?"

"Christos, Yvo. Now look what you've done, you great oaf! Bounced the bloody olives everywhere! You would test the patience of a saint!" he added as their squires leapt to sort things out. "Now! Please, will you shut up and listen?"

"I am sorry, Henry. Truly. But honestly, man. The Romans? Alright – Alright," he added swiftly holding up his hands to Henry's frustrated face. "I'll shut up and listen!"

"Right!" Sir Henry started again, giving his friend a fierce glare as he did so. "When faced with these situations the Romans used a battle formation called a 'Testudo'…a 'Tortoise'. They locked their shields over their heads, and all around them, so that enemy missiles just bounced off them and advanced forward into battle. As well as proving almost impossible to stop, under cover of the testudo all sorts of other tasks could be carried out with minimum casualties. Yes? Good.

Now, our lads are not trained Roman legionaries, and they don't carry the great rectangular shields those boys did. But, if we can get hold of some mantlets, those great boards the archers shelter behind, cut them in thirds and put handles on all the pieces, we will have something like it and with a bit of practice we could achieve the same kind of effect. Then, if we get some good axemen together and some blacksmiths with their bloody great hammers and cold chisels, we could not only flatten or smash down those spikes and blades that did so much damage this morning, but also hack through those chains as well so that the whole bloody thing can be heaved out of the way. And while our blacksmiths are doing their bit for the cause, our axemen could also have a go at chopping the bloody thing up into smaller pieces. What do you think?"

"I suppose the 'Roman' bit came from you, Matthew?" Yvo groaned at the tall Spaniard with a grin. "While our Henry has more brains than I do, not even he could have thought that one up. Though having got that far I can see his hand on the practical side of it: chopped down mantlets, axemen and blacksmiths. You two must be fucking mad! How long do we have before Henry orders another go at that breach? One day? Two?"

"Two days R and R and attack on the third day." Don Mateo said, quietly. "I had it from de Vernaille. He wants the whole of tomorrow and the next day to finish doing a 'proper job' on that wall…and then Henry will order another attack. And this time we will get in…but only if we can remove their

Chevaux de Frises. For with a bigger breach there are bound to be more than one of those bastards up on that bloody slope to deal with."

"Sweet Wine of Christ! Two days! And more than one of those bastard things up there by then?"

"So, Yvo?" His oldest friend asked him, his eyes ice-blue, fixed on him with a concentrated stare: "Yes…or no?"

"Well, I think you are both quite mad. And it's a completely insane idea. Roman Testudo indeed! But…it's the only idea we've got, and if it worked for the bloody Romans there's no reason why it shouldn't work for us. Though what Edward Fitzwalter will have to say when I tell him what we need our lads to do up on that fucking glacis in three days time, I'll leave you to imagine. He will think it as a mad as scheme as I do!" And he laughed. "Now…who's for another clack of this excellent red I picked up on my way here?" He asked grinning at them. "I don't know about you two…but after that little revelation, gentlemen. I *need* a drink! God help us, you two. Everything forward and trust in the Lord!" And they all laughed.

Chapter 4...Second Attack: Siege of Cahors, Toulouse Campaign: July 1159.

Three days later, watched by Henry II, King of England and Malcolm, King of Scots, with their personal divisions in reserve, Henry's army assaulted the north wall of Cahors again, while a swarm of boats led by his southern vassals attacked the south wall across the river with ladders as a diversion. Preceded by a violent storm of rocks and fire balls from the mangonels placed opposite, so that the scaling parties were masked by smoke and flying debris, they went in to the attack roaring their heads off, intent on wholesale slaughter and booty.

Once again it was dawn, and once again the men rushed the great ditch from the northern darkness, just as the sky was suffused with colour, even as the last stars were still shining out above the pale duck-egg green of the early pre-dawn. Giving way to primrose yellow and the softest blush pink, the sun edged its way up to proclaim a new day, heralded by great sheets of gold and crimson that soon flooded the eastern sky with brilliant light.

And as the trumpets were blown and the flags rose, and Henry's army rushed forward again towards the great northern wall of the city with an exultant roar, so the defenders were met by the strangest sight of that early morning assault. For amongst the very first attackers to break from the dense lines of the besiegers were two extraordinary columns of men, like two giant upside-down shoe boxes, their sides and tops formed of garishly painted overlapping boards covered with tough leather soaked and running with water, only the feet and ankles of those carrying them showing underneath as they rushed along in an amazing shuffle that covered the ground with greater speed than could have been imagined.

But no sooner had the assault started when this time de Vernaille's trebuchets opened fire again with great accuracy, bombarding the wall tops and the breech itself with their huge stone missiles, even as the first shoebox advancing underneath their covering fire reached the rickety bridge across the ditch that Henry's engineers had completed four days ago. And as Sir Yvo's men put their feet on it, so de Vernaille's huge missiles whirred overhead to smash with appalling force right on top of the breach where its defenders were already gathering, pulverising scores of them into a bloody gruel that covered the mangled stonework with a violent wash of blood as if a demented artist had hurled buckets of scarlet paint all over it.

Below that the first of the two shoebox testudoes had reached the glacis and started to climb, each man struggling to hold his position as had been practised under their cursing, swearing sergeants in the days before the attack, the massive presence of Edward Fitzwalter, Sir Yvo's Master-at-Arms, for ever at their side. Again and again they had sweated, cursed and struggled to form up and manoeuvre with the great unwieldy sections of cut-down mantlet they had been given to use, those holding them up over their heads as cramped as those holding them out across their waists, while doing their best to shelter the blacksmiths and axemen in their centre.

And while not practising their new formation, they still had to shine and polish their armour and see to the sharpening of their weapons. Staggering around like drunken whores at a wedding with giant cake boards on their arms and playing at 'Romans' was all very well, but they were also Sir Yvo's crack troops, his 'Malwood Lions' as they were known, each one a chosen man, each one bearing the scarlet Lion Rampant of his Lord's House on back and chest, and each one carrying the hopes and honour of Castle Malwood from where they had all set out two months before.

Now was their moment of truth for as they came in range of the defenders at last, they were pelted and shot at with every missile on which desperate hands could easily be laid, as well as fire pots and straw bundles that showered down heedlessly on each testudo as it stolidly mounted the glacis, thumping and bouncing off its armoured back and sides as the testudo brushed them aside with its tough, water soaked boards.

Steadily, with fierce oaths and grunts of effort, Sir Yvo and his men forced their way upwards over the sharp uneven surface of the glacis, while their boards shuddered and rattled to every missile hurled at them as they stumbled on. Nor did they go unscathed as every now and then a spear or bearded arrow would find the throat or neck of one of the men, or pierce a foot or suddenly unprotected thigh so that each shoe box squirmed and writhed in agony as it pressed forward, the men inside covered in the jetted blood of their comrades who, howling in pain or slumped in death, had to be jettisoned and left behind like the obscene dung of some strange painted monster. Twisting and crying out in pain or stretched out in death, their blood spouted from their wounds as the rest of their comrades ground their way up the vast avalanche of scree beneath a deluge of missiles.

And then they were there, right up against the great tree trunk that had stopped them before, and with a wild trumpet blast each shoebox testudo broke apart, the men in the front now standing to rest their boards on the thing itself

18

while others stood over them to let the farriers they had sheltered all the way up the slope wield their great lump hammers and cold chisels against the spikes and sharpened blades that covered each massive timber, and once a dozen clear spaces had been created, so the men stepped over onto the other side, their great mantlet boards shielding those experts who now attacked the great chains holding the Chevaux de Frise in its place with huge cold chisels and mighty sledges until one after another its iron fetters fell apart.

Every time a man fell to spear, stone or arrow, so another took his place, hands slippery with the blood and brains of the fallen, as each seized the dropped sledge or hammer so the way ahead could be cleared for the assault teams leaping up from below to bring their own brand of fighting frenzy to play against the city. And where the gaps had been created by the blacksmiths, so the axemen swung their blades and hewed their way through the obstacle so that others could now move, push and drag each separated length clear of the breach's centre, while still others leaped forward with shield, spear and sword to protect the work gangs from the fury of the defenders...until with a great roar of triumph at last the job was done.

"*Trumpeter!*" Sir Yvo bellowed above the screaming fury of the fight. "Blow the 'Come-to-Me'! Blow your bloody lungs out, boy, and let's get into the bastards!" And so Sir Yvo's trumpeter blasted out the signal for which all had been waiting: '*Tan!-Tan!-Tara!-Tantaraaa!* *Tan!-Tan!-Tara!-Tantaraa!*' And no sooner had the first wild notes soared out like a silver trumpet over the dead, than the youngster standing by Sir Henry twenty yards away beside the other great obstacle did the same, his face swiftly scarlet with effort: '*Tan!-Tan!-Tara!-Tantaraaa!*'...'*Come to me! Come to me! Come to meeee!*'

"*Now boys, bring up the flags!*" Sir Yvo and Sir Henry roared out together. "Let those fucking bastards up there see whose coming for them!" And moments later, when both great House flags had been raised up for all to see, their colours of scarlet, blue and gold shimmying in the breeze, Sir Yvo, Lord of Malwood, opened his throat with a huge roar of violence that could be heard right across to the Royal lines, themselves now beginning to move.

"*Lions! Advance Banners,* Now, lads, up swords and at 'em." And with his giant Master-at-Arms beside him, still holding his great rectangular board on his massive arm and roaring; "*Advaance, Lions! Advaaance!*" And freed at last from the two Chevaux de Frises they had just destroyed, the Malwood Lions leapt forward into the howling maelstrom that was the glacis, unleashed from all restraint, to rend and maul and cut to death all who dared stand in their way.

Don Mateo, his two swords drawn off his back and firmly in his mailed hands, now performed his 'dance-of-death', as light on his toes as any fearless toreador despite his heavy mail and thick nasal helmet. Darting turning, twisting and spinning he hacked, chopped and swept his way through his enemies as if they were grass beneath his scythe. Thrusting his sword through chest and throat one moment, his face sprayed with blood and froth; only to twist and turn the next, while hacking off a limb or rendering a wretched Frenchman headless in a fountain of blood as he whirled his blades up, round and across his armoured front. Within his enemy's reach one moment, swaying away the next; seeming to know instinctively from where each blow would come even before his luckless prey had made up his own mind. Like a mad marionette on springing wires, he leaped and danced and twisted leaving a blood-boltered trail of shattered bodies in his wake.

And just beside him, their great House flags borne rushing into the very heart of the bloody fray came Sir Yvo and Sir Henry, their men all around them, their great coats of mail shimmering in the early morning sun. Split between their legs to the waist for ease of movement and lined with tough leather, their mail armour seemed to flow like steel water as the two knights forced their way up the new glacis that de Vernaille's engines had created, their mail sufficient to stop any close ranged spear or arrow and with double thickness of mail across their chest and back no light fighting bow of those days could pierce them, they seemed invulnerable.

Great kite shaped shields now on their left arms, as their ancestors had held them at Hastings, both men had their swords in their hands, hallooing their men forwards as they climbed, fighting with the skill and economy of long practice. Turning blows on their shields, to push away and open up an enemy before stabbing through the armour, the vicious twist and withdrawal of their blades, guaranteed to draw out their entails; or hacking down on wrist or arm to leave one more hapless defender limbless and spouting blood from severed arteries and fearful cuts and slashes. *Block! Lunge, twist, recover...* until the stones they trod on were slippery with blood and entrails and the air stank of vomit, sweat and faeces as terrified men voided their bowels and urinated as they fought for their lives, or were hacked down and left for dead, their shocked and shattered bodies unable to control their muscles as they spilled their guts out where they lay.

Now, above them was the very lip of the breach itself, a jagged line packed with armed men, beyond which lay the streets and houses of Cahors, its magnificent great buildings and royal palace, town hall, market and cathedral. The whole city lay open and ready to be seized. Only one man and his chosen meisnie, armed in shining mail, with shield, sword and gisarme, and backed by a great mass of stalwart defenders, stood between them and victory: the Lord Baron Sir Thibault de Brocas of Montauban, Narbonne and Gruissan, once supposed leal man of King Henry, now a proven traitor and supporter of King Louis VII, his newly acclaimed Lord and Suzerain. And he it was who now stepped forward beneath his House flag, an enormous emerald banner emblazoned with the symbol of his House, the great black boar's head erased, with scarlet eyes and teeth and blooded tushes that now waved and shivered in the summer's breeze.

"*You shall not pass!*" He roared out, striding forward before his men. "These men and I, and all those who stand around me will not let you pass. You ran yesterday, like sheep before the wolves. Screaming. And so you will today, my Lord of Malwood," he taunted Sir Yvo, with bitter mockery. "And as for you, my Nephew?" he raged at Sir Henry. "My foolish sister's pride and joy? I will fill your bowels with sharpened timber; cut out your stones and fling your manhood to the dogs; and you will beg for death to claim you."

Sir Yvo stopped and looked across at his friends and laughed…at Sir Henry and Don Mateo, and then at his men, stained with blood, helmets and armour battered and torn, and then at the whole host of men already swarming up the glacis behind them and he laughed again. "I always knew you were bad, Thibault. A bloody, traitorous thief and murderer. Now!" He roared at him, pointing down below to the bottom of the glacis thick with men. "*I know you are fucking mad as well!*" And with a huge shout he roared out "*Lions…Advaaance!*" and then his battle cry: "*A Malwood! A Malwood!*" As he hurled himself into the attack, his men following their liege Lord and his great waving Lion Rampant flag. And beside him leaped Sir Henry surrounded by his own leal men from the forest, his own flag bravely waving above his head on that lovely morning, Don Mateo with his Navarrans by his side, and the most bitter struggle for the breach began.

Armoured, helmed and shielded both Sir Yvo and the Baron were well matched. And if the Frenchman had the greater height, Sir Yvo was more nimble on his feet; both men barrel chested and both with thews of iron; but where Thibault de Brocas relied on brute strength to win his battles, Sir Yvo used both blade and point, as quick on his toes as he was with his feet planted firmly on the ground; and both men fought each other like tigers.

Crash! Crash! Crash! on Sir Yvo's shield arm driving him back until he was forced to open himself as he tried to turn and slip away, then leaping forward within de Brocas' reach as he raised his arm for a fourth blow, shield and sword across his chest to force the block before pushing the bigger man back with a violent shove, sword and shield flung outwards as he did so. Then a swift flurry of blows, *Stab! Cut! Thrust!* With point, edge and point that drove de Brocas further backwards, while all around him his men fought and died to seize the breach in a vile slurry of faeces, blood and entrails that slicked everything around them.

21

And then the huge Frenchman was coming at him again, screaming his war cry, "*A Brocas! A Brocas!*" His mouth frothing with rage, using his great sword two handed, with no shield now on his arm, to smash and batter at Sir Yvo. Huge overhead blows that hacked jagged darts and splinters out of the English knight's shield as he drove Sir Yvo backwards, slicing the armour across his shoulders into ribbons of dripping mail and denting his helmet with a vicious, skidding blow across his head that forced the Lord of Malwood to his knees.

But even as Sir Thibault drew himself up to hack down his tormenting adversary once and for all, so Yvo rolled across the stony ground and onto the balls of his feet. Thrusting his long blade out before him like a lance and leaping up off the raddled glacis he drove his blade through de Brocas' mail across his shoulder. It was a perfect thrust, his pointed steel bursting through Lord Thibault's linked and riveted iron and through the flesh and muscle in a spray of blood that made the big man howl with rage.

And so a pause for breath amidst the screaming frenzy of that breach, where their forces reeled and struggled like the Normans outside York at the height of the last Saxon rebellion, the air torn by bellows of rage and pain, shouted battle cries and brazen trumpets, as both sides hewed at each other in mortal, bloody fury for mastery of Cahors.

A pause for two deadly enemies to stand back and breathe and pant, to glare and snort and stamp their feet, their armour sheeted with blood and daubed with great gobs of flesh and shards of bone, while blood from their own wounds trickled down their backs and along their arms beneath their mail, and over their buttocks to run out past their feet.

And then de Brocas was rushing in on Sir Yvo again as if unwounded, returning to the attack with the speed and fury of the great boar he so represented now cornered by the hunt, snarling and roaring, mouth agape and armed with steel to rip and tear his enemy to pieces. But Sir Yvo was waiting for him, and rose up with his sword and battered shield in a solid **block!** that Thibault could not break, straining and twisting, bare inches from each other's faces, snarling and growling like wild beasts, almost blinded with sweat that poured off each man in runnels, until with a mighty **shout!** Sir Yvo thrust the giant Frenchman backwards, flinging his arms apart as he did so, to send de Brocas staggering and stumbling away from him as he leaped forward to flense him to the ground.

But even as Sir Yvo jumped…he slipped on the bloodied offal smeared across the rubble in the breach, staggered like a mighty tree in a violent storm and then fell, his sword spinning from his grasp, his head full of swirling stars…and suddenly he was both helpless and unarmed, scrabbling on hands and knees for his fallen sword, any sword…*any* weapon with which to defend himself from Thibault's fury which was about to fall upon him like a thunderbolt.

Gasping for breath though he was, seeing his enemy fall and his sword fly out of his hand, the Lord Roger de Brocas leaped into the attack sweeping his own great weapon up in both his hands as he rose up to tower over Sir Yvo, and with a great bellow of rage he hewed down with all his strength at the desperate man now kneeling helplessly before him..

It was a killing blow, a brain splitting, eviscerating killing blow delivered by an expert warrior who knew what he was doing. A blow to tell over the winter fires when the snow lay thick and the wolves howled close to the castle walls…a blow that fellow warriors would drink to and boast about for ever.

But it never reached his foe!

For even as Sir Yvo crashed down, both Sir Henry and Don Mateo had seen him fall, but before the Spanish caballero could reach him, Sir Henry dropped his shield and leaping towards his uncle viciously barged him out of the way so all Lord Thibault's great blade did was strike wild sparks off the shattered ashlar blocks with which the breach was strewn, and even as he staggered upright again, his sword more prop than fighting blade, Sir Henry Burley struck his uncle down.

It was his favourite blow.

One that Yvo had seen him deliver many times before, in practice and for real, a vicious upward cut that burst between Lord Thibault's legs, between his split mail coat and sliced his enemy open from crotch to navel. A blow from which there could be no return. A blow that opened de Brocas up like a gralloched deer, and twisting the blade as he hacked into him Sir Henry's sword ripped his whole bowels out upon the ground. A blow that dropped his uncle to his knees in a desperate howl of shock and anguish that left him open to Sir Henry's swingeing, swift riposte, a brutal strike delivered two handed that smashed though Thibault's armour as if it were paper and sent his uncle's head spinning to the ground as his severed body fountained blood up into the air, splattering everyone with hot, scarlet rain before falling forward with a soggy thump upon the torn ground.

Thus was the Lord Baron, Sir Thibault de Brocas, known as 'The Cruel', Lord of Montauban, Narbonne and Gruissan, slain defending the breach of Cahors by Sir Henry de Burley, Lord of the Forest…and with a great roar of triumph the breach fell, and they were in!

Not ten feet from where the Baron had been so brutally hacked down, a young boy cowered and shivered amidst the dead, hiding his tearful face and burrowing into the foul debris of the battle as King Henry's loyal Host poured in and the sack of Cahors began. Soldiers, drunk with victory, running through streets that swiftly flowed with spilled wine as well as blood as they searched mercilessly through the fallen city bent on murder, rape and booty, as much as food and drink...their violent prize for all they had suffered at the hands of the defenders.

Hiding amongst the bodies of the dead and injured, his virgin sword unfleshed, un blooded, Young Roger de Brocas had come to his first battle so proud of his new armour, to crow at their enemies as he had been taught to do and to witness his father's triumph of which he had been assured...only to witness his father's destruction at the hand of his own nephew; his sister's only child, in order to save his friend! And in so doing he had been sprayed with his father's blood...his own father's hot blood...all over his face and armour, his sight blurred with it, thick with it; leaving him both horrified and wracked with guilt for having stood there, mindless, while his father had been so brutally slain before his very eyes.

Eyes now full of bitter tears the boy gathered up his father's battered head and wrapped it in a cloth he found nearby, and also his great jewelled sword which he held close to his bursting heart. But before he left that dreadful place of butchery, that bloody shambles, to find a burial party...before King Henry's men could come for his father's body and throw it naked in the city ditch, as was customary for traitors, or even nailed up for all to see...the young man made himself a promise.

A sacred vow sworn upon his father's head and sealed with his son's last kiss upon his staring eyes and cold and bloodied lips.

That one day he, Roger de Brocas...when once he had received his knighthood from the French King, whomsoever that should be when he was then full grown, and was once more Lord of Narbonne and Gruissan as his father had been, those few lands now left to his family still held safe within the French King's borders. That he, then Sir Roger de Brocas, would bring fire and death upon the man who had slain his father, *and* to all those whom that man loved or cared for, especially Sir Yvo de Malwood who had fought so furiously with Lord Thibault first. Upon his father's head he swore it, and on his blood still wet upon his face now mingled with his tears.

He was a de Brocas, the last in his male line...and one day, **he would be revenged!**

PART II: Castle Malwood, the New Forest: June 30th,1190

Chapter 1...The White Rose of Malwood is introduced.

It was the last day of June and from a sky of blue glass the sun breathed fire out of a cloudless sky, making the yellow-grey stones of the old castle shimmer with the heat; the air almost still, just a cat's paw breeze to ruffle the lily heads now and then that floated pink and white amongst the green pads spread out in great rafts across the lake, the bulrushes standing like dusky sentinels around the edges of the moat, and of the lake that filled it.

Doves cooed dreamily from their cot across the bailey near the New Hall where Bellman the giant boar-hound lay spread out in the cool shadow of the topmost step of its entrance. Eyes closed, great paws twitching, he idly luxuriated in the warmth of high summer as butterflies flickered around the flowers in the castle gardens and the castle bees, on rainbow wings, busied themselves amongst them beneath the solar's windows, loading their legs with swags of yellow pollen, while the swifts screamed on scimitar wings over the roofs and turret tops.

Beyond the cool, black shadow of the tall gate-house that opened out onto the castle bailey beyond the lake, a group of some dozen men-at-arms were drawn up and waiting.

Clothed in brightly burnished mail with domed steel casques on their sweating heads, each soldier wore a white surcoat emblazoned back and front with a single great scarlet Lion-Rampant, armed and tongued in blue. They made a fine sight. Tall, kite-shaped shields, flat topped on their left arms and all carrying the same device, heavy spears grounded at their feet, long swords hanging by their sides they made a fine sight as they stood in two sweating ranks listening to the hard voice of their Master-at-Arms as he put them through their paces.

To the Lady Alicia de Burley looking across at them from her private chamber dressed only in a fine cotton shift, they were the living symbols of her future, the Lions of Malwood, known as much for their bravery and skill in battle as for the leaping scarlet Lions Rampant, with blue claws teeth and tongue, that each soldier carried so proudly back and front, and which she too would soon have the right to wear.

For this was her betrothal day for which all the preparations going on around her were intended. Tonight she would be formally betrothed to Sir Gui de Malwood, the heir of all that surrounded her, and with all the splendour and ceremony that should attend so great and joyous an occasion. Tonight he would claim her heart as his guerdon for the love he gave her, an accolade that he would carry into every skirmish that he fought and every battle, every kingly tournament, and her eyes were like stars.

Her only sadness was that her own parents could not be with her. Her mother, the Lady Anne, had died in childbed when she was only four years old from a fever following the birth of her brother who had died with her. And she had lost her father, Sir Henry, two years later from a festered wound gained fighting in France beside his great friend Sir Yvo de Malwood, Gui's father. But the two families had been close for generations, since both had come up from Rocamadour in the Auvergne to join Duke William's great expedition to seize the throne of England, and had never gone back.

So…with her mother dead, Sir Henry had brought Alicia to Castle Malwood and given her into the care of Sir Yvo's wife, the Lady Margaret, and had named her and her husband as guardians of his daughter, before leaving for France with his closest friend on that fatal last campaign. They in their turn had loved Alicia and brought her up as their own, especially as Gui's birth had been difficult, and the Lady Margaret could have no more children of her own. So she had poured her love into her great friend's child and done all she could to care for her and bring her up as her own. Sir Yvo also.

No girl could have had a more loving family in which to prosper. And though the lady Margaret might long have dreamed that her son and Lady Anne's daughter might form a lasting bond, no one had been more surprised than she when finally it happened.

But Alicia was also the only inheritor of all the Burley estates, both in the Forest and elsewhere, and so the King, Henry Plantagenet, had also named her as a Royal Ward, as was his right, being anxious to ensure so rich a marriage prize did not become a weapon that a powerful Lord might choose to use against the crown. So permission from the King for her betrothal…now King Richard of England… had first been sought. And having thus been granted she, the Lady Alicia de Burley – Royal Ward of the greatest Warrior King in all Europe, and scion of one of the oldest Houses in the land - would thus be hand-fast before all the world to the one man above all others whom she loved with all her heart.

She was *so* excited that she just couldn't wait and giving a little cry as the thrill of it suddenly gripped her, she twisted away from the window, danced across the room and seizing an ivory comb off the top of an oaken chest as she skipped by, she flung herself backwards onto her bed. Arms spread wide, she luxuriated in the sunshine that poured across it from the windows, gazing sightlessly up at the beams above her head as she lay there, her mind a kaleidoscope of whirling thoughts and images.

Then, with a grin, she sat up and began to tug the comb through the tousled knots in her hair. Better to do something useful than bounce up and down like a puppet on a string, her head just filled with dreams!

★

At eighteen Alicia de Burley had blossomed from a gawky, long-legged beanpole with two pimples, scratched legs and a torn shift from climbing trees and chasing round the castle garth, far keener on swords and armour than her stitchery and samplers…into the most ravishing beauty. Secure in herself, clear headed but generous towards others, she had a strong sense of purpose and a keen understanding of what was expected of her, without losing any of her youthful spirit. With her proud family background, innate sense of duty and steely resolve, and a wicked spirit of mischief, she was a lively lady with a passionate, sensuous nature and a warm and loving heart.

And she really was very lovely, both as a person and to look at.

Sitting as she was the showers of golden hair that framed her heart-shaped face shimmered as she pulled the comb through them. Her chin firm and her lips soft, yet beautifully defined, were more framed for smiles and laughter than selfishness and anger. And her eyes, luminescent cornflower blue and thickly fringed with long, curling lashes, were the mirror of her soul: clouded when she was sad, bright and shining when she was gay, deep velvet when she was in passion and, when angry, hard and sparkling with a piercing glare that could drop a man at twenty paces!

Across the bailey the shouted orders and the stamp and slap of mailed feet began once more as the men went through their routine yet again, while the fragrance of the honeysuckle and the white roses that she loved so much she had become known as one of them, rioted beneath her windows where they faced the bailey, filling the room with the very breath of lazy summer. 'The White Rose of Malwood' was how she was known far and wide, and she smiled at the name…both in pride and humour; knowing that in no way could she truly be compared to the beauty of the flowers below her window that she loved so much. His Lion, and her roses; and she chuckled at the thought of them entwined together, as she so longed to be. Gui and Alicia…Alicia and Gui, and her heart beat the more quickly every time she murmured his name.

★

When her hair was as soft and silken as she could make it, she put down her comb and getting to her feet she turned to look around her, and tripping to where her long betrothal gown in all its blue and silver beauty hung against the plastered stonework, she paused to feel the soft richness of the silk and damask from which it had been made, shot through with threads of pure silver and gold, before turning to look round at the room itself where she had spent so many of her growing years.

How she loved her tower chamber with its polished oak flooring and high arched windows that filled it with such light and brightness. From beneath them, on padded seating that her mother had long ago so lovingly embroidered with white roses, her own chosen flower too, she could sit and look out across the great open bailey, part paved but mostly pastured, to the towering Gatehouse, and the thick walls and towers that made Castle Malwood the great fortress that it was. And beyond that to the lake that filled the moat, and to the beauty of the New Forest that surrounded them.

All around her the inner walls of her tower were plastered, white painted, and largely hidden behind beautifully embroidered hangings her father had brought back from France, and there was a carpet, made from a dozen thick wool-fells stitched together, that covered over half the floor and was so lovely to stand on, especially in the winter! There were large wooden chests against two of the walls, filled with clothes and scented herbs, and right against the far wall, facing the windows, was her great bed, with its thick horse-hair filled mattress on leather straps, its fine linen bolsters and great quilted counterpane. Carved by Italian craftsmen, it was the finest in all the castle.

Occupying the very highest story of one of the most massive towers of the fortress, that with others along the broad curtain wall made up the outer defences; her room was considered to be safe from any but the most determined assault. And was close enough to the Great Keep for her to get there easily should the need ever arise…yet far enough away to give some privacy in times of usual haste and bustle.

Indeed, such privacy was not an easy thing to find for Castle Malwood was the busiest centre of Royal and Lordly power in the whole of the Forest. Even the King visited here in the winter for the hunting, as had other kings before him, their trust in the loyalty of the Malwood family as absolute as their willingness to serve the Crown. Thus had it always been. The Malwoods and the Burleys together, since the Conqueror himself had given them their lands. And there was no castle stronger, between Windsor and the sea, in which the king could safely lie as Castle Malwood.

On a level with the wall-walk, with a circular staircase going down to the bailey below and up to the very tower head itself, which rose a further ten feet above the main battlements, her room could not have been more secure She had her own garderobe, hidden within the thickness of the walls, and her carved cherry-wood wash stand, with its marble basin and ewer stood opposite a finely sculpted open fireplace, the zigzag chevrons painted in bright colours, the wide hearth filled with flowers and tall, dried grasses.

Beyond her door, six inches of laminated oak strengthened with iron plates and closed with both lock and drawbar, as were all the tower doors in the castle, lay the passage that carried the wall-walk inside against the outer wall of the tower and then away again across the curtain wall to the next tower, in a defensive line that ran right round the castle. Here arrow slits, one right outside her door, had been cut deeply into the massive thickness of the tower's outer wall, itself some twelve feet of stone and mortar, faced with beautifully cut blocks of ashlar limestone, with more doors and portcullis to block the tower off from the wall-head in time of deadly peril.

In winter, when the rain rattled against the shuttered windows, or the moat was thickly frozen, the snow laying heavy on the battlements like sugar icing and the wolves howled in the Forest, a fire of beech and apple logs blazed across handsome wrought-iron dogs, and she could snuggle down beneath a mound of furs and feel as warm as hot chestnuts. In high summer, with the windows and shutters flung wide and the finest Egyptian cotton sheet, like gossamer, across her silken skin she could be cool as a mountain breeze. Best of all, because it was in one of the oldest parts of the castle, it was somewhat separate from the rest of the fortress, in a tower on its own and therefore less frequented by the servants of her guardian, Sir Yvo de Malwood, and his plump and homely wife the Lady Margaret.

It was here, just after her sixteenth birthday that she and Gui, their son and only child, had first unleashed a passion that had shaken them to the very core of their being. Longed for yet unexpected, and therefore doubly precious, it was here that they had first become lovers.

He had just returned from the North, away up on the wild borders between the English and the Scots. There he had served the Earl of Northumbria under the Lord Baron Sir John de Methley, a distant cousin of Sir Yvo's. Four years he had been away from Castle Malwood, years in which she had grown into a young woman and he into the kind of young Knight all parents dream of. And she had gone North for his Knighting ceremony - she and Gui's parents together, as special guests of the great Earl himself, the Lord Percy of Alnwick, the King's most powerful magnate in the North. He it was who had taken his own great sword and with two light blows of its blade across his shoulders had dubbed Gui 'Knight' to the shouted acclaim of all who had assembled there to witness it.

One look at Gui then, as he knelt there so fine and brave was all it had taken, and her heart was lost forever. She was not sure for whom it had beaten more quickly that day, herself...almost breathless with the sudden surge of emotion that had rushed through her? Or for Gui, when his father had knelt at his son's feet to put on the golden spurs that would proclaim his knighthood, themselves a present from the Earl.

It had all been intoxicating...and marvellous and wholly beyond expectation.

Now, by sight and sound and touch they had brought a love to life in each other that was as deeply gentle as it was all consuming. As full of laughter as it was of tears, as soft and cool as it was hard and fiercely hot, and it was here that she had offered herself to him, and he, with joy unbounded, had so boldly taken her. And flinging herself backwards again onto the broad coverlet on her bed she looked up at the heavy oak beams above her head amazed at the fierceness of their loving, and chuckled at the remembrance of their gaucheness, and their fear of hurting one another..

Not any more.

Secure now in their own feelings towards their union, and those of Sir Yvo her guardian, their loving made her wood-wild; turning her from a gentle maiden into a wanton harlot. Salome, who had danced before King Herod for the Baptist's Head, was *nothing* in comparison to the fair Lady Alicia when seeking how best to please her Lord! According to old Father Gerome such feelings were not supposed to be for such as her. They belonged amongst the borel folk who rutted in their season like the stags of the forest, or grunted like hogs at the trough at feeding time making the beast with two backs! Such things the priest had said, outside of marriage, were mortal sins and would bring God's wrath upon them. Well, not so far!

She smiled, and swinging her legs onto the floor, she hopped onto the carpet, wriggling her bare feet deliciously in the thick, soft fleeces that lay there before pausing and dreamily wandering across to the windows. There she plumped herself down on the padded seating and leaning back she sighed with gentle expectation, gazing almost unseeing across the bailey where the men who had been drilling in all the June heat were just being dismissed.

Today, she and Gui would realise all their dreams and those of both their families. After tonight both their estates would be as one and she would have Gui to herself for ever; would bear his children and would love him till the day she died. Alicia smiled and hugged herself fiercely then, in a sudden burst of excitement, she jumped up, ran across the room and swished her dress off its hanger and holding it against herself, even as she dreamed of being held in Gui's arms, she danced and pirouetted round the room on her toes.

The Lion and the Rose...the White Rose of Malwood.

The two entwined in heart and mind: he, Sir Gui de Malwood, Scarlet Lion-Rampant, strong and hotly armed for love or battle. She, the Lady Alicia, his White Fragrant Rose, her most favourite flower, so sweetly scented, so beautiful, so seemingly delicate and soft...yet fiercely barbed against whoever should become their foes. Her roses sweetly sharp around his lion's claws. Ah, Heart of Christ, let anyone try now and come between them!

She stopped, panting, before going forward and re-hanging her dress, smoothing the silken fabric of which it was made, luxuriating in the feel and weight of it, proud that so beautiful a garment had been created just for her. Then, leaning back against the sunlit wall she stretched deliciously, pushing her firm pointed breasts against the fine cotton fabric that covered them and smiled dreamily.

31

Tonight all the world would be coming to the castle.

Even her Brocas cousins were coming. The Lord Baron Sir Roger de Brocas and his daughter the Lady Rochine, all the way from distant Narbonne, close against the Circle Sea, the glittering Mediterranean; and she grimaced. How strange that Sir Yvo should have invited him? The Lord Baron was the sworn enemy of both their Houses. Indeed it was because of the constant feuding with his family, that Gui's great-grandfather, and hers, had left their French lands all those years ago to join the Conqueror's army in the days of Saxon Harold…and never returned.

Now Lord Roger was coming to her betrothal, to seal ancient family wounds, so Sir Yvo had said, and was bringing his daughter the Lady Rochine with him, with whom she would have to share her bed there being so little room in the castle with so many people coming. Alicia shivered despite the June sunshine. She only hoped they would get on alright, otherwise it would all be very difficult!

She smiled. Cousins from distant France, a country of which she had heard so much, yet never been to; and from the hot and sunny South, the Languedoc; rich with the language of Courtly Love itself, a language that Queen Eleanor spoke and King Richard sang about; and she wondered lazily again about her cousins of whom she had heard so much but really knew so little.

She could hardly wait to meet them!

Chapter 2...In which we learn about the Wicked Baron, Prince John and the Crusade.

Feeling deliciously languorous, Alicia stretched once more then wandered back to the wide window seat and sat down again, holding out her hand in the brilliant sunshine to admire the enormous sapphire, clustered with pearls, that Gui had given her as his Betrothal gift. She loved it, as she did him.

And leaning against the thick stonework, her eyes lifted up to the almost cloudless sky caught by a distant Kestrel quartering the pasturelands beyond the walls for hidden prey. Her mind wandering as effortlessly as the little falcon, as she watched it rising and falling on the air, twisting and hovering as it coursed for mice or voles amongst the distant grasses.

Sir Roger de Brocas, Lord Baron of Narbonne and Gruissan. Her so wicked Cousin!

The son of Thibault the Cruel whose aunt, Phillipa de Brocas, had married her Grandfather, Ralf de Burley...he was supposed to be involved in all sorts of dreadful things, both he and his raven haired daughter, Rochine. Twice he had been placed under a ban by Holy Church. Only the direct intervention of Archbishop Beringuer of Narbonne had recently prevented him from being arrested and brought before the Pope himself.

Suspected of being involved with Saracen slavers trading out of Jaffa and from the great city of Acre itself also, before the Syrian barons had besieged it, he was well known along the Barbary coast, not least because he spoke their language. Some even said that he had met with Saladin himself! She put her arms round her knees and watched as the distant falcon suddenly closed its wings and dropped like a stone out of sight, only to rise again moments later and swing away on swiftly beating wings and disappear.

It had killed!

Just so had the great Saracen leader grasped *his* prey. As swiftly as the kestrel had pounced...so had he, and utter disaster had struck those distant Christian lands as a result.

She shuddered and crossed herself at the very thought of the famous Infidel leader, remembering the awful scenes in the Great Hall when the news had reached them of Saladin's destruction of the massed crusader army at Hattin, and of his capture of Jerusalem. It was said that so many Christian knights had been seized that you could buy one in the souks for no more than the cost of a pair of shoes! That had been before old King Henry had died at Chinon, his most favourite castle.

Then it was that King Richard had first taken the cross, but had been forced to wait until the Old King's death before he could do a thing about it. Now, safely crowned at last, he had set about raising the greatest army ever to leave these islands, and re-claim the Holy Land from the black paynims who had so violently seized it. Thus in this year of Our Lord, Eleven Hundred and Ninety, King Richard's call to arms had rung out across all England.

Such excitement!

A clarion call that had reached into every corner of the land, even to sleepy Malwood where troops were already gathering to join the King before he sailed from Marseilles later in the year. For Gui was going on Crusade, and soon Castle Malwood would be more stuffed with armed men than had been seen since Sir Yvo had last gone to the wars when she was just a child. The year her father had died.

Alicia shuddered at the thought, knowing the great distances involved and the dangers her man would have to face when once he got there. And not just from the enemy themselves, those fierce, hawk-eyed warriors, mounted on swift, snorting stallions that could go like the wind, and fought with curved scimitars and jewelled daggers...but also from the heat and from the many diseases of which she knew so many crusaders suffered from and died. And then there were the Barbary Corsairs! Wild Turkish pirates who roamed the seas like ravening beasts, in great oared galleys driven by slaves who lived and died beneath the lash, packed with fighting men dredged up from every heathen shore. They preyed on passing shipping and undefended coasts without mercy, and the sound of great beating drums always preceded them.

God save all Christian souls from so terrible a fate as to fall prey to Barbary pirates!

How could she not know these things? Seeing as Castle Malwood was the centre of all Royal power in the Forest she knew more even than many of the Lords and gentry who lived around them. Indeed, King Richard himself had been pleased to share his thoughts with Sir Yvo, and with Gui as well, as had been proven at his coronation. And Gui had learned to share them with her too, secure in the knowledge that where Alicia was concerned she was as close as any oyster! And they had been dangerous thoughts indeed: About the safety of England in the King's absence; about Prince John and his lust for power; who should be named Regent? And where the Old Queen stood in relation to her two sons? One who *was* King, by right and the acceptance of all his people...and one who would make himself King by any means possible if he could do so!

Prince John!

The king's only surviving brother, whom Richard had loaded with lands and honours at his coronation...yet all men knew to be faithless, venal and dishonest. Alicia crossed herself at the very thought of him! John of Evil Fame with his sharp, warty face and narrow sloping shoulders; sly, feral way of looking at you with leering eyes, and soft, damp hands with pudgy fingers. *Yuk!*

Five foot five...short, dark and fat with warts, and already gaining a reputation for treachery. So unlike his splendid warrior brother, Richard, as to make those who had not met him before almost gasp out with surprise. Indeed one might almost have wondered whether he was truly sprung from the same loins that had produced those others in his family? He had been spoiled and indulged by his father, whom he had later ruthlessly betrayed; a sulky prince not to be trusted and without doubt, not a man to cross!

And she had met him.

She shuddered at the remembrance of it, brief though it had been, last year when she had been taken up to London to take part in Richard's coronation that September. It had been later that evening, after she had been presented to Richard for the first time, when he had confirmed her as his Royal Ward and had agreed to her betrothal. In return for which, and the public attestation of allegiance from both Sir Yvo and his son, and by oaths given and returned in like manner to those they both had sworn to his late father, King Henry II...Gui would join the King on his Crusade and would bring with him as many fighting men as could be raised and paid for.

It had been a great occasion, and Richard had been every bit as splendid as Alicia had imagined. Enormous, with red-golden hair and beard, and had smiled and talked with her in French, his voice a pleasant baritone with the warmth of the southlands of Aquitaine running through it. Plainly he had been captivated by her sparkling wit and pretty manners, finding her both spirited and comely. A fitting bride he had said, for one of the best and boldest of his new knights, and sprung from one of the loyalist families in all England.

It had been then that she had met with Prince John, who had demanded to meet with this latest of his Royal brother's wards. She shuddered at the memory of it for despite Gui's presence he had pawed at her with his plump hands when she had been presented, running his hands over her breasts and firm hind quarters as if she were a mare, before insisting on kissing her as his Royal right. His breath had stunk, and she had no doubt that he would have forced his tongue down her throat for good measure if he had been able.

Bleah!

And his eyes had lasciviously devoured her. Stripping her naked as she stood before him. He had almost slavered over her! Then, the next day, blessedly, they had left and shortly afterwards they learned that the Prince had been forced to promise not to enter the kingdom for the next three years…or at least while Richard was away! Fat chance of that, Alicia surmised. With the cat away the mouse would surely play, for his fat, be-ringed fingers were already in many pies, and he was known to have friends amongst the southern French barons, including Lord Roger de Brocas, for Gui had told her so, and was believed closer to King Philip of France perhaps than many men realised?

And now the Baron was coming to her home. No wonder Gui was feeling so wretched about his father offering so dread a man his hospitality!

Idly she watched the guards by the gatehouse, stamp and turn, their feet giving off violent puffs of dust at every distant bang of their feet. After all, that's whom they were waiting for, and she felt a sudden delicious frisson of excitement run through her at the thought that any moment her 'wicked' French cousins would soon be here, all the way from Narbonne in Southern France, to attend the betrothal party of a young woman whose own father had been his father's slayer over thirty years before. A violent death, struggling fiercely in the breach of Cahors, and witnessed by his own son. It had made relations between the two Houses impossible.

She smiled wryly.

Perhaps Sir Yvo was right, and it was high time such ancient nonsense stopped, wasn't it? Hadn't the three families been at each other's throats for long enough? Surely now was just as good a time as any to call a truce. And with a broad smile Alicia stood up, leaving her thoughts behind her, and dressed only in the finest of cotton shifts, she ran to her door and called Agnes, her Lady's maid and friend, who adored her wilful charge quite as much as her wilful charge adored her!

★

Closing the door again, as she waited for Agnes to come through with her tire-women and the great bathing tub with all the steaming jugs and buckets of water needed for her bath, Alicia luxuriated in the feel of the warm, scented air that blew from the window over her thinly veiled body.

And suddenly she turned, and with a swift movement pulled her shift up and over her head, throwing it on her bed and tossing her head from side to side to free her hair as she did so. Then, turning slowly round in the middle of her room, she ran her hands over her hips and caressed the tight muscles of her shapely backside, before bringing her hands up to cup her full breasts, loving the warm, weight of them in her hands and smiling at how swiftly their tips, like luscious raspberries, soon pouted hard beneath her fingers.

Gui!....Dear God, how her thoughts were centred on him. And how she *wanted* him! Her whole body trembling with suppressed passion. And turning she spread her arms out, pressing her body hard against the tower wall, grinding her longing into the plastered stones, feeling her loins liquefy with desire for Gui to come and take her, to use her, to enter her and love her as only he knew how. She groaned, and turning her back to the wall she leaned against it, quivering, and bending forward she thrust her hands between her thighs. Her legs weak with passion, her eyes stoned with sudden lust.

'Wood Wild' was how she had described herself, and 'Like Salome!'

She stood then and laughed out loud, a delicious gurgle of merriment. Please, *Please God,* that her marriage would follow her betrothal soon...before Gui left to join Richard for the long journey to the Holy Land...otherwise she felt she would go mad from wanting him so much!

37

Chapter 3... In which we meet Agnes Fitzwalter.

S wiftly slipping her shift back over her head, she pushed herself away from the warmly decorated plaster, and stretching her arms above her head like the great golden cat she was, Alicia opened the door and leaned round to call down the staircase: "Agnes, dearest, where in the name of all the gods are you? It's *ages* since I called. Our guests will soon be here, and I have not even bathed yet, let alone dressed! Come on girl, we have a lot to do before my French cousins get here."

"I'm coming My Lady. I'm coming," a breathless voice called back to her. "But these stupid girls keep dropping things, and this tub is the Devil's own creation, God save us!" And leading a string of castle maids all burdened with great armfuls of towels, soaps and perfumes for their mistress's bath, Agnes bounced into her chamber, an elegant small pair of sheers in her hand, some towels over her arm and somewhat hot of face and body as she mustered her minions, crossing herself as she did so.

"For, I swear if it can catch on one thing it'll catch on everything! I tell you, Judith Cooper," she turned to call down the winding stairs, as sounds of much banging and strife came up the staircase. "If you drop *one* more thing I'll fetch you such a buffet that your ears will ring for a week! And you can take that foolish grin off your face young Maude," she continued, turning on a large, bosomy girl in plain homespun who was right behind her. "For if ever a girl was more clumsy, boneheaded or cack-handed than you, then I have yet to meet her!"

And with a gasp she dropped her burdens down on Alicia's bed while she turned to watch as her helpers struggled in with the great wooden tub they had dragged, bumping and grinding up between them.

Agnes Fitzwalter was softly rounded and cheerful, dressed in a short white wimple and long blue woollen dress with an embroidered petticoat peeping out from underneath. A warm hearted, kindly girl, with good practical sense and a cheerful no-nonsense approach to her sometimes wayward charge! Not as tall as her Saxon father, she had inherited her Southern French mother's dark hair and flashing hazel eyes, as well as her gracefulness, so that she carried her body well, with a straight back and her head held high.

Now a comely young woman of some two and twenty summers, she had looked after Alicia for the past eight years with surprising wit and understanding considering her simple background. But her parents had bred well and the combination of solid Saxon common sense and merry humour had melded with the South French passion and quickness of heart and mind to produce a bright-eyed, determined young woman whose love and loyalty could not be bought with a ton of golden treasure.

Agnes, named for her Saxon grandmother, had been just another of the Lady Margaret's waifs and strays, rescued as a pretty fourteen year old when her whole family had died of fever, leaving the young girl almost prostrate with grief. Her father, Edward Fitzwalter, a giant of a man, had been Sir Yvo's Master-at-Arms until his death. Castle bred, of mixed Saxon and Norman blood, and living with his French born wife, Giselle, Agnes had been brought up to speak French by her mother, herself brought back by her father from the late King's wars after the sack of Cahors thirty years before…where Thibault the Cruel had been cut down by Sir Henry de Burley, Alicia's father, while serving with Sir Yvo in that war for Toulouse…Agnes was unusually talented.

So, when both her parents had died when she was fourteen, the Lady Margaret had known Agnes was special, and had taken her under her wing, giving her the desolate ten year old Alicia to care for, her own father, Sir Henry de Burley having also just died in France. Now that her much loved nurse, Rose, was leaving Castle Malwood to be married to Sir Yvo's former Master-at-Arms, Edward Sergeant, the child, so recently orphaned herself, was sorely in need of loving companionship and youthful understanding. So putting the two of them together had been one of the Lady Margaret's instinctive solutions to a difficult problem, and had proven a huge success.

Since then their relationship had blossomed into a close, warm friendship, complicated neither by Alicia's position as the future chatelaine of a great castle, nor by Agnes's own more humble background, so that Agnes was now as much Alicia's friend and companion as she was her abigail.

Both had struggled together over their letters, as Sir Yvo had decided that if Agnes was to accompany his ward she too must have some formal learning; at least to be able to read and write, and though that might have been considered odd to many men…that *any* girl should be able both to read and write…Sir Yvo considered it a necessary accomplishment for any young woman of Alicia's standing to achieve. Her chosen confidante the same; after all the Old Queen - Eleanor of Aquitaine - was possessed of a formidable intellect and was herself a gifted writer, and what was good enough for his Queen, must surely be good enough for the only daughter of his greatest friend, and also for her companion, abigail or not!

However, it had also set Agnes apart from those whom she might otherwise have married. Popular with all the men in Castle Malwood, as much for her merry smile and bright coquettish ways as for her chocolate curls and firm, voluptuous figure, she would yet have none of them. Alicia had remarked that it would take a rare man to woo her from her side, while Agnes joked that she was saving herself for no less a person than the 'King of France!'

Fiercely loyal to her young mistress and her splendid lover, the more so as he was her master's only son, she now stood beside Alicia with sleeves rolled up above her dimpled elbows, armed with brush, soap and small hand shears: "Well, my love, this is a big day for all of us, " she chatted happily as the girls she had brought with her, and others who followed in a steady stream, busily filled the great wooden tub with hot, steaming water.

"Agnes?" Alicia queried, quirking her mouth and drawing down her eyebrows as she sat on her bed and eyed askance the fine silver handled shears that Agnes was carrying. "Are those really necessary tonight?"

"For any great Lady to attend a function such as tonight's will be," Agnes replied with a grin, fixing her charge with a steely eye, " and then be seen scratching herself between her thighs like a common, flea-bitten tart, would be above all things bad, my dearest. The Lady Margaret would have my hide for it...and that is far more precious to me than the fur between your legs!"

"Agnes!" Alicia exclaimed with a gasp, stifling a smile. "And before these girls too. I am shocked!"

"Now, don't go on so, My Lady." She replied, trying to sound fierce. 'Tis naught but what I have been seeing to with you any time these past five years, so stop your giggling, all of you," she went on rounding on Judith and the other girls with her, who were standing with their hands over their mouths. "And be grateful I don't take these little cutters to the thick thatches I know *you* all have hidden beneath your kirtles!" she ended, swinging sharply round, to crouch down and scuttle forward suddenly snapping with the cutters at their covered loins, so that they shrieked and leaped sharply out of the way, laughing as they did so.

"So," Alicia asked at last, trying to stifle her own giggles, as she watched Agnes laying out her soaps and powders. "How are things going on in the Great Hall, Dearest?"

Agnes stood back and stretched herself, putting her hands on her shapely hips as she did so, smiling broadly. "Sir Yvo is in such a sweat over all the arrangements that he's gone for a ride to cool his head, and the Lady Margaret is in and out of the kitchens like a jack-in-the-box. She is driving Suchard mad with all her instructions and counter-instructions...you know how she is, my love," Agnes continued after a pause, throwing handfuls of herbs and rose petals into the tub beside her as she did so. "If she keeps on giving them it'll be a wonder if we get anything to eat tonight at all!"

She stood back and surveyed her arrangements.

" Now my girl," she went on briskly, turning to Alicia as she spoke. "Up you get, out of that shift and into this water before it gets cold. That blond fur of yours must be clipped. If not then you may yet suffer from the prickly heat, and that soft hollow it's so shyly hiding will smell sour and unloved, and we don't want that do we, my Sweeting?" She ended slowly, giving Alicia a decidedly arch look from underneath her own plucked eyebrows.

"No, you wretch," Alicia replied with a sigh, pulling off her shift as she spoke, and stepping into the scented water. "We surely don't. But I don't have to like it do I?"

"Liar, Liar, Loins on fire!" Agnes replied swiftly, giving her a large soft towel to hold round her shoulders. "Don't you give me that nonsense my girl. You *love* to be pampered. And don't I know it, that have cared for you these eight years past or so"

Then after a while, she said softly, looking up at Alicia's flat belly and the proud thrust of her full breasts, tip-tilted above her: "Alicia, you really are a lovely girl." Adding, almost to herself, as she nestled back to her task, brushing the clipped hair away as she spoke: "A tasty morsel for a king!"

"Even the King of France?" Alicia questioned, mischievously.

"You leave him out of it, you minx!" Agnes reposted swiftly, blowing on her loins. "The 'King of France' is strictly my affair...whomsoever he may turn out to be," she added wistfully. "For with you about to be hand-fast to Sir Gui at last…whom will I have to turn to for life's little compensations?"

"Agnes, you sweet fraud!" Alicia exclaimed, as the girl continued to clip her. "There's young Peter Fletcher and James of Romford who have been after your loving hand any time these past two years…not to mention a host of others I could name! And what about this Jules Lagrasse, I have been hearing about?" she queried, looking down at her friend, with a wicked grin. "He's French, I gather? And you've been seeing a lot of him, you naughty puss. I hear your little coterie of admirers are *very* put out?"

"Well and so they might be," Agnes answered sharply, with a toss of her head. "Peter and James. Bah! They are always fawning after me and begging for my favours with posies of flowers and sweetmeats. Jules is quite different, more sure of himself and–and more determined. If I try to turn him off, he just laughs and comes back with some swift retort. I like that in a man. He is older than me, too, and tougher than others whom I have met, yet with a gentleness that is appealing. A maid likes to feel that her man can protect her"

"Sooo, my little Hampshire Bunny, have you met your match at last?" Alicia asked, her head on one side. "When do I get to meet this young man of yours, who has so swept my Guardian Angel off her feet? I have seen him of course…and his cousin, Lucas Fabrizan. They are some of the men who have come in to us since Richard's proclamation. What does Fitzurse say of them?"

"Alicia, dearest, you go too fast," Agnes said, looking up at her. "I have only met with him a few times…since the Fair two weeks ago. But he seems really nice. He and his cousin came up from South Aquitaine to Normandy after King Henry's death last year, and followed King Richard across to England at the time of his coronation.

"Well…" Alicia said, rubbing the soft towelling across her shoulders, "I can understand that. The King is not a man easily passed over. But how come they ended up here?"

"They went to watch the Christmas Tournament, where Sir Gui knocked the King out of his saddle? And met up with Mercardier, King Richard's Captain of Mercenaries. He gave them a trial, was impressed and recommended they come to Malwood as after Sir Gui's success in the Tournament, he is seen as even more of an up and coming leader than before, and he didn't have a place for them just then anyway. So, they came on here in the Spring."

"They must be good!" Alicia exclaimed. "Mercardier is a tough master and does not suffer fools gladly. Well, Sweetheart. This Jules of yours sounds an enterprising young man indeed. You must introduce him to me, my Love, and his cousin of course, and I will speak with Gui about them. If Mercardier recommended them, then John Fitzurse will have noted that and marked them down for possible promotion."

"Slowly, slowly, My Lady. Please," Agnes said anxiously. "I am still feeling my way with him, and I don't want him startled by too much interest from the future Chatelaine of Castle Malwood!"

"Trust me," Alicia said with a smile. "I can be very unalarming, I promise you. But you are very precious to me, dearest. To all of us, of course, but especially to me and Sir Gui. Where would we have been without you these few years past? But this is the first time I have known you to show any real interest in a man, Honeyone, and there are many rogues about who would just love to claim so vulnerable a heart."

Agnes looked at her and smiled: "I am not exactly fourteen, my Love," she said, grinning. "I am all of two and twenty, and think I would spot a coxcomb by now a mile off! But, talk with him by all means for you are right. My heart is vulnerable. With you and Gui safely betrothed at last, I am aware that time is slipping by me and I would like a man to call my own too! Someone to love me and with whom I can raise a family of my own."

"So, dearest," Alicia said, handing her towel to Judith so that she and Maude could soap her body. "This Frenchman may yet be your 'King of France' in very truth?"

"Maybe, my Lady. Maybe," Agnes said, tapping the side of her nose cheekily. "We shall just have to wait and see, won't we? As for that young Gui of yours," she went on with a chuckle, deftly snipping as she spoke. "He is luckier than he knows, the young devil! For he's getting a King's ransom when he gets you, my own dear Alicia, for there's none more lovely in all this land than you Sweetheart, and well that young varmint knows it too! There," she ended, brushing the last few loose hairs off Alicia's loins with the tips of her fingers, blowing across them as she did so. "Done at last!" And setting aside her hand shears, she ran her soft hands over Alicia's skin.

"Now, come on, you pest. Slip down into the water and let's get the soap off you. Judith is waiting with that soft towel to dry you; Maudie has all your clothes laid out ready on your bed; I have your favourite perfume and the

43

Lady Margaret has your dear mother's sapphire and pearls waiting for you in her chamber when you are ready.

By the time we have finished with you, my dearling, you will look as beautiful as the Queen herself, the King's own mother. And she by all accounts is still really lovely. And this is *nothing* to how you will look for tonight's ceremony, I promise you! All men will desire you, Alicia, but none more truly than your own sweet love. And he'd better look after you as you deserve, young Lady, or he'll have *me* to answer to!"

Chapter 4... *The young Lion of Malwood enters the Lists.*

While Alicia was enjoying the ministrations of her attendants amidst the steaming waters of her bath, her lover and husband-to-be, Sir Gui de Malwood, was talking with his father's Seneschal and Steward in the Great Hall of the Keep, going over the arrangements for the evening.

Entered through The Forework, a set of wide stone external stairs with its own drawbridge and portcullis at the top, the Great Hall was built on the second floor of the Keep that was still the cornerstone of Castle Malwood's defences in those days. The walls, foursquare and some twenty feet thick at the base rose through four levels to tower ninety feet above the surrounding countryside. On each corner were small square turrets that rose a further ten feet or so above the topmost walk way, each one containing a circular staircase from which every level of the massive building could easily be reached. And on every level were a variety of rooms and chambers: dormitories for the soldiers who manned the battlements; elegant guest rooms for visiting knights and dignitaries; together with a host of other offices and simple sleeping rooms as well; and on the very topmost floor Sir Yvo's former family apartments, now occupied by his Seneschal, Sir James Bolderwood. Each room plastered and painted in cheerful colours chosen by Lady Margaret and Alicia together, often to the despair of Gui and Sir Yvo!

The Great Hall itself was an enormous room, rising through two stories of the whole building, and lit by a series of tall Romanesque style double-arched windows on each side recessed into the thickness of the walls. Through these the sun poured its warmth and light in searchlight beams of gold that cast a brilliant pattern of stripes and bars across the freshly herb-strewn floor, great diagonals of dust and pollen dancing and quivering every time someone walked across it.

Finely carved mullions and trefoils decorated every window space, and there were broad seats beneath, well padded with gaily embroidered cushions. Above each recess the stonework had been beautifully carved with zigzag patterns and deep chevrons, all painted in bright colours, while the recesses themselves were white plaster-covered and joyously decorated with birds and animals of the chase.

Overhead a stunning arched roof of huge oaken crucks, like the ribs of some vast ship, stretched above the room. Each enormous cruck springing upwards from the walls on solid stone corbels that had themselves been beautifully carved with bunches of grapes and curling vine leaves, in memory of the French wine lands from whence Gui's family, and Alicia's, originally had come.

Half way along one side was a giant fireplace that in winter took whole tree trunks, and great piles of logs as well, so that the flames would roar and crackle in the hearth, almost roasting anyone who stood or sat too close. Then the smoke would go swirling up amongst the distant rafters as much as going up the massive stone chimney, making eyes water and chests heave and cough when the wind was in the wrong direction.

Now, in high summer, it was empty, soon to be filled with wide armfuls of flowers and leafy branches. As Gui's mother had been busy in the castle gardens as well, so there would be roses all along the tables that night, both white ands coloured, and great lilies, their beautiful white trumpets heavy with the scent of summer, all spreading their perfume amongst the many guests soon to be seated at the boards.

Along the walls were ornate iron sconces for the pine-filled torches that were used to light the huge room at night. Usually only a handful were lit, those around the raised dais on which the family ate their meals, and a few others above the trestles where the castle retainers sat at meat and ate and drank each evening. But tonight every sconce would be filled, along with all the tall wrought iron stands that held a multitude of candle-pins for extra light. Hanging from the very pinnacles of each mighty cruck, on strong chains, were enormous iron wheels with similar candle-pins that could be raised and lowered by ropes and pulleys as required, an idea that Sir Yvo had brought back with him from France. Tonight all would be lit and the whole vast room would be a blaze of shimmering light.

At the far end was a raised dais on which stood a massive long table on finely turned legs. Made from the sawn and polished planks of a single great oak, the first to be felled when the castle had originally been built, it was a magnificent monument to the castle carpenter who had created it. Along one whole side of it, placed to face the entrance of the hall at the opposite end of the building, was a row of beautifully carved wooden chairs with firm seats in red leather, four with taller backs and padded arms of scarlet wool as well. Facing those were polished oak benches with padded covers.

Behind the dais, suspended from the walls on a series of bronze hooks and poles, glowing with a multitude of rich colours and iridescent gold and silver threads, hung a truly magnificent embroidery. A rippling picture of rude hunting action that seemed to pulse with life, as the full panoply of the chase rode violently across the wall from the huntsmen on their horses in full cry at one side with horns and flags and leaping hounds, right to the dying stag, terrible in its rage, brought to bay at the other. When the wind caught it and made the whole thing move and sway, it seemed almost as if all those on it were alive and about to burst from the wall in all their hunting glory!

Hanging from the other walls were family banners, coats of arms, painted shields, tilting helms and great racks of weapons, all bearing testimony to the Malwood's proud and ancient fighting lineage.

Seated right beneath the stag, his chair tilted against the wall, lounged a young man in a fine cambric shirt under a well used jerkin, loosely tucked into a pair of soft, brown leather chausses. Still booted and spurred from his morning's ride across the demesne he now sat, relaxed, while he listened to their Seneschal and Steward, Sir James Bolderwood, outline all the many problems still facing them. Argos, his great white Talbot, collapsed in a heap in the corner, nose on great paws, dozing. But Gui's mind, dwelling far more on his coming betrothal to his own utterly delicious Alicia than to Sir James' moans about the problems of the coming evening, was anything but focused as it should have been.

Gui de Malwood, named after his great grandfather, was twenty two years old with powerful arms and broad shoulders, barrel-chested, with legs like tall tree trunks below a narrow waist; he was built like a barn door! Lean and hard from years of training with all kinds of weapons and riding in all kinds of weather, there was no disguising the fact that here was a young man in the very peak of condition. His face, tanned as much by the wind and rain as by the sun, and his tightly curled black hair only served to emphasise the steel blue of his eyes that betrayed his Norman-French ancestry.

Sent as a young Squire to Baron John de Methley in West Yorkshire, who had marriage connections with his own family and himself served under the Lord Percy, the great Earl of Northumbria, he had returned to Malwood two years past as a fully fledged Knight. Since which time he had been engaged in the Old King's wars in France against Philip Augustus, the French King, and against Henry's own sons, Richard and John; indeed he had been at Chinon when Henry had died there the previous July.

Now Richard, thirty two years old and the foremost warrior of his age, whom Gui and his father had been fighting against so fiercely, was named King in his place and all men trembled. But...the Malwoods had ever held for the King, as all true knights should, and Richard had honoured Gui for his allegiance to his father despite their quarrel, knowing that he and his family had always been faithful to the Crown. Now, with Henry dead and himself crowned King in Westminster, Richard had looked to them all for their loyalty, and the King could not be gainsaid!

Huge and immensely powerful, with the figure and face of a Greek Apollo, hair and beard red-gold in colour and so handsome that he fascinated both friends and enemies alike, Richard was a true tower of strength and fortitude. He captivated everyone with his charm of manner and supreme courage. Fighting was the very breath of his life, and his barons, French and English alike, loved him for it. He could cut a man in half through his armour as easily as he could play the lute or sing a plaintive love song, for Richard was a distinguished troubadour, as well as a fearsome warrior, and regularly took part in the famous singing festival of Provence,' The Jeux Floreaux,' that was renowned throughout the whole length and breadth of France.

No man alive was like Richard Coeur de Lion, King of England, overlord of Scotland Wales and Ireland; Duke of Normandy; Count of Brittany, Anjou, Maine, Touraine and Poitou; Duke of all Aquitaine and disputed ruler of Toulouse.

The finest general of his age next to the Old German Emperor, Barbarossa, and with the same unbounded energy and striking courage. He loved the pomp and panache of his kingly office and adored his mother too, the incomparable, redoubtable, and eternally beautiful Queen Eleanor of Aquitaine.

All men loved Richard...except the King of France and his cronies!

Half Norman and half Angevin, with the hot south French blood of his mother as well, it was said that he could understand all the languages around the Circle Sea. And, though he could speak no Saxon, he was still the true and rightful King of England, and a man after Gui's own heart.

Who would not be awed by such a man?

So when the King had placed his great hands on either side of Gui's not inconsiderable shoulders and, looking deep into his eyes, blazing blue into cool steel grey, and had asked with a smile for both his friendship and his knightly love; how could so great a man, and now his true King by right, be so shamefully denied?

So, Gui had sworn for King Richard Plantagenet, as his father, Sir Yvo had sworn to King Henry before him, kneeling in all humility and putting his hands between his King's and swearing the oath that would bind him, and his, to the King 'til death: "...I swear to become your man from this day forward, of life and limb and earthly worship and shall be true and faithful for the lands I hold of you...

It had been a majestic moment.

And a joyous one also as much because of Alicia as because of the confirmation of his own heritage by the King, and hers of course by association, which Richard justly could have seized as punishment for fighting against him in France. He had a reputation for favouring those who supported him and him alone; but in their case he had chosen not to do so, accepting their loyalty as full recompense for any wrongs committed against him while fighting for his father. So, it was a very solemn moment too. Almost as solemn as his own knighthood, bestowed on him when his long service in the North had come to an end two years before, which his parents had attended, bringing Alicia with them.

That had been an utterly unexpected surprise!

When he had gone North she was still a ragged, long-legged tomboy with a wicked spirit of mischief. Someone he had chased shrieking through the castle orchards; stolen a day's hawking behind old Gerome's back; and taught to fight with sword and dagger. Whom he had rescued from scrapes; mended her kitten's paw when it had got trapped, and with whom he had hunted rabbits with nets and his pet ferret, Nestor. Now she had become the loveliest young woman he could hope to meet, both calm and stately, yet still with that wicked twinkle in her eyes with which she had watched him at every possible moment throughout the whole ceremony as if she could not get enough of him, a smile of such pride and loveliness on her face that she had touched his very soul.

He could still feel the amazing tingle that had coursed through his whole body when he had touched her hands for the first time. Not in the simple friendship of their youth...but as a man and woman, touching and caressing their fingers with a warmth and meaning that had not been there before. That first magical, almost breathtaking moment when a man feels the gentle softness, the warmth and exciting pressure, of a female hand in his that is not that of his mother, his sister or his nurse, but belongs to a woman unknown before that time.

From that moment he *knew* that she would be for ever special in his life and he could not *wait* to get to know this new, and startling, Alicia better. He shook his head in silent amazement at all that had happened since and sighed deeply. Without his knighthood he might never have discovered the new Alicia at all, and certainly not have earned King Richard's favour.

It was like finding a rare and special jewel in his pocket amongst a handful of pebbles off the beach, all of which could so easily have been cast away without another thought as skimmers across the waves! Yet chance had somehow stayed the hand. Now, without realising it, he had fallen deeply in love with her. She was so diverting, and so determined that he would do well and be admired for the man he was as much as for the man she believed he still could be, even when he was in a rage about something.

No treading on eggshells for his Alicia when her man was in a temper! Indeed she had thrown a bucket of water over him once, when he had been snapping and snarling over some silliness or other. Much as she would over two dogs scrapping in the castle yard. And he had been so angry with her! Snatching up another bucket standing nearby, and chasing her up to her room, where he had emptied it all over her too, and together they had fallen and rolled over and over on her bed 'til she had come up on top of him, laughing and kissing him at the same time, the pair of them soaked to the skin.

He put his hands behind his head then and sighed in warmest contemplation.

For that was when they had become lovers for the first time. Unplanned and unexpected, yet so wonderful and marvellous. Wholly inexperienced, yet they had fitted one another like a pair of much loved gloves. Soft and warm and all enveloping. He had no idea that making love to anyone could be so...*so*...fantastic and amazing! Making love with her had been just gorgeous in every possible way. And having done it once with wild and furious abandon, they had done it again slowly and lovingly, as the songs and poems said it should be. The very thought of her stirred him; made him want her. *Dear Lord, but he loved her so!* She would be the most wonderful chatelaine, and mother of their children. Surely he was the luckiest man alive in all England!

"Gui!" The tall Seneschal growled at him at last, waving the sheaf of papers he held in his hand before his face. "You're not listening to me at all! And haven't been for the last ten minutes at least," he went on, his rich voice full of frustration. "Man and boy I've known you, young man," he went on with a sigh. "And you haven't changed a bit. No wonder I get so..so *exasperated* with you at times!"

Sir James Bolderwood was a man of quiet confidence and enormous ability. Tall and still slender, he was now, in his later years, both stately and white haired, with a fierce eye for wrong-doers, but a dry and ready wit, and the rare ability of being able to communicate as easily with the greatest in the land as with the meanest serf on Sir Yvo's broad estates. A man of great strength of mind and nobility of spirit, he was unfailingly discreet and, next to the Lady Margaret, was his father's greatest confidant. There was not anything planned that Sir James did not know about first, and all men trusted him as much for his fairness as his total honesty.

"James!" Gui said, looking up with a gay laugh and a wave of his hand. "That's just not true. I have listened to every liquid word…well almost! About the extra horses being stabled in the village? The accommodation for our guest's retainers; provisions for their servants in the Hall? All sorts of endless stuff! Not bad eh?"

"Amazing!" The Seneschal replied dryly, with mock astonishment. "But, what about the presentations? The meeting and greeting of all your most important guests at the Hall entrance? Who's guarding what and by whom? Well…?"

"Well…" Gui temporised, grinning broadly, "have a clack of this excellent wine, while I think of a good answer," he ended, reaching across to the tall silver pitcher that stood on the table near by. "And you'll feel better! I never knew a fellow, for worrying about things as you."

"Indeed, Dear Boy. Just as I thought," Sir James went on resignedly, picking up a spare goblet as he spoke. "Away with the bloody fairies! Not a clue! I saw you gazing into space, as glazed as any man after his third flagon I assure you. Honestly, Gui. If you get any of this wrong tonight, we'll all be in the suds!"

"Oh, come on, James. Don't badger me so! As long as I'm more or less in the right place, and Alicia is beside me so I can see, hear and touch her, I really don't give much of a fig for anything else. Not my parents, not our many esteemed guests...and especially not the bloody Lord Baron de Brocas and his hell-born daughter! Honestly, James," Gui went on sharply, letting his chair down onto the floor with a bang and standing up. "Father must be out of his mind to invite those two here, and tonight of all nights also!"

"He is certainly a bitter man."

"Bitter? That is the understatement of the year! He may have been only fourteen when his father was killed at the in-taking of Cahors during the Old King's wars, but he has never forgotten that it was Alicia's father who struck Tibault de Brocas down that day, his own uncle. Nor forgiven it either!"

Gui paced the whole length of the dais before turning sharply back towards Sir James. "You know, of course, that they lost practically everything after that? To the victor the spoils, and King Henry confiscated all their lands and castles in the Empire, especially around Montauban, and took away their privileges as well. Henry never was one to forgive a slight easily, and certainly not treason on Tibault's scale! They lost everything that it was in Henry's gift to give them.

All they have now are their lands and castle at Grise, and the Lordship of Narbonne under the Count of Toulouse."

"Mmmm. I know, and Toulouse is effectively Richard's," Sir James commented. "That's what your father was doing out there in '59. Securing Henry's control of the whole County as promised to him through his marriage to Eleanor, and agreed by Louis before he died. But the lands are still disputed and the Lord Baron Sir Roger de Brocas has been very active in the past thirty years since his father was slain before his eyes at Cahors." Sir James ended with a sigh, looking at Gui from beneath his eyes.

"Since when he has gone on to become much valued by Philip, King Louis' son, and his lands are now protected both by the Count of Toulouse, no friend of Richard's, and by Philip Augustus, the so glorious King of France."

Gui finished sarcastically, as he stopped his pacing and swung himself onto the table. "And we all know how much *he* loves Richard occupying his kingdom so strongly that he has little or no control over two thirds of it!"

Sir James came across and stood elegantly before him. "They've had a grudge against your family for generations though, haven't they?" he questioned dryly.

"Absolutely right!" Gui exclaimed, swinging his legs. "The struggle between the de Brocas family and ours, the Burleys as well as the Malwoods, goes back years and years. Centuries! Right back to old Gui de Valance, my Great Grandfather, and Robert de Riveaux, Alicia's, who were given these lands by Duke William on the very night following the Battle of Hastings over a hundred years ago.

They saved the Duke's life at the very height of the fighting, when it was at its fiercest, and all thought the Duke had been slain. It was they told him to take off his helmet and show his face to his men. You've seen the pictures? In the tapestry at Bayeux, that his half brother, Bishop Odo had made afterwards?

"No."

"Well, James, you should do! It's amazing. William had just had his second horse killed under him, by one of Harold's brothers. Robert killed the man, and then stood over William to defend him, while Gui de Valance...after whom I am named!...gave him his own horse and told William to get up and show everyone he was still alive! When it was all over, William called them both to his tent, there on the battlefield amongst the stench of blood-boltered bodies, and gave them their rights to these lands. They were the first of all Duke William's men to benefit from that desperate fight the Saxons called 'Senlac' and we call 'Hastings'. They came to England because of feuding and troubles around Montauban and Rocamadour, where they held valuable estates and wine lands, with that same de Brocas family, changed their names to show their change of allegiance from Normandy to England, and never went back.

De Brocas! God Save us," he growled darkly. "They were a thoroughly bad lot then, and they are a thoroughly bad lot now. They will *never* change! That black-hearted bastard is capable of anything!" Gui said, jumping onto the floor. "Especially now that he is so friendly with Prince John and allied to Philip of France."

"Ah, yes! The King's baby brother!"

"Even so. He is low-minded and deceitful at best, and murderously cunning with it. And he's only twenty two, God help us! He would steal the throne itself if he could. Apart from Richard, only his mother, Queen Eleanor, appears to have any control over him. By all accounts he is *petrified* of her!"

"I had heard he was showing an interest in our Alicia?" Sir James queried softly, reaching for a wine goblet that Gui was filling.

"Just so," Gui said, wiping his mouth. "Ever since we all went to Court last year for Richard's coronation, the Prince has asked after her."

"For himself, despite his new wife...or for the so pleasant Baron Roger?"

"*God's Bones!*" Gui exclaimed, standing stock still. "I had not thought of that. Surely not?" he queried, turning sharply back towards Sir James. "Not even de Brocas would dare to look so high as one of King Richard's Wards...especially as his family have long been tainted by the Crown? God knows what my father was thinking of to send that Man-of-Blood an invitation to our betrothal. You might as well ask the Angel of Death to our feast, as Roger de fucking Brocas!"

"Sweet Jesu!" Sir James exclaimed, with a laugh. "You really don't' like him do you?"

"No, James, I do not!" Gui replied tersely. "He's an evil, black-hearted, smooth-tongued, lying bastard of a Frenchman with no honour, bad background and loose breeding...and I don't trust him either!"

Sir James laughed heartily at that, flinging his arm across Gui's shoulder as he did so: "Well anyway, Dear Boy, don't upset your father over this. After all it is only for a few days and it will all be over."

"Why, oh why, did he ever invite him, James?" he questioned fiercely. "It was not even on his horizon when we set off for London last year, as much for Richard's coronation, as to ask the King for permission to marry Alicia. Later on he was *full* of it! It makes no sense that I can see at all!" Gui said, slipping the older man's arm off him as he turned and went to sit back down on the table.

Sir James, his brows drawing down in concentrated thought, looked hard at the young man now reaching for the tall pitcher to refill his glass. There was so much he wanted to tell him that he could not, as Sir Yvo had sworn him to secrecy.

"Well, Gui," he said with a sigh. "Your father told everyone that this betrothal of yours and Alicia's is *exactly* the kind of family occasion needed to bring this long-standing feud to an end. Ever since that extra meeting he had with the King after you had left, he has talked of nothing else."

"What extra meeting with the King, James?" Gui asked, sharply astonished. "He's not said anything about it to me."

"Mmm, that's why he remained in London after you had all gone home," he said casually, looking at Gui from the corner of his eyes. "And after the Christmas Tournament when you dropped the King on his Royal Arse, they spoke again. It was as much that as anything else that persuaded Richard to agree to your betrothal. He holds you in high esteem, Dear Boy. Gave you his Royal ring I believe. I thought you knew?"

"About the King's esteem...or my father's meeting with him?

"Your father's meeting with him, of course."

"Well, actually, no - I didn't," Gui said softly. "The Old Fox! Now what was he up to I wonder? Ever since then he has gone out of his way to make this place as homely as possible. But he's been very...skittish of late. Like a herring on a griddle. What's he up to James?"

"Oh...I shouldn't' worry about that, Dear Boy, he's often like that before a special occasion. But, actually, he's a bit anxious about one of the guests he has specially invited for your betrothal. The man was due yesterday and hasn't yet arrived."

"He's kept that all very close to his chest. Do you know who it is?"

"Mmmm. Oh, some ancient warrior from his past," the Seneschal replied enigmatically, brushing Gui's question aside. "Someone whom he wished to honour with an invitation to his only son's betrothal. Now don't spoil his fun, Gui. But be patient with him I implore you; for your mother's sake if not for your own."

"Never fear, James. I wouldn't upset our noble Lord and Master over something like that for all the world. But this wretched business with de Brocas and his daughter coming here...that's a different matter. He seems to be almost relishing it all somehow. Going on as if he didn't have a care in the world...

"Well," the tall Seneschal replied, noncommittally. "Of course, while that may be true...isn't it also possible that there is more to all of these preparations than you may yet know of, Dear Boy? Don't you think?

"James?..." Gui questioned him, moving urgently towards him.

"*Ware hawk!*" The older man interrupted him quietly, holding his hand up to prevent him speaking further. "Your father's here, with your dear Mama. I have said more than enough, Gui. More than perhaps I should have done. If you wish to know further, Dear Boy?...You must ask Sir Yvo." And with quiet grace he moved to one side, his grey eyes cool and steady as he watched Gui's father come booming into the Hall, Bellman at his side, followed by his wife, the Lady Margaret, looking decidedly ruffled.

Chapter 6…In which we meet Sir Yvo again…and the Lady Margaret.

At the sight of his large son, still not changed when the first, and arguably most important, of his guests was expected to arrive at any moment, he at once became somewhat forceful!

Sir Yvo de Malwood, now a large, heavily built man of medium height, slightly overweight, with the black hair he had bequeathed to his son just turning silver, and while not built on quite such generous lines as Gui, he still had the same square shaped face and powerful torso. And even though at fifty five the hard muscle of which he had once been so proud had rather gone to fat in these more quiet times, he was till a formidable veteran soldier.

Now, his eyebrow, somewhat grizzled against his more florid complexion, shot up in surprise that his son should still be drifting about, wholly unprepared, when everyone else was running about in ever decreasing circles.

Beside him his wife, the Lady Margaret, looked quite small, not unlike a plump partridge to a lordly pheasant, with short, bustly legs, a round cuddly figure and holding a wooden spoon. She was a kind and gentle soul with a good word for most people and if anyone was in trouble in the village, or in the castle of course, they could be sure of a warm and sympathetic ear. Over the years a fair number of unfortunate youngsters had found their way into service with the Lady Margaret de Malwood as a result of her kindness.

Indeed, Agnes Fitzwalter was a case in point, Lady Margaret having taken her in when her father, Sir Yvo's old Master-at-Arms, and all his family had died of a fever. Agnes had only been a youngster then, about fourteen, but Lady Margaret had trained her into a truly loyal and loving companion for Alicia after Sir Henry de Burley had died in France.

But she was also firm with all those who served her, and ruled her large husband, and her son, with subtle strength such that they would do all they could to serve her and not cause her any more concern than was necessary given the nature of their lives. Likewise the soldiers of the Castle Guard, who knew where their loyalty and their duty lay with regard to the Lady Margaret of Castle Malwood…and woe betide any who thought to take her kindness and her gentleness for granted. She was not the daughter of a fighting Earl for nothing, and could be as sharp and unyielding as Damascus steel if it were truly necessary to be so.

"Splendour of God, Gui!" his father boomed when he saw his son and Sir James together on the dais. "De Brocas and his daughter will be with us any moment and you've plainly made no effort to get yourself ready at all!"

Gui, who had been warned of his father's striding approach by Sir James, his mother following along behind him looking bothered, stood up slowly his face hardening with resolve as he moved.

"Father?" He asked carefully, rubbing his large hands together as he jumped lightly off the dais, before coming and bowing before him as a young man should. "Did you see the King in London the last time we were up? After the Tournament, My lord?" He continued formally. "After the rest of us had all left, I mean. You stayed behind remember? Did you have words with Richard about de Brocas?"

His father stopped and looked at his son, his head turned slightly to one side, his mind racing, eyes subtly shifting under Gui's steady gaze.

"Speak with Richard, eh?...Speak with the King?" and he coughed to hide his confusion. "Yes - of course I spoke with Richard," his father replied, blustering a little. "We both did. So did Alicia and your mother. We were there when he gave you his ring after your fantastic success in the Tournament. How else could we now be doing what we are," he gestured around them, "without first having spoken with the King?"

"Yes, father, I *know* that," Gui replied patiently, looking keenly at the older man as he spoke, before turning away and then back again. "I was there too, remember? But did you see him *again*? *Afterwards*? *After* we had all left to go home?"

His father stood still and glared, while his mother stepped silently away from them both, her face looking suddenly pinched and drawn.

"Yes, Gui. I may have done," he answered slowly, looking round at his Seneschal with a quizzical glance under slightly raised eyebrows, to be answered, silently, with a shake of his head. "But it was on matters of State that do not concern you, my Boy," he went on turning back to look into his son's cool eyes. "And this," he gestured with his hand around the Hall, and at the servants beginning to enter it, "is neither the time, nor the place!" He paused. "This is about de Brocas, Gui. Isn't it?"

58

"Yes, Father, it is! That man, and his daughter, are coming here today. He has a reputation that reeks of evil…and she, by all accounts, is not much better. Yet we slay the fatted calf for him and put her with Alicia. The one person, I am certain, who should be kept as far away from her as possible! I do not understand it!"

"*Gui!*" his father exclaimed sharply, his face beginning to redden while his wife stood behind him, her hand over her mouth in an agony of distress. "You forget yourself! You may be my only son and heir, but you do not stand in my shoes yet. Whom I invite into my own home is for me to decide. *No!*" he exclaimed again, taking a pace forward and holding his hand up in his son's face as Gui made to speak, his eyes hard and glittering. "I know you see this as your concern, Gui, but it is not. Anyway, it is beyond your hands or mine now…and you are frightening your mother, and that I cannot allow! *Leave it alone!*"

"What do you mean, 'beyond your hands or mine'?"

"I cannot say more," his father blustered, suddenly aware that he had said too much. "Only…only that they are due here any minute and cannot now be turned away." softly adding: "Trust me to know what I am about, my son, and all will be well."

"Father, I respect you in all things, you know that," Gui replied earnestly, maintaining as even a tone as possible. "Mother, too, of course. But this is my day too, remember? And Alicia's, and this man, and his daughter by all accounts," he added in sharp disgust, turning away as he spoke. "Are as foul a set of blots on our landscape as can possibly be imagined!"

Then, pacing furiously back again he flung at him: "De Brocas and his kin have been our family's enemies since before the conquest. And since Alicia's father cut Thibault down thirty years ago, even more so. And he is Richard's enemy too! Harbouring the King's foes and encouraging Prince John. He is King Philip's…pimp!" He snarled viciously. "His make-bait and secret enforcer, and yet you have seen fit to invite him into our home! Why Father? Why?"

"*ENOUGH!*" Sir Yvo roared, slamming his fist down on the table and making everyone jump. "*Enough Sir!* I will not have you use such vile language before your mother, and frightening her into the bargain. Suffice it, Gui, that I have my reasons!" He went on, his voice clipped and hard. "*Yes!* The King and I had speech on many things, Gui, aye and made arrangements and agreements too. But not all things that we discussed need be made known to all people. Not even to you, my son. *No, Gui!*" he went on sharply, holding his hand up to his son's face again to forestall him from speaking. "Richard is our Liege Lord and if he sends an emissary we must do all we can to support him…no matter how difficult that may be." He ended, looking at Gui steadily as he spoke.

"What 'Emissary', Father?" Gui shot back at him, his eyes like sharpened needle points

"That is not your concern, Gui!" His father snapped back at him. "The man comes as much at my invitation as for any other reason."

"Which man, My Lord?" Gui threw back at him. "The Baron de Brocas…or this strange 'Emissary' you have just mentioned?"

"I have no more to say, Gui," his father replied, dropping his voice to an almost sibilant whisper. "Just that this 'idea' did not come from me alone!"

"So, the King does have a hand in this?"

"Gui," his father warned, his voice soft, yet dark with menace. "Do not spoil a lovely day with any more of this, please. I said, '*Enough!*', and I meant it. You'll get no more out of me!"

Gui stepped back at that and looked at his father, standing foursquare before him almost bristling with determination, his hands on his hips, his chin thrust forward, his mouth a straight, hard line. And at his mother, standing a few paces back, her eyes wide, like a frighted deer.

"Well, I can see that!" his son snorted, more intrigued than abashed by his father's sudden anger. "But that simply raises more questions than it answers, my dear Papa, don't' you think?"

Both men paused then, eyes locked together, the air tense with suppressed passions, while Sir James stood still as a statue, his goblet easy in his hand and Lady Margaret looked on, anxiety etched into every line of her comely face. A dreadful row now between her husband and their son would be too awesome even to contemplate. Alicia would never forgive either of them!

Gui drew a deep breath.

He knew his father well. He knew that when Sir Yvo spoke in just 'that' way his word was law. Final! And to remonstrate with him any further would only bring a furious rejoinder. And anyway, he was right. This was neither the time nor the place for such a discussion.

Interesting though, his father's reaction.

So...Sir James was right. His father *had* spoken with Richard after they had all gone home. Clearly there was more to all this than met the eye. He drew another breath, his eyes still locked on his father's face. But what? And who was this mysterious stranger whom his father was so concerned about? This, 'Emissary'? His father's face gave nothing away. Nor did Sir James', when he turned to look at him.

The one slightly flushed and quizzical. The other bland as a blancmange. Yet, clearly the King was involved in some way...and it was about de Brocas. So why wouldn't the old buzzard discuss it with him? That in itself was unusual. Since he had been knighted they had *always* discussed things. He sighed. Too much secrecy could lead to disaster, and then where would they all be?

He smiled then, and stepped back holding his hands up in mock surrender: "So be it, Father," he said dryly, looking Sir Yvo knowingly in the face. "So be it! I bow to your superior knowledge and to my King's will *of course*!" He ended, emphasising the last phrase before stepping back.

Sir Yvo sighed and smiled, and came and laid his hands on his son's massive shoulders: "Look. I don't like the man any more than you do, my son. But there are reasons why your mother and I have invited him that I simply cannot divulge. Just trust me....eh? And make sure that Richard L'Eveque is on duty tonight and that he has John Fitzurse by his side... and keep your eyes open. Now...for the honour of our House and my peace of mind, for God's sake *hurry!*"

"I am sorry, Father," Gui replied seriously, stepping back and bowing his head in formal polite recognition of his father's status as he did so. "I will be ready, and I will not let you down."

"I never thought for one minute that you would do," his father said slowly with a warm smile, looking him in the eyes.

Gui grinned then and giving his father a single terse nod of the head, turned with a grin and complete change of mood to his mother.

Kneeling smoothly before her and kissing her hand warmly as he did so he said gallantly: "Mother, I give you my knee, and may I say what splendid form you are in today...if a trifle distrait, my love," he added, standing up once more. "I see you have been with the cooks again, my lovely, dear Mama. You have flour on your cheek, and are holding one of Suchard's spoons!" So saying he brushed her face, giving her a swift kiss and a quick squeeze at the same time, and gently whisked the long wooden spoon out of her hands.

"Now, if I don't go immediately father will have a fit...look at his face! Alicia will be furious and I will be in disgrace with everyone! And poor Suchard will be missing his favourite spoon!" And with a light laugh and wide brazen grin he took himself off before anyone had the chance to say anything further, a fragment of tune on his lips, and twirling the long wooden spoon nonchalantly between his fingers as he went.

Chapter 7...Sir Yvo's secret plans for the Wicked Baron are revealed.

"**R**eally, My Lord," his wife said, somewhat flustered as she watched their large son saunter jauntily away. "What a rascal we have for a son. He has the effrontery of the devil himself, God save us! He's a real cozener. I can't think where he gets it from?" And with a broad smile she looked up at her equally large husband, sneaking her arms around him as she did so, to give him a shy, loving hug.

There was a pause then, while they both watched 'til he passed out of sight, their thoughts miles away. Then, with a little sigh, Lady Margaret shook herself and taking her husband's large hand in her own small one and linking her fingers with his as she did so, she looked up and asked: "Do you think he knows, Yvo?"

"About my speech with the King over de Brocas? No, Sweetheart. I'm sure he doesn't. But he can guess that something's up. He is no fool, our large son. He knows now that I spoke with Richard, more's the pity - but not actually what it was that we discussed. And he smells a rat over our reasons for inviting Alicia's French cousins, which is a shame. But he has not cracked that particular nut yet, my Love. Nor must he until the last possible moment!"

"Why not just tell him, Yvo?" his wife urged. "Since we came back from Alnwick you have always discussed such things with him, why not *this*?" she emphasised. "When so much depends on it. I know your reasons...I just don't agree with them. Nor does Sir James. And you've kept Richard L'Eveque in the dark too!"

"Oh, Margaret," Sir Yvo sighed, drawing his wife's arm through his as he spoke. "We have been through this a dozen times, my darling...and with Sir James as well. He also believes I should talk to Gui. But, in all honesty, Margaret, Look at the boy! He is as straight as a die and wears his heart on his sleeve. He hasn't learned to be a dissembler, like James and me. And *you*, Sweetheart, when you have a need to!"

He would not be able to hide his feelings for one minute. De Brocas would take one look at him and sense a trap immediately. Trust me in this, My Lady. You *know* I am right. And how could I possibly tell Sir Richard, and not my own son? No...it is best that we keep the two of them in the dark for the time being. They will accept the reasons for it all more easily when it's all over and out in the open I assure you."

His wife sighed and nodded slowly. "Then why not just arrest them both the moment they arrive?" she asked, reasonably. "That way it would all be over in one go and we could then go ahead and really enjoy ourselves without this - this mountain of doubt and anxiety looming over us!"

"Because de Brocas is a subject of King Philip's, blast him!" Her burly husband explained simply. "His lands lie beyond Richard's undisputed lands so he is free from arrest. We have had to lure him here...and it has taken time to find the proofs of his treason. *Months!* Quite apart from not wanting to upset the French King on the eve of his setting out with Richard from Frétval...especially as things in France are not wholly peaceful. It would also be illegal without the King's Warrant. It has to be 'right', my darling. And I don't want a bloodbath on my doorstep on the very morning of our son's betrothal, with half the County coming. That would be just dreadful and would ruin everything. The King wants it all done very quietly, and be certain, my Love, de Brocas and his men will fight like tigers!"

"So, Yvo, where is the Warrant?"

"*God's Throat!* Margaret," he exclaimed violently. That's what I would like to know too, and have been in a fret over this whole morning. Where is that man? What has happened to Matthew?"

"Our Benedictine emissary from King Richard? Your old fighting companion who married us and baptised our son?"

"Yes! He has everything with him. John has his spies everywhere, so Matthew has come over from Normandy quietly, on his own with just two of his Brothers for company. He should have been here yesterday. Now de Brocas will arrive at any moment and our other most important guest is not here!"

"Be patient, My Lord. He will be here, I am certain. He has known us both too long and too closely to let you down, let alone his King. But what about your honour in all this, Yvo?" she asked anxiously, looking up at her husband's grim face. "You have invited the Baron and his daughter here in the

64

spirit of friendship. Yet you mean to seize them yourself through treachery. What will men say of you after this?"

"I have no compunction over that, my darling," her husband replied sharply, stopping and turning towards her as he spoke. "None at all! The man is a monster, and his daughter little better. Gui was right about that in every respect."

"But you are putting his daughter, the Lady Rochine, in with Alicia." she said incredulously. "Is that wise?"

"Keep your friends close, my Love, but keep your enemies closer!" He answered her with a smile. "Alicia will be well guarded, I assure you, and the Baron and his men well watched. It is all in hand."

"Is Baron Roger's treason that bad?"

"Just about as bad as it comes, Sweetheart. The very worst because it threatens the whole kingdom, though I cannot tell you all that now. That will have to wait until Matthew gets here. Suffice it that Richard has known of all this for *months!* Why do you think John has been barred from the country after he leaves? Or at least forced to promise not to come near the place for the next three years. Personally I would rather see him behind bars, than foot-loose and fancy-free in France to do what he pleases. And I am not sure that Longchamps will be able to control him once the Queen leaves to fetch Berengaria, and then take her to be married to Richard.

But that is the King's problem. De Brocas is ours, and I have the King's direct orders as to how he is to be dealt with. But God's Blood, I need that Warrant! *And the proofs,* to carry them out...and those I do not have!" And he stamped his feet in sheer frustration, making his wife laugh.

"Oh Yvo," she said after a moment, with a smile, giving her husband a swift cuddle. "I am sure it will be alright. In the meantime, as you say, we must just carry on as we have started and enjoy our son's betrothal with the loathful Baron and his wicked daughter by our sides!" Then, looking up into his face, and hanging on his arm like a young girl she gave him a dazzling smile and said: "Are there any parents more fortunate than we?"

"You are changing the subject," he said with a sudden grin, his heart lightening as he looked down at her.

"And about time too!" she replied, giving his arm a shake. "I have had enough of all this gloomy talk on the very day of our son's betrothal to the most lovely girl in the kingdom."

"Not quite the most lovely girl in the kingdom, Sweetheart," he replied gently, looking down at her, his eyes bright with mischief.

"You old flatterer!" She exclaimed, delighted at his raillery, lifting her face up for the kiss he was swift to give her, a skip in her step as he did so. "Alicia is an absolute darling, and Gui has grown up so - so wonderfully, Yvo. I know the two of you strut and stag at times, but I am still so proud of what he has become."

"What a scamp, eh?" Sir Yvo said with a chuckle. "Heart of Christ, Margaret, but he is a fine lad," he went on, looking down into his wife's wide blue eyes with a loving smile. "We are so lucky you know. That young puss across there," he said, gesturing towards Alicia's tower apartment, "is a real beauty. I never saw such a charmer in my life…except for you, my Life of course," he added archly, giving his lady an affectionate squeeze. "I don't think a daughter of our own blood could have greater love for us than young Alicia."

She paused then, to look around the hall, at all the bustle and rush as the castle servants and a small host of other helpers scurried about to complete their preparations before the first guests should arrive: at the banners of past Lords of Malwood, at the many trophies of war that hung from the walls, and at her own husband's tilting helm where it hung, bright steel sheened with oil, winking in the sunlight that lanced down from the tall windows of the Keep.

"How do you think he will do, Yvo?" She asked softly, her voice small in its sudden distress. "For I tell you, My Lord, this crusading business fills me with alarm."

"Young Gui?" her husband responded quietly, looking down at his wife's anxious face with a warm smile, folding her small hand into his large one. "Don't you worry your pretty head over him, My Lady. He should go far. Not only does he have the King's favour, but he is also the finest young knight I've seen in years. And that's not because he is our son, Margaret. But because he's *really* good! Besides, the boy is the size of a house and wields the heaviest sword in the army. Of course he will be alright!

"But they'll be gone years!" His wife exclaimed sadly. Then, after a pause, she added breathlessly, her eyes alight with sudden excitement: "Why can we not have them properly married…as well as betrothed…before Gui has to leave from Southampton? After all we now have all the authority from Richard that we need. Why wait?"

"God's Blood, Sweetheart!" Her husband replied astonished, stopping dead in his tracks. "That's a *fantastic* idea. We could *all* go with him to Southampton. After all it's not that far to travel, and give our son the kind of right royal send off he and all his men deserve! A wedding and a real surprise party," he added brightly, warming to the idea and rubbing his hands together briskly as he spoke. "That would make the two of them sit up and no mistake!"

And with a broad smile at the humour of it, arms linked round each other, and Bellman padding by their side, stern gently waving, they left the Great Hall at last to the army of servitors that were already descending on it. Out past the massive double doors that guarded the entrance to the Keep they went, now open wide for the occasion as much as for the heat; out beneath the raised portcullis with its rows of iron teeth; across the short drawbridge beyond; down the wide, open steps of the Forework itself and so out onto the main castle bailey at last.

Slowly they ambled across it, pausing to look at the New Hall that had just been completed, with its lovely, wide mullioned windows and gracious rooms, where they and their principal guests would stay that night. Then on to the very Gatehouse of the castle itself, passing the sweating guards who stood there, before crossing the main drawbridge that stretched out onto the first of two small battlemented islands that had been built into the wide lake that stretched in front of Castle Malwood.

Spring fed, dark and clear and chill, it was this lake that kept the broad moat that surrounded Castle Malwood permanently filled, and the castle wells inviolate from poison or destruction. Beyond, from the second island, lay the main causeway that ran at right angles across the front of the main defences, and across which de Brocas would have to pass to enter Castle Malwood.

And on that first little island, they paused, to smile at one another and look down into the sunlit water at the fish that lazed and swam there, and at the acres of pink and white water-lilies dotted in clumps all across the lake; at the tall bulrushes and blue and yellow iris around its edges, and at the pair of swans swimming majestically upon it who had nested there for years. Two people drawn close to one another by years of togetherness, and separation, their love for each other and their family as strong as the great walls that lay behind them, and deep as the waters they had just now crossed

Chapter 8... *In which we learn more about the Lord Baron and the Assassins...*

Five miles down the track from where Gui's parents were standing, a small cavalcade was cantering steadily up the dusty road towards Bartley, having landed with the first tide early that morning at Southampton, broken their fast, then taken the road through the northern edge of the Forest that would lead them through Bartley and so on to Malwood.

They were only a small party: some half-a-dozen men-at-arms in mailed leather, long swords at their waists, shields across their shoulders, two more leading a short string of laden pack horses, with a single man, bare headed and astride a huge black stallion, in the lead. In black gambeson, adorned with gold, and heavy riding boots of black leather, the Lord Baron Sir Roger de Brocas, Lord of Narbonne and Gruissan, was richly armed. His great sword, with grip and quillons entwined with gold, had a huge emerald in its pommel, and by his side, in a bucket-shaped leather holder close to his right hand, lay a great mace of flanged steel chased with gold. And, over all, he wore a green linen cyclas bearing a snarling black Boar's Head, with scarlet eyes, teeth and tongue, and great scarlet tushes dripping blood, the great symbol of his House, deeply stitched with gold and silver thread, which he wore on back and chest, as did his men. But he carried no shield, and his face was dark and bitter, while a few paces behind rode his standard bearer carrying the flag of his House, the Boar's Head erased, Sable, armed and langued Gules on a field Vert.

And riding by his side was the most striking young woman in a long bliaut of softest red leather, belted and split almost to her waist, a long sleeved jacket to match, cut to the waist, over a fine chemise of Egyptian cotton, with long red leather thigh boots that clasped her elegant legs like a second skin.

Her hair, black as a raven's wing, was plaited with green and silver ribbons and coiled on either side of her head, over which she wore a simple coif of white sarsenet, jewelled with pearls and garnets held in with golden pins. The Lady Rochine de Brocas, the Baron's lovely daughter, with eyes of emerald above a straight nose and a mouth made for laughter and soft kisses, was a ravishing beauty with a rich husky voice and a smile to melt your heart...but a heart of stone for anyone but her father whom alone she adored to distraction.

Known to all simply as 'The Lady', Rochine de Brocas was no milk-sop maiden, despite her lush creamy white skin, and seeming sweet disposition. She was a tigress disguised as a lamb. A man-eater, with teeth and claws and murderous heart to match, and woe to anyone who thinking otherwise presumed upon her good nature...for she had none for any but her very closest advisors, and her father.

Now all rode with long stirrup leathers and were well mounted on Spanish Rounceys save the Baron himself who rode his great black charger, Charlemagne. A purposeful, well armed party not to be brooked, and they pushed past all other travellers with scant ceremony and stark looks. And while the Baron was under no illusions as to what his intentions were towards his waiting hosts, for smile and please them with his charm as he most surely would, he had no wish to show his hand until he was completely ready. It was the utter destruction of all those whom he had come to visit with from far Narbonne and Gruissan that he was truly after. A destruction sworn on his father's shattered head thirty years ago, and which after a lifetime of effort, he was now about to accomplish

At forty five he was still in superb condition, better than many men ten years his junior, and his virility was unquestioned, for the Narbonne area was littered with his bastards, and his strength was formidable, for his rather square frame, long legs and barrel chest were built for fighting. Every part of him was thick and muscular, from his corded thighs and bull neck to his great hands with their spatulate fingers and heavy nails.

Most striking of all, was his dark, saturnine face with its deep set, piercing black eyes and thin, cruel mouth. Oh, he could laugh, smile and be as pleasant as any other man, but often his eyes would remain still and cold, hawk-like in their intensity. They never missed a thing, and when the black mood was on him they gave his face a terrifying, hooded look that could make strong men shake, and maidens turn their heads away should they come upon him unexpectedly as he stalked the castle grounds. Dark things were said of the Lord of Narbonne behind locked doors.

Wherever he walked mothers dragged their children from his path and shielded their faces, making the sign against the evil-eye behind their backs, and men drew their mantles closely to them and looked down until he passed, for the Great Darkness was so strong in him at times that they were all afraid. Now the Baron and his daughter were nearing their destination and the culmination of all their months of planning and preparations. For here, at last, was their most perfect chance to restore the fortunes and inheritance of his family after they had been in winter darkness for years. Frozen by his father's actions a lifetime ago, in the days of Henry Plantagenet, and now, with the Crusade proclaimed and Richard of England and the King of France about to journey Outremer, to the Holy Land, their lost inheritance was ripe to be broken free at last.

Ever since the death of his father, Thibault, at the hands of Sir Henry de Burley, he had plotted to revenge himself on Alicia and on her guardian, Sir Yvo de Malwood, whom his father had been about to slay when Sir Henry had cut him down! Whenever these two men had been involved in events affecting his family, it had always been his own that had suffered, never theirs.

Now, assuredly, it was time for them to pay!

So, when he had received Sir Yvo's invitation to attend his son's betrothal, sent in so warm a spirit of reconciliation, he had been quick to accept...for it was all that he had schemed for. He smiled at the memory, and looking round he signalled for a change in pace, slowing their passage to an amble, to rest both themselves and their horses from the long ride up from Beaulieu.

He stretched and shifted in his saddle, turning to look around him at the thick coppices, open heath and great stands of heavy timber that made up the Conqueror's New Forest and he was impressed. Surely this was a rich country, with sheep and cattle everywhere in abundance, happily mixed with the red and fallow deer for which the Forest was so famous, and he coveted it.

And all because of Prince John!

★

The Baron snorted and tossed his head.

Little, warty, deceitful Prince John, whom he neither liked nor trusted, but without whom he would not be here today! God's Bones, but he must have been mad to put any form of reliance on such a little shit! Yet it had been the Prince who had put it all in his mind, after he had helped him hide away some of his chief supporters after the last rebellion. Just after King Henry's death at Chinon. Friends of the Prince, and of King Philip, who had been deeply critical of Richard, and whom the new King of England was now demanding that he, the Lord Baron Sir Roger de Brocas and a subject of the

King of France, should now hand them over to Richard for Justice. And all men knew what that would mean!

So he had refused; saying they were Philip's men and thus beyond King Richard's heavy hand, and there had been a fearful row of true Plantagenet proportions! But de Brocas had stood firm and gained much warm appreciation for his stand from Philip, whose protection from Richard's anger he was swift to claim. Later he had met with John on his estates in Maine, to which he had returned after his brother's coronation - having first been forced to promise not to enter England while his brother was away! The Prince had been raving, not just about his brother's actions, but also over some beauty, a real jewel, whom he had met at Court when she had come up to London from the country with her father for the coronation. But it wasn't until John had mentioned her by name, with sly comment, that he had realised exactly of whom the Prince was speaking.

Then had come the question, from Prince John, about the possibility of preventing his *so* royal brother from ever returning from the Holy Land? That, perhaps, with the help of de Brocas' contacts in Syria...with whom the Prince *knew* he traded secretly...it might be possible to arrange for Richard to be murdered by the Assassins? Perhaps there might be a pay-off?

He was both intrigued and appalled!

The Assassins! That terrifying sect who operated out of Castle Masyaf in Syria, under their new leader, Sheik Raschid-al-din Sinan, whom all men knew as the 'Old Man of the Mountains'. The very thought of whom made even him shudder, for they were fanatics, and had brought about the deaths of many powerful men in the Holy Land. Both Christian and Muslim! Once the Assassins marked you, they *never* failed, and the men they sent to kill did not fear death.

Carefully were they chosen, those Assassins, from among their most faithful followers, for both their youth and skills, and the drug, Hashashshin, was used to prepare each chosen man. To put each youth into such a state of bliss that he believed, *with all his soul*, that death on such a Holy cause would take him up to Paradise, to a garden more beautiful than it was possible to imagine, where the most lovely virgins awaited him and would care for his every need for all time, and the food was such as only Allah would consume! Then, convinced of his prize, and armed with the most frighteningly long pointed daggers for which the Assassins were famous, each was set loose to carry out whatever killing had been determined for him to perform.

71

The Baron shivered again, despite the heat, then smiled and banged his hands together, for it had been shortly after that talk with John that Philip Augustus, his Suzerain Lord, the King of France, had shown an interest too. He had no love for Richard either and would be well suited were the English King to die while serving in Outremer, whether that be by Syrian arrow, Mameluke sword...or Assassins dagger!

And so the plot had been hatched, and the money raised.

So many golden marks from each man of royal blood, then shipped by de Brocas, first to Cyprus in a slaving dromond, where the so called 'Emperor', Isaac Comnenus, still traded with his Arab neighbours in Tripoli, from where the gold had been carried into Syria by camel train...and thus into Raschid-al-din's blood-soaked hands. But while those of royal blood must wait for distant events to run their course, he had not felt so constrained, and when Sir Yvo's invitation to his son's betrothal had arrived so unexpectedly he had seen that as the moment to put his own carefully conceived plan for Castle Malwood into motion.

He ambled Charlemagne forward, looking round at the girl beside him, and at the tough, well armed men whom he had brought with him from the ship, soon to be lying in a closely sheltered anchorage just off Christchurch in deep water basin that was not so subject to tides as elsewhere along the coast.

He smiled as he looked at her, at her profile, at the way she rode her horse, how she carried her body...and her firm breasts, long legs and rounded haunches. She was *such* an extraordinary girl, hot and sensuous and of outstanding beauty. So like her beloved mother, Constancia. He sighed. Now she *had* been exquisite! Warm and loving, adventurous and bold when she needed to be and with a fierce, wild spirit that could shake you like a violent summer storm. So like her daughter, they might almost have come from the same mould.

Constancia had been first seduced by her father, and then by her uncle several years before he had been bound to her. It had made her very 'knowing,' and very good at hiding her feelings. She had been eighteen when he had married her and their first night together had been fantastic! He could *still* remember it! So hot together that it was a wonder they had not both burst into flames! Willing was not the word for it! She had been almost insatiable. Little wonder that he had missed her so much after she had died.

He, a man of experience and known virility, already a seer of some power, and possessed of a great Crystal that had been the gift of the Emir of Samarkand, with whom he had been trading slaves along the coast of Tripoli for years. That's how he had come to know so much about the Assassins...and of the mighty Persian, Hasan-as-Sabah who had first raised them to do his bidding a hundred years ago, making himself their first ever Grand Master, and had run them from Castle Alamut in Khorassan, above the Caspian Sea. It was he who had first had the great Seer Stone created and had imbued it with its power. He it was who had then gifted it to the great Emir of Samarkand, who in turn had gifted it to him.

He looked up at the sky and grimaced.

Castle Alamut, a mighty fortress on a rock, six thousand feet up in a barren landscape of lofty peaks, deep forgotten lakes, steep cliffs and narrow passes. Even the most numerous army could only reach it one man at a time. The most powerful siege engines could not touch its walls. And each evening, from the river and the lakes, rose up a thick and fleecy mist that climbed the cliffs and precipices midway from the top, so that the Castle became an island in a vast ocean of cloud that looked like the haunt of demons, that the people of those lands called Djinns.

It was said not even Saladin himself would go there.

In this dark place, Hasan raised sacred flames through which, like a mirror, he could see what others did and make his presence felt, and on his death had passed his powers on to his successor, Sheik Raschid-ed-din Sinan, the 'Old Man of the Mountains', to whom even Kings paid tribute for fear of being murdered. It was through Sheik Raschid that the Emir had acquired the ancient crystal that, later, he had given to him as a gift of rare and special beauty for personal services rendered, and in the eager expectation of still more to be so. Beautiful indeed...but almost useless, as try as he might he could not get it to work as the Emir had assured him it would do, for the images remained clouded, and he had been forced to remain reliant upon his mind and upon his black hypnotic eyes to get men to do for him that which they would not do for others. Nevertheless, in the end, *serendipity*, he *had* got it to work for him at last, and in a manner more extraordinary than any he could possibly have dreamed of.

Chapter 9......*And The Lady and the Crystal Seer Stone.*

He shifted again in his saddle, his thighs stiff from the several hours' hard riding, and he stretched his great arms above his head, swinging his solid torso from side to side as he stretched them, while he looked across at his daughter...and his eyes smouldered with desire.

Her mother being dead for some ten years, Rochine had lavished him with all her love and attention, coming to prefer his company to that of any other man, and preventing all others from sharing him with her when she was little, except upon the most necessary of basis! So he had not remarried, and in her turn she had made of him a god, coming to desire him as a maiden would another man. Bold, sensuous and seductive, her needs were different, more esoteric and erotic, loving the soft warmth and luscious curves that women have and men do not, while also aching for the living hardness that only a man could provide for her enjoyment.

She'd been eighteen when she had first come to him.

She a maid, with unusual tastes for pain and ecstasy refined from watching, through secret spy-holes from hidden passages within the castle walls, the unbridled lust and passions of others, himself included she had told him later. Even so had she watched until she knew exactly what she wanted for herself...both to dominate and be enslaved in equal measure, and had learned from his favourite whore whom she had cajoled, coerced and then seduced for her to teach her how best to please him too.

Eighteen! The same age as her mother, Constancia, had been when she had first come his bed.

It had been a hot night in June, his fortieth birthday, and she had come to his room wearing nothing but the finest white gossamer that floated like misty vapour round her nakedness, shimmering with every movement that she made, outlining her breasts in all their fulsome, sharp-crested beauty, and her softly rounded haunches.

The hard line of his mouth lengthened as he smiled again and breathed deeply, his eyes half closing as he did so in remembrance.

74

A moment she had stood there, the candles in his great bedroom in the castle, shining in flickering softness behind her. Then it was around her feet and she was in his arms, her cool, inviting body and hot mouth arousing such a fire in his loins that they were soon making fierce, tempestuous love together, oblivious of every convention that should have driven them apart. *Incest!* The greatest taboo. Yet he still shivered in anticipation of renewal, rather than disgust.

Holy Church preached against it of course, yet who were the Church to preach? There were many Bishops he knew for whom Chastity was no more than a written word on parchment; the venal Archbishop Berenguer of Narbonne for one, who was both pederast and whoremaster. And as for the Papacy? The very fount of all church thinking and belief? He snorted in derision. There were as many charlatans and rogues, murderers, pederasts and incestuous lovers as ever in the secular world their flock all lived and died in! And, anyway, the girl had been willing. *More than willing!* She had come to him hot with heart-felt love, her green eyes stoned with lust, her moans and cries of pleasure driving him beyond reason, to greater heights than he ever could remember. Her body a willing sponge that had soaked up all his energies and left them both spent and exhausted on the bed.

He grunted again, and writhed his loins in hungry anticipation, remembering with astonishment all that had happened next. For that was when he had discovered that their forbidden coupling had had an incredible effect upon them both, for Rochine was strangely elated, her body trembling and shaking, her eyes wide open, sunken pools of emerald that mirrored her racing dreams, giving him a clarity of mind that he had *never* experienced before. And, on an impulse he had risen from their crumpled bed and crossed the room to where he kept his precious seer-stone on its exquisitely carved cedar base, and drawing the great crystal palantir from its rosewood box, he had run his hands across its gleaming surface and gazed achingly into its frozen depths.

And, even as he touched it, his fingers tingled as they *never* had before, the wiry hairs on his wrists and arms rising as he did so to fringe the ornate gold bracelet that he wore, covered with dragons and entwined lovers that Rochine had given him that very evening as a birth gift…before giving of herself as well. Then, looking over to where she lay, naked and sprawled out across the bed, he found that she had fallen into some kind of trance, her breathing so shallow that her sharply pointed breasts, lovely in the candlelight, hardly moved as her lungs gently exhaled each soft breath, her head thrown back, green eyes wide open, glazed and staring as in death. While between his hands the huge glass ball had suddenly come alive, filled with swirling clouds that flew around in brilliant colours, slowly clearing as his mind focussed to reveal the empty castle yard, ghostly white in the hard light of the risen moon, with the guards lounging relaxed in the balmy air of that July night, as they stood silent watch over the sleeping countryside.

Even so had he gasped and looked away, his heart hammering in his chest, his hands shaking, thinking it was all a dream. But when he looked again, the sights were still there! Amazing! It was like looking at a picture, though slightly distorted by the curved edges of the giant crystal. *Never* had such an exciting thing happened to him before, and *never* had the Crystal come alive before! It was almost as if he could reach out and touch the men standing there. It had been simply amazing…and so exciting! And since then their knowledge and understanding of how to make the Crystal work had grown, and with it their confidence. Now it was possible, through secret knowledge of men's minds thus gained, subtly to affect and influence anyone, provided that their minds were not as strong and focused as his own.

For the Crystal did not *always* work!

Some there were who could *not* be suborned, and some even he would not dare to try. But mostly he could bring such influence to bear that those on whom he bent his mind and skills became unknowing players of whatever game it pleased Rochine and him to play. Thus had he bent all his efforts to acquire some artefact that would forge that all important link with the family in far off Malwood Castle, and he smiled to himself, hissing his breath through his teeth in mirthless laughter as he remembered the ancient ring that once had graced his aunt's hand, and which his father had spirited away for his own secret amusement and to confound the Malwood family whom he had always detested.

Philipa de Brocas, Ralf de Burley's wife, and the fair Alicia's grandmother, was his father's sister…his own aunt, whom he but vaguely remembered as a pretty, laughing lady who gave him sweets and ruffled his head as a child, and to whom her husband's greatest friend, Sir Alun de Malwood, had gifted on her wedding day, but for her lifetime only, a magnificently faceted emerald ring, set in a heavy ornate band of ancient gold. It was the greatest heirloom of his House, known as the Malwood Emerald, and on the very day of her death had disappeared without trace and for which all had sought to no avail.

No-one knew anything! And throwing back his head the Lord Baron laughed…so startling a red squirrel who had been watching him that he

76

dropped his nut as he whisked away amongst the trees, pausing to chatter with furious anger at the Baron's party before disappearing in flurry of red fur and twitching tail...because he knew all along where it had been!

The nuns who had attended his aunt's funeral in England had removed it on his father's secret orders, and spirited it away to their mother House in France, and despite the fearful row that had followed its disappearance, had kept it safe all those years. So he had tracked it down to their small Priory near Bergerac in the Dordogne, where the family had once held lands, and there had demanded its immediate return. And he sneered and snorted his derision at the memory of the fat little Prioress and her covey of plump French partridges whose inheritance he had so simply stolen.

Now with the ring in his possession it had only been a question of time before he could have affected Sir Yvo, or those around him, sufficiently for him to be sent an invitation to the betrothal of his only son, Sir Gui, to Sir Henry's only daughter, the Lady Alicia...of whom Prince John had told him all those months ago.

Then, almost out of a cloudless, blue sky, and without any effort from Rochine and himself, the much desired invitation had suddenly arrived! Sir Yvo, the old fool, had apparently decided that, 'in pursuance of better family relations', on the eve of the Crusade setting out, 'his only son's betrothal would be a wonderful opportunity to bring their family's long feuding to an end at last!'

He threw back his head and laughed at the simplicity of it all. Better family relations? His only son's betrothal? His eyebrows shot up in amazement at such...such naivety! The man was mad to invite him, of all people, to his precious son's betrothal! Or very cunning? And his dark brows drew together again, concerned once more that all his plans, so carefully conceived with John and Philip, had been discovered. But nothing untoward had occurred, and careful checking had assured him that Sir Yvo's invitation was, *de facto*, a genuine offer of friendship, and so he had accepted.

He looked around him with unseeing eyes.

Of course there had been that monk asking questions at that time. Who had stayed with the Archbishop at Narbonne, but had come across to visit with them at Grise, and he dug his spurs in suddenly, making his horse rear and stamp as he held it down with an iron hand.

Now…where had he come from? That tall, stooped Benedictine, with laboured breathing, a stick in one hand and a basket in the other, seeking herbs and unguents? He had hung around for days, poking into strange dark corners of the castle, asking questions about the Roman remains on which the great fortress had been built, and generally making a pathetic nuisance of himself. His wheezing breath almost as maddening as his endless, stupid questions!

He had even gone into the town and spent some time with those who lived there.

He snarled in his throat. Rabble rousers, malcontents and drunkards. He knew who they all were. Enemies all, but worthless! And then the monk had gone, thank the Lord. *God's Throat*, but he had no time for *fucking* priests! Rochine had met with the wretched man in the end, as much at the Archbishop's insistence as his own, for the Archbishop also wanted to know what the man was doing in their area too, the *so* venal *so* 'chaste' Beringuer of Narbonne, for the Benedictines were not a wandering order. Only with direct permission from an Abbot could a brother leave his home, or at the request of someone great…and this one was soon discovered to carry the Pope's authority with him. Not a man to be taken lightly! The Archbishop had much to be concerned about…as did he!

His forehead creased in thought and a moment later, throwing up his hand, he gave a shout and reined in his horse, signalling his daughter to come up beside him, and with a snort and a jingle the whole party slowed to a walk.

Chapter 10... *The Wicked Baron's black treachery is unveiled.*

"Rochine," the Lord Baron asked, as his daughter drew rein beside him. "Who was that damned Benedictine we had poking his long clerical nose around The Château, and the town, a few months back?"

"Father Matthew, My Lord," She answered him formally in her sun-drenched, husky voice. "Why? Is there a problem?"

"No...I don't suppose so, My Lady," he answered her, equally correct in the presence of their escort, that being usual when they were not alone. "But when we are so close to achieving our plans, it's natural to look over everything for flaws. And he just might be a flaw!"

"Why so?"

"The Benedictines are not a wandering order, Rochine!" he said with some definition. "In fact one of the first Rules of St Benedict was that the brothers were *not* to stray from their House, except when given especial rights to do so! So what was Father Matthew doing making such a pest of himself last winter?"

"Collecting herbs and medical knowledge ahead of the Crusade," she replied calmly. "So many pilgrims and soldiers–of–God died on the last one, that Pope Clement ordered the Church to do something about it. Apparently Father Matthew has a reputation for healing that is second to none, and Clement ordered his release from his Mother House for as long as necessary. Both Philip and Richard want him with their armies..."

"...With a chest like his?" He interrupted briskly. I am surprised *anyone* wants him! Wheezing and whistling like a leaky pump. I wouldn't want him anywhere near me. 'Physician heal thyself,' I say!"

"Oh...he was not that bad, My Lord. But he carries Clement's dispensation and an instruction to all whom he should meet with to give him aid, so he must be worth something. Especially if *both* Kings want him so badly."

"Where does he come from?"

"Spain."

"Spain? What is a Spanish monk doing working for an Italian Pope?"

"He's a Benedictine, Papa. The original Mother House is at Montecassino. So why not?"

"Could he be a danger to us?"

"He is nothing, My Lord," she laughed dismissively. "I talked with him myself on several occasions. Just a bent old man with a head full of ancient ideas. Did you not meet with him while he was with us?"

"No! I did *not!*" He snarled at her coarsely. "You know how much I *loathe* those black crows of the Church. Faces half hidden under their cowls, whining on about Hell Fire and eternal damnation, with their hands ever held out for yet more largesse! And they know too much and see too far for my liking…"

"That, My Lord, coming from you is a little too much!" she replied with a sarcastic laugh. "If there is one man I know who can see into another's soul…it's you!"

"Hmmm. Not always, My Lady. Not always," he replied thoughtfully. "We couldn't reach that old bitch, Eleanor, remember? When we wanted her to rein in her son over those barons he was trying so hard to get his hands on…"

"No…but we fixed Philip!" she said, leaning towards him and laughing. "We got him to stand by you against Richard instead, when he might easily not have done so. And what about the Prince?" She asked smiling at him.

"Dreadful little man!" De Brocas replied darkly. "He was easy. Prince John's mind is *so* like a sewer, that one more evil idea floating in it was never going to be noticed."

"He came to your lure like a falcon."

"More like a buzzard!" he exclaimed, disgustedly. "A lordly falcon that man is *not!*"

"You are invincible, My Lord!" she said then, her eyes shining.

"Not quite, My Lady," he replied softly. "Not without you." Then, leaning towards her, he added: "Will you be ready? We will not have much time."

"I am always ready for you, My Lord," she replied, in her rich husky voice, nudging her horse closer to his and looking into his dark eyes as she spoke. "You have but to ask. You know that. Then, together, we can reach into every mind!"

"Hmmm," He said again, grinning at her sardonically. "I can think of others whom we have not reached. And now we have this monk…this 'Father Matthew'!"

"You haven't tried with him, have you?" she asked him, shocked. "You know the Crystal doesn't work properly on its own. You need *me* for that!" She exclaimed huskily, leaning towards him again, her green eyes alight with mischief and sudden desire.

"I haven't," he said sharply. "He took himself off before I thought it necessary. I just wish we had tried when we had the chance. But it simply didn't seem important at the time. And now…"

"…And now, My dearest Lord," she followed on for him, reaching across to give his arm a shake. "Is *not* the time to get a fit of the dismals. We have planned all this with great care, Papa, and your plans never fail. The monk is a no-body, My Lord. I met with him and we talked of many things…all to do with herbs and medicines, what the Romans had done years ago, surgical practices. All sorts of rubbish. I sent him off to talk with Stanisopoulos. My Greek perfumier?"

"Poisoner and drug provider, more like!" Her father replied, harshly. "You be careful, my girl. That man is not to be trusted!"

"Don't worry. He is constantly watched, and I know where his daughter is! His Nicole. After his wife died three years ago, Nicole is the *only* one he cares about. She is the apple of his eye and is terrified that I may take her away from him, for my own amusement!"

"And the father knows this?"

"No…and he doesn't need to. It's what he *doesn't* know that keeps him so securely on my leash! His own fears trap him…and he knows that as long as I need him Nicole is safe. So he takes every *possible* care to make sure that he remains in my good books at all times!"

"You are good, aren't you?

"I try, My Lord. I do try!"

"All the same, Rochine. Be careful," he advised her, turning to look into his daughter's eyes as he spoke. "It is sometimes the 'little' people who can do the most damage! What about those others whom that monk may have talked with?"

"Who?" she questioned astonished. "That fat Aubergist of the Golden Cockerel, Armand Chulot? He only knows his own name because he hears it called so many times. And Du Guesclin is a spent force since you have laid hands on his son. I left orders he was to be closely watched, but unharmed."

"…Oh, excellent, Rochine!" He broke in exultantly. "I had meant to have Bertrand safely behind our walls before we left, especially after all the fuss over his mother, stupid woman. All she had to do was surrender, not set up a desperate screech like a peacock! Still," he shrugged with a smile. "I soon stopped that! What of the merchant, Soulier?"

"That's another you need have no fear of, My Lord. I have met with his sister, Isabella. Like Stanisopoulos, Guillaume will do anything to preserve her. She is far too young to be of any value to us…yet," she sneered darkly. "But it does no harm for him to know that I have my eye on the girl already! And his wretched brother, Ralf, is already one of my informants…though Guillaume doesn't know it!" And she laughed.

They rode on then in silence for a while, happy to be bumbling along the track, the June sun hot on their backs, the warm scents of dry grass and wayside flowers coming up to them from their horses hooves as they passed by. Secure in the knowledge that their preparations were as complete as they could be. Nervous with expectation, yet cool as ice in all their thinking.

"At least our men are in place," he said, turning towards her, resting his hands on the high pommel of his saddle. "They were taken on as we had planned they should be."

"The Cousins?" she affirmed. "They are good men, tough. They will not let us down. And your special messengers?" She asked, raising her eyebrows.

"Chosen by the Prince, and both alive and well I trust since I sent them forward after all Raheel's hard work with them...*and* sending them with half a dozen of my best birds Those two may look a complete pair of idiots, but they have been well trained and know what they are doing. Young Robin is the only Englishman with the necessary skills this side of the channel that I know of; and Henri will keep him safe. So they'd better get it right!"

"Far better if we never have to use *any* of them, My Lord!" she said tersely. "The more complex things get...the more likely it is that something will go wrong!"

"I know," he said sharply, with a shrug of his shoulders. "But this whole plan of ours carries no guarantee. Sometimes puppet strings break. And there is a greater element of chance in it too. We discussed all this at home, Rochine. Endlessly. It is like chess. If the pawns are not in the right place when you need them...then you may never trap the Queen. Let alone slay the King, her husband!"

"Those Cousins are pawns?"

"Lagrasse and Fabrizan? Certainly! They knew the risks when they set out from Grise. If they get back in one piece they will be well rewarded. In fact you are supposed to have been preparing part of their reward?"

"And so I have done, my Dear Lord and Master," she replied with a grin. "Two of my very best girls, each, I think they were promised? You provide the land!"

"Yes, that is in hand too." He said, looking about him as he spoke. "Land around the villages whose names they bear, and to be held as Freemen, no less! And if they are needed after all...*and* they survive, then they truly will have earned it all," He added grimly. "For it will not be easy!"

She looked across at her father with a sigh...knowing how tense he really was inside, despite his hard, confident exterior. She, better than anyone, knew how he thought and what he had schemed and striven for all his life: To be revenged on his enemies and to make the family safe, and respected. No...*feared*, rather. That all men would do his bidding! She loved him as passionately as her mother had ever done…More, probably! For better or for worse, despite *all* the taboos and restrictions, she loved him unreservedly; she had not been able to help herself. And that made her vulnerable to friend and foe alike, for discovery would be ruinous. But she truly loved the life she led. She found living on the edge of disaster incredibly exciting. A woman holding her own in a man's world, against all the odds? How many could say that? But she had to keep her guard up all the time. Love him or not, he might still choose to discard her if she no longer served his needs. All the more reason to ensure that today went well. Then, with the wretched Alicia firmly in their grasp, she would be better placed to ensure her own safety.

"Do you have the 'fire' safe?" She asked presently, changing the subject. "This storm we are expecting may not do all that you need," she added, her body already tingling at the thought of what would be required of her later. "We have never attempted such a thing before!"

"I know. We can but try. And, yes, it is. Very carefully packed in two closed jars in one of the sumpter's packs. Sweet Wine of Christ, Rochine, but it is dangerous stuff, I tell you. Real Greek Fire ignites sometimes on contact with anything it touches, and cannot be put out by water, that simply spreads it. It has to burn itself out, or be completely smothered in earth or sand, or vinegar!"

"What is it made of, My Lord?"

"No-one knows! It is a secret possessed now only by the Byzantine Emperor and the Knights of the Temple and The Hospital, and no one man knows all its secrets. Not even each Grand Master. And not even *I* would dare to try my mind against any one of theirs. They would destroy me for certain."

"How then…?

"…Did I get it? With extreme difficulty," he replied with an air of quiet satisfaction. "The Knights keep it stored under lock and key at all times. But they do have to move it about from place to place, and I managed to lay my hands on some through a corrupt Harbour Master in Alexandria. It is almost worth its weight in gold. The Muslims are *terrified* of it! Sadly, I do not think it is true 'Greek Fire'…but Arab 'Greek Fire'! A mistake that has already cost the wretched man his miserable life. So, not quite so immediately combustious I understand, which maybe far better for me as I have seen what real Greek Fire can do and it is truly appalling! But our stuff will do just as well, even if it is less instantly explosive. And in the confines of a building will be every bit as ferocious as we could hope for."

She sat back in her saddle then and smiled at him, before saying quietly: "I almost pity the poor fools who are taking us in tonight, My Lord. They do not know what is going to hit them. Wind from the gods themselves, and Fire through their bowels that cannot be put out! Surely we will be avenged on them all at last!"

"Truly, My Lady," he said then, looking across at her, her green eyes smouldering with a desire that he could see was equal to his own. "Together we will be invincible!"

And with a barking laugh, he gave a wave of his hand, along with a whooping shout, and dug in his spurs. With a sudden squeal his mount reared up, crashed back to the ground and then took off along the track, bunched hindquarters pounding, flowing mane and neck stretched out, closely followed by his standard bearer and, moments later, by all the rest, led by his daughter. They could have been the Wild Hunt in all but name, and within moments they had rounded a corner of the track and galloped out of sight, the thunder of their hooves swiftly dying away into the shimmering distance.

★

From high above the square towered gate-house the trumpeters whom Sir Yvo had placed there leaped into life, their clarion calls ringing out brazenly across the drowsing countryside. The Baron's party had been sighted at last, and were even now passing the far end of the village. With a rattle and bang, the guard came tumbling out of the chambers on either side of the castle gateway to form up in the two stiff lines they had been practising all morning, one on each side of the paved roadway that led up to the Gatehouse.

Lifting his head to the sound, Sir Yvo and his wife walked back over the drawbridge and through the entrance passage, to await their guests close to the foot of the broad steps that led up to the New Hall and their own apartments, Bellman still sauntering at their heels.

Sir Yvo looked around him, his sharp eyes taking in everything at a glance: his tall guard commander, Sir Richard L'Eveque, and his Seneschal, Sir James Bolderwood, coming with long strides towards him and John Fitzurse, his massive Master-at-Arms, at the head of his men by the gatehouse. And at the men themselves, armour shining like polished silver, stiff in their ranks, more

85

standing as they had been instructed, weapons in hand, at every doorway and along the battlements above and around the gate-house entrance.

Then there were the rows of waggons, getting loaded to leave for Southampton and then for France with Gui and his men in a few days' time, with their horses cropping nearby, and the three bright flags that even as he looked were breaking from their poles up on the roof as the trumpeters blew their clarion calls loud and clear across the countryside: one with the golden Leopards of Normandy and England, the other the Scarlet Lion Rampant of Malwood, tongue, teeth and claws sharply blue as the sky above them. And lastly Alicia's House flag, the Stag's Head erased Gules, attired d'Or on a field Ermine fluttering close beside it.

All was ready.

It needed only for the Baron and his daughter to arrive, to complete their arrangements. Well, almost, for the King's chosen emissary, and his oldest friend, was still missing. No matter he *would* arrive, and bending his head Sir Yvo kissed his wife on the lips and smiled down at her:

"Perfect timing, my little Lady Love," he said, gesturing to where his men were already drawn up as the leading horse, bearing the Baron himself, standard bearer now by his side, began to clatter across the far causeway. "Our guests arrive, and all is as it should be, save that lump of a son of ours has yet to put in an appearance! Come, my Love, let us go forward and welcome them as a good host should. But not for long. By God's Throat, Margaret, they have more coming to them than they can possibly imagine!"

"Yvo, this is the part I like the least," she said quietly, her head tilted towards him. "This...this dissembling that you have decided to go in for! Oh, I know why," she said, forestalling him with her hand as he was about to speak. "I understand *exactly* what you and King Richard are afraid of. I am just glad that Gui does not know, for I believe we lose much honour by it!"

"Well, Sweetheart, were Matthew here we might indeed have brought it all forward, for in truth I feel as you do. Better to do it now and get it over and done with, than go through the night dissembling and then do it in the morning. But he is not here. And without Richard's Warrant, bearing his Great Seal, together with the papers of proof that Matthew brings with him, my hands are well and truly tied."

"Rather the Baron's than yours I wish, My Love," his wife replied sharply. "Hush now, for Gui is coming to join us at last and he has Alicia with him. So no more of this now, as you love me!"

"What a pair, my darling," he breathed huskily, as he watched his son and his ward walk laughing towards them from Alicia's Tower. "Just look at them, would you? Our son, and dear Anne and Henry's daughter! How proud they would have been that their little girl should have turned out to be *such* a beauty.

I have a feeling, Margaret, that this will be the beginning of something wonderful for all of us. Gui and Alicia to be betrothed, and then married, just as you and Anne so jokingly planned it all those years ago. Richard safe from his brother's plotting and de Brocas and his hellcat daughter securely out of the way at last. The Church commissioners will think that Christmas has come early.

Wonderful, my darling. Surely nothing could be better?"

Chapter 11... *The Lord Baron Sir Roger De Brocas arrives at Castle Malwood.*

Castle Malwood may not have been the largest castle in the land, but it had been strongly built and brought up to date as new ideas of castle defence had come back from the Holy Land. With its great square gate-house and tall projecting towers that studded the limestone walls at regular intervals, each rising some ten feet above the wall-head and pierced with arrow slits on all their outward sides, it was a powerful force to be reckoned with.

Here the main castle entrance, through which an enemy must pass to force his way in, was most heavily defended. With its twin portcullises, meurtrieres in the roof and twin arrow slitted chambers on either side, it was a frightening obstacle. At both ends were double doors of cross-lapped oaken planks a foot thick, strengthened with iron plates, and right in front of all was the drawbridge itself, with a heavy counterweight that swung down into a deep pit behind both doors and front portcullis when the bridge itself was closed. Beyond the battlemented curtain walls lay the bailey, an enormous open courtyard, part paved part down to rough pasture, into which the villagers would flood at times of great danger; and hard against the North Curtain wall, but facing the warm passage of the sun, were ranged a variety of other buildings, including the New Hall.

This was a gracious, two story, stone building with deeply mullioned windows, panelled corridors and beautifully carved stone fireplaces, with massive timbers overhead to hold the leaded roof. Inside were richly adorned apartments and, on the upper floor, apart from the family's chambers, was a beautiful solar for Sir Yvo's family and his guests. This was much lighter and cosier than anything within the Great Keep closeby, and overlooked the sun-drenched courtyard, Lady Margaret's rose garden, and the castle orchards and beehives.

Elsewhere within the Bailey were a variety of other buildings, including the castle forge, stables and quarters for married troops, some thatched others with new slate roofs as a safeguard against the danger of fire, which was very real. Finally there was the chapel, not within the Keep as many were in those days, but outside it, where its beautiful stone work, delicately carved altar screen and lovely tall stained glass windows, made by skilled French craftsmen, could be properly admired.

Three sides of the castle were protected by a great moat, some fifteen feet deep and fifty yards across, revetted in stone and filled by the spring-fed lake that fronted the whole fortress. Across this lake, and running at right angles to the castle's front defences, a wooden causeway had been built out to two small battlemented islands, the closest connected to the main entrance by the huge counterweighted drawbridge, the other by a smaller swing bridge. In winter it was a blank, cold stretch of chilly, black water that often overflowed to flood the lower levels of the village. Sometimes, both lake and moat froze right over so that everyone could slide and skate on them...but now, in summer, they were a riot of flowering lilies, each great pink and white flower with a golden heart, and both lake and moat fringed with bulrushes and tall standing irises, like blue and yellow soldiers.

As the Baron's party clattered across the drawbridge, Gui came with Alicia across from her tower apartment to join his parents, already waiting near the paved entrance to the New Hall to greet their new arrivals. Ostlers ran out to take the horses, and Sir Richard L'Eveque, Sir Yvo's enormous guard commander, tall and languid as ever, with his lazy smile and speech, and his Seneschal, Sir James Bolderwood with Argos, his giant white Talbot by his side, came forward to greet the Baron and his daughter. And as they passed beneath the final portcullis, the Master-at Arms, John Fitzurse, brought his honour guard to attention and saluted, then turned and moved his men, with shield and gavelock in hand, to keep pace beside their mounted guests, fanning out on either side as they reached Sir Yvo's party.

★

Looking round him Lord Roger liked what he saw. The place was as well maintained as it possibly could be! Clean stone everywhere, and well pointed. No crumbling mortar. No weeds or small growths to be seen. It would be a brute to attack. And that huge pit for the counterweight, right behind that first portcullis? Just like the one at home. He never had worked out how to overcome it if once the castle was closed up against him and he had actually to attack it. *Cauchmar!*...Nightmare! And he smiled,

And he also noted the towering Keep, with its massive buttresses and wide batter of solid masonry around its base, and his eyebrows flickered. Truly it would be a pig of a place to try and capture if well fought by its defenders. He shrugged his broad shoulders and grinned...But it was not going to come to that. What damage he intended to create would soon be put right. Then let anyone come at him who would, he would hold this place in their teeth, and he grinned again. With the Malwood–Burley lands under his belt he would be invincible!

And he was impressed with the guard, too.

Their smart turnout, and the fit way they moved, weapons firmly held, eyes alert for every detail. *And there were so many of them!* Not just in the honour guard itself, that was to be expected. But everywhere he looked there seemed to be armed men...and not just in plated byrnies and square casques, but many in proper ringed mail almost to the ground. And there were many bowmen. The whole place seemed to be on a war footing, as if Sir Yvo was subtly flexing his muscles before his French cousin.

He smiled.

For he had two of his own men amongst them, somewhere! He hadn't seen them yet, but he knew they were there. Dear *God*, but he was good! And he made his horse dance and shake his head as he rode across towards where he could see Sir Yvo standing to greet him, with his family and Household Officers standing round him. He snorted in derision, then. Just look at him? Sir Yvo de bloody Malwood!

Feeling so...so full of himself, the fat fool! Posture as the man might, he could have no idea of what was in store for him that night. Could he? And sitting upright in his saddle de Brocas slowed his horse to a walk and looked around him with suddenly sharp, mistrustful eyes: the soldiers walking smartly beside them, eyes to the front; Sir Yvo, boarhound by his side, and his family and principal Officials waiting with smiles to greet him; manure from the stables being carted; a man with a bee-skep in his arms, another with a great sack of something over his shoulder.

All calm. All normal. No waiting trumpeter, and no hint of tension.

He looked at his waiting host, handsomely dressed but now going to fat; at his plump wife wreathed in smiles; the men beside them, one in armour, one white-haired with a great white hound by his side...and at the enormous young man, with keen, hard eyes, and a real beauty on his arm, looking up at him and laughing.

That must be Sir Gui and his bride to be, the fair Lady Alicia de Burley. He curled his lip and sneered. Not if *he* had anything to do with it! But no! No danger there – he was sure of it, and bringing Charlemagne to a final halt he swung off his back, tossing the reins to a waiting varlet as he did so, and came forward, with his hand held open and a broad smile to greet his hosts.

"So, Sir Yvo" he said warmly in his rather harsh voice, taking his host's large hand firmly in his own as he spoke. "I came with my daughter as I

90

promised you I would," he went on, gesturing behind him, to where the Lady Rochine was just walking up from the Gatehouse. "Surely you honour us with so warm a greeting!"

"Welcome, to Castle Malwood, My Lord Baron," Sir Yvo replied in his booming voice. "It is a great occasion to which you have so kindly come," he added, as he took the Baron's proffered hand, looking the man squarely in the face and feeling his strength, before releasing it to introduce first his wife and then his Seneschal and Guard Commander.

The Baron de Brocas greeted all with warmth and grace, smiling his greetings and bestowing a friendly kiss on Lady Margaret's cheek. Then, after speaking briefly with Sir Yvo's Seneschal, he turned to where the massive figure of his Guard Commander was standing, clad head to toe in shimmering mail, with the huge black Lion Rampant and Guardant of the L'Eveque family roaring from his cyclas with its scarlet claws and tongue on its lovely field of Ermine, he was an impressive figure.

"Sir Richard," Lord Roger said. "May I complement you on the turnout of your troopers? They make a brave show and I would be pleased for you to give them an extra stoup of ale each at my expense. It has been a hot morning and surely they deserve it!"

"Thank you, my Lord Baron," came Sir Richard's lazy voiced reply, as he bowed slightly before the older man with a smile at the buzz of pleasure his simple words had caused. "The men have worked hard. They will be delighted." And without waiting for a reply, he gave final a small bow and left to return to his men, his tall frame moving swiftly and smoothly across the bailey, his long sword tapping his heel as he walked.

De Brocas watched him go, his eyes flicking everywhere, his mind a maelstrom of conflicting thoughts. How far could he trust these people with their friendly smiles of welcome? And where were the Cousins, Jules and Lucas? No matter, De Vere would surely find them! Sweet Jesu, but the place was strongly built!

Chapter 12... "...One great use of words is to hide our thoughts...". ...(Voltaire).

Through almost slitted eyes, Sir Yvo watched the Baron like a cat does a mouse, alert and ready to leap in any direction! Now...what was going through that sharp, incisive mind?

A hard man to read, the Lord Baron Sir Roger de Brocas, for nothing seemed to move within his eyes, so often the mirror of the soul. Perhaps this bastard did not have one? And he gave an involuntary shiver. Then, turning away, he brought Gui and Alicia forward to greet him: "I am Sir Gui de Malwood," Gui said, looking steadily at de Brocas, his eyes cold, his mouth in a straight line. "And I, too, bid you welcome to Castle Malwood." And he held out his hand.

Yes...de Brocas thought, with a low chuckle as he took Gui's hand in his, letting the young knight feel the strength of his own broad fingers and thick wrist as he did so. As welcome as an arse-full of fucking boils! Oh, but you do not like me being here, do you, my young bantam, he thought as he felt Gui's response. Firm and hard...but not so hard as it might have been, just enough to make a point! So...intriguing! Big and strong and not afraid to let his feelings show! But far too easily, my friend, he thought. Too simply shown! And he grinned at the young man, eyebrows lifting sardonically as he did so, before releasing his hand and allowing him to step back.

Then, Alicia came forward and curtseyed prettily: "I am the Lady Alicia de Burley," she said introducing herself, as it had been arranged she should do. "And you are very gracious, My Lord Baron," she added, giving him a dazzling smile. "We are all very sensible of the feelings you must have put on one side to be here on this, our special day."

The Baron looked first at Sir Yvo, his black eyes inscrutable, then down at the lovely girl before him, feeling his blood rush through him hotly, wanting her already.

"The death of my father at Cahors was just one of those things that can happen sometimes, My Lady Alicia," he said after a pause. "It could just as easily have been your father, Sir Henry, who was slain." And reaching for her hand he kissed it lightly, looking round him as he did so and smiling at the obvious relief he saw on so many of their faces.

"That is always the worst thing about any strife between our two kings," Sir Yvo responded warmly, putting his hand on the Baron's broad shoulders, as Alicia moved back to Gui's side. "It splits whole families apart, pitting cousin against cousin and even father against son." He stopped then, to look into the Baron's eyes: "I just knew you would feel like that! That the time had come at last to sort things out!"

Lord Roger smiled at him in agreement. Are you glad, in truth...or a cunning dissembler, my so friendly Englishman? he thought. Had it been your son speaking I would have known! But you? Bland, open, so seemingly uncomplicated...and naïve? And all those men-at-arms? Ware Hawk! Roger. Ware Hawk! But is that a great goshawk, with fierce, rending talons or a bumbling buzzard with small ones? We shall see!

Sir Yvo, watching him, paused, wondering then if he had said more than was needful, before adding: "Still, enough of all that. Come and introduce us to your beautiful daughter, and then we can go up to my Lady's Solar in the New Hall and be comfortable, while your things are brought up, and your men shown where they may be put."

★

While they had been talking, Lord Roger's daughter had remained seated on her horse, looking around at all that was going on about her.

Very pretty, she thought, looking at the New Hall in front of her, with its tall mullioned windows on the top floor, its flowers and spiral chimneys. Warmth without smoke! Now that *was* novel! How lovely to be chatelaine of so powerful a castle, and surrounded by such rich lands as she had noticed as they had ridden by. How *good* to be in control of so much wealth! And she almost purred as, smiling warmly, she turned then to watch as her father brought their main hosts across to greet her father's own Guard Commander, Gaston de Vere, as he carefully handed her to the ground.

Rochine de Brocas was certainly a most striking young woman of just over four and twenty summers, tall and slender with hair as black and glossy as a raven's wing and large almond shaped eyes of sparkling emerald.

Her figure was most richly curved, and her skin the colour and texture of creamy satin. She had high cheek bones, with delicately moulded lips set in a generous mouth...and a rich, warm voice with an infectious chuckle that had deceived many into believing her to have a gentle, loving nature. In fact the lady was as hard and sharp as Damascus steel! Yet there was something very compelling and alluring about her, despite her sometimes imperious ways, for she really was very lovely, and no-one, man or woman, on whom she had decided to press her favours had ever failed to answer her desires. With her potions and her philtres, her stunning looks and body, and the sheer force of her personality when dazzlingly released, she was a lady to be taken lightly only at one's peril! And when her sultry gaze ran over Alicia, standing there so poised and graceful, she almost purred with anticipation. Seducing a jewel of such rare beauty would be both pleasurable and exciting. She would have her, literally eating out of her hand before this charade was over.

Then she looked at Gui and smiled, slow, warm and inviting.

Now *there* was a man worth tussling over! So tall, so strong. How wonderful to feel his large hands all over her hot and willing body, and she gave a shiver as a strong frisson of desire ran through her. Such a shame that he was not going to be around long enough for her to challenge, and she sighed, moving towards her father as she did so. Love was one thing, sheer lust quite another!

"Rochine, my love," her father said, holding out his hand to her. "Come, greet Sir Yvo and his family whom we have come so far to visit, and on such an important occasion too." And with enormous pride he turned to face his hosts and said: "Sir Yvo. Lady Margaret...my daughter, the Lady Rochine de Brocas."

With a warm smile on her lovely face, the Lady Rochine de Brocas, lowered her long lashes and sank down in a deep curtsy, her long scarlet bliaut dropping in rich folds around her as she did so. The hand she offered to Sir Yvo with which to lift her up, firm and cool to the touch, the fingers long and tapered with finely chiselled nails.

"My Lady," Sir Yvo said looking down on her, face demurely lowered to him, her jewelled sarsenet coif seeming to float over her plaited cauls. "It gives me great pleasure to welcome you and your father to Castle Malwood on the eve of so important an event for my family." And lifting her up lightly to her feet, pausing only to admire her beauty, he kissed her on both cheeks. Then taking her arm he went on: "I know that you must have had a long and

94

tiresome journey to get here, my dear, but I hope the entertainments we have arranged for your visit will give you something by which to remember us. Now, Alicia, my love," he said, turning to his ward. "Take your cousin and show her to your chamber, where all she needs to refresh herself before the evening has been provided.

"My Lord, I thank you for your welcome and your kindness," Rochine replied, her voice rich and warm. "I have indeed been looking forward to meeting the Lady Alicia for some time now, ever since my father received your invitation. After all Sir Yvo," she went on, giving the older man a dazzling smile and cheeky squeeze, "she is my cousin, in very truth, and it isn't *every* day that a girl discovers that her long lost English cousin is so beautiful."

"A compliment indeed, My Lady," Sir Yvo replied, smiling back at her, as everyone laughed at her unexpected sally. "Coming as it does from one so beautiful herself. I thank you." Then, turning to the Baron beside him he added: "Your daughter, My Lord, is as lovely as the morning and as sweet. I am so pleased that I have put the two of them together. I see she has brought no tire-woman with her..."

"...No, Sir Yvo," her father said, interrupting briefly. "We decided to travel swift and light. It is the way I like to do things!"

"Well, I had thought that might be so, Lord Roger, so I have arranged with Agnes Fitzwalter, Alicia's friend and abigail, to assist your daughter in all things, should she need it. And," he added, almost as an afterthought, "I have also arranged for extra men-at-arms to stand guard over the two of them tonight. There will be many strangers about, from the village, of course, and beyond it. Half the County will be coming, and Alicia's tower room is separate from our apartments. She always has a guard at her door, but two such lovely girls doubles the danger of a casual intruder, and I would hate anything to go wrong while you are with us!" and he looked into the Baron's black eyes and smiled.

So...just you bear *that* in mind, de Brocas, you smug bastard, he thought. I do not intend to make anything easy for you tonight!

"That was really kindly, Sir Yvo. Nothing could be better!" Lord Roger said, looking across at his daughter with a smile. "Security is also a problem at home in Grise, or Gruissan as it is better known there, so we are comforted by your kindness."

So...am I being warned? He thought, looking around him again, and back at the wide entrance of the castle, black with shade against the sizzling background of the sun-filled courtyard, with the broad lake, sparkling beyond it. No! That fat fool is as innocent as the day is long. Look how empty his eyes are? Splendour of God, but it is a long way across that open causeway! We must be quick tonight.

"You are very quiet, My Lord," The Lady Margaret, said then, looking up at his saturnine face and still, black eyes. "I know you are far from home, but we will do all we can to make your stay here with us as comfortable as possible."

"Oh...do not worry about me, My Lady," he said, thinking her to be even less knowing than her large husband. Sweet Lord, but she was as different from his Constancia as a plump partridge to a hawk!

"I was just miles away. Thinking how lovely this place is and how pleased I am to be here."

Sir Yvo looked at his wife and beamed. This was exactly how they had hoped it would be. How he and Sir James had planned it.

Everything calm, everything normal. The courtyard full of sunshine, his home decked out to look its very best, his men in gleaming mail, and his guests both relaxed and smiling. It could not be better. If only the Baron knew what they had planned for him, the treacherous bastard? All that he and King Richard had schemed for so carefully in London, and that he had later so thoroughly discussed with Margaret and Sir James at home, was even now all falling into place.

He just trusted that Gui...and Sir Richard!...would forgive him for not telling them both all that had been planned and organised. *But he was so right!* Just look at the boy! Try as he would, there was still resentment in every line of his face and body. Had he been told, truly, what was afoot, he surely would have shown it and the Baron simply *must* have smelled a rat!

He sighed, then and ground his teeth. The trap, so carefully laid for this Man-Eating Tiger was now baited and set...it only needed Father Matthew to arrive to trip it, and it would snap shut on both the Baron and his daughter, and two great evils would be cleansed. God Send him! Where *was* the man? And he looked past all those standing nearby to the long empty causeway beyond the gatehouse, his brows faintly drawn together in frustration. No matter. The man would surely come! And with a bright smile he turned to beckon Alicia forward to greet her cousin with a kiss on each cheek, and warm words of welcome.

Now she was as sultry piece! And as tricksy as her father by all accounts. 'Keep your friends close and your enemies closer!' Pray God he was not making a dreadful mistake in putting the two of them together? He must have a word with Sir Richard and double the guard on those two tonight. He smiled; Johnny Foxglove and Davey Oates would do excellently: tough as nails and long in service with the family. And those two Frenchmen, those 'Cousins' as well, nothing could be better; and sweeping his guests forward, he laughed.

Linking arms Alicia led Rochine away to her rooms in the old tower, closely followed by the castle servants helped by some of the Baron's people with The Lady's baggage. Black and golden heads bobbing together in the warm sunshine, arms now around each other's waists and bright with tinkling laughter, the two girls quickly disappeared from view.

Chapter 13...The Tiger enters the Lion's Den.

Pleased with what he had accomplished, Sir Yvo stepped back to beckon his guest forward and the two men walked towards the broad flight of steps that led up to the entrance of the New Hall, Gui following behind with his mother on his arm.

So far, so good!

At least they now had the Tiger in their den without him taking fright and trying to rush right out again! That would have precipitated an immediate armed response and led to the very kind of bloody skirmish that he and King Richard had gone to such lengths to avoid! To have seized the Baron in such a violent way...or even *killed* him!...without the Royal Warrant to protect them, and while Philip's goodwill was still so necessary for the Crusade did not bear thinking of! Nor did the King's anger! Almost Sir Yvo mopped his brow in relief as he and the Baron made simple, uncomplicated conversation as they walked along together.

★

Through all those exchanges Gui had watched his father's guest through narrowed eyes. Watched as he had ridden in and dismounted; watched as his men had raced to carry out his orders; watched as his daughter had arrived. Lord, but there was power in the man, and not just from his physical strength either, though that was formidable enough he thought wryly, giving his right hand a surreptitious shake. And his square frame would make him a horseman of rare ability. It would surely take some charge to thrust Lord Roger from his saddle! And those shoulders were made for fighting; for wielding his sword or battle axe; for bearing the full heat and burden of his armour throughout a long and bloody day.

But it was his eyes that really made him so extraordinary. They never seemed to move, yet he was sure they watched everything.

I don't trust you, Baron Roger! He thought. I don't trust your honeyed words and I *don't* trust your smile that never lights up your eyes...and I don't trust your black eyes either! No, My Lord Baron, he decided grimly.

You are *not* the man for me…and your Guard Commander, de Vere, needs watching too, as do all your entourage, I think! Nevertheless he had passed off his father's introduction carefully enough with a cold smile of his own, knowing as he did so that the Baron was no more enamoured of him than he was of the Baron. So be it. They would watch one another like a pair of moulting hawks, talons gripped and curved beaks ready to rip and tear, yet safely jessed by custom and good manners. His father need have no fear of any overt rivalry between the two. But it was there. Oh, for certain, it was there!

He must have speech with L'Eveque about the extra guards that his father had already mentioned, before things got so out of hand he simply forgot! With so many people all over the castle, keeping his eye on the eight more who had just arrived would not be easy, especially with some others of the guests bringing their own escorts with them too. Yet he wished to know what they were up to all the time!

Sweet Wine of Christ! But Alicia's determination to retain her tower rooms, convenient enough in the past, was now proving to be a real problem. His rooms in the New Hall were at least near those of his parents, but if anything should happen to Alicia, for whatever reason, then it would take him time to get there.

Miles away with his thoughts, he was swiftly brought to earth by his mother's voice and having bowed to his father's guest, murmuring some polite shibboleth as he did so, he took his mother's arm, and following behind the two elder men, now deep in conversation, he walked her up the broad stairs that led to the New Hall his father had built against the north wall of the castle. This was not where the party would be held. That would be in the Great Hall of the Keep itself. Nowhere else would do for such a mighty gathering as had been planned. But as a quiet place to take stock and meet especial friends, for entertaining important visitors, or for the family to gather on less formal occasions there was no better place than his parent's new apartments. Passing through the arched doorway and the small hall beyond, they mounted a further flight of stairs, all built in stone for fear of fire, and so to a long, broad passageway where the stonework had been part panelled, part plastered and then painted in warm colours, or with birds and beasts of the chase.

At one end was his parent's bedroom, with its lovely wall hangings and great carved beechwood bed, in between was his own set of apartments, with some others for occasional guests, and at the other end was the solar. This was a magnificent room, with its tall mullioned windows facing south, and real glass in every pane and not the thin plates of horn as were used in almost every other part of the castle. Indeed the Keep had mostly thick oak shutters, through which the wind howled in the winter time, making the place abominably draughty. Smokey too! His mother had always *hated* it. No wonder she had been so pleased with his father's decision to build afresh outside the Keep's great walls!

Truly, Gui thought, as he followed his father and the Baron into it, it was a most handsome room bright with embroideries on every wall, and a huge, thick carpet from distant Persia that his father had bought back from Venice years ago. There were broad window seats with fleecy cushions, and a number of sturdy chairs with padded backs and arm rests, as well as several tables and four great iron-bound chests.

Now it was filled with flowers and brilliant sunlight, but at night there were sconces on the walls for resin torches and numerous wrought-iron brackets on tall stands for candles. In the middle of the wall opposite the windows, was an enormous fireplace. Not as large as the one in the Great Keep, but large enough certainly to heat the whole room in winter. Then, when the north wind battered outside, with sleet and snow beneath its wings and the wolves howled from the Forest depths, all was snug and warm within. A lovely feeling, and it was ideal for entertaining special guests whom Sir Yvo wished to impress. But Gui had no desire to be closeted with the strange, dark-visaged Lord Baron of Narbonne and Gruissan if he could avoid it, if only because he might give something of his thoughts or feelings away to him without realising it.

So he made his excuses, and left to seek out his friend and his father's Guard Commander, Sir Richard L'Eveque, before any more time should slip idly through his fingers.

Chapter 14... The Lady and The White Rose together.

U p in her own chamber, Alicia and Rochine really did appear to be getting on extremely well, and sitting opposite one another on the broad window seats, they were soon in close conversation as they sorted out the various family relationships that now bound them both together.

Then, while Alicia went from place to place in her much loved room to show off her treasures, Rochine cleansed herself of the worst of her journey with the hot water, scented soap and towels that had been brought up to them. She was also at her most vivacious as she bent all her efforts to captivate her young cousin, keeping Alicia both interested and amused by telling her about her home at Gruissan near Narbonne, and of her journey North with her father to come to England for the first time.

And there was wine to drink too, warm as the summer sun itself, a fine red Bordeaux that Gui had ordered sent up to her room in a beautifully chased, gilt-lined silver decanter, with cool water from the castle springs in a finely etched glass jug to take with it if they so desired. However both girls had been drinking it as drawn down from the cask, unmixed with 'Adam's Ale,' from tall Venetian goblets of delicate blue-green glass, decorated with gold filigree round each rim that were the pride of Sir Yvo's collection. And into Alicia's glass, left on a side table nearby while she happily chatted over her shoulder from across the room, The Lady tipped some powder from the special ring she always wore for just that purpose. A pretty gewgaw of pearls and topaz whose top swivelled on a tiny spring, and whose contents fizzed briefly then vanished into the wine that had subsumed it.

This, combined with the warmth from the sun, and the heat and the excitement of the day, suddenly appeared to be making Alicia feel just a little woozy, though in truth she had not taken much. Nevertheless, soon her head began to droop and her conversation falter, and gliding to sit beside her cousin, like the predator she truly was, Rochine stole her arm around Alicia's slender waist and bent her head towards her, deliberately sending the heavy perfume she was wearing wafting gently over her. Alicia, slightly in awe of her older, more worldly cousin, was wooed by this; flattered and delighted with such kind and sweet attentions and snuggled herself onto Rochine's welcome shoulder as girls so often do.

The scent from her favourite white roses and from the honeysuckle that rioted below her window; the steady, lazy droning of the fat bumble bees that buzzzed and bumbled there; the red wine of Bordeaux - albeit doctored by The Lady - and the strong warmth of the sun all combined to make her feel drowsy. And, as their conversation slowly flagged and fell silent...so Alicia felt the first touch of soft lips on her neck. She turned her head then, her blue eyes huge in her face and slightly glazed, and as she did so her lips brushed Rochine's, sending lightning jolts of sudden passion coursing through her and making her cry out softly, her whole body quivering with a wild pulse of fire that made her head spin even more. Again Rochine brushed her lips against Alicia's, and again, letting her tongue dart out and touch them lightly every time she did so, like a snake tasting water on a hot day.

Then, taking her cousin by the hand, Rochine stood her up and held her in her arms, feeling her breasts push against her own as she did so.

Alicia, overwhelmed by her cousin's strange attentions, felt herself sinking, falling, swooning. The room was spinning, Rochine's green eyes sparkling, her lips were parted. Soft lips, warm lips, wet lips and suddenly she wanted them, was reaching for them, straining for them even as her hands felt for Rochine's full breasts to hold them, lift them, cup them, mould them against her own.

Eyes closed, her breath coming now in sharp gasps as her heart and lungs became suddenly suffused with passion, Alicia took Rochine's head in her hands at last and kissed her deeply, thrusting her tongue into her mouth again and again as she did so, lashing Rochine's tongue with her own, teasing it, tasting it, sucking it into her mouth until both girls were panting with desire and Alicia found herself standing, holding Rochine in her arms, breast to breast and thigh to thigh, in as passionate an embrace as ever she had done with Gui.

It was a few moments only...a minute maybe, perhaps two...before, with a gasp, Rochine parted from Alicia, gently allowing the younger girl to sink back down, breathless, eyes closed, onto the cushioned window seat...while she moved away, languidly straightening her own dress as she did so til her own heart and lungs had settled, and she was coolly in control of herself once more, no longer panting.

Looking round at the state in which she had left her cousin, and in which she had aroused herself as well, Rochine smiled wickedly, and turning the heavy gold pearl and topaz ring she was wearing on her left hand sharply clockwise, so that the top flew open, she blew the remaining powder that was in it out of the window. With a swift puff of her lips it was all gone, and a moment later she turned back to the girl still leaning, eyes closed, and breathing heavily, against the sun-drenched plaster of the window seat. It had been *so* easy to drop the powder from her ring into Alicia's goblet, while the silly girl had been rummaging in one of her chests for something special to show her sophisticated new French cousin, chattering all the while. A powerful Eastern aphrodisiac she had brought with her specially: it was a well practised old trick of hers, and never failed. There had been plenty of time, and this little one was so innocent of any trickery. She looked down at her and smiled again. Why rush something so delicious…when it could be so gently savoured first? Surely her body was every bit as lush and inviting as she had imagined it would be.

"Alicia, Alicia! What's the matter?" she cooed over her, taking her young cousin's hand in hers, and leading her over to her bed. "Come and lie down for a moment. You nearly fainted. It must be the heat and all the excitement. What came over you, my love?" She went on, solicitously, laying Alicia down and pressing her cool hand gently against her cousin's forehead: "There, Sweetheart. How hot you are? I'll leave you now, while you have a little rest and I am sure you will feel fine in a moment. Too much wine and sun, my love…and all the excitement as well I expect. I will be back presently, Alicia. But just now I must see my father and make certain he has all he needs for tonight, and now seems as good a time as any. Sleep well, and I will join you again later after I have had that bath your Agnes has promised me. If not I will see you in Lady Margaret's solar before we all go across to the Great Hall."

She turned then to walk away, but seeing the girl lying there so seductively spread out, she returned and sat down beside her again. Then, swiftly reaching over her she kissed her softly on the lips, and caressed her breasts, briefly squeezing and twisting each swollen tip, now taught beneath her touch, where they pressed so sharply hard against the soft material of her dress, making Alicia moan and shake her head. And all the while she let the perfume with which she had anointed herself behind the ears, and between her own firm breasts, drench the girl's senses once again, til with a smile she rose up to stand looking down at her cousin, still lying there with her eyes closed, her face and neck flushed with sudden passion.

"Alicia, I'll find that companion of yours…Agnes Fitzwalter," she said quietly, her green eyes glittering with success. "And send her along to make sure you are alright and to help you dress. I have been doing it so long for myself that I do not need a dresser, but she could help with my hair if she likes.

"Do you have to go?" Alicia asked her drowsily from the bed, eyes flicking open but still unfocussed. "I feel so strange," she mumbled. "So...so, floaty! Will you be alright in your own?"

"Now, don't you worry about me, young lady," Rochine answered her briskly, turning back towards the door. "I'll soon find my own way. What you need is rest. I'll see you in the solar, before dinner. By the way, I am so glad you liked the bracelet I gave you. It is very old you know. One of a pair. My father has the other one. I gave it to him long ago as a birth gift, from a bazaar in Morocco when Papa had gone there to conclude some business with the Emir. Be sure you wear it on your arm tonight. I'll be terribly hurt if you don't!"

And with a secret smile of quiet satisfaction on her lovely lips, she softly kissed her cousin's forehead, closed the door and slipped away.

Suddenly exhausted, Alicia lay on the great counterpane that covered her bed, uncertain as to whether she had really kissed Rochine and fondled her...or if it was all a wild dream? Whatever else had happened, her body was certainly in a keen state of arousal. It made her wish that she could feel Gui inside her right now, rampant as the great scarlet lion he wore so proudly on his chest. And thrusting her hands against her aching loins she clamped her thighs together and curled herself into a ball.

And thus it was that Agnes found her when she came along to her room to dress her for the evening, still in a ball, still with her hands between her thighs, but with a radiant smile on her lovely face.

Chapter 15...The Game's a'Foot!

That night the castle was en fête with a vengeance.

Not since Gui had returned from Yorkshire had there been so many people. The tables were packed with a glittering company and groaned beneath the weight of food that had been produced. Laid in the form of a giant hollow square below the dais, every table was covered with fine white napery that brilliantly set off the richness of the silver-gilt spoons, and bone-handled knives and spikes that lay beside each place

But only the High Table were there the great silver platters before each guest that had been part of the Lady Margaret's dowry; elsewhere there were only the usual trenchers on wooden plates, And only the High Table was set with the beautiful blue and gold glasses that Sir Yvo had brought back from Venice ten years earlier, everyone else below the salt had horn beakers in silver holders, or leather jacks for ale and cider.

Behind the guests on the dais and round the walls of the Great Hall, the castle servants stood in immaculate surcoats and hose with the Malwood Lion-Rampant richly emblazoned in scarlet on back and front. Some held tall silver pitchers of red and white wine, with a napkin of pure white linen over the arm to catch the drops, while others just waited to be called, each there to serve the needs of the guests before him.

The great room itself was lit by hundreds of candles in bronze and silver holders both on the tables and beside them, as well as those suspended from the great wheels that hung down from the rafters. And there were scented pine torches sputtering and hissing away in freshly blacked iron sconces on the walls. The light was almost dazzling, winking and sparkling off the bright eyes of the guests, their jewels, the polished silver, their glasses and their shining faces, animated by laughter and the flowing conversation.

Truly it was a gargantuan feast that Sir Yvo and his Lady presented that night for there were meats and delicacies of every kind: great haunches of beef and mutton, spiced pasties, sucking pigs and venison from the King's own forest. The Boar's Head was borne in on a huge silver charger by two of Suchard's lustiest helpers, preceded by the man himself and two of the castle's foremost trumpeters, with two more following behind, whose clarion calls brought all to their feet with cries and shouts of praise.

Already carved and jointed, with every slice put carefully back in place and then glazed and decorated with fruit and parsley, it was a magnificent thing to see, and taste. In addition, Suchard, whom Sir Yvo had brought back with him from France, had himself cleaned and polished its brutal curved tushes especially for the occasion, finishing him off with a late apple from the Lady Margaret's stores stuffed into his cruel mouth. The Boar's Head was followed in procession by Swans, skinned, cooked, carved and their skins cunningly put back with all their feathers in place; and a stately peacock too, fantastic in all his blue-green glory, with tail raised and spread for all to see and catch the light that blazed out on every hand. Each new wonder greeted with fresh cheers and laughter.

There were also fish of every sort from the red flesh of the salmon to the grey-white flesh of the pike…but not the one from the castle moat who had managed to evade capture for so long that Sir Yvo had forbidden anyone to fish for him! But there were carp and whiting, eels and lampreys and a great sturgeon, fresh caught that morning and brought from Southampton by fast carrier especially for the occasion. The list seemed endless: capons in lemon, larded pheasant, duck and partridge with heavily spiced pasties of forced rabbit and stewed sparrows. Gravy with this; delicate sauces with that; and a wide variety of fresh vegetables from the castle gardens.

Finally there were the deserts: jellies of different colours, blancmange, fruit pastries of every different sort, open tarts with fruit in fine custard, fresh strawberries, peaches and apricots, great cheeses with apples from deep storage still crisp and sweet, cheese cake with nuts and honey, raisins with pistachios, small bowls of sultanas and the Lady Margaret's finest glazed fruits and marchpane, and jugs of thick cream from the castle dairy.

As Gui watched the courses come and go, he was not surprised that his mother had been in such a state about all the arrangements, and he wondered if there were any people left at all in the village that night, for by God there were an awful lot of them about the room already! Some of her orders must have gone out months ago, particularly those for the spices and special nuts and sultanas. Bringing them all together must have been a real nightmare. Still, Alicia and Agnes had helped a lot, and he had found the three of them, on more than one occasion, up to their armpits in flour and pastry having a heated argument with Suchard the Master Chef over the preparation of one thing or another. Why the poor man was still here after years of his mother's meddling he would never know, for they were always fulminating about one another, alternating with Suchard running out in a fine Gallic temper, threatening to leave, and his mother having mild hysterics at the thought that this time he really might!

Thank God he was a man and could get on his horse and leave them all to sort it out. Poor love, rather her than him any day!

★

Seated at the High Table on the dais, just to the right of his parents, he and Alicia were the very centre of attention.

He, dressed in the very height of fashion that night, looked truly resplendent. The long, dark red silk overdress that he was wearing over a purple bliaut, itself worked in thick gold thread with its collar and deep, long sleeves in brilliant cloth of gold edged with ermine and studded with pearls, shimmered in the candlelight, and every time he moved, his brilliant yellow silk under tunic with tight sleeves to his wrists, danced and glimmered like tongues of living flame, as it flickered out from between the slashed pleats that hung to his waist.

And round his neck he wore the beautifully enamelled St Christopher, on its chain of thickly twisted gold, studded with gems that Alicia had given him as her own Betrothal gift, as much to keep her in his heart, as to keep him safe on his long journey to the Holy Land.

She, in a blue silk and damask dress that matched her eyes perfectly, pleated and reaching to the ground, with puffed shoulders of blue and silver with long deep trumpet sleeves on which the scarlet stag's head with golden antlers of her family had been gloriously and richly embroidered with pure gold thread, the whole also edged with ermine as befitted her rank. Laced criss-cross over her breasts, a chemise of dark blue silk with tight fitted sleeves to her wrists beneath, over which she wore a diamond patterned corselet of silver and gold that looked absolutely stunning. Her hair hung in thick golden plaits to her hips, thickly entwined with blue and silver ribbons, with huge butterfly bows to match at each end, and on her head she wore a simple wimple of finest blue sarsenet, edged with sapphires and pearls and held in place by a beautiful band of intricately twisted gold of different colours, a single cabochon sapphire in its centre, a present from Gui's parents brought all the way from Constantinople itself.

107

Round her waist she wore a wide braided girdle of finest blue and silver suede with huge blue and silver tassels that swung just below her knees; and around her slender neck, sparkling in the candle light, she wore her mother's great chain of sapphires in beautifully worked nests of mixed gold set with milky pearls and diamonds, and on her hand the great sapphire, with clustered pearls, that Gui had given her the previous evening to match that upon her forehead.

Sitting next to her, her hand clasped in his own, Gui found it almost impossible to keep his eyes off her, and her perfume and the warm, clean woman smell of her was intoxicating. Her breath smelling softly of mint, that she had chewed after brushing her teeth with fresh hazel twigs, she looked good enough to eat! However, there were times during the evening when a tiny shadow seemed to cross her face, and she would look vaguely pensive and uncertain.

"Are you alright my darling?" he asked her during a pause between toasts. "Because you were looking rather - bothered? - just now and I *so* want you to have a really lovely evening with no problems for that busy head of yours to pause over. Let others sort them out for a change."

"Oh Gui, don't worry about me," Alicia replied, turning to him with a brilliant smile. "I'm having a marvellous time. It's so lovely to be the real centre of attraction for a change, and it's just wonderful to see everyone enjoying themselves so much in our honour.

Dear God" She breathed huskily, grasping his hand fiercely, her eyes devouring him. "But I do *love* thee, Gui de Malwood, my *so* Dear Lord and Master. My own very gentle, perfect Knight."

Gui sat back and smiled down at her, his heart just bursting with love for her also. Overflowing. His strong brown hands deeply entwined with the white porcelain fineness of her own, and he brought her hand up so that he could kiss each slender finger as she spoke.

"Stop worrying, Gui, I'm fine. Truly. It's just that I *so* want you to myself and I can't have you! Indeed, I shan't even be able to see you tonight later at all, which is a great shame because I want you so badly it hurts! The sooner they all go the better," she said, gesturing at the assembled throng with a laugh. Then, after a moment's hesitation, and looking at him closely, she asked: "What do you know of my gentle cousin, Rochine? She whom they call 'The lady'?"

"Not a lot. She's the only bud on his branch. About twenty four. Lives in their Château at Gruissan, that we call Grise, near Narbonne with her father; has a distinctly wild reputation, not to say downright unsavoury…quite unlike your Grandmother, Phillipa de Burley, who though wild at times was honest and true in every other way which this one I don't think is!" he added with a grimace. "Looks like an angel, but definitely is not! In fact, I think, quite the opposite! I didn't want her anywhere near you, but father overruled me. Why?"

"Well…" Alicia said, after a further pause for thought and moving to whisper softly in his ear. "I swear she tried to make love to me this afternoon when we were alone together!"

"*What?*" He exclaimed, suddenly shifting in his chair, trying to gain a glimpse of the Baron's daughter further down the table.

"*Shush*, Gui!...don't make a fuss," she hissed at him, taking his hands in her own and stroking the back of them with her thumbs. "Nothing happened, my darling. It's against all the teachings of Holy Church anyway, but I know about such things from what the soldiers say…"

"Soldiers?" He exclaimed again.

"Yes, silly. *'Soldiers!'*" She replied laughing. "You know? Little men in armour type people? Carry big swords and fart a lot? They are *always* talking about such things, Gui. Especially those who have come back from Outremer, and have seen a bit more of life than a few wild days out in Southampton! Remember, I have been around soldiers all my life."

"What 'things', Alicia?" he asked, intrigued.

"Oh…just 'things', she said enigmatically. Then, after a pause she added mischievously: "Like three-in-a-bed?" looking up at him from underneath her brows and smiling at his look of amazement. "I have learned *more* from listening to the, supposed, 'whispered' conversations of your men outside my door over the years, Dear My Lord, than you may care to imagine!...*And* from talking with the castle girls from the Forest, like Maudie and Judith and Luscious Laura whom Richard was so keen on a few years ago!" she added with a wicked grin, watching his eyebrows go through the roof. "And Agnes of course."

"You *hussy!*" He replied shocked. "Some 'innocent' you were in your room that afternoon then, you Jade! When I threw that bucket of water all over you!" Adding with a secret smile: "You just wait 'til I get you on your own, my Lady! And Luscious Laura as well…eh?"

"*Gui!*" She answered him, horrified. Then relaxed with a smile as he threw back his head and laughed, before digging him sharply in the ribs. "Who else was I to turn to for knowledge and advice, you wretch? My dear Mama died when I was only little, and I could hardly ask your mother!"

"But The Lady?…Rochine de Brocas?" he repeated, dropping his voice instinctively. "Tried to make love to you?…"

"*Yes!* – No! I don't know. I'm not sure. She was certainly *very* friendly, my darling! But nothing happened I assure you. Well I don't think so? It was just so unexpected…and strange," she went on, squeezing his hand lovingly. "But it was so warm and close in my room, that in the end I decided it was all in my mind and blamed your not being there for kissing her the way you kiss me.

"Is that what you did?"

"I don't know, darling. Truly! All in my mind, I expect. Comes of wanting you *so* much! See what you've done to me?" she asked, laughing gaily up at him. "Some sweet 'innocent' I am, that's for certain!" And bending towards him she kissed him softly in the candle light.

★

Sitting on one end of the huge table just ten paces away, Baron Roger leaned back in his chair and watched them through narrowed eyes black as pitch, his mouth a tight gash, his brain seething.

Go on, my little pigeon. Enjoy him while you may for you will not have him for much longer. I have set in train such events this night as will tear your ridiculous community apart. He leaned forward again, staring empty eyed across the Hall, rolling his glass between his large square hands as he did so, his mind filled with his thoughts and impressions of the day. Pleased that his plans seemed to going well, and delighted that the two men whom he had sent on ahead with such care had been taken on as he had planned they should be.

Jules Lagrasse and Lucas Fabrizan!

Both had worked for him for several years and were two of his best trained and most trusted men-at-arms. Vicious, amoral and dedicated. He had seen them both now, and de Vere would speak with them too, later on. They were there in case everything went really badly wrong and he had to get out fast!

He drank from his glass and grunted.

Not that anything should go wrong, of course. His plans *always* worked. But so much hung on the effective outcome of tonight's attack, and there was so much that just *might* not work this time, that he had been forced to make careful arrangements just in case. And then there were his two message carriers! That had been almost the most complicated part of all, and the most expensive. Anything involving Prince John always was, and the irony of it was that none of it might ever be needed! He growled in his throat, looking down at his glass as he did so. By God's Bones, but it had *better* go well! His men were in place; his daughter was prepared; he had all the foul ooze he needed to fire the building; his personal arms were ready and his ship lay waiting, snugly moored in sheltered waters. What could go wrong now?

He drank again, deeply, then abruptly beckoned a varlet to re-fill his glass, his dark eyes fathomless. Intense. Making the servant shiver so that the wine he was pouring suddenly spilled over the edge onto the floor.

"You *fool!*" the Baron hissed violently, almost striking the man, now desperately apologising for his mistake. "You *ignorant* peasant! *Canard!* Had you been one of my servants, I would have had your skin for this! *Get out of my sight!*" he gestured furiously, mopping at his clothes with his napkin. Then, realising he was drawing unwarranted attention to himself, he smiled at those around him whom he had startled with his outburst. "It is nothing, nothing!" he said calmly, tossing it off with a laugh. "Just this fool of a varlet has spilled the wine on the floor and splashed me a little," and turning he waved the man away again, this time with a smile, before looking round, and searching out his daughter sitting a few places further away and talking animatedly with her neighbour, with whom she was flirting outrageously.

My, but she was a handsome piece! Fantastic! And their coupling that afternoon had been fiercer than ever. Never had the crystal felt so alive! Never had the power flowed *so* strongly. It had made the hairs on his arms stand out like sentinels. He could still feel it coursing through his veins. They had done their work well. Tonight a storm would come, he could feel it. What came next would all depend on Rochine.

If she played her part with Alicia tonight then all would happen as he had intended, and all the months of planning and plotting with Prince John would have paid off, and they would have all the riches and success their hearts desired. He looked around the Hall, his black eyes deep-set, hooded in their intensity.

Soon this would all be his.

He smiled. And that ridiculous mountebank Sir Yvo de Malwood and his foolish wife would be gone. The man was absurd! This whole little community was absurd, with its kindness and its friendliness and candour. "*Bah!*" he snorted with disgust. They did not do such things at home in Gruissan. He rubbed his hands together and grinned. Oh, but there would be changes when he was Lord of Malwood!

He snarled deep in his throat and drank again, looking at Gui darkly as he did so. The boy! He thought, watching him kissing the lovely girl seated so closely beside him. What of the boy? He grimaced. Would he be a problem, with his great broad shoulders and tall muscular body? He had met young men like him before. All brawn and muscle, but nothing in the loft! He would try his mind on him later; see what he was made of. But he didn't foresee a problem there. And as for the girl, Alicia? She was surely grist to his mill *any* day. He only had to reach out his hand and she would fall into it like the rich peach she was. Between him and The Lady there was nothing they could not do. And throwing back his head, he laughed.

It was all just a question of time.

And with a slow, deep smile he raised his glass in mock celebration to the Hall and all around him and drank deeply, imperiously ordering one of the servants standing nearby to refill it, while through the window ahead of him he could see the Western horizon already filling with deep storm clouds, just as he and Rochine had gloriously striven that afternoon to achieve.

The game's a'foot; the dice are on the roll, let every player stand his shot.

112

Chapter 16... The Lull before the storm.

In a moment between conversations Rochine watched her father drinking.

Dressed in a beautiful bliaut of deep crimson silk trimmed with ermine that plunged between her breasts under a beautiful jacket of finest cloth of gold lined with white sarsenet, cut to the waist, she looked stunning and revelled in it! Her slender neck decorated with dark rubies and diamonds on a heavy gold chain that simply glowed like drops of blood against her creamy skin, her hair in braided cauls threaded with ribbons of cloth of gold, beneath a golden snood studded with pearls, no-one that night was more magnificently dressed.

Knowing what he was thinking and what they had done together that afternoon, the mere memory of it enough to stiffen her breasts, she smiled also, pushing her hands down hard between her legs as she did so. Sweet Life but he was so good to be with. So hard, so demanding! There was none better, and she had sampled many. Men and women both, and never had she thought anything about it. It was really very simple. She truly loved him! Even knowing that everyone else would condemn such wickedness, the Church especially, she still loved him. She sneered, and her lip curled wickedly. Hadn't Queen Eleanor, King Richard's own precious mother, supposed to have had a rabid affair with her Uncle, Raymond of Tripoli, while still married to Louis of France? The Church? Bah! She didn't give a fig about the Church, anymore than her father did!

Who were *they* to preach chastity and obedience? Fifty years ago it hadn't been a problem. She thought, sipping her wine. Then priests could marry. Since then 'The Church' had changed its mind. Now priests couldn't marry...so they had 'housekeepers' instead or abused little boys! What rubbish! And the Church was disgustingly venal. How else had her father got them both out of trouble the last time there had been a row about their relationship, save by bribing the Archbishop of Narbonne with golden marks and pretty girls? And as for the Papacy? That was surely awash with Satan's brew! Hadn't her father told her of a Pope who had seduced his own sister when she was just thirteen? Pope Sergius III...her father had a head for such details, as did she! The wretched girl then had a son who then became Pope himself. John...John?...John XII who, Sweet Wine of Christ, *then took his own mother as his mistress!* And revenged himself on his enemies in his spare time by

113

hacking off their limbs! Mother Church, indeed! *Such* hypocrisy! She snorted with derision. Life was for the living, and she just *loved* the living of it.

But *Dear God*, what a terrible collection of people there were around her! So dull! So lacking in life and expectation! Were all Englishmen like these? No dash! No sparkle! The man whom she was sitting next to, Rupert de La Roche? was plainly dazzled by her to the absolute fury of his very plain wife, Elaine, sitting too far from her husband to make any difference. So she had teased him mercilessly, fluttering her eyes, breathing at him a little too closely, rubbing her breasts against his arm and her foot against his: 'Oh, Sir Rupert' this and 'Oh, Sir Rupert,' that while fluttering her eyelashes at him until he was goggle eyed, like a petrified rabbit, and his wife was incandescent!

She gave a chuckle in her deep, husky voice. It had been glorious.

Then, tilting her head, she sipped her wine, and looked at Gui over the golden rim of her glass, and squeezed her thighs tightly. Now he *would* be good. In fact he was probably the largest man she had ever met, being both broader shouldered and taller than her father. What a shame he was not going to be around long enough to find out whether she really could take him away from her sweet cousin, Alicia. It would certainly have been fun trying. Only soon he would be dead and she long gone with her father and his fiancée, and she looked at the lovely girl beside him, laughing up into his face, with the blonde plaited cauls twined with blue and silver ribbons, and her mouth tightened into a thin line as she did so.

Now there was a charming piece, and ripe too!

Breasts almost as full as her own and a passionate mouth. Smooth thighs and tight buttocks from riding. That afternoon in the girl's room had just been a starter, leaving her suitably lubricious she was certain. She smiled to herself at the memory. It had only been a few moments, but enough to convince her that seducing Alicia would be both delightful, and easy. Her father would have no cause to be displeased, and she almost purred at the thought. She would have her eating out of her hand before long, *that* she was determined on. Then, when all that they had schemed for happened tonight, it would be the easiest thing in the world to get her to leave with them.

She mustn't forget the drug she would need to fix the guard's night drink, though. Perhaps Jules or Lucas could help with that? Perhaps they might even be the very men chosen for the guarding duty that Sir Yvo had talked of? For though she had not spotted them when first they had arrived, she

114

knew her father and De Vere had found and spoken with them since, and Jules had told him of his growing relationship with Agnes Fitzwalter, Alicia's friend and personal handmaiden. Even the soldiers whom they had brought with them, mingling cheerfully with the rest of the castle guard, had told them what was going on between Jules and Agnes. So anything was possible, and she had the drugging posset with her now, in its small glass philtre straight from her little Greek perfumier, Dmitri Stanisopoulos, hanging from a fine gold chain between her breasts.

She pressed her hands against them to be sure that it was still there, its hardness nestling in their warmth. Soon now she must leave the hall and find Gaston de Vere, her father's Guard Commander. He would help her to do the rest. Then all they had to do was wait.

After that they would be away and gone back to their great Château at Gruissan, the very seat of her father's power; and from where no-one could do them harm. The very idea was ridiculous. The Château was immensely strong. Unassailable, and many, *many* miles away! After this night's work had been concluded, and with Prince John's support after Richard's departure on his ridiculous crusade, her father would marry the girl and inherit everything. Then she could get rid of her through Valerian Dodoni and Wazzim as she had already planned and have her father to herself again.

But what about children? Her father would need an heir, so how would that work?

She ran her hand over her belly and touched her breasts. She shuddered What a horrendous idea! Pregnancy alone was bad enough...but pregnant by her father? While it wouldn't be the first time such a thing had happened: sisters with brothers, like Egypt! Or even sons with their mothers, like the Greeks! But *not* with her...not like Pope Sergius, that would ruin everything! Not even the Archbishop of Narbonne would be able to help them then, and anyway she would not suffer it herself...not even for her father! The swollen belly, the sickness, the pain? She shuddered again. She had seen it all before so many times. Love him as she did, she knew such awfulness was simply not for her.

Better to leave that to some other chosen concubine who like Abraham with his wife Sara, would give birth into her hands thus making the child her own! Six thousand lovely, fat golden Bezants that was for certain. She shrugged her elegant shoulders and smiled wickedly, rolling her long-stemmed glass between her hands as she did so. She would have all the fun, her father's little blonde sow all the travail! Live for the moment and let the future take care of itself! That was her motto. She just had to get the girl away from here and all would work out well. She drank smoothly of the deep red wine in her glass and then threw back her head and laughed.

Dear God! But life could be good sometimes!

★

Gui heard Rochine's sudden laughter and looked over at her as she turned back to her table companion, nudging Alicia as he did so: "Look at her making cow's eyes at poor de La Roche. His wife must be spitting blood and splinters. Look at him, poor man, he looks stunned!"

Alicia smiled. "Elaine's furious. Look at the 'looks' she is throwing him! No wonder, poor dear, she's not exactly the prettiest girl in the room anyway, and beside Rochine she is as plain as a pikestaff! Whatever did Rupert think he was doing marrying her?

"Lands and money, my darling," he replied wickedly. "Lands and money. Same as why I am going to marry you of course! Why else would I saddle myself with so impossibly demanding a wife?"

"Gui, you abominable man!" she responded swiftly, giving him a hearty kick under the table. "Take that for your pains, you wretch!" He laughed and kissed her swiftly behind her ear as they struggled happily together.

"By the way, dearest, where did she slip away to this afternoon?" He asked her presently, looking round the great bustling room with its myriad lights and brightly chatting people. "Your fine French Cousin? I couldn't find her anywhere, nor her precious father either. Not in their rooms, not in the Castle garth, nowhere. I don't trust that man one little bit!"

"I've absolutely no idea. Perhaps they went for a walk around the moat, it's pretty enough and there are several glades leading off it full of flowers just now that give a lovely view of the castle."

"Perhaps," he said, mollified. "Certainly the next time I did see them they seemed to have just come through the gatehouse. Maybe that is what they had been doing?"

"Anyway, darling, after our little tryst earlier she left me to rest and I didn't see her, or her father again 'til just before I met you in your mother's solar in the New Hall. I dressed first and left just as she came in for her bath. I left her with Agnes to go to your mother's room for my pearls and sapphires. That was before we all came together here. I thought she looked a little flushed when she came in, but perhaps she had been running, not wanting to be late?"

"Running?" Gui exclaimed derisively. "That one? Not everyone behaves like a hoyden, my love. I shouldn't think she's run anywhere for years. She just glides about quietly and pops up when you least expect her. If you ask me she's a real bitch! You say you got on rather too well together this afternoon," he went on mischievously. "Then perhaps a little 'pillow talk' might just be the answer. Those two are up to something, I am sure of it," he went on earnestly, casting a swift glance to where the Baron was seated. "*Sweet Jesus*, Alicia, but I wish I knew what was going on in that black, inscrutable mind of his." And signalling the varlet standing behind his chair to refill his glass, he turned to watch the hearty manner in which their guests were all so obviously enjoying themselves, his mind filled with thoughts of Alicia, of leaving home to follow his King to Jerusalem…and of their two so unwelcome guests around whom there was so much secrecy! Not least his own dear Papa still waiting, with scarce concealed impatience, for his unnamed guest to arrive and his mother doing all she could to keep him calm!

"Gui?" Alicia asked quietly, after a moment: "Did you mean that, about 'pillow talk'? She was *very* friendly with me this afternoon," she added, tugging at his sleeve and looking up at him coyly through her long eyelashes, her heart beating swiftly at the remembrance of it. "And you know how girls like to talk together. She just might let something slip."

"You little minx. She really got to you, didn't she? You watch your step, My Little Lady. That kind of stuff is condemned by the Church. Sapphic love and all the goings-on on the distant Isle of Lesbos!…"

"*Gui!*" She answered him shocked. "How do *you* know of such things? Of the Fair Lady Sappho, her pretty Greek island and her educating the daughters of wealthy Greeks?"

"Don't look so surprised, my darling, I have heard the tales myself. There was a South French squire serving with Lord Percy up north, from near Grasse. Where your perfumes come from? Pierre de Menton. He had one of her poems. Anyway, my Angel," he went on sarcastically, giving a soft shake. "How do *you* know such things?"

"What on *earth* was he doing in Yorkshire, poor boy?" she said, suddenly changing direction. "That's *miles* from his home!"

"*What?*...Oh...some family reason or other. Favourite uncle recommended Yorkshire to his father, or something....Look, I thought you wanted to know about Sappho? So stop trying to divert me, you Jezebel!"

"I do! I *do!*" she said, tugging at his arm with a smile. "Please go on...it's just I was distracted by your friend coming from so far away."

"Well...she was Greek. Sappho that is, not my friend! And very famous for her poetry, all about love and marriage. And love between women," he added dropping his voice, almost to a whisper. "Anyone who puts in a marriage poem to the bride that 'she was moist as wet grass' is not writing a ballad just to extol marriage! Anyway, 'The Church' decided she was just too much of a good thing and in Constantinople and in Rome they had all her works gathered in and ceremoniously burned."

"*Sweet Lord!* What an extraordinary thing to do!" She exclaimed, astonished. "When was that?"

"Oh...years ago, Sweetheart. During the time of the Conqueror, I think. 1070 or something, not long after this castle was first built. The Church believes in love and marriage, of course, as I do," he said, looking down at her lovingly. "That leads to children and the next generation. That's good! Anything else, like same sex love, is simply bad, *and must be fiercely discouraged!* He ended with a flourish. "The priests thought Sappho's works were dangerous...so they burned them all. Simple!"

"Hmmm," Alicia said, thoughtfully. "What about Kings? I hear William Rufus was pretty loose about whom he bedded? And some of the Bishops themselves are no better. Seems to me there is one rule for Kings and priests...and another for the rest of us! What about the Lady Rochine then?"

"Just you go carefully, my darling. Don't get drawn into anything you know you can't handle. I don't know that I trust her any more than I do her father, and he really makes my flesh creep... And I don't want any 'pillow talk' between the two of you unless I am there to share it!" he added with a wicked smirk, dropping a kiss on her lips as he spoke.

"*Gui!*" She responded, shocked. "Nice girls don't do things like that!" she said, archly. "Father Gerome says that is how the Greeks and Romans behaved, and look what happened to them! And anyway...you'd never cope. We'd wear you out long before you could do the same to us!"

"You cheeky cat!" he responded, drawing her close to him again and kissing her soundly. "My, but Gerome is a knowing one, and no mistake," he replied thoughtfully a moment later somewhat amazed. "I had no idea he had so much learning. Here was I thinking him no more than a simple country priest...yet he's been telling *you* all about the ancient Greeks and Romans! I hadn't supposed him capable. So that's where you learned of Sappho and her famous island school for girls?"

"Sir Yvo insisted I be properly educated and encouraged to read widely, like Queen Eleanor."

"Hmmmm...I doubt he meant you to learn about Sapphic love, my darling! I wonder what else you know?" He asked, grinning mischievously down at her.

"Nothing that a '*nice*' girl would wish to own up to, *that's* for certain!" She said, peeping naughtily at him through half closed fingers.

"Who said you were a *nice* girl anyway, you vixen?" he responded, pointing to his shoulders with a smile. "What would Father Gerome say about the marks on those?"

"That you had clearly been mauled by a fierce wild beast...*Me!* And he would look mournful and shake his poor old head saying he doesn't know what has happened to young people nowadays, call me a real hussy and give me a dozen 'Hail Mary's'. Then the poor dear would want to know when we are getting married.

Oh Gui," she said, holding his hand and kissing him. "When *can* we get married?" she pleaded, batting her eyelids at him. "I *hate* all this hole in the corner business...if you see what I mean?" she added fiercely, seeing the dangerous quirk in his eyes.   "All this pretending that nothing is 'going on' when everyone *knows* that it is. I want you when I want you, you irritating man, not just when we think no-one's watching!"

"After tonight, my darling, as soon as it can be arranged. But whether that can happen before I sail for France, I really don't know," he added gloomily. "You are still King Richard's Ward, and your marriage cannot be concluded without him."

119

"Without the King?" She was genuinely surprised.

"Or someone given his direct authority" he added archly. "Like me, for instance, or my father."

"You *wretch!*" she berated him, giving him a rap on his knuckles with the back of her spoon. "You were funning! How you do tease me."

"Like a trout to a fly, my darling. Every time"

"Like you, me and Rochine?" She questioned silkily

"What do you think?" he asked, leaving the question hanging.

"I think you're a rogue and a charlatan, but never mind My Love," she replied softly, shaking her head and kissing him lightly, "You know I would *never* do anything you wouldn't like me to!" And smiling serenely up at him as if butter wouldn't melt in her mouth, she promptly changed the subject.

"Incidentally, do you like my new bracelet?" she asked, showing him the heavy gold arm ring that Rochine had given her. "It's a betrothal gift. It's beautifully ornate and heavily carved. She says it is very old; one of a pair she bought from a bazaar in Morocco. Her father has the other one"

"Very pretty, darling," Gui replied carefully, studying her wrist. "But I'm not sure I like you wearing anything that woman may choose to give you. She may sound as if she comes in friendship, Alicia. But it is my belief that they have something very different in mind. My father was very mysterious this afternoon about their being here. And Richard and I have put men all over the place to keep an eye on them…"

"Do you want me to take it off, Gui?" She suddenly asked him anxiously. "It is very heavy…and chunky. I could easily make that a reason for removing it. I just don't want to offend her."

"No, my darling. That might give rise to awkward questions while they are both still here. When they are gone will be soon enough. But look, Sweetheart," he said sharply, giving her arm a shake, as a sudden extra buzz and bustle of interest flew all round the room. "Father is getting up at last…so is Gerome. This is the part of the whole proceedings that we have both been waiting for, so pay attention!

120

Chapter 17... In which the Lord Baron first tries his wicked hand.

Father Gerome, the village priest and Sir Yvo's Castle Chaplain, a gentle man much loved by all and Gui's former tutor, had indeed risen to his feet together with Sir Yvo, who hammered for silence before moving to the very front of the dais so all could see what was happening. There the Lord of Malwood took a great parchment hung with scarlet ribbons and seals from Sir James, first showing it to everybody before breaking the seals and handing the whole great parchment over to the little priest beside him, so he could read its contents out to all those before them in the Great Hall.

The early part was full of powerful legal statements to do with the King's rights and privileges regarding wardship and marriage, especially with regard to Alicia's inheritance and of the entailment of the de Burley estates in her name. This was all with respect of her betrothal and future marriage to 'His trusted and well beloved servant, Sir Gui de Malwood,' and so on, and so on, and so on. And as soon as their names were mentioned both Gui and Alicia stood up and moved over to stand before Sir Yvo and the old priest at the front of the dais as he worked his way through the document, both swearing love and allegiance first to each other with kisses and blessings, and then to the King.

Then, *at last*, with a broad smile, Father Gerome arrived at the very heart of the matter.

Holding up their hands for all to see, and taking the two ends of his long silken stola, the very symbol of his Office as a priest, he gently bound their hands together and, while everyone held their breath, he proclaimed them formally betrothed: "Let no man part asunder those whom the Good Lord has joined together," adding in a loud aside, with a wicked grin for so Holy and beloved a priest, "And praise God we get these two married soon, because I'm fed up with all their naughty tricks and cannot keep the pair of them apart any longer!"

At this there was a wild burst of cheering and stamping of feet from all of those gathered there, together with much ribald comment and nudging and winking from those who knew the true state of affairs between the two lovers, but had spent many weary months pretending not to! Then, while his mother remained watching from the high table her face full of love and pride in her family, Gui's father moved across and solemnly kissed Alicia on both cheeks and then once more for family, welcoming her to their hearts amidst much 'oohing' and 'aahing', especially from the ladies present as he did so.

So, finally, it was over, and they were a formally betrothed couple at last…and everyone went wild, hammering their fists on the table tops, stamping on the floor, and leaping up to toast the happy couple. While they both stood, huge smiles on their faces and enormous love for each other in their hearts, beneath great showers of rose petals cast down upon them from all the open galleries above. Now at last it was time for the entertainments to begin and for the guests to mingle freely with each other, and with the villagers who now came pushing their way forward to join in the fun. So, while the tables at the far end of the hall were cleared away in preparation for the dancing that was soon to follow, and the musicians were tuning their instruments with a weird cacophony of tortured sounds, in came the jugglers and acrobats whom his father had engaged to amuse everybody. Gui smiled at the scene and laughed. There were certainly going to be a lot of sore heads in the morning, and not many would be listening to Old Gerome when he stood to take the Chapel Service!

It was while he was watching all this that he suddenly noticed that Rochine de Brocas had disappeared. Her father was around, looking as inscrutable and impenetrable as ever, but his beautiful, raven-haired daughter was missing. Calling over one of the wine stewards he asked if he had seen her, but was only partially relieved to discover that she had been seen making her way towards one of the many garderobes with which the castle was provided. Nevertheless it was still some considerable time before she re-appeared, now with a light shawl across her slim shoulders, and by then he and Alicia had risen from the table and moved down into the hall, she to talk with some of her many friends who had come in from the surrounding countryside for their betrothal party, and he to mingle with his father's guests and generally keep an eye on things. So it was from the deep shadows of one of the cross arches beneath one of the overhead galleries, that he now watched her cross the hall to her father's side, smile and exchange a few words with him, before moving away to join others who were getting ready to dance.

"Now, where have you been to my little Lady?" he murmured softly to himself.

"Where indeed?" came a drawled question from right behind him.

"*Splendour of God!*" Gui exclaimed leaping round and thrusting his hand down towards where his sword should have been. "By Jesus, Richard, but you gave me a fright! How long have you been lurking in the shadows?"

"Oh, a while, My Lord," came the slow, laconic reply from their tall guard commander. "A while! It is my personal watch command tonight as you know, hence the military regalia" he added shaking his mailed shoulders. "Standing Orders that we dress accordingly when on duty, and quite right too!" he said. "Anyway, I like to know what is going on when It's my time on the roster. I missed some of the good Baron's men earlier this evening, especially his Guard Commander, Gaston de Vere, whom I found later talking with one of the Cousins. Can't say I like the fellow much, Gui! Personally I wouldn't give him barrack room if he begged me on his knees. Where he is about, there will not be mischief far away. Yet the Baron trusts him with his life!"

"But you don't trust the Baron." Gui ended for him quietly.

"No, Gui. Which is why I too would like to know exactly where The Lady, as they call her, has just come from? And it's why I have put Dickon Fletcher and two of his finest bowmen up in the gallery above us with strict orders to keep a sharp bead on both of them!"

"So, Richard, you missed her too?"

"Yes, Gui," he said, relaxing as he turned towards him. "I saw her going out and followed her, but just then all those fool villagers, mummers and tumblers came brawling in and in the crush I lost sight of her. By the time I got onto the top of the Forework staircase she was no-where to be seen. She could have gone to her room for that shawl; to one of the loos about the place; anywhere."

"No matter, Richard. It does my heart good to know that you are about your Lord's business tonight!" He said with a smile, and clapping him on his armoured shoulders he went forward to find Alicia, confident in the watching eyes he knew were guarding them, and equally determined not to drink any more wine that night. There was plenty of good spring water to be had, and he wanted a clear head in the morning. That was a good enough reason for anyone!

Then suddenly, with a great blast of sound, the musicians struck up and everyone took to the floor. Up down, turn around they all went, Lords and commoners together, holding hands and changing partners as they bobbed and weaved amongst each other. This was not the stately dance of the Court, this was the wild music of the country: of pipes and tambours, crumhorn, drums and flutes, of hot sweating faces wreathed in smiles and the broad laughter of common friends and families…and the noise ebbed and flowed around as everyone danced and stamped their feet, laughed, cuddled, drank, sang and kissed one another. This was English country hospitality at its very best, with Gui and Alicia in dazzling form as they swung, bounced and weaved through the reels, clothes a shimmering rainbow of colours, arms waving and legs jumping to the joyful swirl of the music.

Eventually they'd both had enough, and leaving the hot crush on the floor they returned, breathless, flushed and laughing, to their seats on the dais where the wine stewards standing there came forward to refresh their glasses. Gui resolutely stuck to water, despite the startled eyebrows of some of their friends nearby, while he and Alicia sat back, still holding hands, their bodies as close to one another as their chairs would allow, and watched their guests enjoying themselves.

As Gui looked around the Hall his eyes fell on the Baron, standing somewhat apart towards the further end of the Great Hall, and was amazed to find him pointedly staring at him. God's Bones but he could be a frightening looking fellow, with his deep, sunken eyes, hooked nose and straight gash of a mouth, more like a steel trap than flesh and blood…and suddenly he got a whiff of real danger, a sense of evil and of deep foreboding that seemed to press down on him, making the noise and general hubbub of the party going on around them fade almost to nothing as those great black orbs caught and held his gaze.

And as he looked he felt himself go cold and clammy.

He tried to speak, but his throat wouldn't work. Tried to move, but his limbs would not obey his urging, and all around was fading into shadows. An opaque mist that shrouded reality, through which he could see nothing…and then, in a wild moment of terror, he found himself swaying on the very edge of some terrible abyss, poised upon a pinnacle of unimaginable height surrounded by a cloying, terrible darkness so thick and palpable that he began to struggle even to breathe, as if his very life was being squeezed out of him. His heartbeat sounded like a mighty drum, but deep and muffled as on a funeral march, and black despair began to grip his soul as he felt and heard those very heartbeats slow, and in his ears a voice cried out in terror.

And all the time the Baron's eyes stared at him through the darkness, huge and pitiless, without hope, as he fought to seize Gui's mind and turn his will to match his own implacable imagining; and as he stared so did the world around him start to spin, the great whirling pit of drunken memory that led to sickness and oblivion, but here could lead him on to sacrifice his very soul instead. And in his torment he cried out again for help with all his heart.

Then, almost without realising it, a picture began to form in Gui's mind: Alicia and he together upon a verdant hillside entwined in love beneath a blazing azure sky; cloudless, free, with only the larks spiralling above them, the brightness of their song bringing with them the fragrance and tranquillity of such a Summer's day that all men dream of, and all the warmth and hope and love that such a day could bring...and with a sudden 'lurch' everything came back into focus.

Everything stopped spinning, the awful blackness vanished and his world returned to normal. The Hall, the dancers the music all as it should be, as in his mind he had been dragged from it; and he found himself leaning back in his chair, Alicia's hand clutched fiercely in his own and her lovely face bent over his in urgent consternation. Sweat like ice lay on his forehead and he was gasping for breath. With a fierce struggle Gui thrust himself upright and stared wildly round the Hall, but of the Baron there was no sight. With seeming ease, despite the watchers all around, he had simply disappeared.

Chapter 18...How Alicia showed her love for her Lord.

"Gui! *Gui!* What's the matter darling?" Alicia asked urgently, chaffing his hands between her own. "Why did you cry out? You look so pale and you're sweating. You're shivering, as if you have a fever." Then, briskly taking charge of him, she said: "Come, my Love. What you need is some fresh air and a little loving from your own true heart!"

And taking him by the hand she walked him from the High table and down the whole length of the Great Hall, making their excuses and weaving their way between the many merrymakers as they went, then away through the outer defences of the Forework, past the guards who were standing there, down the long flight of stone steps that led down to the Bailey, and out into the dusky darkness of a close summer's night. Once down the broad steps and away from the great flaring beacons in their iron baskets that stood on either side at the bottom, she turned towards him and held him close in her arms, pushing her hands up over his broad back and shoulders, pressing her soft body against him. 'Til lifting up her face to his at last, she kissed him warmly, nuzzling his neck softly with her lips as she did so.

"Shush, sweetheart, Shush," She said to him softly, as he tried to speak. "Don't worry, just let me hold you." And for a while they stood there in the close, airless darkness while she gentled him with soft endearments, for he was trembling like a stallion ridden to the very limits of its strength, rubbing his shoulders and his back with her hands, comforting him with her nearness and her touch.

"Oh, my darling! *darling!* What happened to you in there? I thought you were going to break my hand you gripped it so hard. And you cried out, and went so pale. You frightened me!" she ended, pressing her body tightly against him once more.

With an effort he steadied himself.

"I don't know, Alicia. It was terrible," he said, turning away from her to walk round a moment. "I suddenly found the Lord Baron looking at me. His eyes seemed to go right through me, to wash over me as if nothing else in the world mattered. Then it seemed I found myself balanced on a thin pinnacle of rock above an abyss so deep that there was no end to it, surrounded by darkness that seemed to choke me, with everything spinning around me as if I were drunk and about to fall down. I felt sick and dizzy and in despair," he went on, momentarily looking down. "It was awful. I heard a voice cry out. It must have been my own!"

He looked down into her eyes, now brimming with tears, her hand held up to her mouth in horror. "Oh, my Love," she gasped. "So that's why you cried out! How terrible. Come, Sweetheart, hold me tightly and feel my heart against yours. It's over now, and I'm here to love you as I always have been and always will do."

"*That's exactly it*, Alicia," he went on in a sudden rush of words. "Just as I was about to fall into those huge, black, staring eyes…into what seemed a terrifying, bottomless pit…you rescued me. Your *love* rescued me!"

"I rescued you?" She whispered, her eyes huge in her face. "Oh, my darling, how?"

"He was staring at me through this dark cloud," he told her urgently, his hands on her shoulders as he spoke. "All I could see were those eyes. His eyes. Black eyes, deep eyes, dark and terrible. Everything else had gone. I was teetering above this vast abyss, the whole world spinning round my head. I knew I was about to fall, and if I did I never would get back. I cried out for help, Alicia and..and suddenly, I felt you there beside me. I felt your nearness, my darling, and the warmth of your love, and I saw us lying together on some beautiful high place, wrapped in each other's arms, everything around us drenched in bright sunlight, fragrant, tranquil, lovely and all at once, with a sort of 'lurch', the world returned to normal. Everything stopped spinning, I was back in the Hall, and you were there beside me holding my hand. But when I looked again to find him…the Baron had disappeared and my mind was clear and free. It was the strangest thing. Honestly, Alicia, if it wasn't for you I think he would have won!"

"Oh, my darling. How horrible how dreadful!" She exclaimed softly, holding him close in her arms. "Well," she said firmly after a long pause as she squeezed him hard, straining her lithe body against him to assuage his fear and hurt. "I *was* there and he *didn't* win! You are my champion, dearest of men, and *no-one* is going to take you away from me! Not least a rotten old French Baron!" she added, stroking his broad back with her small hands and murmuring soft endearments to him, while she ruffled the back of his head and kissed his eyes and face.

Then, gently easing herself out of his arms, she took his hand and silently pulling him behind her, she moved out of all immediate sight round the corner of the Great Keep, right round behind one of the huge stone buttresses supporting it that reared up into the hot summer darkness, and turned him to face her. Bending forward, in a series of swift movements, she unlaced her silver corselet, and slipping her arms out of their puffed sleeves she slid her dress and her chemise off her shoulders so that her breasts were free to his touch. Taking his hands in hers, she held them against her, covering them with her own, making him cup her breasts, leaning back against the warm stones of the massive building as he did so.

"Feel my flesh, Gui. Feel my heart beating," she whispered. "It beats for you, my darling. No-one but you. I am a real woman. *Your* woman. Not a dream, nor a figment of your imagination," She gasped as he handled her, delivering delicious, unbearable torture that made her whole body quiver. "You hold the strings of my heart between your strong fingers, my dear sweet Lord, and I won't *ever* let you loose them, not as long as there is breath in my body!"

And, wrapping her left leg around his thighs, she clung to him fiercely, drawing him towards her so that she could kiss him deeply, thrusting her tongue into his mouth to savour him more strongly. She wanted him so badly, to feel him inside her, stretching her, filling her to the utmost, driving into her again and again as only he could do. Her whole body was on fire, aching for his hands to rove all over her, his mouth, his lips, his wicked questing tongue. But now was not the time. Love was what he needed, now...not sex. That would come another time. What he needed now was reassurance, gentleness and understanding.

Softly, with infinite grace and gentleness, she released him, panting: "Gui, look at me," she said, holding her breasts out to him, supporting them underneath with her hands. "I have loved you and wanted you almost as long as I can remember, since before you went to Yorkshire. You are kind and gentle, yet hot and demanding as well." She went on, her breasts gently swaying as she moved them with her hands.

"You know how to make me feel a Queen. Even when you have been busy you have always found time for me, to show me that you love me and, in this world of men, you have always shared your thoughts with me, and your hopes and fears. All I have to give you is my body and my heart and mind and those, my darling, I offer you in full measure. My soul belongs to God, but everything else is yours. You are my Lord, and I will always be your

Lady…and your willing slave!" And taking a step towards him she reached up with her hands for his face, and pulling him gently towards her she slowly kissed him with infinite softness. Butterfly kisses with the very breath of love fluttering in each tremulous wing beat. "You are my heart's desire," she breathed into his face. "I will *always* be here when you need me. I shall *never* leave you!"

With that he bent down and lifted her up in his arms, kissing her breasts as he did so, loving their soft firmness and the silky smoothness of their perfumed slopes, while Alicia threw back her head and gasped at every wild touch of his tongue and mouth as he held her against him.

"My Lady," he said at last his voice husky with desire. "Your Lord is certain that no man could be less deserving of his Lady's love than I. *Oh, heart of Christ, Alicia!*" He cried out in a sudden agony of spirit, "I love you so much it hurts. Dear God, but I shall miss you when I've gone." And putting her down he took her face between his big hands and kissed her long and deeply, feeling her hands go round his neck as he did so, as she kissed him back as fiercely and passionately as she was able, until at last they rested, her head pressed sideways against his shoulder, eyes closed, his arms enfolding her in a crushing embrace against his heart, unwilling ever to let her go.

"You are the sweetest, most beautiful, loving and *most* wonderful girl that any man could ever hope to find," he murmured into her hair. "Pray God, Sweetheart, that old Gerome will marry us right soon, for more of this I cannot take!"

"Nor me," she replied, ruffling his head. "I am not made of ice either. Now come on, my love, we must be getting back. Help me, please, darling," she added with a light chuckle, "or else I will go wood wild and spread myself for you against these very stones I want you so badly, and that would be disastrous for any moment now someone surely will discover us. We have been missing for ages, and they're bound to be looking for us."

They both laughed as picking up her silver bodice from the ground she handed it to Gui who draped it over his arm while, with a sigh, he first helped her pull her chemise and her dress back over her arms and shoulders, followed by her silver corselet, hiding the succulent fruits of her body once more beneath a covering of luxurious silk and damask cloth.

Then, checking that they were both presentable, they moved out of their shadowy bower, arms wrapped close around each other, bodies pressed

129

together, and walked slowly back towards the steps of the Forework that led up to the Great Hall. Pausing briefly at the bottom to look around them, the flames from the two great flambeaux that had been placed there suddenly flared and twisted as a vast hot breath of wind came gusting at them out of the West. Sending the flags still mounted on the Gatehouse wildly fluttering and tugging at their ropes, frisking Alicia's dress and Sir Gui's long scarlet silk over gown, as it swirled and rushed about them…before just as swiftly blowing itself out again, leaving the air around them as hot and breathless as it was before.

And in the distance a sullen growl of thunder rumbled from a sky now strangely yellow into which dark clouds of black and grey were swiftly spilling.

Beyond the castle's massive walls the whole forest seemed to sigh and shiver as the sudden wind rushed through it, sending boar and deer deeper amongst the trees and the wolves to their dens. And in the fields and pastures all around loose cattle were called into barn and byre for safety, or lay down together in the open fields, while sheep clustered beneath strong walls and hedges seeking shelter from a storm that all could feel was coming.

Chapter 19... *The storm clouds gather around Castle Malwood.*

From where Gui and Alicia were standing they could hear the men urgently calling the cattle in, and the sound of dogs rounding the sheep up from the castle orchards to pen them up within their barn. And big Nick, the massive castle blacksmith, was already beginning to dampen down his fires and close up the doors to his forge to prevent any great wind from blowing his charcoal into white hot incendiaries that would set the whole castle garth aflame. So their appearance was not a moment too soon because just as they turned to mount the stairs they met Sir Richard coming down towards them fully armed, two of his men close behind him, each with a torch brightly burning in his hand.

"Well met, Gui. I was just coming to find you," he said swiftly, wholly at odds from his usual lazy style, making Gui stop immediately. "Quite so, Gui," he said firmly. "Serious stuff, Dear Boy. I've just come down from the tops and the men up there are worried," he continued, gesturing to a point way above them. "Apparently there is a great storm building to the West, Gui. From up there you can see it clearly. Huge cloud platforms black as pitch, unlike anything I have seen before, and the wind is rising. Already the men are calling the loose cattle in where they can reach them, and Ned is bringing the sheep in from the orchards. I know it sounds silly, Gui, but the men are a little afraid! Even big Nick is closing down his forge as we speak. I think we are really in for it this time!"

Just then the rushing breeze that had died away a moment before, now gusted back again into fiercer life as suddenly as it had disappeared, while the sky around them had now turned to brass and ochre. And though the intense heat of the day had faded with the coming of evening, it had left the air close and thick, heavy, charged with an energy that made the very hairs on the arms stand up and the skin prickle; the atmosphere pressing down with a stifling sense of weight and breathlessness. Even as they stood there talking in the queer half light, the hot rush of wind that had sprung up again tugged at Alicia's silk dress as it teased and quested round her, making the distant flag ropes flack noisily against their wooden poles. For several minutes it blustered and wuthered around the castle until, just as suddenly, it died away again to nothing...and in the far distance the air trembled with the sound of thunder, a soft thud and rumble on the very edge of hearing.

Gui felt the wind fade away, heard the distant roll of sound and looking round him sighed. "Bad you think?"

"Mmmm. Could be, Gui. All the signs are there. Looks really nasty from up top. I can see why the men are scared. Don't want to lose one up there to a violent wind or lightning strike."

"Bit dramatic, Richard, for a summer storm? How feeble are these lads of ours? Are they babes and sucklings, or the fighting Lions of Malwood? Good grief, whom do I have in my forces that is afraid of a summer storm?"

"Me!" Alicia replied in a small voice. "I hate the thunder and lightning. They always make me quiver like one of Suchard's jellies."

The two men laughed. "We will make an exception for you, Dear My Lady," Sir Richard replied gallantly, sweeping her a bow. "Your bravery in taking on the burden of care for this great bear of a man is unquestioned. I salute you! And completely excuse you the fear of any summer storm, be it the fiercest in living memory or not...and that, Dear Boy, is just what the men are all afraid of!"

"Why do they think that?" Gui asked, as the two men behind his guard commander murmured a growled assent.

"Oh, the usual portents," Sir Richard went on, looking around him. "Birds doing strange things; crows flying early to their nests," he added, pointing at the flocks of crows making their doleful way back to their roosts. "Cattle lying down, sheep gathering in clusters; hens not laying and so on. The old men say it was such as this before the great storm of '65, when boats were blown inland and the three great oaks in Castle Field blew over."

"Old men will say anything for an extra stoup of ale!" Gui said, looking around him and up at the rapidly darkening sky. "Still, Richard," he said, testing the air with nose and finger. "There is certainly going to be a storm; it's hot and sticky enough and the colour of the sky is not good. It's been close all day, until just this last moment or two. So, yes, they're probably right and there will be some form of grand celestial upheaval. However, Richard, storm or not, I don't want to bring any man down from up there.

With de Brocas here they have a job to do come rain, shine or mighty storm," he added heavily with a grin. "But whether of such a fury as that in '65, I am in some doubt. However; my so Noble Guard Commander," he added clapping him on his mailed shoulders. "Make sure no man is on his own; that they have their waterproof capes and something warm to drink. And be sure that you check them out yourself. I would do too, but tonight I just can't. Where are our principal guests, the good Baron and his so lovely daughter?"

"Inside, enjoying themselves. He and Sir Yvo seem to be on bosom terms."

"They would be! How that man has cozened my father I do not know, but he seems blind to his danger. Well I am not. I have had a taste of the good Baron's metal tonight" he added looking down at Alicia, "and it was not a pleasant experience! So watch them, Richard. I trust them not an inch! Have you arranged the guards?"

"Yes, as you requested. Davy Oats and Johnny Foxglove outside Alicia's door, Lagrasse and Fabrizan in the guardroom below."

"The Cousins? The two who came to us through Mercardier?"

"Yes, Gui. They are two of the best."

"That will please Agnes," Alicia said, with a dig at Gui's ribs.

"Hmmm. Are you sure they are ready for this? We know very little about them."

"They have shown themselves to be quick thinking and thorough."

"What did Fitzurse say? I'd heard one of them had been seen talking with de Vere, the Baron's Guard Commander,"

"So have many of our men, Dear Boy," Sir Richard replied, reverting to his usual lazy drawl. "You told them to mingle with our *so* welcome visitors, and so they have mingled. Fitzurse sucked his teeth and scratched his head, but was happy enough, provided we put two of our own men right outside Alicia's door, which he has done. Good men, both. Brave and resourceful. You know what he's like. He doesn't trust anyone easily and foreigners not at all!"

"Not a bad trait just now, I'd say!" He replied, somewhat grimly, looking up at the thickening sky now turning charcoal. Then, turning back he said: "Oh well, Richard, if you are happy…and Agnes is happy," he went on smiling down at Alicia. "Then who am I to cavil at it? It's your decision."

"Well, in that case I am willing to give them a try."

"Excellent…but, er, just keep a weather eye on them, eh?"

"Oh…*very* droll, Dear Boy. Your natural wit is only exceeded by your extreme personal beauty!"

"Yours too, Richard!" Gui replied with a laugh, adding: "Oh, and make sure all those on guard elsewhere in the castle also have something hot to drink before they go on duty, and make sure that they are changed regularly. I want them alert, not drowsy. Who is the Sergeant on duty tonight?"

"John Fitzurse…our redoubtable Master-at-Arms, as your father requested earlier."

"Of course he did," Gui replied swiftly. "Now he *is* the very best! I would stake my life on him. Get *him* to check up on those two Aquitainers…and on those poor frightened bunnies up there," he added pointing to the Keep's great fighting tops. "And mind, Richard, if there *is* a problem I am to be called immediately. You know where to find me. No," he replied with a smile at his raised left brow and unasked question, "I will be in my *own* quarters this night. The Lady Rochine shares with Alicia, more's the pity! Good hunting, my friend." And with a bang on his armoured chest he sent him on his way before turning to put his arm back round Alicia's shoulders.

"There will be a storm tonight, my darling," he went on pointing to the now rapidly blackening sky, still underpinned with grey and white. "I can feel it building. Up there, where the great racks of clouds are growing higher and higher, the storm giants are preparing to hurl their thunderbolts and lightning rods down upon us! I know you hate these storms, Sweetheart, and I know I won't be near you tonight. But it is only a storm, Honeyone, and this is the strongest castle in a hundred miles and has weathered any number of terrible storms…including the Great Storm of '65! So stop worrying. You will be fine."

"I know that, really," she sighed. "But it would be so much more fun if you were there to share it with me. I am told," she went on smiling wickedly, "that the best way to conceive a son is to make love in a thunderstorm..."

"Yes," he interrupted laughing. "And according to Father Gerome, the Greeks swore by a West wind up their mares' tails to be certain of a good foal in the spring as well! A good try," he added kissing her swiftly. "You're a cheeky puss, my darling. But at least you will have Rochine with you, and for all that I do not trust her she must be better company for you than a feather pillow." And he laughed down at her again, squeezing her shoulders as he did so.

"Now come on, we'd best be getting back inside," he went on sweeping her up the steps beside him as he spoke. "We have been out here for ages, father will be wondering what on earth has happened to us, and with this lot brewing up like the Devil's own cauldron," he continued as they walked up the Forework stairs, "those of our guests who are not staying may well want to get away before it breaks. And those who are staying had better start to batten down the hatches, for I have the feeling that Richard is right, and the heavens may really fall in on us tonight after all!"

Just then, as they reached the entrance to the Keep, right at the top of the Forework, the sky suddenly flashed and flickered for the first time, making Alicia shiver, and minutes later the first real stamp of giants' feet thudded in the distance and reverberated across the countryside. Swinging Alicia round Gui paused again beneath the jagged teeth of the portcullis, raised high above their heads, to look out across the darkening countryside and towards distant Southampton Water. "Some miles away yet, but it is surely coming our way. Thank God we are not out on the deep tonight, because I am certain there'll not be much that could live in the kind of tempest that may strike us.

Then, with a sharp glance at the two guards who were standing there and a brief salute, he and Alicia turned and walked back across the tough drawbridge that separated the Great Keep from the Forework, and passing under the raised portcullis they disappeared from sight.

Even as they did so another distant growl of thunder rumbled across the heavens like huge bowls across a wooden ceiling, as the wind veered into the West and began to rise, pushing the clouds ahead of it in towering black mountains and coming now in violent squalls that flogged at the castle, turning the broad surface of the lake into a seething mass of white horses and heaving lilies, and sending the guards high up on the turret tops and above the gatehouse scurrying urgently for shelter

This was now no cat's-paw breeze, but truly as the borel folk feared, the harbinger of a great storm. Each distant crash of thunder louder than the last, as the sky slowly turned a vile purple-ochre edged with deep black, the line of monstrous black clouds boiling up from the horizon, shot through with zizzling sheets of lightning, seemed like towering mountains a-float upon a sulphurous sea.

Shortly after that the party broke up, their many guests streaming away on horses already half maddened by the growing darkness, while those staying for the night made their way to their own apartments or gathered in hushed groups in the centre of the Hall in the Great Keep, comforted by each other and by the massive strength of the huge building that enclosed them. Before long however Sir Yvo's servants brought up more wine and ale, along with a variety of sweetmeats, and with that the musicians struck up and the party suddenly got going again to a background of distant violent bangs and flashes.

Chapter 20...The Baron shocks Sir Gui with an unexpected gift!

While Alicia took Rochine off with her to her tower bedroom, Gui conducted his father's principal guest to his own suite of rooms in the New Hall, where his clothes for the night, and sundry other belongings had been carefully laid out for him by the castle servants. There he made sure the Baron de Brocas had all he needed before turning to leave as swiftly as possible, with the Lord Roger seated on a chair as one of his own men began to pull off his boots.

After what had happened to him earlier in the evening, Gui had no wish to linger in the Baron's company for any length of time beyond what was absolutely necessary. Yet just as he reached the door, de Brocas called him back signalling his servitor to go to another room.

"Sir Gui," he rumbled deeply, after the man had gone, stretching his toes out before him in their party hose. "You are a remarkable young man. Come take a glass with me of your father's excellent Burgundy. I have seldom tasted better." And reaching for a tall silver-gilt decanter that stood on a polished wooden chest beneath one of the windows, he poured two glasses of the deep red wine so beloved of Gui's father.

There was no way now, without giving the very gravest offence, that Gui could refuse the older man's offer, certainly not in his own home. So he took the proffered glass with a slight incline of his head and a brief word of thanks, then stood quietly watching the baron over the rim of the fine Venetian glass as the man drank with obvious enjoyment, before delicately sipping from his own.

What was this extraordinary man thinking? What had he truly come for...all the way from Narbonne? And what was his father hiding from him? Why, all through the evening, had Sir Yvo constantly asked the guard if any, unheralded, visitor had arrived? He had been jumpy all night. And his mother had been little better! But every time he had tried to raise the issue he had been firmly told: 'It's not your concern'; and that: 'Nothing is wrong, my son!' In the end he had given up and gone out to check for himself. But all for nothing!

Then there had been that strange mental encounter with the Baron...harrowing, frightening, and from which Alicia love, like a giant sunburst, had rescued him, and whom he was damned if he was going to call 'Roger'! 'My Lord', would do fine...and the bastard could like it or lump it!

He sighed. The sooner they were gone from Malwood the better. And from what Alicia had said, the daughter was little better than her dear Papa, the so good and 'friendly' Baron! Tried to make love to her? The woman was little better than a common trollop. He smiled. No...'common' was not fair! 'Uncommon', more likely!

De Brocas watched him guardedly before speaking. How had he managed to resist him? He was both puzzled and annoyed. He *had* him. He could feel him teetering on the edge of that abyss, just ready to fall over into his grasp...spinning like a top...and then somehow he'd just slipped away! Vanished from his cognizance, and he'd been left...with nothing! Bird-song and blue sky. Rubbish! He looked at Gui with greater speculation. Perhaps it was the girl...perhaps she had more power in her than he had realised? Or was it her love for this young man that had saved him? He would have to be more careful about how he approached this 'boy's' mind again. One more such failure, and he never would break through! It had happened before.

"You are an interesting young man, Sir Gui," he said at last. "If you can keep that dark head of yours on those brawny shoulders, you should go far. There are not many who can resist me," he said looking at him from his deeply hooded eyes, lifting his glass as he did so. "I salute you!" And he drank deeply, savouring every drop, until his glass was empty.

Gui watched him. You bloody bastard! How dare you taunt me! Well, I think I have your measure now, you *sod*! Love conquers all, they say and tonight Alicia and I proved it. You will *not* catch me unawares again!

"May I re-fill your glass, My Lord Baron," he asked him then, quietly, completely ignoring his earlier comments. "I must away to my bed, for we have a full programme for your entertainment tomorrow, and I do not want a thick head!"

"Thank you...Sir Gui," the Baron responded, pausing over his name, with a quirk of his lips. "You prefer formality?"

"I am no dissembler, My Lord Baron," Gui replied gravely. "Nor do I intend to dishonour my house in any way. But, formality has its place and I think we would both feel more comfortable if we stick to what we know, rather than drift into an arrangement that neither of us really means."

The Baron laughed.

"Maybe you have the right of it, Sir Gui. And certainly you are no dissembler, and for that I thank you. At least we both know exactly where we stand. No...wait, I pray you," de Brocas said swiftly, as Gui made a further move to leave the room. "I have something for you." And he turned towards a small open chest that stood on a side table nearby, not far from a beautiful polished rosewood box with ornate gold hinges on either side, that he caressed briefly with his hands as he passed. "I promised you a betrothal gift this afternoon, but so far have not had the chance to give it to you."

Gui, who had watched his every movement round the room, stepped back and started to demur: "My Lord Baron, I had not expected such generosity. I am not sure..."

"...That you should accept a gift from such an enemy to your family as you believe me to be?" the Baron finished for him. "Come, come Sir Gui. Do not be so churlish. This gift is heartfelt, I assure you, and your father and I have now settled all our differences. I do not hold him responsible for my father's death. Nor Sir Henry. As I said earlier, things happen in the heat of war that are beyond our control. Either your father, or Alicia's, could have been slain by Sir Thibault that day," he continued, his face giving nothing of the hatred and fury that was consuming him. His true feelings masked - rigidly controlled. He had a role to play and a task to accomplish first before he could allow his true depth of loathing for all that this young man represented to break free at last.

"I know that you do not like me, but this is something that even you would be proud to own. Furthermore," he went on, quietly, lifting something from the small chest as he spoke, "I rather think this belongs to your family anyway?" And so saying he placed a small, dark blue velvet bag into Gui's hands, tied close with a fine cord of twisted gold and silver thread, before stepping back towards the window, his wine glass in his hand, to watch the effects of his gift on the tall young man before him.

Holding his breath somewhat Gui untied the thread and then, very gently, tipped the contents out onto the palm of his hand.

Swiftly The next moment he nearly cried out in shock, involuntarily closing his hand as he did so to prevent himself from letting the contents of the bag fall onto the floor. Clenching his fist he turned away from the Baron to face the window, unable at first to take in what it was he held there. Then, very gingerly, he opened his hand again and looked at what the Baron had placed in his hand, almost afraid it might actually have vanished! But it was still there! An enormous emerald set in a heavy ring of beautifully wrought gold. It was the most magnificent thing he had ever seen in his life and he stood amazed, mouth open, too stunned at first even to speak as it just lay, fatly, in the open palm of his hand. The faceted surface of the huge stone winking and flashing at him in the candle light, green fire running round inside its mystic depths 'til it leapt out at him with dazzling brightness.

Dear God in Heaven! Sweet wine of Christ! It was the Malwood Emerald!

Gifted to Alicia's Grandmother, Phillipa De Brocas, for her lifetime on her wedding day by Gui's own Grandfather, Sir Alun de Malwood, it had mysteriously disappeared the very day she had died and had never been seen since. There had been a terrible, *terrible* row - a row to end all rows that had revealed nothing. The great stone in its beautiful golden setting, the most precious heirloom of the Malwood family, had quite simply vanished into thin air.

Now...two lifetimes later...it had re-appeared as if out of nowhere and he looked at it again. It was very old, Roman some people said, and had been found by old Gui de Valance, before he had changed his name, when the first Castle Malwood was being built, and had been in the family ever since. Grandmother Phillipa had been dead these past thirty years...yet here it was, in his hand. He simply couldn't believe it!

He turned swiftly towards the Baron and looked at him, not knowing where to begin, or even whether he wished to begin anything anyway. There was silence between them.

"How?" he exclaimed at last, taking a pace towards where the Baron was standing. "*How?*" he repeated more strongly, holding the ring up to him. "This disappeared from my family thirty years ago when Grandmother Phillipa died. Off her very finger before she was wrapped and shrouded. How did you

140

find it, My Lord Baron? I know the family searched high and low for this...*yet you found it!* How?" he questioned more softly.

"Be careful, young man," Lord Roger growled darkly. "How I came by this is not your affair. My Great Aunt, the Lady Phillipa, was a de Brocas long before she became a Burley. We are not considered an unimportant family in France, you know," he added silkily. "You would do well to remember that before you come demanding information of me to which you have no right! I thought you would be pleased to have so ancient a family heirloom returned to you?"

Gui ground his teeth. The man was impossible, and he was right. How he had come by it really was none of his affair. And if he did not care to tell him, he could hardly batter it out of him, least of all while he was a guest in his own home.

"I crave pardon, Lord Baron." He said, bowing. "But I *do* have a right to know. *Every* right, if only because this jewel," he went on, holding it out on the palm of his hand, "was in the possession of my family generations before it was gifted to your great aunt on the occasion of her marriage, and for her lifetime only. However that is a matter for my father to discuss with you, Baron, not me. It was just that I was so surprised to discover something that everyone believed to have been lost for eternity. Of course I am thrilled to receive so wonderful a gift," he continued, bowing to the Baron's generosity. "And I thank you greatly. The whole family will be amazed and delighted. I hope, later perhaps, that you will feel able to give us some idea of how so rare a jewel was re-discovered. Alicia, especially will be astounded. She has long admired her Grandmother."

And bowing once more before his saturnine guest, he turned and left immediately, striding off to his own rooms, his head in a complete whirl of confused thought and wild speculation, while the Baron, whom he had left standing by the window watching the storm gathering its forces overhead, raised his glass to the burgeoning heavens and threw back his head and laughed.

Chapter 21... The Lady fails to twist The White Rose to her desires.

Upstairs in her tower room, with windows and shutters firmly closed against the storm, Alicia was lying back in her bed propped up against her pillows, in a long night-gown of finest Egyptian cotton, beautifully embroidered with silver, red and gold roses that Agnes had laid out for her, watching Rochine letting down her thick, glowing black plaits that had been coiled on the sides of her head all evening.

She was feeling delightfully light headed, the wine and the rushing excitement of the evening reacting with one another to make her feel buoyant and frothy.

Yet she was uncertain also, aware that something strange had happened between them earlier in the afternoon without really understanding what. Something she had heard about through her classical studies with Father Gerome, and which she had talked and laughed over with Gui that very evening. But though she had talked with her friends and listened to the men's secret conversations, clearly she had never experienced such things herself. Nor was she at all certain that she wished to do so either. She did not feel that the delights of Sapphic love were quite for her. What might be fine for ancient Greeks nearly two thousand years ago years ago was not necessarily fine for good country girls at home in England in 1190! Though they were clearly interesting, as she had discovered!

And then there had been the equally strange experience that Gui had had with the Baron during the evening celebrations. Alicia understood none of it. Just horrified for her splendid lover and humbled that it should have been her love that had saved Gui from the Baron's sudden apparent wickedness. Though she too was not comfortable with the Baron's dark eyes that seemed to follow her everywhere with an intensity that almost made her skin rise up in goose bumps, she was not afraid of him, even though perhaps she should be!

She shivered, making her rub her arms briefly. Clearly Gui was not happy about the man being here and was not keen on him, or his daughter, staying any longer than was necessary...nor was she at all certain that she wanted them to either. Yet she was intrigued by her French cousin. Rochine was different from any of her other friends. She was experienced, more mature, and had travelled with her father beyond the Circle Sea. Whereas she, Alicia de Burley, had only ever been as a far as London, and that only once: let alone to France! She was bold also, and outspoken for a woman of their time. Yet there was a hint of danger in The Lady, as she was known amongst her entourage. It surrounded her like an aura, that subtly excited Alicia and made her heart beat faster.

Outside the wind was battering at the shutters, which rattled against the horn windows every time the wind struck them, the draught from imperfect seals making the candles that stood on chest and table flicker and gutter wildly. Those that were in the two great iron stands, like crowns, on either side of her bed also twisted and waved, casting weird leaping shadows on the plastered walls and ceiling of her room, while the thunder growled and stamped and threatened, getting closer all the time as the lightning sparked and flickered more often, each flash making Alicia wince.

Reaching for one of the silver wine goblets that a servant had brought up earlier in the day she savoured the dark, red wine, like blood, that filled it and drank deeply. She hated the thunder, no less than the lightning that preceded it, and she reached smoothly over to re-fill it from the chased silver wine-pitcher that stood on a fine wooden table beside her bed. Then she lay back again against her pillows to sip at its warm contents, the wine running through her like fire, as over her goblet's silver rim, she watched Rochine slowly unlacing the fine corselet that covered the top half of her dress, while the lighting flashed behind her and the thunder banged and grumbled.

Standing sideways on, Rochine worked her long fingers down her body, eyelet by eyelet, aware of her cousin's eyes glinting at her in the candle light, 'til the cloth of gold corselet was free at last. Leaning forward she gently loosed it from her dress and dropped it to the floor. And all the time Alicia watched her silently, aware only of the rapid beating of her own heart as Rochine turned to face her, a deep smile on her face, and slowly pulled her rich, deep red silken bliaut off her shoulders. So different from the leather she had worn when she had arrived, she gently freed it from her arms and let it fall to the polished wood floor, so that it lay like a still pool of blood around her pretty feet.

Alicia ran her eyes down Rochine's naked body, taking in the creamy texture of her skin, the firm boldness of her heavy breasts, her areolas dark and swollen, crowned with taut nipples like ripe blackberries, the rich swell of her

143

hips and the suppleness of her thighs…and gasped. It was a small involuntary sound, but it made the other girl smile.

She was shaved!

There wasn't a hair on her body, nothing under her arms; and her loins were completely smooth! The soft folds of flesh that nestled there below her mons like plump fruit ready for the picking. She was startled rather than shocked, the sight of Rochine's nakedness making her even more aware of the dark-haired girl's beauty and the differences between them. And Rochine smiled at her, her almond shaped green eyes shining in the soft candlelight, as she turned towards the chest that lay against the far wall that Alicia had given her to use, her breasts bouncing gently as she moved, her firm, rounded buttocks glowing in the warmth of the candles that burned and flickered in their holders.

Slowly she bent forward, the luscious fruits of her body swinging freely as she picked up one of the enamelled flasks that lay there, and filling her hands with thick aromatic oil she rubbed them gently over her breasts and naked loins, deliberately turning so that Alicia could watch her every lubricious movement. Then, stooping briefly to extinguish the light that flared beside her, she turned back towards where Alicia was lying.

"These too, my pet?" She asked softly, gesturing to the crowns of candles on either side of the bed.

"No," Alicia breathed her reply. "No, Rochine, not yet," she said, putting her goblet down and whisking the sheet up over her chest. "The storm frightens me and I want to talk with you. Discovering a French cousin one knows so little about, especially one with a *wicked* reputation is so exciting," she said with a smile. "And we have had no real chance to talk since this afternoon. But had you not better put on a nightgown?" she asked, eyebrows raised, as Rochine moved towards her. "I am sure Agnes put one out for you of the most beautiful sendal. Where did it come from?"

"From Cathay!" Rochine answered her casually. "I thought everyone knew *that*. The silk comes first to Constantinople then to Venice, and I have a friendly Venetian trader who always brings me the best he has. Anyway, why a nightgown, Alicia?" she asked, gracefully sitting down on the edge of her bed, "does my body embarrass you?"

"No, of *course* not," Alicia replied swiftly...feeling that in actual fact it did very much, well 'awkward' perhaps, rather than embarrassed...while drawing her knees up and hugging them over her finely embroidered sheets and quilted counterpane. "But in England it is expected that we should cover ourselves when others are about. Except our close family, I suppose," she said musingly. "Agnes would be *terribly* shocked, and as for the Lady Margaret," she added, mischievously, "she would be *horrified* if she thought I was parading myself naked in front of strangers - let alone naked and..and shaved," she almost whispered, hesitatingly.

"Not shaved, Sweetheart," Rochine said softly, with a wicked smile. "Plucked!"

"*Plucked?*" Alicia exclaimed, horrified

"Yes, my love. Plucked, with bronze tweezers, and *mighty* horrid it is too. Takes ages and is excruciating. But *so* much more lasting than simply being shaved. Aren't you also?"

"*No!* Simply clipped," she said appalled, surreptitiously moving her hand to ruffle the short, wiry fur that covered her loins. "But why..why..*everything?*" she asked, shocked. "In truth, Cousin, I have never *heard* of such a thing!"

"Because where I live, Alicia, it is so hot most of the year that being wholly smooth is both much nicer..and cleaner. It is the way the Arabs keep their women...and they are seldom ill. My father insists on it with *all* the girls and women who work in the castle amongst the many guests and visitors we have...including me. And we bathe every day as well! You cannot work for the Lord of Narbonne in Castle Grise unless you are properly cleansed."

"But *every day?*" Alicia almost cried out, shocked. "From where do you get so much hot water? Ours has to be carried up from the kitchens, and it is a *frightful* business, so it doesn't happen often I assure you, I wish it did as I love to be clean. But today was special, so everyone made a big effort. *But washing every day?* Isn't that supposed to be awfully bad for you?"

Rochine laughed, then, coming close up beside her cousin with her deep chuckle she said: "No, Silly! It is *good* for you, and easy for me as we have a wonderful sunken Roman pool at Château Grise that is always filled with hot water from underground. No dreadful clumping baths! It's *lovely*, Alicia. And look at me. No spots or bumps or boils. Feel my skin," she went on, taking Alicia's hand and sliding it over her thighs as she spoke. "See, it is smooth as silk, and that is not just from the oil I use either. And my breasts," she went on, bending forward and moving Alicia's hand up and over their warm slopes, sighing softly with pleasure as her hand brushed across their hard crests. "And between here too," she added, dropping her voice and sliding her thighs open as she spoke.

Alicia was stunned.

Not just by the bold way her cousin was revealing herself, but by her own reactions, which were not as shocked as perhaps they should have been, not least because she found herself wondering not just whether Gui would like her to be smooth and soft as well...but whether *she* would? She shook her head then. Too much, too soon, and with a light laugh she slipped her hand away before Rochine could place it there.

"Rochine," she said then, startled, as her cousin moved languorously away from the bed. "Truly your skin *is* soft and you *are* very lovely. But isn't this all a bit..." she stammered slightly, "...a bit *bold* before a stranger?"

"But I am not a stranger, Alicia," Rochine said softly, her liquid eyes sparkling in the candlelight. "You are my little English Cousin. I am *family* now, remember?"

"Well, Honeyone" her cousin replied hastily, "of course you aren't. A..a stranger I mean, because as you say you are my Cousin. But I don't truly know you yet, so you are also rather strange. Oh, Rochine," she said laughing, covered in confusion. "You know what I mean. It is just that I am not used to so bold an attitude," she went on, resting her chin on her hands. "You almost make me blush!"

"Because I am not afraid of my beauty or because I am standing here beside you without any clothes on?"

"Both, I suppose," Alicia replied, laughing again. "You are what Lady Margaret would call 'brazen', and poor Father Gerome 'lewd'. And what they would think about you being..being..." she hesitated, "smooth all over, I hate to think. Brazen would not be in it," she ended with a chuckle of her own. "More like harlot!"

"And what about you, little Cousin?" Rochine asked her, smiling, standing tall in the soft candlelight, running her hands gently over her oiled and scented body. "Do you think I am brazen and lewd? Like a harlot?"

Privately Alicia thought she looked stunning. She also made her feel extremely provincial, almost innocent. Yet 'Sweet Innocent' she was *not*. She and Gui had been lovers for nearly two years. But were they innocent lovers? Alicia felt that Rochine considered her untutored...even ignorant. That she had spent her whole life so far in an agricultural backwater while she, Rochine, 'The Lady', had been to strange and unusual places with her father that Alicia could only dream about...and bathed in a Roman Pool every day!

"I think that you love to shock and, yes, I am a little shocked. Perhaps startled would be a better word. And I envy you your experience, while lacking the courage to experiment for myself." She answered her, watching the way Rochine's body moved, her soft creamy skin gleaming softly, her full breasts with their dark swollen berry tips moving deliciously as she glided round the room almost dancing, the plump smoothness of her loins. "Exotic is what you are, Rochine. Very. But lewd or brazen? *No!* And as for harlot? I have never met one, except for the girls who hang around the barracks sometimes and they, my so beautiful Cousin," she said with her rich chuckle, "are nothing like you on earth!"

Rochine stopped, and turning towards Alicia she held out her hand to the girl: "Then join me," she said huskily, her eyes shining. "Take off that ridiculous nightgown and dance with me to the music of the storm, she added her figure suddenly lit up with a violent flashes of lightning followed by a mighty *bang!* As the storm stamped its way ever closer. Each violent flash of light seeming somehow to flash-freeze her every movement, casting stark black shadows across the room and flaring her alabaster skin into startling relief. "Come, Alicia," She beckoned again, holding out both hands. "Let me enjoy looking at you as much as you have enjoyed looking at me. You have enjoyed looking at me, haven't you"

Alicia swallowed hard, heart jumping in her throat, her body panting. She was *so* tempted. Tempted to tear off the fine cotton that covered her, if only to show her cousin that this country girl from England was every bit as beautiful and sophisticated as her clever French Cousin; her thighs as smooth, her breasts as beautiful, their crests as taut and swollen; her skin as soft and creamy-white. Then she shivered and shook her head, her blonde hair flowing over her white shoulders in a shimmering cascade as it caught the candle light.

"Yes, Rochine!" she said, looking her in the face with her shining, sunburst smile. "I would be lying if I said that I don't enjoy looking at you, for you are very beautiful. But, no!" she said firmly and clearly into her cousin's mocking eyes, "I will not join you. That is not my way, Rochine," she added shrugging her shoulders. "I would only make myself look foolish in your eyes, as well as mine," she added definitively. "And in the morning I would feel ashamed. I wouldn't know what to say to you, and Gui would think I had gone moon-mad."

"You would tell him?" Rochine asked incredulously, coming to plump herself suddenly down on the end of the bed.

"Of course," Alicia said, startled, looking at her cousin, chin on hands. "I tell Gui *everything*. He is my best friend as well as my lover. He shares everything with me also. We have *always* done so since we were children, and will expect to do so after we are married. Is it not so with you?"

"*No!*" Rochine exclaimed, privately horrified at the thought. "Nor would my father *dream* of sharing everything with me either. We must all have *some* secrets. That is what makes any relationship so exciting, the finding out of hidden things!"

Alicia sighed: "Well, I think that the truth *is* important, *and* being honest with one another even more so. That is almost more important than being truthful. For you can be truthful without necessarily being honest with a person in every way. But honesty makes being truthful an essential!"

"What a little Philosopher you are my love," Rochine said smiling, reaching out to stroke Alicia's cheek with her long fingers, adding with a sigh: "Well, I suppose then that I had better find my sendal nightgown that your Agnes put out for me, if I am to share my English Cousin's bed tonight. I feel that I have rather shocked you, Alicia," she continued with a laugh, as she stood up and turned away to where Agnes had laid it out for her. "So, for tonight at least, my love, I will obey the proprieties of life. See," she added a moment later, slipping the most exquisite green silk nightdress over her head, with a huge scarlet dragon embroidered all over it. "How does that suit you now?"

Alicia thought it was breathtaking. Not least because it threw Rochine's whole body into such sharp, exotic relief. Alicia smiled. The girl might just as well *be* naked the material was so fine and softly clinging. In fact she was if anything even more alluring with her nightdress on than she had been with it off!

"Well, budge up, Sweetheart," Rochine said, sliding in beside her. "Then, perhaps you could at least give me a cuddle. If that would not be treading too much on your sensibilities," she added mischievously. "I too am far from home and lonely, my love, and this storm is beginning to wind itself up," she said, giving an involuntary shiver after a particularly violent flash and much closer, vicious *Bang!*. "I hope your room doesn't leak, Alicia. If there is one thing I *hate,* it is getting out in the middle of a stinking wet night and paddling about in the rain inside my own room!"

"Oh, come on then, silly!" Alicia exclaimed, chuckling, opening her arms. "I promise you, despite the occasional draft, my chamber does not leak, and of *course* I will give you a cuddle. Truth to tell I could do with one myself, for I do not like thunderstorms one little bit, and there is nothing better when a big storm is on than to snuggle down with someone's arms around you and feel all warm and safe from everything!"

Holding Rochine in her arms was a totally new experience indeed, making Alicia feel strangely motherly as she looked down at her cousin's head resting on her breast, her shining hair, black as night spread over her shoulder, the warmth and fullness of Rochine's own body pressed so firmly against her own.

What an extraordinary girl!

Bold and forthright one moment, breathing hotly over her and swamping her with her perfume and her ideas…the next cuddled into her like a little child. She felt Rochine's head move more firmly against her and the faintest touch of a kiss and instinctively she bent her head and kissed her cousin's forehead softly in return, loving the warm, clean, perfumed scent of her, smiling as she felt Rochine's hand curl round her breast. Like a baby. And loving the weight and security of her cousin in her arms, she closed her eyes and despite the storm, worn out with all the excitement of the day, she went to sleep.

Rochine lay there in the flickering, noisy darkness dismayed and angry.

149

This afternoon, she had thought that seducing the girl would be easy. Now, she was not so sure. Alicia should have been sufficiently tempted this evening in their room to 'play', but she had resisted. Perhaps she should have used her powder after all? Even more so since her father had also been balked earlier by Gui, for he had told her all about it, suspecting that the love the girl had for her large fiancé had been the key to his escape! Well...he might just be right! She had expected Alicia to dance with her at least, and from there to touching, kissing and making love would have been easy. But she had simply said, '*No!*' And that had never happened to her before, and she growled softly in her throat. Well, we shall see, my fair Lady Alicia...we shall see! *This struggle is not over yet!*

Chapter 22... The Devil's Cauldron bursts over Castle Malwood.

As the storm relentlessly approached the castle on huge giant's feet, the hills and fields an iron causeway, each massive pace more thunderous than the one before, so it rose to its height.

Harried by great winds that howled out of the West, and lit by great jagged streaks of lightning that lanced through the sky in antlers of searing white fire, the storm fell upon Castle Malwood with unrestrained fury. And while the thunder rolled and boomed around the surrounding hills, and hammered the castle with vast, deafening bursts of sound, so the wind roared and gusted around the weathered stone in shrieks of rage, hurling roof tiles, thatch and whole sides of simple buildings away into the seething night as if they were paper, as it fought to tear the whole fortress from the very ground itself.

In the Forest the trees creaked and groaned in the tumultuous wind, tossed wildly by the fury of the tempest, their branches bent, whipped and stripped of their leaves to be sent whirling into the air like giant handfuls of confetti. Whole trees ripped out of the ground and laid flat in rows, or cast wildly across the forest floor. Huge branches of great oaks and chestnuts smashed off their trunks, while in the fields lone trees were struck by lightning which in an instant turned their sap to super-heated steam, blasting them apart, and sheep and cattle were flung about like farmyard toys.

Suddenly, through the vast roiling darkness, a huge bolt of lightning seared through the sky with the *sizzzling* sound of ripping canvas, and... ***Flash–BANG!...*** struck the New Hall with demonic, blazing fury. Lightning strike and thunder both together like the very Crack-of-Doom! A monstrous, crashing detonation that stunned the senses, and filled the air with sharp sulphurous fumes, shaking the whole building to its very foundations, making it rock and shudder as if it were at sea.

And with it the shutters of Sir Yvo's bed-chamber were burst asunder, shattered glass and timber from the monstrous explosion flying in all directions, while the frames and broken shutters burst into flames as they were hurled, like scarlet blossoms, across the room setting fire to everything they touched; and with a great shout, Sir Yvo came instantly awake, and seizing hold of his wife's arm he shook her furiously before leaping out of bed

"Get up Margaret! *Get up!* The whole room is on fire. The castle's been struck and we must get out! Quick, *quick*, my darling!" And as she struggled to take in what was happening, so he thrust his feet into a pair of leather slippers, and seizing a rug off the floor began fiercely to beat down the flames that had been scattered round them.

Swiftly dragging on an over-gown of finest sendal, the Lady Margaret rushed across the room to open the door. But, try as she might, she could not get it to move. The latch worked, but the stout oak of which the door was made would not give an inch, and she shouted out to the two guards whom Sir Richard had placed outside their door: "Help! *Help!* Wilson, Jackson! Open this door for us. It is jammed, and our room is on fire!" But there was no response, no answering shout, no friendly crash against the door to burst it open. No aid at all.

"*Yvo!*" She cried out sharply in distress. "*The door won't open!* And there is no answer from Wilson or Jackson!" And banging on it in growing desperation she shouted for their help again, as her husband continued to beat at the flames until they were mostly hammered out. Each extinguished patch filling the room with foul smoke and making them both cough and splutter.

"Sweetheart," he called out to her. "Keep any flames with this!" He shouted, pushing the singed rug he was holding into her hands. "And do your best to keep them away from those wall hangings. I will give those men a shout myself! The door is thick and the storm loud. They may not have heard you," and he gave his men a mighty shout of his own while striking the door a terrific buffet, shaking it as a terrier would a rat!

"Nigel, David! To me lads, *to me!*" he roared out in his largest voice. "Come and give this door a battering. Lady Margaret and I are stuck in here, the door has jammed and our room is on fire!" And he bellowed again: "Help*!* *Help!*" Giving the whole door and its oaken frame a terrific shaking as he strove to wrench it open. Again he shook the door, and again...even hurling his own considerable weight against it, but its oak frame, recessed as it was into the stone of which the room was built, resisted his every effort.

Resting for a moment, leaning against the stubborn wood and panting from his efforts, he became aware of a thick, viscous substance slicked with oil that was creeping from under the door in an ever increasing dark flood that stuck to his slippers, and ran over his feet and ankles. Every step caused him to slip and slide in its foul, slimy mucous flood, and the stench of it was strong and sharp. Suddenly, with a wild cry, he leaped back gasping, his eyes opening wide in shock.

"*Yvo! What is it?*" His wife called out desperately, running to his side, the flames around them forgotten in her fear and haste.

"*Sweet Wine of Christ!*" Her husband hissed at her, his fingers stabbing at the ever growing pool of black-gold fluid that was still oozing out from under the door. "It's what we call 'Arab' Fire, Margaret! Like *Greek Fire* though not so deadly. But in here it is the Devil's own brew. Dear God, how has it got here?…" And leaping forward and banging ferociously against the thick unyielding wood, he shouted out fiercely above the storm: "Who's out there? Who's doing this? *Open the door, I say!* It is the Lord of Malwood himself here, and his Lady. The room's been struck, and is on fire behind us. If that filthy stuff ignites we will both be roasted!"

Then from beyond the sealed door, came a crowing burst of harsh laughter and a sudden rush of more oily liquid, its sulphurous fumes making them both cough and splutter violently. And at that voice, Sir Yvo gasped in recognition: "*It is de Brocas!*"

"Baron Roger?" His wife squeaked, her eyes opening wide in horror.

"*Yes!*" he snarled at her in frustration. "Baron Roger! This door is not stuck, Margaret. He has somehow got the spare key and locked it! Look, see? Ours is on the floor."

"*Then use it Yvo!*" she screamed at him, her hands fluttering in distress, even as her husband swooped to pick it up, fumbling with it furiously as he struggled to push it into the lock

"*It won't go in!*" He called to her desperately, still struggling with it. "He has turned his key and then jammed the lock with something. This thing is *useless!*" and he hurled it furiously against the wall.

"God aid us, Yvo!" she replied, putting her hand to her mouth. "Why did you not seize him this morning while you had the chance?"

"*Because Matthew was not with us!*" He cried out bitterly. "It had to be *right!*" Then turning back he shook the door again and shouted: "Is that you de Brocas? Stop this nonsense. Unblock this door and let us out! Where are my men?"

"Dead! You fucking bastard! What else, you fool? Do you think I'd be out here on my own otherwise? They've gone to their fucking Maker," he swore obscenely through the door. "As you will too!" And he laughed.

"You bloody bastard! Open this door and let us out. Killing us will not yield you anything except extreme pain and trouble!"

There was a pause and then the Baron's shouted voice came back to them through the door: "Wrong, de Malwood! **Wrong!**" Baron Roger bawled back at him. "Your deaths will give me *everything*! I will be revenged on you and yours for my father's death; and I, the Lord Baron Sir Roger de Brocas, Lord of Narbonne and Gruissan, will claim my own at last!" And he laughed and banged on their door, cruelly taunting them by rattling the keys he held in his hand against the woodwork.

"Roger! Open this door and help us." Sir Yvo shouted back at him. "For pity's sake, man, before we perish!"

"Help you?" De Brocas' voice came back to them with a harsh burst of laughter. "*Help you?* When I have gone to such trouble to trap you? I think not," he roared. "I really think not! Else you might think I had gone mad!" And his laughter came to them high and broken. Then, spitting with rage, he added harshly: "You fool! I *want* you to perish! And '*Pity?*' You fat moron! Was it 'pity' that struck down my father in Cahors, you vile English hog? Was it 'pity' that robbed my family of all it held dear?"

"That was 'War', de Brocas, you treacherous bastard!" Sir Yvo raged back at him, hammering on the door. "Your father made the wrong choice! He backed the wrong King, and paid for it with his life! He died trying to kill me, knowing the risks of betraying King Henry from the start. By God's Throat, you black-hearted murderer, but you will pay for this, I promise you!"

"How, you fat *prick?*" The Baron's sneering voice came through to them. "*How?* You will both be *dead!*" And he laughed again, a dreadful crowing sound that made poor Margaret shudder.

"Hold me here if you must, de Brocas," Sir Yvo roared back in anger. "But let Margaret go free. For Mercy's sake, Roger. She has done you no harm!"

"*Mercy's sake?*" he howled back at him in fury. "Are you mad?" And he laughed again, high and long. "'Mercy's sake'? Was it 'Mercy's sake' that made your family great and cast mine into the gutter?" de Brocas roared his reply through the door. "What kind of fool do you take me for? To let the old Sow go free when I have the Hog trapped here and his fucking Shoat down-by in his room? Never! Now you will *all* pay, I assure you! All save one!"

"One?" Sir Yvo shouted back over the fury of the storm and the growing roar and crackle of the flames beneath him. "Only one?" Sir Yvo called back again, his voice almost cracking as he did so, ending in a great bout of coughing from the smoke that was beginning to fill the room, making his chest heave and his eyes water.

"Yes, you *oaf!*" The Baron spat back at him. "All save one. Your son, your own fucking piglet, will die as you will, you smug bastard, roasted alive in his bed!"

"*Nooo!*" Lady Margaret screamed out in anguish, clutching at her husband's arm. "No! Not our son! Not my Gui!"

"Even so, you fat *Sow!*" came back the sneering, hateful voice, thick with spite and anger. "Roasted in his bed like the great sucking pig he is, squealing for his mother! I'll even put an apple in his mouth before I leave!" He mocked her ruthlessly. "But the girl…the fair and beautiful Al-ic-i-a." De Brocas shouted back, his voice relishing every syllable of her name. "Whose father slew mine and sprayed his blood across my face - She will be mine. She I will take for my amusement!" He taunted her cruelly. "*She I will have for my own!*"

"*Nooo!*" Lady Margaret howled again in anguish, like an animal in pain. "Not Alicia! Not my precious girl! Not both my little ones!" And she sank down at her husband's feet, sobbing piteously into her hands, her clothes dabbled in the filthy mire that now almost surrounded them.

"*Yes!* You fat, old Sow. You fucking *whore!*" De Brocas screamed venomously. "It will be *my* seed your precious girl will have thrust into her belly. It will be *my* child her fine tits will suckle, and it will be *my* name," he shouted out exultantly, "that she will carry for the rest of her sad and miserable life! And it will be *your* lands, Yvo, you fucking *bastard!*" He screamed at them, now beyond all reason: "Yours and Cousin Henry's together that I will rule over!" And through the door they heard the Baron's crow of harsh laughter rise again, loud above the storm.

155

"King Richard will never allow that to happen, you madman…"

"Richard, you pathetic fool?" de Brocas hooted back at him. "*King fucking Richard?* He will be dead before the year is out, and John will rule in his place and he will give me *everything!*" And he banged his fist on the door and howled with mad laughter as he rattled the keys again in utter derision. "Alicia; her lands, your lands…*Everything!*" And he roared with laughter again.

"*Margaret!*" Sir Yvo called out sharply, covering his mouth with his sleeve. "Margaret! Come with me, Sweetheart," he went on, drawing her up from the floor, her night clothes and legs thick with the sulphurous, oily fluid that had flooded through from the passage beyond. "He is beyond reason. A wild lunatic! Come, my poor darling, swiftly, before he sets that filthy stuff alight…or it ignites itself from the flames around us. See how it is already beginning to steam!" And grabbing her by the hand he dragged her back towards the smashed and smoking window. "Quickly now, my Love! Get some air and look below. There may yet be a way out from here. Be quick, Margaret! And see if there is anyone down there who can help us?"

Coughing in the ever increasing smoke, he helped his wife to the open window, and while she leaned out, gasping for air…he dashed back across the room to where his baldric lay across one of the many chests that stood around the room.

Leaving the great blade in its soft leather sheath he swiftly drew his dagger, and with tears now coursing down his face, he staggered back to the window.

"It's no good, my Dearest," Margaret said, turning to face him. "There's no way down from here that I can see, and it's far too high to jump! I called out, but there's no-one to hear me. Yvo…there's just no way we can get out!"

"Yes there is, you big silly!" Sir Yvo said to her softly with a great smile. And putting his burly arms around her to shield her from the flames that were leaping up from below, he turned her so that he could hold her close against him, her head pressed tightly into his shoulder.

"Oh, my darling. Don't cry," he said, rocking her in his arms as great heaving sobs racked her soft body. "Shush…shush now. Of course there's a way out my *beautiful*, so wonderful wife," he went on gently, his left hand caressing first her head, and then her back, his fingers feeling their way lightly over her ribs beneath her soft, plump body.

"I have loved you, my most precious darling, *all* my life long. Since the very first moment I saw you all those years ago, my angel, beside the stream in your father's orchard. Oh my Margaret. My Sweeting," he whispered to her, the tears running freely down his face. "Forgive me, for this."

"For what?" she asked him, looking up into his eyes as she spoke, the wind whipping her hair about her wildly. "For what, Yvo, my perfect Knight?" she asked him again, taking his head in her two hands and kissing his eyes, wet with tears. "For what, my dearling?"

"For this, my *most* beautiful Lady," he breathed at her, as he kissed her in return. Brushing each eye closed with gentle butterfly kisses. "For everything, my darling, darling girl!" And holding her tightly to him with his left arm he drove his long pointed dagger up between the fingers he had placed on her ribs, and with a single mighty thrust, he pierced her wildly beating heart. With a gasp her eyes flew open, her whole body leaped and shuddered in his arms as he caught her to him fiercely…and then she was still.

"Sweet Jesus," he sobbed, holding her crushed against his heart. "Receive her soul into your safe keeping." Then looking up from the shattered window into the very heart of the storm, he howled in anguish to the heavens in all their raging wildness: "Dear God, forgive me for what I have done…and in your loving mercy *may I be revenged!*"

And even as Sir Yvo cried out the lightning flashed again and again, huge hammer blows of jagged blue-white fire that struck down out of the heaving sky as the storm passed directly overhead, the searing streak of each monstrous bolt followed immediately by Satanic blasts of thunder that made the whole castle seem to stagger and reel like a mighty ship crashing down upon a reef.

With that first shattering **BANG!** the Baron seized a flaming torch from its nearby sconce and with a great roar of triumph hurled it down against the naphtha soaked door, and with a fierce roar the flames leaped up and shot under it, burning more furiously than anything he had known before. Leaping back in sudden terror, his eyebrows singed, his own hands seared with fire, he heard a single terrible cry of mortal agony that for a moment made him cower down and cover his ears.

Then standing up he shouted out: '*Burn! Burn!*' giving another dreadful crow of wild, raucous laughter as he hurled the two empty flasks away from him and swiftly turned to leave; and with those final, mighty crashes came the rain.

Vast torrents of water that sluiced off the roofs and poured out of the gutters and gargoyles around the battlemented walls in huge spouts and waterfalls of freezing, rushing white water that turned the cobbled yard into a seething lake in moments. Rain that flew in horizontal sheets as the wind shrieked through it like a dozen banshees screaming for the tormented souls of the dead, hurling the water before it like steel rods as it crashed down upon the countryside below.

Up in the Gatehouse, and in the turrets way above the Great Keep, the guards cowered against the far corners of their guard-chamber and howled their fear into the teeming darkness as hurricane force winds battered at the building, ripping tiles off the roofs as if they were paper, and hurling them away into the streaming darkness like spinning plates, while the lightning fell in huge jags of blinding light and the thunder crashed and roared above them, their ears left ringing from each thunderous assault.

Chapter 23...*The Wicked Baron leaves the young Lion for dead...*

With that first horrendous crash Gui came instantly awake, sitting bolt upright in his bed as he felt the whole building tremble, clinging to the carved bed-posts as his room rocked to each successive strike. Then, leaping naked off his bed, he flung himself at the door that led out into the stone corridor beyond, and raising the latch he tried to heave it open, only to find that the door was stuck fast, immoveable, and nothing he could do would shift it.

Sweet Jesus, it was jammed.

No! *God's Throat!* It was *locked...and* jammed, for his key was there on the floor of his room, and struggle as he might he could not get it back into the lock again to turn it...and he wasted precious minutes struggling with the latch until with a crash it came away in his hand and he fell into a spitting heap on the floor.

The Baron! He cursed. It *had* to be him! But what about the guards? Sweet Wine of Christ, what a bastard mess! And what about Alicia? Where was she this very night but in the arms of The Lady?

And suddenly it came to him, a thought so brutal as to stun his body rigid in mid stride. *Splendour of God! They want Alicia!* For her inheritance? Not possible unless both he and his parents dead...and then only through marriage! *God's Blood!* So that's what all this is about! He wanted her for marriage! By the Torch of the Gospels, it was the only thing that made any sense and he was appalled by the thought, not least because he knew it to be true!

As long as they were both alive Alicia's inheritance was not an issue because when she married him it would all be transferred to his control. That was how the laws of property worked in England! *But if he, Gui, was dead...and his parents?* Then that would change everything! Whoever held Alicia then, with everyone else slain, could do as he liked! Forced marriages were not unusual, given a venal priest!

159

God's Wounds! *The Fucking Bastard!*

Somehow he must get out of this room! And soon, before he became trapped and unable to make his presence felt in any way, and looking round desperately for some kind of lever he could use against the door, he suddenly saw his fighting axe that young Simon Varter had just finished burnishing but clearly forgotten to return to the armoury. God Bless the boy! But he would reward him for that, and seizing it in his hands he hewed at the stout timbers that bound the solid oak door together with all the force at his command.

Crash! Crash! Crash! Each massive blow delivered with all his power and concentration, given extra strength borne of his desperation, and at the fourth blow he felt the door give, and hurling himself at it from across the room, he burst it off its hinges and fell amongst its ruins into the passage beyond.

And not a moment too soon!

Thick smoke already filled the corridor, the glow and flare of crackling flames lighting up the scene with a terrifying intensity that made him think of Hell-Fire and the Pit. With blood running down his legs and shoulders from the cuts he had received when he broke through the door, Gui looked almost as spectral as the scene on which he was gazing. Standing by the drooping, twisted hinges he glanced briefly round him, taking in the slumped bodies of the two guards outside his door and the orange, flickering glare that lit up the passage beyond. Dead or drugged? He bent down to feel them, his fingers coming away covered in blood, and there was even more of it spread out across the floor. Dead then, poor bastards! Stabbed or gutted? He didn't have the time to find out, but dashing back into his room he pulled on a pair of strong leather breeks and his heavy work boots, and picking up a brown leather jacket, he stepped out of his room.

And almost immediately he smelt it!

Something strange in the air...unusual even. Oily, slightly resinous, with a hint of sulphur...or saltpetre? He could not place it, though he thought he should know what it was. He paused then, briefly, like a hound questing a faint scent on the breeze, before ignoring it and turning to lope, with his long stride, towards the crackling light, still carrying his axe in both hands, coughing and choking in the smoke as it thickened the nearer he got to the fire. Then, rounding the corner that led directly to his parents' room, Gui came to a sudden stop for there outside their room, silhouetted against the blazing door of their bedchamber was the Baron himself, Lord Roger de Brocas.

Two dead men at his feet, their bodies untidily slumped either side of his parent's doorway, and two flagons of some sort in his hands, the contents of which he was still throwing at the flames that covered the door to his parent's room. Flames that instantly roared up even more fiercely, roiling black and scarlet-orange, curling up to cover the stone ceiling in a violent burst of fire that was almost white in its intensity and drove the Baron backwards, his arms held across his face from the heat as he did so.

"*Burn! Burn!*" He could hear him shouting as he hurled the two empty flasks at the fire, dancing and capering madly; and with a great roar of triumph he turned...only to find Gui standing there before him, barring his path, his great fighting axe already swinging in his hands.

Rage, pain and hatred burned in Gui's heart then from the clear knowledge of what de Brocas had done to his parents and had tried to do to him, and he knew now what it was that he had smelt moments earlier: *Greek Fire!* Greek Fire, that the crusaders made and carried in clay pots to hurl over their infidel enemies. Greek Fire, that no water could put out, now burning, live and unquenchable, here in Castle Malwood! No! This must be Arab Fire! More oily, more resinous. Not so explosive; slower to burn but no less deadly in so confined a space.

"*You foul bastard, de Brocas!*" He shouted at him, above the roar and crackle of the flames. "Arab Fire! You filthy, treacherous, murderous *dog!* You hoped to kill us all and, but for this!" He roared at him, shaking the great weapon at him as he shouted, "You might have done so too!"

"*Ho! You pathetic boy!*" Baron Roger shouted at him. "You fucking dung hill cock! Do you think you can stop me now? Do you think you can stop all of this?" he added, sweeping his arms towards the fire. "I have done for your fucking parents at least," and he threw back his head and laughed. "Yes! They're *dead!*" he jeered at him. "The Hog and his fat Sow, burned to a crisp like overdone pork! Shame about the crackling!" and he sniffed the air mockingly, laughing as he saw the look of pure hatred that flew across Gui's face. "All that remains is the fucking *shoat!*" He snarled then, staring intensely at Gui as he spoke, seeking out his eyes. "The striped piglet...and roast sucking pig is such a delicacy for any feast I know!

161

"Don't try your mind games on me, Baron." Gui roared at him through the smoke. "You tried to bend me to your will this evening. But my Lady's love prevented you. You cannot harm me now. She has cracked your power over me for all time.

"And where *is* your precious Lady?" de Brocas spat back at him, crouched down like some great, loathsome toad. "Your darling, sweet, Al–ic–ia? Eh? Eh?" he mocked him bitterly. "In my daughter's arms *you fool!* That's where she is now. And soon she will be in mine, and you will be but a memory to her. She has a ripe body, *Boy!*" he sneered. "I can't wait to plunder the little bitch myself! Her fine tits in my mouth," he crowed. "And my thick cock stuffed in her wet cunt to the very hilt," he added, gesturing coarsely. "And she bucking madly on the end of it!" And he threw his head back and laughed, a wild, demonic crow of pure malice.

"You Devil's spawn!" Gui raged at him, bouncing from side to side on the balls of his feet, his great axe swinging free. "*I will be revenged on you for this!*"

The Baron's eyes glittered in the flaring light from the flames behind him, hard as granite, filled with bitter hatred and he waited, crouched down on his toes as his enemy moved steadily towards him. No coward in battle by any means, Lord Roger knew the dangerous fix he was in should Gui once get close enough to him with that swirling axe of his to pin him down. Like in a corner. There was only one way out of *that*, and it would not be pleasant! Of course the boy was good. But he had met many just as good as he and beaten them. Such big men were often slow. Slow of foot and mind. He did not doubt his skill to win, and he had a surprise in store for his enemy of which he could know nothing!

For his part Gui watched the Baron carefully as he came on knowing, even though the man was unarmed, that he faced an opponent of great skill and strength. Only a fool would think he had an easy kill before him. Then, suddenly Gui moved, feinting left but really swinging right, bringing his great axe round in a lethal shimmering arc to cut murderously at de Brocas' open side. Yet even as he swung the Baron swayed aside, the huge blade whirring past him to crash against the wall, jarring Gui's body right to his shoulder ends and striking bright sparks of fire that flared briefly in the smoky gloom.

And Baron Roger mocked him.

"A noble try, bantam! But you will have to do better than that if you wish to split my heart in two!" And with a swift jerk, from across his back he pulled a short crossbow, thick bolt with short green fletchings already firmly held in place, and before Gui could speak again he held it out before him and pulled the iron trigger. Gui, who'd seen the brief flicker of movement seconds before, just had time to fling himself sideways, before he was struck a hammer blow as the short deadly quarrel smashed through the leather of his coat to bury itself, up to the feathers, in the thick muscle pad of his left shoulder, right into the very joint itself. It was a cruel blow. Agonising! And with a wild cry of pain Gui crashed to the ground, almost letting his axe slip from his hands as he did so.

"You useless lump of *shite!*" the baron crowed, leaping towards him through the smoke. "Did you think I would come here unarmed? You pathetic idiot! *Bedlamite!* Out of my way; I have better things to do than waste time with a yapping cur like you!"

But Gui had been brought up in a hard school, and struggling to his feet he still barred the Baron's way, his giant body as much a barrier as the axe he still swung with his right arm and shoulder, 'though with blood welling out in thick gouts from beneath the bolt so firmly struck into him, it was only a matter of time before he fell again. But time was something the Baron did not have, because behind him the fire was gaining in fierceness and fury, and even now might still consume them both! Lurched to one side, Gui swung his axe around him, dizzy with pain and shock, while the Baron danced aside, for though the young knight before him was wounded he was still extremely dangerous, and he had no weapons of his own left with which to fight him. If he once strayed within the young man's grasp he was a dead man.

And the boy *was* good! Very good. He snarled. But was he good enough?

Gui watched him, conscious of growing dizziness and pain, but he was not finished yet for even as the Baron moved again, trying still to edge past him, he brought his axe round in a reverse blow of dazzling speed, then back across his front, and out again, each blow forcing de Brocas involuntarily backwards until he hit the wall and had nowhere else to go. Gui, striding forward each time, *knew* that he had his man, for when he swung his axe again, nothing could avoid the blow he would deliver. And his enemy knew it too, not ever expecting Gui, with an iron bolt so deep in him, to be capable of such fast moves and, giving a wild cry of fear, he threw up his hands to ward off his final end.

The bloody boy had been good enough after all!

Up went the axe, its sharpened blade flickering in the leaping firelight, up over his shoulder, from where it would fall upon his enemy like a great thunderbolt from Zeus himself…but the blow never fell! For even as Gui leaped forward to close the gap between them, axe swinging high over his shoulder as he moved, he slipped in his own blood that all the time had been flowing out from his shoulder, and from the many other tears and rents his body carried, and with a jarring crash he fell sideways, rolling on to his knees as he landed in preparation for his enemy's next move.

But that move never came for, with a groaning roar, one whole section of the ceiling above Gui's head suddenly gave way, and a huge roof truss crashed in smouldering ruins across his back, felling him instantly and knocking him senseless beneath its weight, his axe flying out of his grasp as the beam smashed him to the ground. Clambering swiftly over the debris, the Baron capered madly beside Gui's fallen body, spittle flecking his lips, his eyes glaring wildly as he danced.

"Farewell, Sir Knight." he shouted, kicking him savagely as he lay senseless on the floor. "Your fucking life has run its course I think. Where's the murderous dog now, eh?" he shouted, kicking him again and again. "Right here beside you, you miserable, fucking piece of *shite!*" he shouted, bending down to his ear.

"I get the girl, and *all* her fine inheritance…you just get *dead!*" He ended, standing up again. "*Dead*, you fucking Bedlamite!" he screamed down at him, spittle flying from his mouth. And giving Gui a final brutal kick between his legs for good measure as he lay helpless on the floor, he stalked away from the inferno he had created and scuttled from the ruined building, while behind him the flames took firm hold and ran along the floor in broad streams of liquid fire, towards the Baron's helpless fallen victim.

Chapter 24......And tries his wicked hand again!

Minutes later, having seized those of his belongings that he most needed from his own rooms, handing them to his men as he did so, The Lord Baron Sir Roger De Brocas dashed through the pouring rain from the doomed building to the great tower where his daughter was staying with Alicia...and where, in the guard rooms at the foot of it, the Cousins had been so innocently placed by John Fitzurse. Inside, the men had a cheerful fire burning, and were sitting on stools with horn beakers of mulled wine in their hands, and as he entered they leaped to their feet.

"Do you two know what to do?" De Brocas growled at them urgently.

"Yes, My Lord!" Jules replied instantly. "The Lady told us when she came here for her wrap. We are to go up and deal with the two men outside their door, then run up onto the tower-top and drop the two portcullises to cut the tower off from the rest of the castle, while you get the girl away with you!"

"Yes. Then what? Hurry man. *Hurry!*" He said, urgent to get things moving.

"We shift the bodies, come back down here, clean ourselves up from top to toe, put on clean clothes as well -you taking the bloodied ones with you – take the potion your daughter has prepared for us, and wait to be discovered."

"Is the potion safe, My Lord?" Lucas broke in anxiously, as the lightning flashed violently outside followed by yet another terrific, rolling crash of thunder. "She does not mean to kill us?"

"*Kill you?*" de Brocas almost shouted at him. "*Are you mad?* We need you both to stay here in case anything goes wrong. Don't be so bloody foolish! Of course it's safe"

"How will we know?"

"If we don't get clean away with our prize, then *all* the world will know it, for she will be back here screaming her head off!"

"What happens then, My Lord?" Lucas persisted.

"Then, you jackass," his cousin broke in sharply. "We carry out our orders, as arranged. As we have been given them! Stop being such an arsehole, Lucas! You *know* what happens next: we do our best to stick near the little lady like glue; do all we can to get chosen for the Crusade troop and keep alert for instructions when the Lord Baron has another go with El Nazir. If all else fails, we go with the others down to Bordeaux and then slip away into the night, and then home! That will be the easy part!"

"*God's Blood*, but it doesn't sound fucking easy to me!"

"*That's enough!*" The Baron snarled, grasping Fabrizan by the throat and shaking him fiercely. "Your orders are clear. I didn't hear you complain, when you were chosen for this mission! You were keen enough then! Now, *get up there and do not fail me*, or we will all be doomed, and I shall be certain to make sure you die first! Any moment now we may be spotted, despite all the confusion. Now, Get *out!* Both of you. *Go!* I will be right behind you."

With that the two men rushed upstairs, Jules leading, drawing their long daggers as they went and shouting, "*Fire! Fire!* The castle is on fire!"

Above them came more shouts and sounds of wild confusion as the men placed outside Alicia's room reacted; with Johnny Foxglove running up to the tower-top for a clearer view, his friend turning to see who was coming up the stairs shouting. And so it was that Davy Oats was the fifth person to die that night, for as Jules bounded into sight calling out his name, so he stabbed him through with his poniard, brushing Davy's arms open as he attacked, and bursting his long pointed blade straight through the man's mailed jerkin into his belly, cruelly twisting it as he pulled it out. Then as Davy doubled over in agony, unable even to cry out, he stabbed him again through the neck and killed him, his hot blood rushing out over his hand. Then, while his cousin rushed on up to the top of the tower, Jules dragged the dead guard through the open door behind him onto the wall-walk, before running to follow his cousin up the stairs.

Above him Lucas was having a tough tussle with his opponent, who had turned as he heard footsteps rushing up the stone spiral just in time to catch the glint of drawn steel in the flashing darkness before his unknown assailant was on him. Both were hard men, and of equal strength and they reeled from side to side across the top of the tower, hands gripping hands as Lucas strove to stab with his long blade, and Johnny Foxglove fought to prevent him. In the end, it

166

was Jules who rescued his cousin, running up behind him and pulling Foxglove backwards. Even then there was still a fierce struggle until Lucas finally managed to stab his blade upwards through poor Johnny's throat and into his brain, killing him instantly, throwing him to the ground, his life's blood flooding out across the stones.

Together the Cousins then ran to the heavy wooden spindles that held the two portcullises up on either side of the tower, and strove to throw off the ratchets so that they could both crash home onto the wall-walk below them. Meanwhile, the Baron had reached Alicia's door, and was thundering on it with his gloved hands.

"Quick, Alicia. Rochine, quick! *Fire! Fire!*" He shouted, desperation sounding in every word. "Open the door! Lightning has set fire to the castle and the whole South wing is one great mass of flames. You must get out immediately!"

Rochine, who'd been waiting to hear those very words for what seemed half the night, shook Alicia violently awake, pointing wildly to the flickering ruddy glow that could be seen through the shutters as she did so.

"Alicia! Alicia! *Quickly, my Love!*" she shouted at the sleepy girl, dragging her out of bed. "Get up and put some clothes on. My father says the castle is on fire and we must get out or be burned in our beds! Here," she went on, sweeping Alicia's over-robe off the floor where it had earlier been tossed and thrusting it at her. "Cover yourself, my darling. My father needs to come in." And waiting only a moment while Alicia, still dazed with sleep, slipped it on, she drew a fine silk surcoat over her own slender shoulders, running across the room as she did so and snapping back the bolts that held the door closed.

With a crash it flew open, and in a few deep strides the Baron rushed across the room, and flung open both window and shutters. At once the wild tumult going on outside burst on their ears, the room filling with the acrid smell of smoke and burning, the walls lit by the lurid light of the fire.

"Quick girls, the castle's on fire and we must leave at once. Throw something warmer over those clothes, it is pouring with rain outside. You will be drenched through in a moment and it's freezing cold. The smoke's so thick that it's hard at times to see just where one is going.

"Why?...What's happening?" Alicia stammered, still half asleep.

"Have you heard nothing, My Lady? De Brocas shouted at her. *Look!*" And dragging her over to the windows he threw them open and showed her what was going on.

"The castle's on fire, and you must get out *now!*" He exclaimed loudly, turning away to grab up some of Rochine's belongings, while she hastily dressed herself. "Before the fire takes hold of the whole building. Already the walls are beginning to crack in places from the heat, and the lead is running off the roofs in molten rivers. Don't worry about your things, just throw something on and get clear!"

"Lord Roger, *wait!*" Alicia cried out then, now fully awake and resting her hands on the windowsill, leaning out to gaze, horror struck, at the fire. "What about Gui and his parents? Help me," she went on desperately, turning back and holding out her hands to him. "I *must* go to them. Help me, *please!*"

"It is too late, My lady," he replied harshly, grabbing her and shaking her fiercely, not wanting to give her a moment to slow down and put her thoughts in order, while Rochine, now dressed, rushed about gathering things up as she went.

"What do you mean, '*It's too late?*'" Alicia questioned him sharply. "This is my home. I must go to Sir Yvo and find Gui, or Sir Richard. They will know what to do. Now please *Let me go!*"

"It is too late, Alicia! Too late!" the Baron went on, shaking her again as he spoke, dismayed by her determined reaction. "I tried to get through to them from the far end of the corridor that links their rooms with the lower hall…but the heat and smoke were too great. They drove me back. See," he continued, his voice rising, as he dragged her back to the window, gesturing towards the fire that now lit up the whole night sky. "The windows are great blazing eyes of flame. *Nothing* can survive in there," he emphasised brutally. "I had the greatest difficulty in getting clear. There is smoke and debris everywhere. Look at me! See, my cape is burned and so am I, and my hair singed. I was the last one out, I promise you!"

And in truth it was a terrifying sight. For by then the whole South wing was a raging inferno, the flames towering up into the night, leaping and twisting, with everyone screaming and shouting and running madly about, men and animals both, and the smoke billowing out from every angle,.

From end to end the New Hall was ablaze, with huge plumes of dense smoke boiling up into the flame-lit sky, itself alive with sparks, which were drenched out almost immediately by the rain now falling in torrents. The flames themselves however, driven by the wind, kept leaping forward unabated, licking up towards the walls of the Great Keep itself. Vast columns of roaring fire, accompanied by the bang and crash of timbers and bursting stones, sounding clearly to her as she gazed in horrified wonder at the appalling scene before her.

"No, Baron!" She said at last, firmly pulling herself out of his grasp, and running back into the middle of the room. "The New Hall has gone, that I can see. But the Keep is untouched, as is most of the rest. The whole castle is *not* on fire. None of our men will leave Castle Malwood until the last, and nor will I. I *must* find them! And anyway, Gui may not be dead. He *cannot* be dead! I will not *let* him be dead!" And flinging open one of the great cedar wood chests that stood against the wall, she seized some clothes out of it and started pulling them on over her nightgown.

"Alicia, dearest," Rochine pleaded with her, flicking her head fiercely at her father as she spoke, even as she helped her cousin dress. "You've seen what it's like out there. The whole South wing has gone. My father has been there, Alicia, and look at the state of him? Singed and burned everywhere! If he says the family are lost, Sweetheart, then they are lost," she went on putting her arms around the girl who had now broken down into pitiful sobs. "You cannot stay here, my love. You must leave, now, before the fire sweeps through here as well!"

Suddenly Alicia turned in Rochine's grasp, pushing a little away from her, and with a swift gesture swept her arm across her face, wiping her tears away.

"No! Rochine, It's no good. *I just can't do it!* You must go, and your father of course, but this is my home and I am *not* fleeing yet. I have a responsibility here. These are my people too," she added, rushing to look for some sort of cloak against the rain. "And I'm not about to abandon them just because the whole place seems to be going up in smoke and flames around me. Even if Gui and his parents truly are dead, I'm still not going anywhere. This is my home!!" she cried out. "There, dressed at last!" And whisking up a thick cloak from a nearby chest, she turned and prepared to leave the room.

169

Pausing by the door to look back at her cousin and the Baron, still standing in the middle of the floor somewhat stunned, she hesitated. In her mind she believed that what the Baron had said might well be true. They might all be dead indeed? Certainly the fire was big and fierce enough. The whole New Hall, so recently completed, and many of the buildings nearby were clearly one giant mass of flame. Rochine seeing the hesitation, now ran across to her and taking her hands between her own strong fingers, she drew her down to sit beside her on the bed.

"Oh, Alicia," she urged her, looking into her eyes and shaking her hands in emphasis as she spoke. "You *must* come with us. You *cannot* stay here! Oh father," she said, giving him another fierce gesture of encouragement behind Alicia's back. "Tell her she must come with us now if she is to be saved!"

Thwarted in his immediate aim, and quite unprepared for Alicia's steely resolve, the Baron smiled at Rochine's cleverness, and kneeling down beside Alicia, while his daughter held her there by her shoulders, he placed his hands on either side of her head and looked deep into her eyes. Blue ones, large as cornflowers, stared into black ones, dark as night, as de Brocas strove to take control of her mind. Breathing slowly and deliberately, despite the urgency of the moment, he stared into her very soul, and looking into his deep and silent gaze, Alicia was lost.

"My dear child," he said, his voice dark and slow, measured and insistent. "You are a brave and spirited lady, but you must believe me when I say that Gui, Sir Yvo and his wife are dead. They are burned in the flames. I heard their cries and saw their rooms ablaze. There is no hope for them, my child," he went on in a slow, and richly sombre voice, brushing her forehead as he spoke. "Gui, Sir Yvo and his wife are dead! Do you understand, Alicia? *Gui, Sir Yvo and his wife are dead!*"

Alicia felt her head spinning, and then herself falling, drowning. There was a faint resistance as she remembered what Gui had told her earlier that evening, but Gui was dead, wasn't he? 'Gui, Sir Yvo and his wife were dead! Were dead! *Were dead!*' And she allowed the deep, rich, warm persistence of the Baron's voice to wash over her, cleanse her, heal her. She felt no pain, no misery of heart or soul, but she was falling: falling into those eyes, those deep, black, penetrating eyes...and all at once she just *knew* that she must go with them; that the Baron would look after her. Rochine would look after her, would love her. They would both love her. They were family, weren't they? To whom else could she turn? Gui, Sir Yvo and his wife were dead! Gui, Sir Yvo and his wife were dead! Were dead, were dead, were dead

Chapter 25…How the Baron and The Lady stole the White Rose of Malwood.

Then, as if from no-where, Alicia saw a man looking at her.

Tall he was, black-robed, with warm kindly eyes, deep brown and clear, looking at her from an open, smiling face with high brows and a hawk-like nose with his hands held out to hold her…and even as she saw him, into her mind came a picture of her and Gui together on some clear, high place beneath an azure sky, the sun shining brilliantly warm upon their faces. Kissing, holding close, loving…and with a horrendous, graunching rumble the two portcullises thundered down their stone grooves beyond the room to hammer down on to the wall walk with an enormous '*crash!*' that shook the tower to its very foundations, and with a wild cry Alicia leaped to her feet.

Dashing the Baron's hands away from her face as she did so she ran to the centre of the room and looking at him and his daughter she shouted: "**Stand back and let me be!** What is going on, here? Those are the portcullises! Who has released them?"

For a moment both Lord Roger and his daughter were too shocked to move, almost as if themselves had been turned to stone.

"*You Devil!*' Alicia snarled at Roger de Brocas, as with a gasp of shock she finally realised what he had been trying to do. "You *cannot* hold me! Not now…not *ever!* And as for you, you *witch!*' She shouted, rounding on her tall French cousin. "Stand back and leave me alone! There are guards at the foot of this stair, and others not too far away," she continued, whisking herself towards the door, which the Baron had not closed fast behind him. "Gui had them put there especially to guard me. Make one move towards me and I will have you both in chains!"

Before her was a sudden frozen tableau: Rochine standing, like a statue, one arm by her side, her other hand up to her mouth in shocked surprise. The Baron still crouched down before the bed where he had been holding Alicia, his hands still outstretched from where she had pulled herself away from him so suddenly, stunned into disbelief that for a second time that evening he should have been so inexplicably baulked of his prey. But not for long! Even as Alicia turned back to reach for the door, so the Baron came to life, his deep, harsh voice filling the room above the wild noise and rumpus going on outside.

"Stop her, Rochine!" He shouted out fiercely. "The door! *Quickly girl!* The door! Once let her out and we are lost!"

With extraordinary speed, Rochine flung herself across the room and seizing the edge of Alicia's cloak just as her hand was at the leading edge of the door, she hauled back on it with all her strength and with a wild shriek of surprise, Alicia flew backwards into the French girl's arms. There she struggled fiercely to break free, shouting out for help as loudly as she could to the soldiers she still believed to be there on guard: "To me! *To me!*" she screamed out desperately. "Aid me! *Aid meee!*"

Once she almost broke free from Rochine's grip, seizing the hand nearest her mouth and sinking her teeth into it as she twisted herself violently out of her cloak, her own hands scrabbling in desperation for the edge of the still partially open door. But, by then, the Baron was at his daughter's side, and once he had Alicia in his grasp there was no denying his greater strength and speed.

Seizing her from Rochine, he grabbed her by her arms, and dragging her clear of the doorway, still kicking and screaming, he flung her bodily down onto the bed, while Rochine, panting and dishevelled, and clutching her wounded hand to her chest, crashed the door closed at last.

"*You fucking bitch!*" she screamed at Alicia, the blood running down her dress from where Alicia had bitten her. "You bloody little *whore!*" And striding across to where Alicia was now struggling to sit up, she hit her open handed across the face as hard as she could. A swingeing blow that snapped the girl's head away, the marks of her fingers rushing up in scarlet wheals across the whiteness of her skin. Then, reaching across her father for Alicia's hair, she seized a great handful of it and shook Alicia like a sewer rat, before bringing her hand round and hitting her just as hard a second time.

"*Enough!*" The Baron snarled, grabbing Rochine's hand before she could deliver a further stunning blow. "We need her unmarked, remember? And safely away from here as swiftly as may be done! There is no time for such foolishness now!"

172

Alicia, tears streaming down her face, rubbed her cheeks where Rochine had hit her, dashing the tears away with the back of hand as she watched the swift play of emotions between the two. "You will *never* get away with this!" she cried out then, struggling to her feet. "Any moment my people will come searching for me. The guards whom Gui and Sir Richard have placed at my door will be here to rescue me!"

"Be silent, you little *fool!*" Rochine snapped back, tying a white cotton bandage over her injured hand, torn from one of Alicia's fine Egyptian shifts, tightening it with her teeth as she spoke. "There are no bloody guards! The two outside have both been *slain!* You will find their blood spread across the stones outside your door, and on the roof above. Who do you think released the two portcullises? St George? The two below the same!"

"Killed?…" Alicia said, horrified.

"…drugged, stabbed, dead. Who cares, *you little bitch!* I put the potion in their mulled wine myself when I came back here during your pathetic party," she sneered at her venomously. "This tower is now cut off, and in the hands of our men. No-one is coming to rescue you. They're all *dead!*"

"You *liar!*" Alicia, snarled back, hatred making her voice dark with menace. "You have no idea who is dead and who alive in this castle. Nor whether Sir Gui has been slain as you suggest. But, be certain of this, my Lady. *I am no whore!* I am Ward to King Richard of England, and the betrothed wife-to-be of Sir Gui de Malwood with his blessing. If you drag me with you the King's vengeance will seek you out and destroy you. Be sure of it! Now, release me to go and find those whom I love. You," she added, with a contemptuous wave of her hand. "You, may go where you will, you are no concern of mine!"

"Do you think we care what you say?" Rochine shouted at her, pushing her back down again onto her bed. "You are coming with us, you little whore," she emphasised, sneering. "Pathetic Gui's little plaything! *Dead Gui*, now!" She jeered, laughing into Alicia's face, ashen with pain and hatred.

"You will have to kill me first, before I will set foot outside this door in your filthy company!" Alicia screamed back at her, her eyes bright with tears of rage and complete distress.

"That will not be necessary," the Baron broke in silkily, as he came and leaned heavily over her. "You will come with us, Dear Lady, come what may," he breathed at her, his voice no more than a sibilant whisper in her ears. "Leave with us you shall…and alive, but not conscious, I fear. Far too noisy!"

And with a terse order to Rochine to call de Vere and his men to them at once, and before Alicia could make a move, he pinioned her body beneath his own, and seizing her head in a vice-like grip he covered her nose and mouth with a large cambric handkerchief, pressing down on it remorselessly.

Alicia, unable to move or even to cry out, gasping desperately for air, sucked the handkerchief into her mouth, her body flopping and thrashing beneath him like a landed fish, her eyes almost bursting out of her head until, all at once, her body collapsed and she lay still. Instantly de Brocas released her, whipping his wide handkerchief from her nose and mouth as he did so. Then, tilting up her head he swiftly poured the contents of a small phial that he had brought with him, down her throat. Moments later he laid her back onto her bed, propping her up with a number of cushions, so she would not fall over. No sooner had he finished, than with a clatter of feet and chime of metal, Gaston de Vere came running into the room with three of his men, swiftly followed by the Lady Rochine.

"Right, Gaston!" de Brocas ordered him crisply, gesturing with his hands. "Clear this room. Leave nothing of value behind. We must have *some* gain from this adventure of ours at least! Rochine, make sure this little pigeon of ours is properly dressed for the journey. Bind her hands, and gag her! We leave immediately and nothing must stop us, least of all some desperate girl's screams or cries for help! So…move, *all of you!*"

With that, all was organised bustle and drive as de Vere and his men raped Alicia's room of all its value, including her mother's precious sapphire and pearl necklace that she had worn that very night. Then, within minutes, they were leaving, Alicia trussed up in her thick cloak like a hapless chicken bound for market, mouth gagged and eyes rolling in her head. Her hands were also bound, so that she might neither cry out, nor seize hold of anything as they hustled her from her room, down the spiral staircase, and out into the roiling, smoke-filled air of the castle bailey.

All around them showers of bright sparks flew up into the coal black sky, only to fall back as wet sludge from the rain pouring down, and there were people everywhere: grooms waiting to run their horses off to safety; soldiers doing their best to rescue what they could from the blazing buildings; servants snatching bundles up from the ground, and hundreds of others just standing there in the teeming rain, all gazing upwards at the towering flames and vast twisting plumes of smoke. Quietly, but with no obvious haste, the Baron's men

174

formed up, drifting their horses along towards the gatehouse with practised ease, but with none of the pack horses with which they had arrived, as he had no desire to have anything with them that might draw some sharp- eyed guard's attention. But with so much going on all around, there was little chance they would be noticed.

Throwing Alicia up before him, Lord Roger quietly idled Charlemagne over to where his men, led by de Vere, were waiting; Rochine following immediately behind. Then, with a soft clatter they were off, by-passing the people who were gathered in the lower courtyard beneath the Keep, including Sir Yvo's tall Guard Commander as he strode past them calling orders.

So steadily, with nerves of steel, breath rasping and their hearts hammering in their chests they walked their horses beneath the tall Gatehouse, desperate to set spurs to their horses' flanks, but determined not to bring unwarranted interest to their actions from the guards all around the great building. Then they were under the double rows of iron portcullis teeth, beneath the murder holes high in the roof above, through the double gates, swung open on their massive pintles, over both bridges…and onto the long, open causeway at last, every moment expecting a challenge to be flung at them followed by a storm of arrows.

But, despite their orders, the guard were all gawping at the fire, too busy watching Castle Malwood burn to be bothered by yet more of Sir Yvo's guests leaving…and so no challenge came. They let them go, while behind them the whole south wing of the castle was now one vast torch of towering flame that could be seen for miles. Other parts of the castle, especially the Keep itself, though steaming from the heat, were relatively untouched except by smoke, and L'Eveque had organised a bucket chain to save what few buildings he could of those on either side of the New Hall.

But the Hall itself, Sir Yvo's pride and joy, was lost in the roar and fury of the blaze, and the spectacular bang and crash of falling timbers and exploding masonry. For the Gatehouse guard, so close to what was happening, the noise and heat had drawn them away from their duties, and the frantic efforts of a tight group of men desperately struggling to break down a side door into the fiercely burning building had grabbed their attention. Indeed, even as they watched, the men, led by Big Nick, the huge castle Smith, disappeared inside leaving everyone waiting to discover if ever they would get out again. So no-one saw the Baron and his party leave, or if they did, saw only what they expected to see - just another small group of guests escaping from the fire into the rain-soaked, roaring darkness of the night.

Chapter 26... The Saracen's Head receives some early guests.

For Alicia, that journey from Castle Malwood lived ever after in her mind as one of the very worst experiences of her life!

An absolute nightmare!

Bundled up before Roger de Brocas like some sack of old cornmeal, her cloak wrapped round her as best she could, her body received scant protection, and she was soon soaked to the skin. But the shock of what had happened to her, along with the potion she had been forced to swallow, was all too great for her mind to cope with and she lay supine against the Baron, too numb to do anything but breathe, as he held her body against him to prevent her from falling off,

'Gui was dead, Gui was dead, Gui was *dead*!' Every beat of the horse's hooves seemed to drum it into her. But, 'he wasn't, he wasn't, *he wasn't!*' Was no less an insistent beat in her heart, as the realisation of her abduction by the Baron and his daughter forced itself into her consciousness. In her drugged state everything simply subsided into a strange blur of mixed sound and colour, swirling patterns that formed and re-formed behind her eyes and sounds that ballooned and shrank in intensity, until even the horses and people around her ceased to have any reality. She knew not where she was going, nor why, nor even the manner of her passage.

She knew only that she was alive and captive.

Yet, surely this was all a dreadful nightmare? Any moment now she would wake to find herself safe and well in her own great bed at Castle Malwood. She shivered uncontrollably, her teeth rattling together like knuckle bones in a dicing cup, and in the end it was the sluicing water that brought her back to a more conscious understanding, and with it the true hideousness of her situation. For with sopping wetness and the cold, came cognisance, a steady return to sentience and thus, ultimately, to reality...and with reality came anger and an almost unbearable pain that people to whom so much trust and kindness had been shown should have betrayed it all so vilely, even unto death!

To Alicia at that moment it seemed that all the people whom she had ever loved and known, or had ever loved and known her, were gone along with her home, in a roaring sea of flames, and only dust and ashes were left. She was too numb to weep, but the horror of it made her struggle wildly and cry out, though the sound was muted by the gag that de Brocas had tied across her mouth, lost in the wind and the thunder of the hooves and storm.

'Bastards! Bastards! *Bastards!* she screamed in her head, the last word torn from her mind and transformed into a wild cry of muffled rage and a sharp twist of her body, momentarily throwing the Baron off balance so that he gave her a fierce buffet across the head, making her ears ring, even as he struggled to retain his grip on her flailing body. Undeterred, she bucked against him again, and again he hit her, and again, only much harder this time with his closed fist against the top of her head as he would an angry horse, until she felt sick and dizzy.

"*Keep still,* you little fool!" he shouted at her. "Or you'll force me to let you go and you will surely be trampled to death under our hooves! So, as you value your life, Madam," he spat at her. "*Keep still!*" And he squeezed her floppy body even tighter against himself.

Seized, bound, gagged and crushed almost beyond breathing...Alicia was borne away in to the howling wet darkness, her mind in chaos, as much from the buffeting she had received as from the drug that Lord Roger had mercilessly forced down her throat before leaving. She felt small and alone; helpless against the forces ranged against her, and all the time the Baron and his party hurtled through the forest without seeming pause or hindrance from either land or weather. And that was no mean feat indeed, for it was pitch black, pouring with wind driven rain, and *everywhere* there were trees down. Just a barely definable lightness above them showed the place where the track wound its way between the woods that lay so thickly on every side.

Often they had to slow to a mere walk to pick their way around sudden obstacles. Once a flock of sheep blocked their way, broken loose in the storm and wandered off in the way only sheep can. And once it was a cow, knocked dead by lightning and swept away by the rain, its great body jammed across a ford so that the stream waters, already swollen by the torrential rain, cascaded all over it. And everywhere the ground was littered with smashed branches, the shattered limbs of whole stands of ancient timber, and a zillion torn leaves, mute symbols of the wild savagery of the storm.

Then suddenly, after what seemed like an age of travelling, the rain stopped and almost immediately there was a loud shout from de Vere up ahead, and she could feel the Baron reining in, slowing to a long striding walk as, with clatter of iron hooves on slippy cobbles, they turned off towards the wide courtyard of a large wayside Inn. But even as they turned, Alicia caught a glimpse of a black face, with pointed armoured helmet and chain-mail coif, holding a great curved scimitar swinging darkly above her head, sufficiently close for her to duck. Immediately she stiffened both her mind and her sinews, and for the first time since being dragged from her room, she felt a flicker of real hope in her heart.

She knew where she was!

By God's Good Grace, de Brocas had chosen the *one* place on his entire route that she knew like the back of her hand. The Saracen's Head at Lyndhurst! With its large open fireplace and tap room filled with tables, stools and benches, and broad stairs and gallery leading to its many rooms and passages above, it was a popular place to stay, for Lyndhurst was the only town of any size in the whole vast expanse of the New Forest. And Alicia smiled secretly to herself, for the Saracen's Head was owned and run by friends, and good friends too, for the Innkeeper was Edward Sergeant, Sir Yvo's old Master-at-Arms in her father's day, and his wife was her old and much loved nurse, Rose. Now, with God's Will, she might yet break free and escape the Baron and his daughter who had so rudely seized her, and in the roaring darkness borne her so cruelly away.

"*Ho there!*" de Vere shouted as the Baron rode into the inn's cobbled yard behind him, Alicia still held tightly in his arms. "Ho there, the Inn! Open in the Lord Baron's name, Sir Roger de Brocas!" And while two of his soldiers leaped from their horses and battered at the door, de Vere ran up and held out his arms to seize hold of Alicia from the Baron's keeping.

Swinging himself easily off his magnificent black charger, Lord Roger stepped swiftly to where his daughter was also just slipping from her own horse's back.

"Make sure of the wench, de Vere!" The baron called back as he gave his daughter a hand to dismount. "We don't want her escaping now and screeching her hurts all over the countryside."

178

"Leave her to me, father," Rochine said grimly as she strode to where de Vere was holding Alicia drooping in his arms. "I'll make sure the little bitch stays silent I assure you! Go now, My Lord, and see that the rooms arranged for us are ready. We must get her out of these soaking clothes as soon as possible, or she may fall ill, and that would be the very last thing we would wish to happen now."

"How will you manage?"

"Don't worry!" She snapped back, seizing hold of Alicia as she spoke. "Trust me to know what I am about. Draco can help me. He will not blanche at a little blood letting," she snarled, giving Alicia a shake as she did so. "I will do my part, I promise you!"

"Very well, Rochine," her father replied staring into his daughter's angry green eyes. "Just don't leave her marked...and don't kill her either!" And with that he was gone again, running swiftly across the inn yard just as the stout oaken door that led inside was cautiously opened and the russet, tousled head of a tall, broad shouldered man peered round the side.

"Who shouts so boldly on a night like this?" He demanded, pushing the door wide open behind him, and stepping through onto the broad stone flagged steps that lay before the doorway, a drawn sword in one beefy hand and a flaring torch in the other.

"What Baron is it who calls for aid in the King's own Forest?" he questioned again loudly, holding up the torch so that its flickering light fell on the faces of two of De Vere's men. "*You two!*" He ordered sharply, shortening his sword arm as he shouted, "Stand back from me and say what you do here at this time of night, and in such a violent manner. Speak now before I cut you down!"

"I am the Lord Baron Sir Roger de Brocas, friend of King Richard of England," de Brocas said clearly, stepping menacingly out from the shadows, fiercely signalling as he did so to the two troopers who had been hammering on the door, to stop and step behind him. "I have rooms arranged for the night, and horses ordered too," he continued, his black eyes glittering in the torch light. "Who are you?"

"Robert Forester, late of King Henry's army out of France," the tall man replied fearlessly, now resting on his sword, his eyes coolly looking over de Brocas and his men. "Served all over Normandy and Aquitaine with the Old King, and am cousin to Rose Sergeant, whose husband owns this inn. He is

179

away from home and his lady is caring for her son who has the fever. I am here in his stead, and I know of *no* orders for rooms or horses!"

"*God's Blood*, you *varlet!*" the Baron snarled back at him, taking a step forward and dropping his hand to his sword. "How *dare* you address me so! Much more of this and I will have my men seize you!"

"Softly, my Lord Baron," the man replied, his voice full of quiet threat. "This is not France, and I am no peasant for you to threaten in so bold a manner. This is England and I am a free man and the Saracen's Head is a free holding. You do not hold sway here, my fine French Lord. So speak more softly, or you may yet taste my steel," he went on, lifting his sword from the ground. "It will not be the first time this blade has let out bad French blood!"

The Baron stood back then and throwing his head back he laughed: "Enough of all this nonsense, Englishman!" He roared. "I have stood here long enough bandying words with you. As I see it you have two choices. You may do as I have ordered: Send your ostlers to help my men with the change of horses, show my daughter and her cousin up to their rooms as arranged, and give us all food and water...Or," he continued, gesturing behind him, "I will unleash my men!" And with a signal of his hand his men all drew their swords, laying them over their shoulders and settling themselves more firmly in their saddles in preparation for an immediate attack.

"They will be worse than the Flemish Wolves whom Prince John is pleased to use on visits such as this," de Brocas threatened darkly. "They will tear this place apart, I promise you. Let us in and we will be away before the dawn. Deny us and we will destroy you! We are come from Castle Malwood, and if you know Sir Yvo and his family, and do not wish to enjoy the King's displeasure in this business, Master Robert Forester, late of King Henry's army out of France," he said sardonically. "You will let me and my daughter and her cousin in at once, and provide food and shelter for my men. Or by the King's Grace, you will rue the day that you were born, *I promise you!*"

Robert looked down into the fierce face of the Baron de Brocas, his eyes flicking sideways to take account of the others in the Baron's party...especially the well armed and mounted soldiers who were even then pushing their horses forward and menacingly swinging their swords, and he pondered. He had seen such men before...and he knew all about the Prince's 'Flemish Wolves'! Bloodthirsty mercenaries who cared for nothing but their pay! And while he liked neither the look of these travellers who had arrived so suddenly out of the storm, nor the tone of voice used towards him...he had no desire to have them turn Rose's home into kindling, which he had no doubt

180

they would do given only half a chance! Also the casual use of the Malwood name, and of Sir Yvo and the King, spoke of comradeship, not strangeness. And he knew force majeur when he saw it staring him hotly in the face, so there was a pause, while both men stared angrily at each other, the horses fidgeted with stamping hooves and the baron's men waited for him to order their attack.

Then, lifting his sword onto his shoulder, Robert stepped aside, and opening the door wide behind him, he waved the Baron through to the large room that lay beyond.

"Of course you must come in," he said then, as de Brocas pushed past him, his hard body brushing across Robert's chest. "I will send some varlets to look to your needs, and men to help with the horses, and I will speak with my cousin about the rest. In truth, My Lord, there are two rooms that do not have guests in them and Edward Sergeant has an unusual number of fine horses in the stables above the yard. Maybe they are the ones you requested? Hey! What ails the lass?" he questioned suddenly, as he saw Rochine and one of the Baron's men supporting Alicia between them as they came out of the rushing darkness. "We already have one case of the fever in this house. Mistress Sergeant will not want another!"

"*Hush!* You foolish man," Rochine hissed at him. "This is my cousin. She has no fever, but a falling branch caught her as we rode along through the storm. God alone knows how we got here without more injuries, the wind has been so violent. Do not worry over her, she is a poor mazed creature at the best of times anyway," she went on sadly, crossing herself and casting her eyes up to God. "Her wits have always strayed from her since her birth, poor child. A few hours rest and she will be fine, I promise you."

"But she is bound!" Robert exclaimed sharply, taking a step towards them both, as he noticed the straps that still secured Alicia's wrists.

"Of course she is bound!" Rochine answered swiftly, stepping sideways to shield Alicia from Robert's gaze, her green eyes staring boldly into his puzzled blue ones. "If we do not do this, then she has been known to harm herself when the fit is on her. Be assured, Master Forester," she went on, her voice softening with her gaze, to melting sweetness, laying her hand gently on his arm as she spoke: "We who love her well know how best to care for her. Just get one of your abigails to show us to our rooms and all will be well I promise you."

And giving him a lovely smile she turned away, crooning over Alicia's slumped body as she wrapped the cloak closely about her, and swept past him to the foot of the stairs where, looking back at him over her shoulder she said forcefully: "*The abigail*, you silly man! The abigail! My cousin needs warmth and rest, and without one of your girls to show me where to go, that cannot be. Hurry now, before the fit comes on her again!"

Momentarily Robert Forester paused, his sharp eyes full of questions, his brow furrowed with uncertainty. While what he had been told made sense...he knew about mazelings...it did not 'feel' right somehow. He watched her pause upon the first step, the girl on her arm still drooping against her, her eyes unfocussed, her arms almost floppy at her side. The soldier with her, also holding the girl firmly in his grasp. Too firmly? Too forceful? He was not sure. Watching them Robert was aware of a heightened sense of urgency...almost of danger, and everyone seemed momentarily frozen in their places: The girls on the stair; the men around him who had followed them in; the Baron's leading man, helmet in his hand, head thrust forward...and especially the Baron himself who seemed almost poised for action, his hand on his sword and his eyes black, penetrating, seeking almost to devour his very soul.

Robert shivered and shook his head.

Then, turning away from the three figures on the stairs, he clapped his hands and called loudly for help, which appeared almost instantly as a number of maids and other servants came through from the rooms beyond, to offer help and sustenance to this weary band of travellers. The sound was both sharp and sudden...and, just as suddenly, the little tableau around him broke into movement: Rochine walked up the stairs, closely followed by a pretty abigail in white wimple and blue dress; de Vere put his helmet down and moved to join some of his men; the Baron turned to stand before the fireplace where he kicked a pile of smouldering logs into blazing life...while the remainder of his men banged and stamped their way into the inn, alert for food and wine, or good English ale, the threat of sudden action no longer on their minds.

With one further sharp look around, Robert Forester opened an iron studded oak door that led to the back of the inn and disappeared.

Chapter 27... The White Rose in torment.

From the moment Alicia had ridden past the swinging signboard into the wide inn yard she had been on tenterhooks of expectation. Even being hauled unceremoniously off her horse like a worn sack of oats and then dragged upright by Rochine had not unduly shaken her, as she was certain of almost immediate rescue.

"Now, my Lady Fair," Rochine had hissed violently in her ear, as she had taken hold of her from her father. "*One* word from you... *One* sign that you are about to scream or make a run for it, and you will feel this bodkin of mine pierce your breast!" And with a twist of her arm she had shown Alicia the needle-pointed dagger she always carried hidden up the long sleeve of her dress.

"But your father said..."

"...My father says a lot of things, you little *whore!*" she hissed at her venomously. "My sooo sweet *Cousin!*" she added a moment later, with biting sarcasm, pushing the dagger against Alicia's breast until she heard the girl gasp. "But it is *I* who have you in my hold, *not* him, sweetheart! And I would cut your pretty tits off, before I would let you threaten our safety now! Do you wish to die, Alicia? Struck through to your heart? You and all the others in this wretched place?" she hissed at her, shaking her head fiercely towards the inn as she spoke.

"No!" Alicia mumbled desperately through her silken gag, shaking her head vehemently. "*No!*"

"Then be *still,* you little *bitch!*" She spat in her ear. "And all will be well, for you at least!"

"What do you want with me?"

"Your silence!" Rochine shot back at her, pressing her dagger back against her cousin's breast until she gasped again. And silent she was!

Nevertheless, Alicia remained confident in the strength and willingness of her old nurse, Rose Sergeant and of Edward her formidable husband to help her. She was equally secure in the knowledge that the Baron and his daughter had no idea that she was known to the Innkeeper and his wife, nor that she

183

knew the Saracen's Head like the back of her hand. Certainly she had never mentioned it to Rochine when they had been talking together before the party…when they had been together in her room. And she thanked God for it! Just let Rose or Edward get one sight, or sound of her, and she would be free. She was sure of it. Not just because of the love he and Rose had for her…but because he had been Sir Yvo's Master-at-Arms, had fought with him all over France and to whom he owed both his life and his livelihood also. They would not fail her, and her body stiffened in expectation.

Rochine, feeling her suddenly tense, immediately swung her away from the light, and pushing her into Draco's arms she seized Alicia's face and whipped the silken gag away from it. Then, before the girl could react or cry out, she forced her teeth apart with her leather covered fingers and thrusting the metal end of a small flask between them, squeezed a swift burst of fiery fluid down her throat, forcing more in, no matter how much the girl spluttered and spat it out, 'til her mouth was filled and she was forced to swallow. Then the door had opened…and whatever dreams Alicia's might have had of immediate rescue died with them.

She had no idea who the man was? She had never seen him before in her life! Where was Edward Sergeant? Where was Rose?

By then, held fast in Draco's grasp, and swiftly surrounded by others of the Baron's escort, there was no-one to see or hear her gasps and desperate struggles as she fought for her freedom, like a butterfly in a spider's web. Try as she might, no amount of bucking or kicking could get her free and with her mouth filled once more with silk, and her throat gagging and retching, she could not scream out either. And as she struggled…so the potion that Rochine had forced down her took effect. Everything around her seemed to slow down and lose its everyday form and structure: voices became an indistinct mumble of sound and her arms and legs seemed to be weighed down with lead, until every movement became a dreadful effort, beyond her strength to achieve, like wading through treacle or crossing a soaked field of freshly ploughed clay in heavy boots!

Faces, in weird visions of colour, came and went before her eyes in exaggerated form and shape: eyes like huge plates of coloured glass; faces vast as pink moons; mouths like caverns, and speech like the booming surf on a rockbound coast. And so she had been brought in and almost carried upstairs to her room above, her thoughts scrambled in a whirling torment, the room spinning and wheeling and twisting around her until, with the suddenness of a candle flame extinguished by a summer's breeze, her eyes closed, her mind shut down, and she was plunged into dreamless, impenetrable darkness.

What seemed hours later, Alicia came dizzily awake to find a child looking at her from a pair of huge, solemn blue eyes thickly fringed with long blonde eyelashes, A somewhat grubby child in short kirtle and pink chemise, with an equally grubby thumb thrust firmly into her mouth and a stuffed rabbit under her arm.

Alicia goggled at her in amazement.

It was an Angel-Child! A girl Angel-Child, small and rosy cheeked; barefooted and dressed in a long blue kirtle that hung almost to the ground, with a small stuffed rabbit clutched safely under one arm. And no wings! Why were there no wings? She thought, looking puzzled. And did Angel-Children have little stuffed bunny rabbits with black button noses? Did Angels have children? She smiled foolishly and giggled at the wicked thoughts of Angels making babies! Where would they put their wings? She held her hands out to the Angel-Child. Tied hands. Tied hands? She looked at them uncomprehendingly and wriggled them. Why did she have tied hands? She shook them again, waggling her fingers, and giggled at the Angel-Child, and stuck out her tongue. The Angel-Child sucked in her breath and smiled. Just like me! She thought, the idea swimming lazily round her head.

That's it! That's me! I've died and gone to heaven and this is me as a child, with Flopsy tucked under my arm. Look! It's even got the same furry body as my Flopsy had, with blue buttons for its eyes, a black button nose, a sloppy smile and a *huge* white cotton burst for a tail. And she giggled again, reaching out to touch this strange Alicia-Child, mumbling Flopsy's name as she did so...and gasped as the little figure moved suddenly away, its blue eyes opening wide in fright.

And it suddenly became desperately important that this miraculous child shouldn't go.

It was important that the Alicia-Child, with the soft furry rabbit in her arms should stay and talk with her. But she knew this child, didn't she? Or was it the rabbit she knew? A Rabbit-Child, with too many thumbs and huge blue eyes and a white fluffy tail. She giggled foolishly and blew raspberries, making

185

the Rabbit-Child laugh. Almost cross-eyed with concentration, she reached out her hands and slowly said her name: "Al–ic–i–a. Al–ic–ia, Honeyone."

"No! Mar–ga–ret!" The little Alicia-Child said carefully, pointing to herself. "I'm Mar–ga–ret!" She enunciated again with great care, each syllable coming out with sober clarity. Then, first pointing to herself and then to her she said: "*I'm* Margaret. *You* are Alicia. Lady Alicia de Burley…and you're funny!" And she chuckled at her cleverness and daring.

Alicia lay there stunned, her world still going round and round in circles, as she struggled to force her brain to work properly. What was she doing here? How did she know this child? And how did this child know her? Why were her hands tied she wondered, holding them up amazed? Then bending to look owlishly at the tight knots holding them together she shook them in the air again and giggled. And where were her clothes? Why was she only in her underskirt?

She groaned and held her forehead in her hands, her eyes closed against the dreadful pain that suddenly lanced across her brows. Why did her head feel so…so *awful?* She *never* had headaches! It felt as if the castle blacksmith was humouring out Gui's armour…! Castle? Blacksmith? Gui…Gui?…*Gui!!* And with that came full, blinding recognition and remembrance, and she gasped, struggling then to sit up, moaning piteously as she did so.

"You *are* Margaret!" She croaked out at last. "Margaret Sergeant. And this is the Saracen's Head at Lyndhurst. Sweet *Jesus!* And I *am* the Lady Alicia de Burley! Oh, Dear God, Honeyone," she groaned again, sitting up. "Help me, little one! Help me! Where's your Daddy? Where's Edward, and your Mummy, Rose?"

"Mummy's with Peter. He's got the fever and Daddy's gone to fetch more herbs from the monks at Beaulieu. He left two days ago. Father Matthew, the Master Herbalist from Ellingham Prory has been looking after Peter until today. He's not long been gone. He said…"

"*Sweetheart!*" Alicia broke in desperately. "Quickly, little one, *Quickly!* Take me to your Mummy now. There is not a moment to spare!" and swinging her legs over the side of the bed, she instinctively reached out for the little girl's hand…only to see the child back away, eyes like saucers in sudden uncertainty and fear, stuffed rabbit grasped in one hand, her whole little body poised for flight, like a deer at a waterhole who hears the crack of timber in the forest and fears a hunter! For one heart-stopping moment Alicia thought the child was going to scream. Her eyes closed and her mouth opened, she saw

186

her take one almighty breath, knowing that she was too far away to reach her, and knowing that any sound at that moment would ruin them all.

But…nothing happened!

Even though it had been a long time since she had last seen Alicia…training will out, and Margaret knew well enough who the half-naked lady with the tied hands truly was, and to know that her mother, and her father too, regarded this woman with deep respect and affection. And fear of her mother's anger was a far greater spur to her intent…than fear of the funny lady with tied hands and naked breasts! So she shut her mouth with a snap, opened her eyes and took the funny lady's hand, and moments later she and Alicia were out of the room, along the narrow gallery and through the end door that led, via a maze of little stairs and passages, to her parent's apartments at the very rear of the inn.

Gasping for breath, Alicia was led along still feeling frighteningly wobbly on her feet, like being on a ship at sea in a cross current, and just as queasy! Without hesitation Margaret led Alicia right to where her mother was kneeling down beside her son's pallet, a wet flannel in one hand, and a small glazed mug full of steaming liquid in the other. Beginning to turn with hot words of anger on her lips, fuelled by anxiety, with which to rip into her daughter…who'd been told under *no* circumstances was she to go anywhere *near* her brother's room!…the woman took one horrified look over her shoulder, and was struck dumb at the sight before her.

For there, out of nowhere was her own Lady Alicia, half-naked, in only her underskirt, and with her hands bound together with the silken ties that Rochine had devised before they'd left Castle Malwood some scant hours earlier! It was a wonder she did not drop the mug of hot physic she was holding in her hand, and indulge herself in a swift burst of strong hysterics! Many would have done so. But Rose Sergeant was not one of them

Tall and finely built, with her flaxen hair piled up on her head, dressed in a long bliaut of cream woollen cloth embroidered with wayside flowers and grasses, she was an arresting sight. Her eyes bright with anger at her daughter's intemperate arrival, she looked what she was a determined, mature, good-looking woman in the midst of ministering to a sickly child, and annoyed at being so unnecessarily interrupted by a youngster who had been warned and should have known better!

"Mercy, Mary, *Mother of God!*" She spluttered out after a moment's complete shock, during which she very nearly *did* drop the mug she was holding! "My Lady? *Alicia!*" she gasped putting the little mug down on a table, and getting swiftly to her feet she almost ran across the room to greet her. "What brings you here? And dressed like…like *that?*" She stammered, appalled. "And…and *tied!*" she continued, automatically undoing Alicia's bonds as she stood mute before her, her hands held out in supplication. "Here, cover yourself with that," she said, putting a long woollen wrap round her naked shoulders. "If one of the servants came in here for anything, my lovely, they'd have a fit!"

"Oh, my Rose," Alicia replied in a rush, tears flooding her eyes, and reaching for her hands as she spoke. "You have no idea what has been going on! And I haven't the time to tell you it all now, but I must get away from here immediately. *Immediately*, my precious love! Any moment my absence may be discovered and the hunt will be up…"

"…What hunt, my Lady?" she interrupted her, amazed. "And where's Sir Gui? Surely…"

"This *is* about Sir Gui, Rose," she replied urgently. "These people who have seized me…"

"What people, my Lady? Who has seized you?"

"Those from whom little Margaret has just rescued me…"

"From here? In the Saracen's Head? Sweet Jesus, Alicia. What are you saying?"

"Oh Rose! *I don't have the time to tell you,*" she answered desperately. "Just trust me that it is so indeed. There are bad men below. Wicked *Frenchmen!* Who are like to murder you all if I do not escape from here at once!"

"But…but you are among friends here, my Lady," Rose Sergeant went on, shaking her head in confusion, still holding onto Alicia's hands. "No–one would dare to harm you under this roof. The King's Grace would not allow it!"

"The King's Grace, my love, is in France," Alicia replied sharply, with raised eyebrows and a swift shrug. "And below stairs are a party of well-armed and murderous Frenchmen who will stop at nothing to seize me and hold me close. If I do not flee from here they will tear this place apart and kill everyone they can lay their hands on! Believe me, Rose. They will do this!"

"*Christ's Mercy, Alicia*!" she whispered, horrified. "My little ones as well?

"*Everyone*, Rose! They have already murdered Sir Yvo and his wife…"

"*No!*" She gasped her face ashen with shock.

"*Yes!*…and set Malwood Castle ablaze, probably from end to end by now."

"And Sir Gui, Sweetheart?" She almost whispered, her tears already beginning to flow.

"I don't know, Rose!" Alicia cried out then in anguish, raising her fists in frustration. "*I don't know!* They say he is dead, killed in the fire, and it might be true. They certainly think it is so and, God knows, the fire was fierce enough to burst the stones apart. But I don't know that I believe them. I don't *want* to believe them. And when they told me that everyone was killed and I should go with them…I couldn't do it, Rose. *Wouldn't!* So they forced me from there. Drugged me, bound me and dragged me from my home!"

"*Drugged you?* Who are these people, Alicia?" She cried out, her eyes round with horror.

"My French Cousins!" she said fiercely, shaking her fists in rage. "The Lord Baron Sir Roger de Brocas and his daughter, the Lady Rochine. You have heard of them I know…"

"Yes, of course I have my Lady. His Great Aunt, the Lady Phillipa, married your Grandfather, Sir Ralph. But why?"

"*I don't know why!*" she wailed. "I only know that you have her great nephew and his daughter below stairs eating their heads off, while waiting to set sail from Southampton tomorrow, and thinking me to be tied up and dead to the world upstairs with one of her foul potions! And when they find I am gone, Rose, all hell will break out around you. I *cannot* let that happen. You must help me to escape before that happens, Sweetheart. *You must!*"

189

"Of course I will help you, my Lady," Rose answered her swiftly. "Sweet Mary, what a time for my man to be from home!" she cried out, turning round to call her daughter to her. "Margaret!" she said gently, hunkering down before the little girl, holding her shoulders with both hands as she did so. "Go you swiftly now, my poppet, and ask Master Robert to step upstairs at once! Go only to Master Forester and tell him that Peter has taken a turn for the worse, and that I need him in my parlour immediately! Now go, Honeyone," she urged her, turning her to face the door. "Quickly and quietly my dearling, and you shall have a whole sugar plum to yourself when you get back!"

"Still tempting with sugar plums, then?" Alicia asked with a sudden chuckle, remembering her own childhood, as the little girl bustled swiftly away, her rabbit still clutched under one arm.

"They never fail!" Rose Sergeant said, looking round with a smile as her daughter disappeared. "They didn't fail with you, my Lady...and they don't with her either! Now, my dearest, come quickly and let's see what I have will fit you, for it is certain that you cannot go junketing about the Forest like that!"

With that the two women set-too with a vengeance, and by the time Robert duly arrived with young Margaret in tow, narrow eyed and anxious about little Peter, Alicia was dressed and ready for the road. Robert stared, as well he might.

"You're that woman they brought with them!" The tall russet-haired man said when he had got over the shock of seeing her standing there. "I thought you said young Peter was ailing, Rose?" he asked then. "Who is this woman? They said she was a mazeling."

"Well, Robert Forester," Rose said, getting to her feet and putting her hands on her hips. "A mazeling she most definitely is not! This young lady, whom you saw being brought into this inn, is the Lady Alicia de Burley, my very own sweet nurseling, the chosen bride of Sir Gui de Malwood and King Richard's own Ward! And those blackguards below have murdered her guardian, Sir Yvo and his wife, *and* Sir Gui for all we know, set Castle Malwood afire and stolen her away!"

"*Dear God!*" The tall man said, sinking onto a stool and crossing himself. "And I've been giving them of our best since they arrived..."

"…And you must continue to do so," Rose said urgently. "They are desperate men, Robert. And too many for us to fight, especially with Edward away from home, so the longer they can be kept busy downstairs the better!"

"My Lady," he said, turning to where Alicia was standing. "I had no idea. I am so sorry. I thought something was not quite right, and I didn't like the big man's attitude, nor the way his men were behaving, but I have seen what men like them can do when they have a mind to it, and it seemed better to let them in than to have them put us all to the fire and the sword."

"Which they would have done, Robert, assuredly." Alicia replied with a grim smile, giving him her hand. "Have no qualms, over this. You saw what they wanted you to see. They are good at it. But I must get away, *now!* Before that hellion, my *so* sweet cousin, finds that I am gone."

"Go now, Robert," Rose said urgently pushing him towards the door. "Saddle my chestnut mare, Sunburst. She is both fleet of foot and courageous. The best in our stables next to Gingerbread, and Edward has him. Quickly now," she went on, holding the door open for him to leave. "We will be right behind you. Where will you go?" she asked Alicia, turning towards her.

"Home! Back the way we came. It is the only way I know."

"No! You can't do that!" She counselled her urgently, pausing to settle her daughter, now drooping with sleep, into a big chair nearby. "They are bound to follow you, and follow you hard. All it will need is for you to make one error and they will be onto you like bees to a honeycomb! No my lovely, you must take the second turning to the right after you leave the town's edge. It is a shorter route through the Forest to Malwood, and known only to those who live here. It is the road taken by Father Matthew and his party."

"Father Matthew?"

"The Benedictine Herbalist from Ellingham Priory. He was on his way to your betrothal ceremony, but stayed to help with Peter. He saved the boy's life."

"My betrothal ceremony?" Alicia asked amazed, as Rose hurried her along. "I don't understand. Who?....Why?.."

"There is no time now for any explanation, Sweetheart," Rose said swiftly, as they scampered down a short flight of stairs. "Suffice it that he has been this way before and knows us all well. He left not more than a few hours ago, a horse and small tilt cart and two other brothers with him, all determined to reach Malwood before nightfall if possible despite the storm. He would have been with you yesterday, had it not been for Peter's illness. Pray God you meet up with him. No Baron, be he ever so bold, would dare to seize you while you are under the protection of Holy Church!"

Alicia who was none too sure that anything would stop de Brocas from achieving his ends, smiled at Rose's words, knowing they were warmly meant. She just didn't know the nature of the foe whom they were up against! Nevertheless, turning swiftly, she hugged her fiercely. "How can I ever thank you, my Dearest Rose?"

"By getting clean away, silly! Now…hush!" she whispered. "We are at the yard's entrance. Robert should have Sunburst standing for you just outside. Go now, swiftly, my darling. And God's Blessings be on you tonight!"

"How long do I have…"

"…Before they follow you? Not long I expect. But don't worry, Honeyone. They will have to saddle-up first, and in the darkness and all the rush, there is bound to be some confusion. We will do our part, I promise you. Remember, the second turning on the right. Now, *go!*" And with that, Rose opened the door, and Alicia slipped through into the sighing darkness.

Outside the rain had stopped at last and the cruel wind had died down to a stiff breeze. A large moon was showing between the still hurrying clouds, its pale silver light turning the wet cobbles of the inn yard into shaded pools of quicksilver that shimmered and moved as the trees of the Forest, which came close to the building at that point, bowed and dipped their branches over them. Stepping softly out of the yard door, Alicia flitted across to where Robert held the chestnut mare tightly by the bit, the reins already over her head as she stamped her hooves, nervous of the darkness and the twisting shadows all around her and she snorted, missing the warmth and safe comfort of her stable.

"Will she be alright?" Alicia asked him, watching the mare as she nervously flicked her ears backwards and forwards and scraped at the cobbles with her left forefoot.

"Don't worry, my Lady. She will be fine. She's just a little anxious. Once you are up, and she can feel your hands on her mouth, she will be fine, I promise you. She'll not tip you off, and she's as brave as a lion."

"It's not lions, I want this night, Robert," she chuckled. "It's Pegasus himself! Now, come on. Give me a leg-up and let's get this play on the cart! There isn't a minute to lose!"

And indeed she was right, for just as she was struggling to thrust her feet into the stirrups, there was a great shout of rage from within, and moments later the outer door was flung wide open with a crash, spilling bright yellow light and shouting men out across the dappled yard.

"Stand clear, man!" Alicia shouted to Robert at Sunburst's head and, sitting back deep in her tall saddle as any knight would, she pointed the mare's head at the yard's wide entrance and stabbed in her heels. With a scream Sunburst reared up as she fought for purchase on the silver wet stones and then, with a great shout and a mighty buffet from Robert's hand on her hindquarters, she was away in a shower of sparks, tail streaming out behind her, thundering down amongst de Brocas's men as they fell over themselves in a mad panic, some to try and escape the mare's flashing hooves, some to try and stop her by waving their arms or reaching out to grab at the reins as she hurtled towards them.

In the end, only one man managed to get a hand to Sunburst's bridle, but Alicia was ready for him. Slipping her steel tipped boot out of its stirrup so she could take him on the chin with her stiffened leg like a lance, she struck his face a fearful blow, and with a dreadful cry he was tossed away as she flew past him. Then she was out of the inn yard and away, leaving a wild tangle of furious, yelling men behind her as she galloped off into the night.

Behind her in the inn yard everything was rage and turmoil as de Brocas and de Vere struggled to bring order from the chaos Alicia's sudden flight had created.

All had been peaceful for several hours since their arrival. Rochine had overseen Alicia's bedding, stripping the wet clothes off her and roughly towelling her supine body; leaving her half-naked, in only her underskirt, so that if she did wake up she would think twice about running away. Since then she had been up several times to check on her, cruelly twisting her flesh with her hard fingers to be certain of her cousin's unconsciousness, and each time she had been satisfied that the drug she had so brutally administered was still keeping her fair cousin suitably sedated.

Meanwhile food had been brought in by the inn varlets and serving girls under the steady eye of Robert Forester, and the fire had been built up so that it blazed brightly in the great hearth, spreading goodwill and humour amongst all those gathered there, for despite it being June the great storm and freezing rainstorm had driven a sharp chill into everyone. The Lady, in particular, was in sparkling form, hanging on to her father's arm and laughing up into his face with all the joy of a young girl with her lover.

Wine was brought and quaffed from wooden cups and horn beakers, and ale and rough cider from large leather Jacks dark with age and usage, while trays of meats and fresh white bread, the best the Inn could offer, were brought round by the serving wenches, themselves chosen as much for their looks and bold natures as for their skills at serving. Having been dragged from their beds to serve the needs of such important foreign company as the Lord Baron Sir Roger de Brocas and his daughter, just newly come from the betrothing party of the noblest local family in all the Forest, the girls were determined to do their best to please, so there was soon all the makings of a rollicking good party.

Then...in a moment, all that had changed.

Rochine, having disappeared upstairs once more to check on their all important captive, was suddenly screaming with rage from the stair-head: "The bitch has gone, father! *The bloody little bitch has gone!*"

194

"What do you mean, '*Gone!*'?" He demanded furiously, running up the stairs towards her. "She *can't* have gone. You left her drugged, tied and half-naked in a locked room. She can't possibly have gone *anywhere!* Show me!" And forcing his way past her he rushed into the room where Alicia had been placed.

"*God's Blood, Rochine!*" He roared at his daughter, now standing ashen faced before him as her father thrashed around the room, lashing out at the walls and throwing the empty bedclothes at her face. "*Where is she?* How could she have got out of a locked room?"

He stared in fury at his daughter, his eyes narrowing with rage as he watched her drop her head: "Now, don't tell me, daughter," he said then, lowering his voice to a deeply menacing whisper as he moved to walk round her, now standing petrified in the middle of the room. "Don't tell me it was not locked," he went on, grabbing her hair and twisting it in his powerful hands. "I really do not want to hear that, my Lady!" He went on, each word accompanied by a further vicious twist of her hair till her neck was almost turned sideways against her shoulders.

"She was drugged and tied, my Lord," she cried out to him, her eyes watering from the pain. "I thought she was safe for another hour."

"*Sweet Wine of Christ, Rochine!* But I will have your hide for this," he snarled at her, flinging her head away. "You did not lock the fucking room!" Then, turning, he leaped down the stairs, two at a time, roaring for de Vere to bring up the horses with all possible speed, ordering some of his men to search the Inn, and others outside into the yard to try and stop her should she try escaping from the Inn. And for several minutes there was true pandemonium as de Vere and the handful of the troopers he had with him spilled out into the inn yard, almost falling over themselves in their eagerness to carry out their orders, with the result that they were an unbalanced, disorganised mob by the time they realised what was happening, and totally unprepared for the chestnut thunderbolt, all flying hooves, mane and tail, that crashed amongst them moments later.

Only one man managed to lay a hand on the fleeing girl's bridle, and he received such a kick that his head was nearly ripped off, leaving him minus a tooth, and his face torn from eye socket to jaw-line where the girl's steel tipped boot had raked him. And the wound poured blood through his clutching fingers as he crouched down sobbing with pain on the cobbled yard, while de Vere harried the rest to bring up the horses. But of course they had been changed from those they had ridden earlier, and somehow all were in the corral,

195

not in their stables as they had expected, and had to be caught up and saddled before anything further could be done.

Inside the confusion was just as great, as de Brocas bellowed and raged at those few men still left inside after de Vere and the others had rushed out into the night.

"Bring me the man Forester and that fucking whore, his mistress, the owner of this...this *hovel!*" He raged. "They must have aided the little bitch! *God's Blood,* but I will have his guts out upon this floor and the woman's tits flayed! And this whole wretched hovel razed to the ground in a heap of ashes, and everyone within it! Upon my life, I swear it!"

"Not this night, my Lord Baron," came a soft reply from above him, "And not in this house either. We do not suffer such wickedness in England. We protect our women from such filth as you. And you will have to see your daughter dead first before you can see my guts, my Lord Baron."

And coming slowly down the stairs was Robert Forester, one huge hand pinioning the Lady Rochine's arms behind her back, the other holding his sword in such a way, that he might indeed almost cut her head off with a single stroke should he so desire; and half way down the stairs he began to shout in the hugest voice that many had heard: *"Ho, the house!* Ho the house! Robbers and bandits are loose amongst us! *Rise Up!* Rise Up! Draw swords and fight! *Ho the house!* **Ho the house!**" His great voice booming and rattling round the inn 'til it seemed certain they would hear it all the way to Southampton.

And with that there was the most unholy, wild flurry of noise and commotion as from every door along the gallery there issued forth a stream of guests. Many of them, already aware that something wrong was happening, from all the shouts and yells that had been going on some minutes before, were already dressed and armed for no man, be he ever so hardy, would walk the Forest tracks or lead his sumpter mules and pack ponies without some weapon by his side. In moments it seemed to the Baron and his men that there were a dozen armed men glaring down at them from the gallery above.

"Take your daughter, Baron, and leave this house at once! While you still have life and limb to do so. Or do you and your bully boys chance your arm this night against these men and I? We are all good Englishmen here..."

"...*And Normans!*" Came another great voice, rich in its tones, and dark with anger. "Now...what thieves and vagabonds cause such a hurly burly in my house, that I need almost to be thrown from my horse as I return? And why do I find it filled with armed men who would be better off asleep than fighting?" And into the room below, from the door opposite the main entrance to the inn, stepped a huge, dark-haired man. A veritable giant of a man, with a bull neck and weather beaten face, arms like the knotted branches of an oak, a long sword hanging by his side and a club the size of a weaver's beam in his mighty hands.

His sudden appearance behind the Baron's men brought immediate silence. Even the Baron, no small man himself, was momentarily quelled by both the enormous size and powerful presence of this unexpected adversary.

"I am no vagabond, and my men are not thieves!" The Baron spoke haughtily, drawing himself up to his full height, loosening the muscles across his broad back as he did so. "I am the Lord Baron Sir Roger de Brocas, come from the betrothal of Sir Gui de Malwood. You must be Edward Sergeant, with whom arrangements were made for me to stay in this place," he stated, his hot black eyes staring at the giant innkeeper standing loose-limbed before him. "I had heard you kept a good house. I see I was misinformed!" Then, switching his burning glare to Robert Forester, he ordered furiously: "Put up your sword and release my daughter at once! I see we will get no justice here. There will be no fighting either. We leave in pursuit of certain property entrusted to me by King Richard himself!"

And turning to his men, who had been standing in gawping immobility before Edward Sergeant's massive bulk, he snarled: "You dolts! Move yourselves! And you, you parcel of Forest swine," he raged at Edward and those who had rushed to support him. "You have not heard the last of this, I promise you!"

And as Rochine came running down the stairs so his men rushed out into the night, and with a final blazing glance around him, de Brocas swept out, closing the door behind him with a crash and leaped up on Charlemagne's back to chase after Alicia into the Forest.

Chapter 30...*How the Lion was saved from the Baron's Fiery Furnace.*

I t was the heat that brought Gui back to his senses.

That and the thick smoke that rolled and billowed down the stone corridor in choking waves, making him cough and splutter violently. His breathing was taut and laboured, and he felt crushed beneath the weight of the huge beam that had fallen across his back, together with the chunks of smashed masonry and plaster that had come down with it. Yet, miraculously, not only was he still alive, but, as he struggled desperately to free himself, he realised that he was no more badly injured than before, for there was sense and movement in all his limbs. Though his left shoulder, where de Brocas's bolt had struck him, was in agony, for the head was still lodged there, forced even further into the joint by the huge beam lying across him.

By some quirk of its construction, as the ceiling had given way the great timber that had struck him had twisted as it fell, and only given him a glancing blow, before lodging firmly across the wide passageway. And, though he'd collapsed as though pole-axed when it had hit him, it had finally come to rest with one corner wedged against the far wall, where it met the floor and the other end jammed into the masonry just above his head. This had left a small gap between the great wooden truss and the floor, and it was there that he lay, like a beetle beneath a giant's thumb, pinned firmly to the hard stone flags yet still just space for him to breathe and move his arms and legs.

All around him the building was creaking and groaning, the rumbling sound of falling masonry and the roar and crackle of the flames as the fire spread coming clearly to him amidst the ferocious heat, leaving his face streaked with grime as the sweat poured off him through the dust that had cascaded down when the ceiling had collapsed.

Luckily, however, the fire had spread away from him, down the stairs from his parent's room to the Hall below which, from the warmth beginning to

198

radiate from the far wall, must be burning fiercely. If he didn't manage somehow to wriggle free soon then either he would be roasted by the fire or choked to death by the smoke. So, as the heat increased so he began to struggle frantically, scrabbling with his hands at the stone flags until his nails were ripped and his hands were torn and bleeding as he fought to free himself. But try as he might he was totally unable to move his body in any direction. Yet, unless he could get free soon, or someone came to his aid, then he would surely die, for either more debris would fall on him or he'd finally be overcome by the heat and the bitter acrid fumes from the fire now raging unchecked beneath him. Either way, it was only a question of time before his strength gave out and he collapsed into a fatal stupor.

Dear God, but he'd been so close to splitting that bastard in two! There was absolutely no way he could possibly have escaped...and the bloody man had been armed after all! He winced in pain, as the broad-headed crossbow bolt so firmly lodged in his shoulder, grated against the bone every time he moved. At least as long as it was stuck there he would not lose too much blood. What cursed misfortune to have slipped at such a crucial moment! And in the flaring darkness that surrounded him he grimaced fiercely.

God's Blood, but he must get free somehow! And with a burst of renewed energy he tried once more to heave his body up against the beam with all his remaining strength, but to absolutely no avail. He simply could not get a purchase on anything, either to push upwards, forwards or back, and with a sob of frustrated rage he slumped down again, exhausted.

★

Outside was a scene of near pandemonium as everyone hurried desperately to save what they could before the flames engulfed everything.

Horses were being led away at a run from the stables and soldiers and servants were scurrying round with boxes and bundles of baggage and trappings, all flung out in the first few moments after the New Hall had been so fatally struck. But of Sir Yvo, the Lady Margaret, and Sir Gui there was no sign, and in all the confusion no-one paused to give the Lady Alicia a thought. Her rooms were not in any immediate danger, and she'd always resisted interference anyway. She would surely be along presently, and maybe she would know where Sir Gui was. For where she was concerned, he was never far away!

Sir Richard L'Eveque was sleeping in his private chamber on the South side of the Great Keep when he was told that the castle was on fire. Despite the fury of the storm, with its howling wind and torrential rain, he was soundly asleep and had no idea there was anything amiss, so it was some time before a breathless messenger could force his way through the milling press to tell him what had happened; as with a thunderous crash on his door one of his men burst it open and stood panting, soaked and dishevelled in the doorway, to deliver his message.

"*Splendour of God, man!*" Sir Richard cried out, leaping up for his sword in his half-awake state, believing the castle to be under attack. "What the hell's going on?

"*Sir Richard!*" the man shouted desperately, rushing into the room. "Come quickly, My Lord. The castle's on fire! The New Hall is going up like a torch and we can't find Sir Yvo or any of his family!"

"Sweet Jesus, Thomas! I thought the Hounds of Hell were at the gates at least! Calm down man! Here, throw me those trousers and give me my working jacket. You'll find it in that cupboard over there, and for pity's sake stop gaping like an idiot and tell me calmly what you know."

"It was when the storm passed directly overhead," Thomas Ringwood, one of his chosen men replied, panting as he helped Sir Richard on with the tough leather jacket he liked to wear when he was working. "A huge bolt of lightning struck the New Hall right above Sir Yvo's rooms. A streak of blue-white fire it was, followed by a huge ***Bang!*** he said, waving his arms in the air. "Then, almost immediately, the building was struck twice more, Sir Richard...and in the same place. We thought it was the Devil's work, My Lord!" And with a white face, still shocked at what had happened, the soldier instinctively crossed himself.

"For God's sake get on with it, man," his Guard Commander said, giving him a hearty shake. "The Devil's Work indeed! For Heaven's sake, stop being so foolish! This is not the first storm we've had here. No, and not the first time the castle's been struck more than once either! So what happened to cause such a terrible fire?"

"I've no idea, Sir Richard, it was unbelievable! Within minutes it seemed the place was ablaze. The fire spread so quickly that we only had time to rescue a few things before we were driven back by the smoke and flames. I never saw a fire take hold so quickly! "

"What about Sir Gui and his parents?" L'Eveque shot back at him, tugging his long, leather boots on as he did so.

"*We cannot find them!* The main stairs are impassable, the rear staircase has already collapsed and the flames are spreading. The building will soon be aflame from end to end, other buildings nearby are going up already. The Master-at-Arms thought you'd best be called immediately, Sir Richard. You know the building better than anyone, and we have no plans for anything as bad as this. The courtyard is full of people, animals and clutter, and it is proving hard to get them organised."

"Where is Sir James?"

"Not in the castle. He went earlier with some of the guests..."

"*God's Wounds,* lad, so he did!" Sir Richard exclaimed, interrupting him. "Sir James said he was staying with the Lorings tonight at Sandford. Thomas, find Peter Rudyard and tell him he is to ride at once to Sir Nigel Loring's castle and bring Sir James back with him straightaway. A small escort of four men, Thomas, and they are to ride like the wind. Right," he added as he straightened up, banging his feet hard down on the floor to settle his boots more firmly. "I'm dressed now, so let's go and sort this bloody mess out. There is a little known way in from the south side. Sir Yvo had it put in specially, just in case! You know what he's like. It leads up to the second story; to the corridor that leads to all the family rooms, but the outer door is locked and he has the only key, so we'll just have to break it down! Go find Fitzurse and tell him to collect all the men that he can find by the Chapel steps, and to gather up some tools, and we'll see what can be done. And Thomas,"

201

"Yes, my Lord?"

After giving young Rudyard his orders, see if you can find Big Nick. He is just the man we need. Then come back and join me! Now *move!*' And flinging a mantle round his broad shoulders Sir Richard ran out, taking the broad steps of the Keep's Forework two at a time as he rushed out into the teeming night.

★

Forcing his way past the people who had gathered in the main courtyard, he arrived before the seat of the fire, skirting a small mounted party of departing guests as he did so, one with a woman held close against him. Obviously they were getting out before it was too late, but in the fury of the moment he did not have time to check that they were alright, and without another thought he ran on to where his men were gathering round the chapel steps.

And truly it was a daunting sight, with smoke billowing out of the windows, and from the main entrance of the New Hall, with great flaming gouts of fire leaping out across most of the great building, lighting up the immediate scene as it if were day. And with them the crash and bang of falling timbers and masonry, each sending huge flames and showers of sparks searing up into the night sky, the sparks, like a myriad fire-flies, extinguished almost at once to fall as a filthy black rain that soiled everything it touched.

But though the central and western end of the Hall was a raging furnace, the eastern end was still largely intact, and by God's Grace the roof had not yet collapsed. If they moved fast there might just be a chance of breaking in and making their way through the hidden gallery that Sir Yvo had ordered to be built to join up with the main passage at the back of the building, where it lay against the main curtain wall. There the walls were very thick, and though Sir Yvo's rooms were above the centre of the blaze, Gui's were further back and he might just still be there, probably injured, otherwise he would surely have escaped by now.

And the heat was ferocious, making it impossible to stand anywhere near the main building and causing even the mighty walls of the Great Keep to steam and other more simple timber buildings smoke such that any loose spark might cause the fire to leap all over them with scarlet claws like the monstrous great beast it truly was.

Pushing his way across the yard, Sir Richard was up to the Chapel before he realised it, and there waiting for him were some ten or fifteen men fronted by his giant Master-at-Arms, John Fitzurse.

"Right, John," he said urgently, "come with me and bring six of the men with you. You others take their cloaks and mine and go soak them thoroughly. God knows they're fairly wet already, but I want them absolutely pouring water. Next," he went on as three of his men ran off to do his bidding. "We'll need two heavy mauls, a couple of sledges, and a pickaxe for good measure. Also several torches. I don't care *what* you have to do, just get them, and meet me back here as quickly as you can. Try the forge, it's as good a place as any. And if Big Nick is there, so much the better, he can come too, he has more muscle on him than any of us!" And the men laughed, as he had intended they should; the less anxious they were the better they would perform.

"Right, lads" he went on, his slow, lazy speech helping to keep them calm. "The rest of you organise a bucket chain from the moat to the outside buildings. Keep them soaked as best you can," he went on, gesturing around him. "This rain will ease soon, I can feel it, and we must prevent any more of the castle from catching alight if we possibly can. Concentrate on those with slated roofs, they are the newest. Let the thatched ones go! Press everyone into service whom you can find and keep the water flowing. We will only have one chance at this, and time is running out, so *let's go!*"

And while the rest of the castle guard ran to execute Sir Richard's orders he, together with the men Fitzurse had chosen, rushed from their places towards a narrow side door recessed into the south wall of the New Hall. A tightly knit purposeful group joined within minutes by the men whom he had sent to soak their cloaks, and with their now sopping mantles over their heads to shield them as much from the smoke as from the fierce heat, Fitzurse and another of his men attacked the door with the hammers that had been collected for the purpose, while others held their spitting, hissing torches out of the way.

Moments later they were joined by the castle Smith, Big Nick, an enormous man with muscles bursting out everywhere, his usually friendly face now grim in the extreme. Still dressed for the party in blue and green part hose and a fine woollen jacket, he had paused only to throw his heavy leather apron over his head before running over to join the others still desperately struggling to smash open the door. Putting Fitzurse, whom he topped by several inches, gently aside and the other man with him, Big Nick picked up one of the sledge hammers and flexing his back, dealt the oak door before him such a massive, smashing *whack!* that he actually made it bounce in its hinges and dust fly everywhere. Just three more such almighty blows, and it began to sag and splinter, and laying his shoulders to the shattered timbers he gave it just a single great heave, and with a crash it fell inwards. Pausing only to take a few last desperate gulps of air, and covered swiftly with a well soaked cape, he plunged into the fiercely burning building and disappeared, followed immediately by Sir Richard, and then by all the others whom Fitzurse had chosen.

Inside, the heat of the fire could clearly be felt through the thickness of the walls, which were already becoming warm to the touch; the narrow passage in which they found themselves running immediately to a straight flight of stone steps leading steadily upwards until they rounded a corner and disappeared from sight. Holding one of the torches they had brought with them, Nick led them at a run up the stairs, round the corner and on up a further narrower flight that ended abruptly in an apparently blank wall of solid ashlar masonry.

Here they all paused, confused.

But, moving ahead of the giant smith, Sir Richard rammed the torch he was carrying into an iron bracket placed there in the side wall for just that purpose, and seizing the hammer that Nick was still carrying, reversing it as did so, he pounded with the handle at one of the finely cut Ashlar blocks half way up the wall from the bottom that had deep runic letters carved in it. And at his third attempt, the stone moved; there was a sullen click and one whole section of the wall, some five feet high and three feet wide, swung outwards while the men stood back with a gasp, and Sir Richard grinned round at them.

Instantly however they were assailed by a great blast of hot air and choking smoke, but drawing their streaming mantles closely around them and bending low to get the best of the air, they pushed forward into the wide corridor that lay before them. Coughing and spluttering Sir Richard unerringly turned left and together they made their way along the passage, with eyes streaming and ears alert for any sound that might indicate the presence of young Gui de Malwood. But all they could hear was the roar and fury of the fire, the sharp crack of exploding timbers and the crash of falling stones as the roof began to give way above them.

Suddenly, with a muffled shout of excitement, Sir Richard reached the shattered ruins of the door leading to Sir Gui's room, and though the room was empty, the smashed and splintered remnants of his door all pointed to some very strange goings on, swiftly confirmed by someone stumbling over the bodies of the two men whom Fitzurse had put there to guard Gui's room and bar it from intruders. Nevertheless they had to leave them and push on as they still had not found anyone alive, and unless they did so soon, they would all have to turn back or perish where they stood, for the smoke was getting thicker and already there was the glare and crackle of flames from up ahead. Not only that but the whole building was groaning and crying out in agony, the wall nearest the fire almost too hot to touch. If the roof fell in now then they were all doomed, for the wall would go with it and they would all fall to their deaths into the very heart of the fire below.

"*Come on!*" Sir Richard shouted desperately. "We only have a few minutes left, maybe not even that. We'll just go to the next corner, and if we can't find anything there, we will have turn back."

Choking and stumbling they pushed on to the bend, only to find their passage practically blocked by a huge mass of fallen timber and smashed masonry: "It's no good, Sir Richard," Fitzurse called, tripping over a pile of rubble. "We can't go any further, the way is blocked. The smoke is too thick and the flames beyond are coming this way!"

"You're right," Sir Richard replied urgently, pushing past Fitzurse's bulk to see for himself, almost choking as he did so. "We must go back! There's nothing for us here. Sir Yvo and his family have surely perished, for their rooms are beyond that blockage which is already a seething mass of fire. There's no point in hanging round here any longer. Come on, let's get out while there's still time!"

They were just on the point of leaving when Thomas Ringwood, who had called for him at the start suddenly called them back.

"Wait my Lord! *Wait!*" he shouted over the roar and crackle of the fire, tugging frantically at Sir Richard's arm. "*Look!*...Over there!" he went on pointing furiously. "I'm sure I saw something move, there by the corner of that pile, under that huge beam. There, right against the wall!"

"Impossible, man!" his Guard Commander replied, turning aside. "There's nothing there at all, only shards of plaster and old debris from the roof. Come on, we must get out of here now!"

"*No, My Lord!* Wait, Sir Richard!" young Thomas pleaded desperately, rushing forward. "*Please!* I can see something there. Looks like a man's foot! *Look!*" He cried out, pointing frantically. "See? It moves! *I am sure of it!*"

"Sweet Wine of Christ, Thomas, you're right," Sir Richard shouted then, coming up beside him, and handing his torch to one of his men. "*Quick!* Move this rubbish out of the way, let us see what we have here."

★

Gui meanwhile had given himself up for lost, having already passed out twice from the heat, the difficulty of breathing in his crushed position and from the creeping weakness of his wounds. Then suddenly he heard the voices, especially Thomas Ringwood's, and though unable to cry-out he had made a last desperate effort to move his feet and legs, and it had been that desperate twist of movement that had caught the young soldier's eye as he had turned to go. Dear God, but he'd double all their pay for this. Young Thomas particularly deserved some special reward. If they ever managed to get out of this God Awful mess alive he'd see to it in the morning. Right now, however, he just wished they would get on with it and pull him free, and with that thought still in his mind he passed out again.

★

Unfortunately rescuing their Lord was more easily said than done, for though they quickly managed to clear away most of the fallen stones the problem of how to move the massive timber that was pressing down on him was not so easily solved. One false move and it could still crush him completely, yet if they did nothing soon, they'd *all* die!

"Quick Fitzurse, find something with which to wedge up that bloody great truss, if it slips even an inch more he's done for. You, Thomas," Sir Richard ordered briskly, "see if you can find something else we can use as a lever. The rest of you shift as much rubbish away from that beam as you can without touching it too nearly. And for Christ's sake be careful."

Rushing back to where Sir Gui's room was, Fitzurse and young Thomas Ringwood quickly returned with some of the thick oak pieces from the door Sir Gui had shattered when he'd escaped, and while Sir Richard wedged one of them against the underside of the fallen beam to prop it up a little, Fitzurse slid the other against the edge of it and prepared to bear down with all his weight.

"Now when I give the word, heave down on that timber of yours, and pray God it doesn't snap. You two, grab a foot each and pull hard at the same time. We haven't time for any niceties, and he wouldn't thank us for any either. We'll only have one chance at this, so let's make sure it works first time. He's out cold anyway, so at least he won't feel a thing!"

In the smoke and glare of the fire, with the stone flags themselves now beginning to smoke and steam with the heat of the inferno beneath them, Fitzurse stretched his muscles, and with a great shout bore down with all his strength on the thick oaken slab he'd wedged beneath the beam. The pressure was enormous, yet so also was the weight that he was trying to shift, and as his muscles bulged hugely, his face went puce with the effort and his leather jerkin split across his back...but nothing moved.

"Again, man! *Again!*" Sir Richard called out, and hurling himself beside Fitzurse, he joined with him in giving it another go, and with a mighty shout they bore down on the lever together with all their strength, eyes bulging with the effort and, at the last possible moment, they felt the great timber shift, and wriggling and fighting they forced the beam upwards, while two of their men thrust some stones underneath to keep it up. A moment later they were forced to let go, unable to bear the weight any longer, and they sagged over, bent double, panting for breath in the filthy air and heat of the passage.

"It's not enough, My Lord", one of his men shouted out. "We still can't shift him!"

"Here, Sir Richard," Nick's deep voice broke in. "Let I see what I can do." and so saying the huge smith moved forward, pushing his way through the others before pausing briefly to assess the problem before him.

"Now, John," he rumbled darkly, in his rich Somerset burr moving the big Master-at-Arms aside again as if he were a baby. "Youm let this dog see the rabbit! Now, yarely my boys, yarely! One more heave, and we'll sort it!"

Sir Richard, who had stepped back to allow the giant smith room to move, looked round at his men with a smile.

"If Nick can't move it now, then no-one can," he gasped out as the smith bent to pick up the fallen timber they had been heaving with. Placing it once more hard up against the huge, jammed beam Nick turned and spoke: "I can do this, but you will only have seconds to pull him out. Ready, my boys? Now, you *bastard*!" He said tersely to the huge balk of timber before him. "You'm goin' to give moi boy, if it's the last thing oi bliddy well *do!*"

And with that he rubbed his huge hands together briskly, gave a huge shout, and bore down with all his massive strength on the lever.

For a moment nothing happened.

Then, with a frightful, rending groan, the whole mass began to move, forced up from the floor by the giant smith, the muscles of his neck standing out like thick cords of rope, the sweat pouring off the rictus of his face...as beam, rubble and fractured stones all lifted off the floor together.

It may have been only a few more inches but it was enough, and with the race of desperation the men standing by dragged the trapped body of their young commander free, even as Big Nick let go, and with a mighty crash it all smashed flat back onto the floor in a swirl of dust and debris.

With blood running down his face from the rough scraping it had received and trickling from his scalp where it had scored itself against the rough hewn timber, Gui lay like a bundle of rags at their feet, De Brocas' quarrel still buried deep in his shoulder. And, though he looked as if the whole Army of Islam had trampled all over him at least he was alive, and with God's Grace they might yet all manage to escape unharmed.

Pausing only to pick Gui up by the armpits, his feet dragging along the stone passage, L'Eveque and his team turned and raced back the way they had come, while the flames burst through the floor at their backs, and the whole corridor behind them became a mass of white hot fire that flowed over the place where they had been just moments before and still threatened to engulf them.

Within moments they had reached the space where they'd first entered the passage way, and bundling Gui roughly through the narrow opening first with all possible speed, they all piled through themselves, L'Eveque being the last to cross the threshold. Hauling the stone section on its heavy iron pintles back into place with a bang to shut off the flames, Sir Richard picked up the torch, still hissing and spluttering in its blackened sconce where he had left it; and with the giant smith leading the way again, they all stumbled back down the steps half dragging, half carrying Gui along beside them, his eyes rolling blankly in their sockets, his head lolling about on his shoulders.

By that time the wall nearest the Hall was too hot to touch, the mortar binding the stones together exploding outwards in spurts of overheated lime and sand that stung their blackened faces, and singed their clothes whenever it struck them, til with a final rush they were at the open door, and willing anxious hands were there to pull them out.

Chests heaving, retching coughing and stumbling with exhaustion though they were, there was no time to rest and pant for the roof was now tottering on its last supports, vast columns of twisting flames leaping through it, and it was sagging dangerously in the middle. If it went now, before they managed to get well clear, they could still all perish for their lungs would be incinerated by the sheer blast of heated air that would burst out from its fall. Furthermore, though they had managed against all the odds to bring Gui out alive, he was still clearly in a bad way and would need immediate attention if he was to survive.

"*Move back! Move back!*" Sir Richard shouted, waving his arms as Gui was rushed off to the relative safety of the Chapel. "The roof is about to go! *Well done*, boys!" he shouted at them all, turning round to them as he spoke. "*Bloody well done!* And as for you, Nick, you gurt big lummox," he added with a huge grin, giving the man an enormous buffet across his back. "That was *magnificent!* That new forge you've been wanting this year past? Consider it done! Now, Fitzurse," he added turning back to his Master-at-Arms, and banging his hands together. "Pull *everyone* out, and make sure they bring their water containers with them. Now, move back! *Move back!*

Like a dark wave, the people who had congregated in the courtyard rolled back from the immediate vicinity of the fire…and not a moment too soon, for with an almighty, thunderous roar the roof and top storey of the great building fell at last. The noise almost indescribable as towering white hot flames leaped and twisted up into the night turning it to day, and the people instinctively cowered back, covering their mouths and faces to protect themselves from the searing blast of heat that rushed out at them. But though the heat was intense, neither the stables nor any of the other slate roofed buildings caught fire, the constant dousing they had received preventing their timbers from actually blazing up…though every other thatched building nearby had perished, adding their flames and smoke to the inferno so that it really did look as if the whole castle was fiercely burning.

And with the fall of the roof, it stopped raining, and the fire ran its course at last.

Though it leapt into life again from time to time, as chunks of fractured masonry fell into its glowing heart, the flames themselves began to die down steadily until, by the time the grey light of an early dawn began to steal across a clear blue rain-washed sky it was a dull, hellish glow that winked and glared at the appearing day, huge plumes of grey-white steam and smoke curling and twisting into the sky, and everywhere a fine layer of ash and sludge.

Chapter 31...The White Rose is dismayed!

A licia, meanwhile, was completely lost!

Chapter 32... The Lady Alicia's adventures on Sunburst.

She had left the Saracen's Head in a ferment!

Feet straight down in long stirrups, riding as any knight would have done, her back supported by the high cantle of her saddle into which Robert had so unceremoniously pitched her, Alicia had burst through the men trying to stop her like a charging boar scatters the hounds. Head down, she had rocketed past another horseman just entering the yard who'd had to rein his mount back almost onto its very haunches to avoid her, and then she was away through the little town like the wind. Hooves pounding the sodden road as loudly as her beating heart, she sped into the night. Body crouched as far over Sunburst's withers as her high saddle would allow, she urged the chestnut mare onwards with hand, heel and voice; clods of earth and torn grass flying in all directions; mud and water splashing her face as they raced away from Lyndhurst together, the silver-white light of the moon showing in fitful bursts between the ragged streamers of cloud left over from the storm.

She was free! She was free! She was *free!* She exulted as she left the town behind, twisting and turning in her saddle to see whether, even now, she was already being followed by the Baron and his men, for of his hot pursuit she was completely certain. But not yet, she prayed... *Not yet!* And she forced herself to slow down to an easy canter, so as not to miss the second turning that Rose had told her of, conscious of the absolute importance of not missing it in her desperate rush to avoid re-capture.

Even so she very nearly did!

And might well have done so had not Sunburst been suddenly startled by the ghostly shape of an owl swooping out from a low tree beside her head just as she was passing. With a wild hunting screech, on great white silent wings, it had swept past making the mare veer violently, and toss her head to show the whites of her eyes in sudden fright.

"Whoa! *Whoa!* Little Lady," Alicia called out to her, pulling her up and leaning forward to pat her steaming flanks. "Steady now! *Stead-y!*" she went on firmly, as Sunburst continued to stamp and tittup across the track. "That was only a silly old owl! Calmly now, calm-ly! Yes, you big baby, it frightened me too," she went on talking, gentling her startled mount as she spoke. "There. That's better," she said presently, bending forward to rub and pull the mare's ears. "All right. We'll walk a bit until you feel ready to press on. Sweet Jesus! Where's that blasted turning? We've already been past one, so the next cannot be far away. God aid me, but I must be running out of time!"

All around her the forest seemed to breathe and sigh as if it were alive, the trees scattering raindrops everywhere as they swayed and swooped to the wind, now dropped to a gusting breeze from the howling gale of a few scant hours ago. The swish of leaves and branches, coming to her like the billowing skirts of some great lady passing by, the trackway littered with broken fragments, and soused with water that sprayed up every step that Sunburst took, and sodden leaves covering it like scattered petals after a wedding. And all the while the moon's harsh silver light flickered across them both like a guttering candle as the clouds from the broken storm wrack flittered wildly over head. First lighting the way...next plunging everything into deepest darkness.

And the great forest was alive with sound.

The constant swish and swirl of the trees themselves, of course, with the sudden crash of falling branches, but also the hoot of an owl, the snuffle and squeal of boar rooting for food, the bark of a deer, and, once, the terrifying, eldritch screech of some poor creature being slain in the night. Rabbit, faun or shoat. She knew not. But it had been close, and made every hair on her arms and scalp rise up in startled fear, making Sunburst skitter and jump with sudden nerves for wolf as well as boar lurked in the forest, beside the lordly stags and their hinds. Wolf, fox, stoat, weasel, polecat: killers every one! And though she was sure the last bear had been killed long ago, there were always tales of fell beasts that roamed the forest seeking whom they might devour. And there were outlaws. Desperate men who would not hesitate to kill and rob if their prey were weak and they thought it worth their while.

She shivered and rubbed her arms, conscious of having no weapon of any kind with which to defend herself, not even a knife! And she strained her eyes to see the way ahead, and her ears for any distant sound of the pursuit she knew must be upon her any moment. And all the time that she was walking the mare...she had the strangest feeling that she was being watched from amongst the trees!

It had only been a feeling at first. Just a heightened sense of awareness...of danger...which she had easily shrugged off. Shadows that were nothing. Shapes in the darkness that looked like faces, or men hiding - but were only the trees and bushes. Sudden hands and bony fingers across her face – that were just twigs and branches. And a constant pattering that she though was raindrops falling from the trees all around her...but that strangely stopped whenever she did. And on every side small trees and bushes, and great clumps of fern and brambles pressed close to the track, menacing in the rushing, silvery darkness, making her heart beat faster.

Then had come the first sound of a twig snapping!

And after what seemed just moments later, came another. Sharp sounds that no wild animal should make. Certainly no small animal...and in–between was silence, so thick you could almost cut it. So now she was achingly conscious of *every* rustle and crunch in the undergrowth that pushed up at her on every side, each sound making her shiver and the mare nervous. So it was with extreme relief that she saw, at last, the place she had been looking for, where another trackway branched off right from the main one she had been following.

Narrow it was, and almost hidden beneath the drooping branches of a tree, half blown over by the storm. Had she been riding hell–for–leather along the track she must certainly have missed it, and she silently blessed the owl that had flown so suddenly out in front of Sunburst's head. So, swinging herself off the mare's back she paused to examine the ground, dropping down on her hunkers to examine the forest road more closely, drawing in her breath sharply at the sight of clear, deep tracks left by some two wheeled cart that had clearly passed that way not long since, the narrow lines of its wheels still clearly indented in the soaking ground. And the marks of wheels were not the only spoor that had been left behind.

"Sa, sa, my little one," she muttered softly under her breath as she squatted down on her haunches, her boots squidging in the mud, Sunburst's reins held firmly in her fingers. "See," she continued chatting to her horse, as much for companionship as anything else, as she traced the pattern of hooves, feet and cart wheels in the trampled ground. "Others have been here before us! Pray God it is the good Father and his merry men, because I see muddy footsteps here amongst the wheels and the hoof prints. So, we must go this way swiftly, or we may yet be caught by the so wicked Baron...and that is not a fate I even wish to think of!" And so saying she led her mare around the drooping obstacle, her hair catching in some of the torn twigs and branches, Sunburst's mane also snagging as she dipped her head to pass them by. Then they were both through and swiftly re-mounting the mare, she kicked Sunburst on again into an easy canter, aware of her isolation and her helplessness should she be suddenly attacked.

And ever present, as she rode further into the whispering darkness of the ancient forest, was the feeling that she was not alone. That someone, or something, was following her every move. She could almost imagine that she could hear its breathing, and she shuddered in her creeping certainty. Once she even stopped to call out: "Who's there? Show yourself!" But only the sighing trees and rustling bushes answered her.

Then, away in the distance, over the sound of wind and trees, she heard the pounding of hooves and the wild cries of men, and knew that the pursuit she had so long dreaded was close upon her. For just a moment she sat frozen with fear as she strained to learn whether the chase would hurtle past the distant break in the trackway or pause, as she had, to examine the ground. With a wild flutter of her heart she heard a distant halloo...and the sound of hooves stopped. Sweet Wine of Christ, they must surely see now where she had turned off. Any minute now they would be onto her. And suddenly she was galvanised into action, jagging in her heels and driving Sunburst forward again along the track as fast as she was able, laying herself down as close to the chestnut mare's neck as she could, ignoring the swish and smack of every twig and leaf that struck her as she rushed by.

Ducking beneath low overhanging branches, weaving round some obstacles and jumping others that lay across her path, her thighs gripping Sunburst's sides, she was suddenly caught unawares by a mighty tree that had fallen right across the track. Branches, like giant arms thrusting up in all directions it filled her horizon, and there was no way round it. The only possible chance was to jump it where a gap had been created by one huge limb being shorn off at its very root...and Alicia had only a moment in which to collect herself before she must push the mare forward to attempt the jump.

With only a brief pause to balance herself she took a deep breath, circled Sunburst to keep her moving then fiercely drove the mare on, bending forwards as she did so, the reins loose in her hands to give the mare all the space she needed to stretch her neck and throw up her head as she made her jump. Closer and closer they flew until with a great cry of encouragement she stabbed in her heels once more to lift her.

"Up! *Up!* My Beauty!" She called to Sunburst then. "Fly, Honeyone*!* *Fly!* You *can* do this, sweetheart, you *can!* Now...*Fly!*"

And, like some great bird, Sunburst bunched her haunches beneath her young rider and with one great spring she took off, soaring over the tree before her, her hooves thrashing through the broken branches as she leaped, leaves and mudded divots flying in all directions, Alicia's face whipped by twigs and loose tendrils of ivy as they crashed through. Then they were over, and with a wild whoop she and Sunburst thumped back onto the soggy ground, their great obstacle behind them.

"*Good Girl!*" She praised her, pulling her back to an easy canter and leaning over to thump her withers. "You *goody girl*, you! Who would have thought you could have jumped so *beautifully?* Not even Pegasus himself could have done better. Who trained you, you clever girl? Whoever it was deserves a golden chain for their pains! Good Girl! *Good Girl!*" She said to the mare again with a warm chuckle, leaning forward to pat her shoulders and pull her silken ears through her own still trembling fingers. "What price the bloody Baron and his men should run straight into that tree? With all the gear they are carrying, and on that bloody great charger of his, Charlemagne, they'll *never* get over as we have done! Now, come on, Honeyone. *Kick on!* It's high time we came upon the good Father and his little band. They surely cannot be so far from us now?" And with that she rode into a wide clearing, silver-white in the moon's shimmering brightness, but eerily empty...and from which no main track issued again!

To all intents and purposes it was a dead-end.

Not that there weren't numerous pathways leading out of it. There were...but all in different directions, and horse, cart and wagon tracks were everywhere. In the moon's light, and without local knowledge, it was impossible to know which trackway to follow, as all were similarly marked. So she was stumped, but desperate to move on, and dismayed that Rose had not told her which way she should take once she had got to this great clearing. So...offering up a silent prayer to the gods of all trees and forests, Alicia took the first trackway that best led off in the direction she believed she must go. And kicking Sunburst into a gentle canter she pushed on again, ducking down to avoid branches damaged by the storm, now hanging low across her path, and shaking off the cascading droplets of water that burst over her every time she nudged a tree as she passed by.

Trackway crossed trackway, each leading to an agony of indecision as she came to them, but she could feel time pressing in on her, not knowing whether the Baron and his men were still following her or not. Once there was a fierce, wild outbreak of shouts and cries some distance behind her...and she had paused, her heart in her mouth, ready to flee. But distance was very hard to judge in the Forest, especially at night, when sounds could carry so far, and so she swiftly moved on again. And moments later the sounds stopped, and all was still once more.

This way and that she and Sunburst turned, once losing the path altogether, so they had to back-track the way they had just come to find it again. Sometimes galloping where the track was straight and hard, sometimes even at a long striding amble, but usually at an easy canter…and always pushing on as best she could, her fear of capture as great a stimulation, as her determination to reach Castle Malwood and safety. Finally, with a deep sigh of resignation, they came to yet another unmarked crossway and stopped.

There was no denying it. She was lost!

"Oh, Sunburst," she said, leaning over the mare's shoulders, exhausted. "We are both hopelessly and completely lost in a forest as big as half the county, filled with unknown dangers: Wolves, foxes, boars, angry French people and, for all I know, Honeyone, even bears!" She put her head in her hands and sighed again. "What *is* a girl meant to do now?"

And then, quite distinctly, she heard a branch snap behind her, followed by the sound of something heavy moving off through the undergrowth. Her head shot up and she gasped, twisting desperately in the saddle to try and spot where the sounds had come from, her senses swamped by a sudden and appalling fear, while Sunburst, unsettled by her rider's wild feelings, jibbed and skittered nervously beneath her. But at that very moment a great streamer of cloud covered the moon's face, and the whole forest was instantly plunged into a stygian darkness.

Alicia was terrified!

Almost whimpering with fear, the hair rose along her arms and crawled up the back of her scalp as the sound seemed to rustle past her, before just as suddenly disappearing again. All her earlier anxieties of being followed returned a hundredfold, and Sunburst jerked forward as her feet dug into her flanks, her head tossing wildly at her rider's rising alarm. Again a branch snapped, almost it seemed alongside her, followed by a wild crashing of trees and branches and she had a brief glimpse of broad antlers against the sky, now moonlit once again, together with the sudden sound of hooves…then silence, save for the dipping and sighing of the trees around her. Alicia, scared almost out of her wits, sat bolt upright in her saddle, her hair on end with fright, herself panting with fear as she tried to gentle her startled mare, looking this way and that into the impenetrable darkness which had just then closed in around her once again.

"*Dear God!*" she gasped, relaxing back down again, her heart hammering fit to burst. "It was only a silly old stag. Startled by a rooting boar or…or something! A…bear? Are there bears still in this forest?" She asked her mare in a hoarse whisper, her voice still trembling. "Or…Outlaws. Or," crossing herself desperately as the thought swept over her, "even the Guardians of the Forest themselves?"

She knew all the old tales! She had heard them all from Rose as a child and now she shivered, her whole body shaking with sudden fear at the very thought of the mythical figures, half-man half-animal, of badger, fox and wolf; boar, bear and lordly stag who were supposed to keep watch over all that happened in the ancient forest and would punish with a dreadful death all those who angered them or broke the laws of Herne the Hunter, the ancient god of the Forest from before the Romans came. And with that thought, the moon sailed clear of the last broken streamers of the storm that had so lashed the lands around them, bathing everything in its hard, cold, silver light, so all around her the trees were blackly silhouetted against the sky and the crossed trackways, now bright with the moon's harshness, stretched emptily away from her. If the whole ghostly hunt had swept by her at that very moment, she would not have been surprised!

"Oh, Sunburst!" She exclaimed, as her heart settled down again, leaning forward to pull the mare's furry ears once more and pat her neck. "What are we to do now? God alone knows in what direction Castle Malwood lies. Or where Father Matthew is…whomsoever *he* may turn out to be? Or even that bastard Baron and his bloody daughter? We could be *anywhere* for all I know! And I am tired, hungry and frightened! Oh, how I wish that Gui were with us now. He would be sure to know exactly what to do. This is just all too much for me!"

Then, suddenly, and without any warning of there being another living soul within miles, a great black horse, huge in the moon's stark light, came up beside her out of no-where - as if it had come out of the very ground itself and her whole body trembled, even more so as strong hands suddenly seized hold of her! And, even as she screamed violently in sudden terror, a soft bag was cast deftly over her head. Shocked beyond measure, she was powerless to resist, her wild cries and shouts for help muffled by the soft thickness of the bag that now covered her right down to her shoulders. Sunburst's reins were twitched from her nerveless fingers, and her hands were swiftly bound before her with strong cords.

She was caught!

Chapter 33...In which Father Matthew utterly confounds Alicia...

Thirty minutes later, after clumping and bumping about like a sack of potatoes and more twists, turns and backtracks than she could possibly remember, the man leading her finally brought the mare to a halt, and once more she felt strong hands reaching round her waist, and with no more than a soft grunt she was lifted, seemingly feather-light, from her saddle and placed gently on the ground. There her hands were swiftly unbound and the bag swept off her head at last so that she could look full into her captor's face.

It was a monk!

Sitting on a convenient log before a small fire, and looking up at her...but still a monk! And she was speechless. Expecting the coarse, leering features of common outlaws...or, worse, the smug, gloating face of de Brocas and his men! She saw instead a strongly built man, tanned of face, somewhat ascetic features with deep brown eyes that gleamed with intelligence and twinkled at her beneath a high domed forehead. And after all her desperate imaginings she was never more shocked in her life, into both immobility and open-mouthed silence!

Dressed in the black habit and cowl of a Benedictine, his face was dominated by a hawk-like nose and the mouth, firm above a determined chin, was open in a warm smile of welcome. And she gasped! For this was a face she knew - or..thought she knew? Yet she was equally certain that she had never seen him before in her life either and for a moment she was totally bemused. Just stood there and goggled at him, at the small fire burning cheerfully before him, at the steaming bowl of something warm and delicious he held on his knees, for her nose wuffled at the delicious, meaty smell of it, and at the chunk of fresh white bread he held in his hand.

And without speaking, her thinking still incoherent, like an automaton, Alicia took a similar bowl of broth that someone handed to her out of the darkness and sat down on a convenient log opposite.

"*Father?*" She squeaked, shocked to her core. "Father..Matthew?"

"Yes, my child." came the steady reply in the man's light, musical voice, with the hint of Spain and the hot Mediterranean in every word…and a raised quizzical eyebrow.

"But..but after being so swiftly snatched I was expecting an Outlaw! A..A band of Outlaws!…" And her voice trailing away to stunned silence as he pointed over her shoulder, and smiled.

Turning round she found she was on the edge of another wide clearing where, not twenty paces from the log on which she was seated, another fire burned brightly. Behind it was a large tilt-cart, its long upright shafts supporting a great tarpaulin that had been stretched out to make a sort of awning in front of the fire, over which a wide stockpot was hanging off a stout iron chain, itself suspended from a blackened iron tripod. Here two other Benedictines were tending both fire and pot: one large with fat arms and legs and a merry face, and one small and wiry, and both with thick studded sandals on their feet, and both with their wide black cowls thrown back to reveal their tonsures.

However, it wasn't the Brothers who had so horribly caught her eye, strange though it was to see them there. It was the rest! For seated round that other fire, on a collection of logs and tall kegs, or leaning over it silent at that moment, lounged nearly a score of the toughest looking men that Alicia had seen outside Sir Yvo's lock-ups! In dark clothes of leather or rough woollen cloth, some in mailed jerkins, long boots on their feet and cloth hoods over steel caps, many with stout staves in their hands, they looked competent and menacing. Some had long swords at their sides, others carried axes and billhooks. A dozen were leaning on longbows, the quivers on their backs stuffed with arrows.

And all paused to look at her as she turned round.

Finally her gaze settled on the man most obviously their leader. Not a huge man like Edward Sergeant or John Fitzurse, but a man of medium height and build. Square chested, his legs thrust into tall, black leather boots; the firelight glinting off his polished corselet of riveted mail that hung down below his waist he had a presence that many other men lacked, and wore a conical steel helmet with thick nasal protector.

Longsword and shapely poniard hanging by his side, one strong arm flung over his horse's neck, the other bent to fondle the rough head of a giant wolf hound busily competing for his affection, he was every bit the leader. And she was at his mercy. What such a band were doing in the King's New Forest, in company with a Benedictine monk and his Brothers whom she had been so desperately seeking since fleeing from the Saracen's Head, she neither knew nor understood. She just felt so overwhelmed by everything that had happened to her that night she promptly burst into tears, dropping her food bowl heedless on the ground as she bent forward in both mental and physical agony, her head in her hands, her whole body shaking to her sobs as she rocked backwards and forwards in utter misery.

To Father Matthew sitting opposite her, the urge to rush to her side and comfort her was almost overwhelming, but the tall Benedictine resisted the impulse with all the training at his command, waiting quietly, still as a hunting goshawk in a tree, until the first paroxysm of despair had passed, and with tear-stained face the terrified girl before him finally looked up. And even though his head was in shadow, Alicia felt the force of the tall Benedictine's eyes on her as she finally wiped her own with the back of her hand and turned back to the monk in the long black habit, who was still patiently waiting to address her.

"Father, what is happening? Who are these, these *Outlaws?*" she hissed at him desperately, gesturing over her shoulder. "And why are you here? I have been seeking you half the night. Now I am completely lost, when I *so* need to be at Castle Malwood. Soo need to be there, Father. And now I have been seized by Outlaws! Please, Father. Please help me!"

"Outlaws?" He questioned her, astonished, putting his piece of bread down onto a wooden platter by his side. "Well I suppose you might think that, my dear. They certainly look the part!" Then, calling across to the half-armoured man beside his horse he said: "Allan? Our young guest thinks you are all outlaws!" And the men sitting or standing around the fire laughed, before turning back to get on with the jobs they had been doing when Alicia had turned round.

Jumping up then, and almost stamping her feet with rage Lady Alicia de Burley swung round to face them, her eyes sparkling with tears in the firelight, as she boldly shouted: "Don't you *dare* laugh at me, you...you...*bullies!* My home is on fire; those whom I most love have been murdered and I have been kidnapped, drugged and chased for my life by a bunch of wicked French killers; half terrified out of my wits and, finally, bagged as if I were a common thief and dragged bumping and lumping through this beastly forest as if I were a sack of meal, to be dumped at the feet of a bunch of ruffians. *What do you expect me to think?*" She ended fiercely, swinging back towards the dark monk again before adding, with a horrified look on her face: "No! You *horrid* man...you are playing games with me. It's what you *wanted* me to think!"

221

"Ho there, Allan. I am a 'horrid man' now, and you're all 'ruffians',," the tall, dark habited monk exclaimed, putting back his cowl and laughing.

" 'Ruffians' indeed!" and he chuckled again, before looking up at her from his seat by the fire. "And 'Horrid man'? Well, my Lady, perhaps I did deserve that a little," he said then, looking at the tears hanging from her eyelashes. "I am really sorry, my child. It was meant to make you smile. A little. Come you now, My Lady Alicia de Burley, and sit down and eat your broth that Brother William has taken such trouble over," he said, picking up her bowl and holding it out to her again. "He's the fat one...before it gets cold. Lucky it didn't spill when you dropped it. The other is Brother James, the wiry one who is a wonder with horses. And, no, these are not 'Ruffians' my little Lady Bright Eyes. These are the King's own Verderers and he," he added, pointing towards the half-armoured man, now smiling at her from beside his horse, "Is Allan-i-the-Wood, the Under Sheriff of the New Forest."

"No, he's *not*, Father!" she said firmly, sitting bolt upright. "I have *never* seen him before in my life. John de Grey is the Under Sheriff to Sir Jocelyn Upton. Him I know well. So who pray are these 'Ruffians' then?" she questioned haughtily, still angry and distressed by his untimely joke. "I know de Grey's men, every one of them, yet these men are strangers to me! And - and how do you know my name? *No-one* has called me 'his little Lady Bright Eyes' since my own dear father died! Oh Father!" She wailed in despair. "What is happening to me? And.. and - who are you?" And sitting down with a thump she buried her face in her hands and cried

Again the tall Spaniard waited until his guest had stopped weeping, while signalling to one of his brothers to bring a bowl of hot water and a towel for her to wash her face and hands, giving him her bowl of food at the same time, now gone cold and with odd bits of grass and stick in it too, for him to replenish it properly.

"Well!" The tall monk replied at last, when she had stopped crying and sat back up again, wiping her ram across her face as she did so, his dark brown eyes smiling gently into her hot, sore blue ones.

"First wash your face, my child, and your hands," he said gently handing her the bowl that the wiry Brother James had brought. "What would your Rose say were she to see you now? And, see, Brother James has brought you a fresh bowl of pottage and some of Brother William's best baked bread to go with it. In very truth, Alicia," he went on in his warm, lilting voice, ignoring her shocked expression at the familiar use of her name. "You have had a truly desperate night in every way. And the very night of your betrothal

222

to which I also was bidden.

But please show some gratitude towards those who have so bravely saved your life from de Brocas's angry steel, and at some cost to themselves," he added, noting the shock on her face at the casual use of the Baron's name. "For they have lost three good men in the doing of it this night, and several badly injured, and only did so because of the love they have for King Richard and for your own lovely Rose of the Saracen's Head - and at my insistence!"

"Father!" She whispered, shocked to the very core of her being. "Father...please, who are you? How do you know so much of me and of my family? Things that only someone really close to my father could possibly know; sweet words I have not heard in years. Yet I know I have never seen you before. Please, Father, if you have any kindness, any love in you for me. Please tell me who you are and what you are doing in the Forest so far from anywhere, and on my way to my Betrothal? I do not understand!"

"All in good time my 'little Lady Bright Eyes'," the tall monk said, pressing her bowl into her hands. "When you have eaten and had some of this mulled wine," he added putting a large horn beaker wreathed in steam and rich with the scent of cinnamon and oranges beside her. "I will explain everything to you, I promise. For in truth you both need and deserve to know as much as I can tell you just now. More I cannot say until I reach Castle Malwood, which I am as desperate to reach as you are, my dearest Lady Alicia de Burley. But you are safely among true and loyal friends I assure you!"

And for some time after that there was a more comfortable silence between them as both ate hungrily of the meaty broth the two brothers had prepared, wiping their bowls with the hunks of fresh bread they had beside them and drinking their mulled wine, while all around her the forest breathed and rustled and the men behind her talked quietly amongst themselves, cleaned their weapons, cared for their wounded and kept guard over the camp.

Finally Alicia sat back and stretched her arms towards the fire before them, warming her hands off the flames that spurted and flared up amongst the wood, grateful of the warmth after so chill and wet a journey. "Oh, Father, thank you! I so needed that, and I am sorry I have been such a wet blanket. Such a cry-baby. I am generally much stronger than you might think," She said contritely, looking across at him, leaving her bowl by her side. "But I have had a truly ghastly night. More so even than you may know about," she went on with a shudder, hugging herself beneath the cloak that Rose had given her when she had left the 'Saracen's Head'.

And thinking of all that had happened since she had got up the previous morning, she shivered again. *Sweet Jesus!* Just less than a day had gone by, and yet here she was in a clearing in the Forest, surrounded by armed men whom she had never met before and talking to a Benedictine monk...whom she'd never met before either, yet was somehow certain she had seen...and who seemed to know all about her? How strange life could be! Then, looking across into the man's warm brown eyes she smiled wryly and sighed, bending down to pick up her beaker of mulled wine, holding its warmth between her hands as she did so.

"*Of course* I am grateful to Allan Wood and his men, Father, and am appalled that three have lost their lives on my account and others have been injured That truly is a desperate thing and saddens me greatly, and I will do all I can to help their families. But they *did* frighten me, Father. And I don't *have* to like being smothered in a foul smelling bag, do I?" Then, suddenly overwhelmed by her thoughts and feelings, she covered her face with her hands, rocking herself in distress and cried out piteously: "Oh, Father! Help me! All dead! *All gone!* How could they? How *could* they?"

"The murders you mean?" He asked her quietly, standing up while she recovered herself. "Sir Yvo and Lady Margaret? And the burning of Castle Malwood?"

"You know?" She whispered breathlessly getting to her feet, her chest almost panting.

"Oh, my poor child," he said, his brown eyes dark with pain. "The whole Forest knows what has happened there this night!" And, opening his arms to her grief at last, he caught her as she flew into them, holding her close to his own heart as her body shook with her distress and she wept bitterly into his shoulder, her small hands clawing into his black robes as if she never would release him.

"Never fear, My Lady Alicia," the tall monk said grimly, as he stroked the sobbing girl's head. "The Baron will not escape this night's wickedness. That, *on the Cross*, I promise you! Not today maybe, nor even tomorrow. Maybe not for weeks. But he will pay I promise you. Even if, God Help Me, I have to cut him down myself!"

"You, kn-know, the Baron?" she stammered, lifting her head in amazement and dashing the tears from her face.

"The Lord Baron Sir Roger de Brocas? The *so* good Lord of Narbonne and Gruissan…and his equally charming daughter, she whom all call 'The Lady'? The lovely raven haired Lady Rochine? Oh yes! I know them of old, my Lady Bright Eyes. And I know how much they hate both your Houses. Yours *and* Sir Yvo's," he added, putting her gently from him and holding her tear-stained face gently in his hands so he could look into her eyes. "It was *he* whom Allan and his men drove off tonight, though he lost three good men in the doing of it. The Baron and his daughter both, and a wild parcel of their soldiers. You will not have cause to fear them again to night. *I promise you!*"

"Oh, Father, I do hope not," she whispered, the air hissing through her teeth. "I do hope not! Such dreadful things have been done this night, Father. Dreadful, *dreadful* things! You do not know the half of it! They murdered all the guards, and told me Gui was dead also. But I did not believe them. They wanted me to go away with them, back to France. But I *would* not, so the Baron covered my nose and mouth with his handkerchief until I passed out, then drugged me, gagged me and tied me up!"

"He drugged you?" he said, sitting down again. "I am amazed he had the skill!"

"No skill, Father. Brute force!" she went on, taking a fresh, hot bowl of broth from Brother James as she sat down opposite him once more.

"He thrust some sort of phial into my mouth and poured some vile muck down my throat, then held my mouth closed so I had to swallow it. *Bleah!* Disgusting! He dragged me out as the whole castle went up in smoke and flames around us. She said, shivering at the memory, and shook her head as if to rid herself of the images that still filled her mind. Then, after a pause, while they both dipped more bread into their broth and ate it hungrily, she raised her face and examined the man in front of her closely: the studied ease with which he ate his food; the long, clean fingers that spoke of scholarship, not earthly toil; his air of complete assuredness; the way he, a monk, addressed and handled her, a woman, when so many others would have turned their faces away for fear of 'contamination'! So unlike any monk she had met before. *And how did he know so much about her?*

Finishing her broth with a smile, and wiping her last piece of bread all round her bowl, she sat back and spoke: "Father. Forgive me, but…"

"…But you are not sure you really know who I am beyond my name," he said, deftly interrupting her, passing her a full beaker of mulled wine at the same time. "Nor how I come to know of you and your family. Nor, my dear Lady Alicia," he added with a lift of his brows. "How I come to be here at all! Yes?"

"Well…Yes!" she said, smiling, sipping from her beaker in between her words. "And no…because I do know your name at least, you must be Father Matthew, unless The Forest is harbouring more than one party of Benedictine monks and their tilt cart this dreadful night? Rose told me of you before I fled from Lyndhurst after escaping from the Baron and his vile daughter who also drugged me, Stripped me half naked and left me tied hand and foot on a bed!"

"That was careless of her to leave you so…"

"…So stripped and tied?"

"No, my child," he replied in his rich musical voice. "So unguarded! I am sure her sides will be smarting tonight. Her father will have given her a sound whipping."

"Are you a mind reader, Father? As well as a rescuer?"

"No, my Lady. But I know the Baron. He is not a nice man, I can assure you! Harsh even to those whom he loves, if such is possible for so twisted a man. And he does love his daughter and she him also. More than a daughter should I think," he added, startling Alicia with his comment. "But enough of that Man-of-Blood for the time being, my little Lady Bright Eyes," he said with a warm smile at her sudden confusion. "What can I tell you of me?"

"Oh, everything Father!" she exclaimed then, her eyes fixed on his. "You seem to know so much about me, yet I know almost nothing of you: not who you are? Why you are here? Why you were coming to Malwood?…or why I am so sure that I know you - when I know inside I have never met you? Nor, if you know so much of me and my family, why have I not heard your name spoken of before?"

"So many questions, My Lady.

"So many secrets, Father Matthew," she said looking him in the face. "Too many for one poor Forest maid to cope with," she added with a sudden smile that lit up her face like a sunburst. "It is time you answered me, I think. Don't you?

"How like your mother you are...Alicia. Just then your smile so reminded me of her. She was a truly lovely lady, the Lady Anne. Your father never really got over losing her, you know. I have often wondered whether that isn't why he died? Oh, I know he had a fever. But fevers can be defeated if the will to do so is really strong. Show any weakness and it can overwhelm you. He died in Sir Yvo's arms, far from home and no loving lady to come home to."

"There was me, Father. I loved my Papa dearly. Could he not have come home to me?"

"Oh, My Little One; who can know what goes on in a fevered mind? In his delirium he may have seen your mother calling to him...and just gone to her? Truly he loved you dearly, but the Lady Anne was his whole life!" He exclaimed quietly, poking the fire as he spoke, his mind far away for a moment, while Alicia herself just gazed at the flames as she drank her wine.

Then with a deep sigh, the tall monk sat back again and looked at her with a smile. "Now, enough of such past sadness," he said then smoothly, with a twitch of his eyebrows. "My name *is* Father Matthew. I am the Master Herbalist of Ellingham Priory, an Alien House to which I have been attached for many years and which, for various reasons I prefer to keep to myself for a while yet; and I was on my way to your betrothal party at Castle Malwood..."

"...My betrothal party?" she cut in urgently. "You mentioned that before, but not why? I mean why you, Father? I had no idea that Sir Yvo and Lady Margaret even *knew* anyone from Ellingham Priory, let alone had invited anyone. The place is some distance from us, and very small. We have almost nothing to do with it! Yet you seem to know them well...and me?"

"My dear lady Alicia," the tall herbalist said, looking at her over the flames, his brown eyes dark with memories. "I have known Sir Yvo almost all my life! *And* your parents, God Bless them both. And *you*, my little Alicia, since just a week after you were born!"

"*No!*"

"*Yes!*" He said mimicking her surprise. "I have known Sir Yvo since we were young men. I was not always a monk, my Lady! My home was in Spain, in Navarre, and in Spain we fight the Moors. They still occupy almost half my country. My family held lands in and around Pampalona and around Castile, and I was born and bred to be a warrior, as was Sir Yvo...as is Sir Gui. We were two gay Caballeros, young knights together, Sir Yvo and I. Meeting by chance…"

"How?

"Oh…that is still something I wish to keep as a surprise, my Dear. Oh nothing dreadful, I assure you," he said swiftly, seeing a look of sudden dismay cross her open face. "But I will bide my time on that, my Lady."

"So-so you knew Sir Yvo then, in your fighting days? Father…what then is your real name?"

"My real name is Don Mateo de Silva de Pampalona. A Spanish Hidalgo of great family, lands and honours; now a humble Benedictine monk, Father Matthew of Ellingham Priory…and elsewhere too maybe?" he finished with a smile. "I do not wish to reveal all my secrets in one go, my little Lady Bright Eyes. Then you would have nothing left to look forward to from me!"

"And my Father? My dearest Papa? You knew him too?"

"Sir Henry de Burley? But of course. He was a fine man, Alicia. A *fine* man. He would be soo proud of you today! He and Sir Yvo were David and Jonathan together…Roland and Oliver. You seldom found one without the other near by, your father and Sir Yvo. Wherever one was the other was never far away! And he fell in love with your mother about the same time that Sir Yvo did with his Margaret. I was with them when they married…

"…My parents?"

"Watched them fall in love, and I was with them just after you were born. Such a lovely baby you were, my dear. And so *hugely* loved and cherished!" He smiled at the memory, looking at her across the fire, sitting in amazement, while he reached down and threw a few more pieces of wood onto the flames before picking up his own re-filled beaker from somewhere beside him.

"I christened you: Alicia-Margaret-Louise. Of course I had hung up my spurs by then. Choosing to mend men's bodies, and their minds, rather than rend them limb from limb. Too much killing…too much blood! Too much wandering. I lost the taste for it I suppose." He mused, looking into the fire. "God was calling me to do something different with my life, and I joined the Benedictine Order…To stay in one place for a change!" He smiled at the irony of it.

"But, Father," she asked, her brows creased in thought. "Given that the Benedictine's are not a wandering Order, what then are you doing here in the Forest, so far from anywhere and on your way to Malwood? I am intrigued!"

He sighed then and leaned back to look up at the night sky, now completely cleared of the massed ranks of serried cloud battalions that had so covered it earlier; at the moon sailing across the vasty heavens, and the myriad stars that could be seen all round it, now just beginning to pale. "I found I had a talent for curing people, and a lively interest in the herbs and barks and flowers used to do so. And I found that I was a good listener; that if I was careful, and caring, people would tell me things; and I learned to keep my counsel! Then as my thirst for knowledge and understanding grew, so did my reputation for healing and for seeking out the truth, and suddenly I found myself travelling again: first at the Lady Abbess's request to Romsey, where I still go to hold Mass for her and her nuns; then by my Bishop and, most lately, by the Papal Legate for all England,…and finally the King himself.

"By King Richard?"

"Certainly, and by the Old King, his father, before him. I have also met and spoken with the Pope himself!"

"The Holy Father?" She asked incredulously, her eyes lost in wonder.

"Even so, my Child." He said simply, looking into her open face. "Pope Clement. I had a commission from him to carry out in France."

She paused then, and looked across at him as he drank deeply from his horn beaker, then down into the flames as they flickered and twisted in the fire Sometimes greeny blue; sometimes red and orange. How lovely they were, and she stirred them with a stick.

Now here was a puzzle indeed, she thought as Brother William, with his jolly smile and soft rubicund face and figure silently re-filled her own beaker. When St Benedict had established his Order, he had determined, by decree, that no Brothers should be allowed to leave his House, except by special order of the Abbot of his House…or by some other more powerful intervention. So…Father Matthew must be very special indeed to be so far from home - and known both to the King himself, and to the Pope! What then was he doing here? Why, if he was coming to her Betrothal had he not arrived? And why all the secrecy? Why, also, if he was so well known to her, and to Gui's parents, had she never met with him before…nor heard his name mentioned? Yet she remained certain that, somewhere, somehow, *she had seen his face!*

Across from her, Father Matthew sipped his hot wine and watched her, his bright eyes missing nothing of the emotions that coursed across her face. How much should he reveal of what had brought him here? And how much should he keep hidden?…And how long before she worked out where she had seen him before? And by the Torch of the Gospels…what was the situation at Castle Malwood now?

"Father," Alicia said then slowly, feeling her way through to the next questions she needed answering so badly. "Forgive me. But what *are* you doing here, merrily jauntering about in the Forest at the dead of night? I mean, why didn't you come straight to Malwood? And how come you are so thick with Allan Wood and the King's Verderers..and..and so *many* other questions! Not least, how come, if you have been known to both families for so long a time have I *never* met you, nor heard your name mentioned?"

The tall dark Benedictine looked at her for a long time then, and smiled, both at her perspicacity and her determination to press forward with such difficult questions: "Alicia, those are all excellent questions and fair ones too. Some I can answer now, and I will do so willingly, I promise you. Some will just have to wait until we get you home. Will you accept that, my Lady?"

"Well, Father," she said quietly, through slightly gritted teeth. "You really don't give a girl much choice, do you? So, of course I accept. Just don't think it'll all go away will you? For I promise you, it won't!"

"How like your father you are, my dear. He was just as determined and just as clear in his thinking…"

"…Father," she interrupted him gently. "You are avoiding my questions!"

"Well, not exactly avoiding them as putting them off somewhat! Still, nothing ventured, nothing gained as they say, so here's the best I can do! Alright?"

"Alright, Father." She said, and settled herself more comfortably to hear his tale.

Chapter 34......And makes some more things clear.

"I met Sir Yvo and your father many years ago when we were all young men just setting out on Life's unknown journey.

We were all young knights together then, the three Caballeros, and I fought for King Henry, as they did...as well as for my own lands against the Moors beyond Navarre. Then, about twenty years ago or so, as I said, I hung up my spurs and became a Benedictine, and took Holy Orders as well, some time before they both got married...and long before you and Sir Gui were born and baptised.   And then...oh for all sorts of different reasons, I chose Ellingham Priory to set up home, so to speak. It is an Alien House, as my Mother House, the Monastery of San Salvador of Leyre, is in Navarre - near where my is my real home, Pampalona, and I chose Ellingham as much because it was near both your families as for any other reason, and as there are only a handful of brothers there, two of whom you have met, I am my own Abbot," he chuckled "And recognised as such by the Holy Father...

"...The Pope?" Alicia squeaked, astonished.

"The every same, my child," Father Matthew went on with a bow and a twinkle in his eye. "So I was able to christen first Gui, and then you too. Two such lovely children and in such happy circumstances...though he did bawl lustily when I poured the water over him! And with Ellingham so close to the western borders of the Forest I visited whenever I could when you were very little. But, as you so rightly said, the Benedictines are not a wandering Order, so it was not often that I was able to get away. Not least because of my work on medicines and cures, and the demands on me, as a priest at nearby Romsey Abbey..."

"That place is full of nuns!" Alicia commented.

"But of course it is full of nuns!" He said with a smile.   "It is a Benedictine Convent."

"And not very wise nuns either, I think," she added with a chuckle. "At least they seemed mightily 'wet' when we had some stay with us at castle Malwood a few years ago...Full of superstitions and fears: spiders, bats, frogs, and bulls; all sort of rubbish. Lady Margaret got very fed up with them!"

"Yes, Lady Bright Eyes, But then Romsey Abbey is a Convent, as I said, so of course it is full of nuns! But they need a priest for confession and the Holy Mass, and they are at heart 'good people'…even though very silly at times!" He agreed, adding: "So, apart from Romsey, I found myself being called upon more and more to help sort out difficulties far and wide, and was given special authority, first by the Papal Legates, to journey overseas and collect all the herbs and barks necessary to further my research; and then by the Pope and the King. Too many men had died on previous Crusades from sickness and from sour wounds. Prince Richard, as he was then, particularly wanted to know what could be done to do things better. That took me to Constantinople and beyond: Persia, India and of course to the Holy Land itself…"

"To Jerusalem?" Alicia interrupted him, her eyes big as saucers at mention of so wonderful and Holy a place.

"Yes, and mighty smelly it is too, I assure you! Though the market is fantastic and the King's Court simply amazing!" And he smiled at the remembrance of it all.

"So? Go on!" She urged him.

"Well, back then to Rome to report my findings to the Curia itself, and then to Chinon to meet with King Henry, and his Queen, Eleanor of Aquitaine…an incomparable beauty and possessed of a most powerful intellect. And, of course, King Richard, only he was Prince Richard then. But I have known the family since he was a baby."

"A baby?" She asked amazed.

"Yes. The first war of Henry's reign, in Toulouse, started in '59. We were *all* in that campaign. Sir Yvo, your father and me: three gay Caballeros, all part of Henry Plantagenet's household, and in and out of his quarters all the time. Richard was born in '57. A lusty babe, always struggling to be first to his mother's knee, or to his father's, the Queen nursed him herself for some time!"

"My father? Sir Henry?" She asked eagerly. "Did you know him then? And my mother?"

"Yes, my child, I did. Both of them"

"Am I like her, Father?" She asked wistfully. "It was so long ago now, I can barely remember her, except for her smile and her laughter, and the scent she wore.

232

"Your mother was the *most* beautiful Lady, my dear Alicia," he said softly, smiling across at her and taking her hand for a moment. "She was always bright, the Lady Anne, with a warm smile and a joke on her lips. Your father adored her. You are so very like her." And he sighed.

"He always seemed such a big man to me, my father," she said then, looking into the fire, her thoughts miles away. "With a deep voice and arms like tree trunks; that I *do* remember…being tossed in his arms. And he loved horses…especially Alexander, his favourite charger."

"Do you remember him?"

"Mmmm. Yes! He was huge, the rich colour of a fresh conker just out of its spiky shell; with big flicky ears and a hairy nose that '*harrumphed*' at you and nudged you for titbits! Papa always had an apple or a sweetmeat for him somewhere," she said with a chuckle. "As I do myself for our horses! And then of course he took him to France," she sighed then, looking up: "And that summer was the last time I saw them. I cried *so* when I heard my father had died, I thought my heart would break. Sir Yvo and Lady Margaret brought me up then, and gave me Rose to love, and now Agnes Fitzwalter…she was my nurse from when I was ten…and she is now my closest friend. I adored them both above all beings, save their son, Gui," and she groaned deep in her heart as she thought of him.

"He is my life on earth, Father. Tonight…last night," she said, looking up to see the first, faintest hint of the pre-dawn stealing greyly across the rain-washed sky. "Was both the *most* wonderful…and then the most *terrible* time of my life!" And she sighed again and was silent, rolling her warm beaker between her hands as she gazed again unseeing into the fire, while Father Matthew watched her.

"I never dreamed 'Life' could be so difficult. So-so complicated, Father," she said after a while, looking up at him. "Or that 'things' that happened so many years ago to others could have so devastating an effect on me now! You, my father, Sir Yvo…the Old King, and now *his* sons, Richard and John."

"The one who is King and the one who would like to be so! They are a turbulent family, our Plantagenet kings."

"So, that's where you met with Richard for the first time," she said after a while, looking up at him. "At Chinon. And King Henry too…and the wicked Lord Baron de Brocas?

233

"The Old King Henry? Yes, but the de Brocas you know was only about fourteen then. It was *his* father who was causing the problems. The Lord Baron Sir Thibault de Brocas, known as 'The Cruel', whom your father put down at the siege of Cahors some thirty years ago now, right at the start of the Toulouse war."

"My father killed him?"

"Yes! Fighting over Sir Yvo, who had fallen in the rush to seize the breach. Thibault would have cut him in half if your father hadn't hacked him down first. I was there. Saw Sir Yvo fall, but could never have reached him in time to save his life. Sir Thibault was right there standing over him, sword raised for a truly awful killing blow. There was no saving him. Then came your father, leaping like a tiger and barged de Brocas to one side and then slew him with his two favourite blows: split him up the middle, from crutch to navel, with a vicious uppercut and then hacked his head off with a perfect return blow, two handed, right to left. I can still see it now, and hear it: the deep '*thwok!* of your father's final blow, Thibault's head flying off in a spray of blood, and his butchered entrails everywhere…"

And for a moment there was silence as both looked at the fire, their minds far away in distance and in time.

"So you were right there, Father?" she asked, taking a sudden quick breath and looking across at him. "Beside them?"

"Almost. Close enough to see it all."

"Is that where the feud started?" she asked. "With Thibault's death?"

"No! It had been going on for years. Constant raid and counter raid; legal fights over land and property; dirty, underhand dealing; treachery and murder. All sorts! The de Brocas family is full of bad blood. Enough to drive your ancestors, and Sir Gui's, to move north from Montauban and Rocamadour permanently."

"Yes. That much I do know. They came to England with Conqueror William, and stayed here, in the Forest."

"Well, that business over Cahors did for de Brocas and his family once and for all. Thibault changed sides at the last moment, backed the wrong King and lost everything, including his life. He always was a fool! Anyway, his family were tainted after that, for treasonously supporting the French King…Louis VII it was then…when Henry Plantagenet was their true Liege Lord. De Brocas

234

had sworn to hold Cahors for Henry, and then changed sides. Louis apparently promised him the earth and he, the ass, believed him. The really bad thing was that his son, Roger…now the Lord Baron you have come to know so well!..was there when you father cut Lord Thibault down.

"No!"

"Hmmm. Afraid so! Picked his father's head up, and his sword, and scuttled off drenched in his father's blood before anyone could stop him. So of course that just made an already bad feud even worse."

"So what happened then?" Alicia asked intrigued.

"In those days Lord Thibault de Brocas had lands everywhere, but mostly around Montauban, and Rocamadour…where your family held land also!…And all was in King Henry's gift, so of course the family lost everything, and were forced to move right down to Narbonne where he is now in alliance with the Count of Toulouse and the good Archbishop Berenguer. A prime article if ever there was, that one, the good Archbishop; and a man whom the Pope has his eyes on for permanent removal to the furthest, meanest part of the Holy Roman Empire where he can do no more harm!

Anyway, there from his new base at Château Grise, young Lord Roger - now the Lord Baron de Brocas courtesy of the new French King, Philip Augustus - was already making a name for himself by thrusting his sticky fingers into every nasty pie he could find, and constantly fomenting trouble in the hopes of getting his lost lands back. But King Henry would have none of it. He used me to gather information, and your father and Sir Yvo and their men to help carry out the instructions that followed. We made sure De Brocas was not a happy man!"

"So what happened then?"

"Well, my Lady, this is where it gets very complicated and - and very political. And it is a part of the story that I really cannot divulge to you at this time," he said very cautiously. "At least not until I know what has happened to Sir Gui! Suffice it to say that I am not here by accident, *nor* without the King's knowledge…*and* his blessing. More I cannot say!"

She looked him in his face then, the tight line of his mouth and the fixed steady gaze, and knew that she would get nothing more from him than that. Not by accident, and not without the King's knowledge or blessing. So King Richard had indeed had a hand in all this somehow? She sighed, frustrated. She'd got so far…but not nearly far enough! Yet she was not dismayed as much that had not been clear before now was...especially why de Brocas hated their families so badly.

"But, Father," she asked ingenuously, looking at him from the corner of her eyes. "That does not explain what you are doing here. Nor how you come to know Allan Wood or Rose and Edward.

"Well, in all my travels, my Lady," he said after a pause. "I still have to come home to roost from time to time. That is my Benedictine duty, and despite my Papal warrant I still need show myself to be a dutiful Brother monk. And, every time I come back, I always travel to Ellingham from Beaulieu, through the Forest. And that means going through Lyndhurst..."

"...And that means The Saracen's Head! Mmmm, very convenient, Father," she said, smiling, her eyebrow cocked up at him quizzically.

"Why so cynical, my Alicia?" he asked her, poking the fire with a stick. "It's over thirty miles or more by track and roadway from Beaulieu to Ellingham, and the 'Head' is about half way. Everyone passes through Lyndhurst at some point or other on their way from Poole to Southampton, or up to the King's great castle and cathedral at Old Sarum, and so the 'Head' is a natural meeting place for exchanging news and views. And popular, too, Rose and Edward have made sure of that. Why else do you think de Brocas chose it? And sent orders to hold two rooms against his coming?"

"I don't know."

"Because I told him to!"

"*You told him to?*" She gasped at him, mouth dropping open in shock, swiftly covered with her hand.

"Yes, my Lady! I did, when I was down at the Château Grise, last winter; or Gruissan as they call it. There I met with the daughter, 'The Lady', as she is known and told her about my search for herbs and medicines. Posed as an ancient and doddery old priest, with wheezing breath and shaky on my limbs; you would have been amazed," he said, laughing at her shocked face. "Didn't want anyone to think I might pose a danger, and didn't want to meet with the man himself, he might just have recognised me from the old days."

Alicia could only sit there and gape, her eyes almost bursting out of her head at the extraordinary tale she was hearing. So this lovely, seemingly mild mannered and scholarly monk was a Royal and Papal spy! Not only that but de Brocas being here was planned... but by whom...and for what purpose? She looked across at the tall Benedictine and shook her head, astonished by all that she was being told.

"So, in the process of telling her what you did, you also told her where your Priory was...and how wonderful the Saracen's Head was as a place to stay!"

"No...not where my Priory was. That might have been dangerous, but about the Saracen's Head? Yes I did."

"Why?

"Ah!" he said then, suddenly aware that he had let slip far more than he had intended. "Can't tell you that..."

"...Until we get back to the castle!" She finished for him with a smile.

"As for Allan and his men? They were deliberately close to hand, for reasons I cannot give you just now...but just in case.

"Just in case of what, Father?"

"Just in case you get your pretty little nosey nose chopped off, young Lady Bright Eyes!" He said, laughing. "Suffice it that Allan and his men were brought in especially because we needed to be certain that nothing would slip out, and we were not sure of the loyalty of the Under Sherriff, nor some of the Forest Verderers."

"Who's 'we' Father?" She asked sharply.

"What?" he replied startled.

"This mysterious 'we' that's suddenly appeared in the conversation? Who are 'we'?"

"Hmmm. Can't say, My Lady," he replied, startled by her sharpness of mind. "Not now!"

"Oh! Another 'wait until we get back to the castle' thing?" She countered swiftly.

"Yes," he said, laughing. "I expect so!"

She sighed. Clearly she wasn't going to get anything more on that subject! So who could 'we' be? And what was all that about the loyalty of the Verderers?...And *where* had she seen him before? She sighed again. "Was it because of the Baron?" She asked then. "About the Verderers, I mean?" She added, seeing him look suddenly confused

"Oh no!" He replied swiftly, somewhat surprised. "Because of Prince John!"

"*Prince John?*" She gasped again. "Is *he* involved in all this, Father? That dreadful little man?...No! Don't say it!" She added, as she saw his face close up again. "'Can't tell you that until we get back to the castle'!"

"Well, my Dear," he said then, sitting back and crossing his arms, his hands lost in the depths of his wide black sleeves. "You surely are just as sharp as I had thought you would be, given your heritage. Sir Yvo would have been proud of you!"

"That's lovely, Father," she said, gazing down again into the flames as they jumped and flickered amongst the burning sticks. Then, looking up at him a moment later she asked: "But something went wrong, didn't it? Or I wouldn't be here!"

The tall Benedictine sighed, and disgustedly threw some more pieces of wood onto the fire, while she waited for his response. Then, after looking into the busy flames for a moment, he said: "Yes. Lots went wrong really: Little Peter fell ill, we were hit by the storm of the century, my message didn't reach Yvo, and then Saffron got injured!" he added pointing to the lovely dappled mare quietly cropping in the clearing, one foreleg heavily bandaged. "Quite simple really," he added, looking at her then. "Because of Peter's illness I couldn't leave for Castle Malwood when I should have done. And he really was very ill, my Lady, so ill that I could not leave him when I wished to. So I sent a message on ahead to Sir Yvo and bundled the child's father off to get more herbs and stuff from the Cistercian Herbalist at Beaulieu..."

"...Which is why when I turned up Edward was not there to greet the 'noble' Baron, and his unexpectedly drugged cousin? Nor Rose either!"

"And when we did get away...it was into the teeth of the worst storm in living memory! Next poor Saffron got a dreadful bang on her left foreleg, poor old lass...and here we all are!"

"What a mess!"

"What a mess indeed, my Lady. And I still cannot really tell you what it is all about either..."

"…'Til we get back to the castle!' Yes I *have* rather got that point, Father," she said, smiling across at the older man, now looking both concerned and very fed up. "Still, there's no point sitting here feeling mumpish. What's done cannot be undone now, as I have heard Lady Margaret say so many times, Bless her. So you had better tell me more about *him*," she said, pointing to the compact man leading towards them what was clearly now, in the drab light of early morning, a dark chestnut; his keen eyes alight with humour, the huge wolfhound she had seen earlier, now frisking by his side.

"That's Allan-i-the-Wood. The new Under Sheriff, remember? It was his men who found the baron and his troopers thrashing the forest searching for you. They couldn't get past some great tree that was blocking their path, when Allan and his men caught up with them. There was a stiff and bloody fight, because of course the Baron's men were all armoured while many of Allan's fellows were not, during which he lost three of his men as I told you, before they finally managed to drive that wretched Frenchman off. Allan's men came to guard the King's deer...not fight wild French bandits to the death! So be gentle with him. It was he who found you and brought you safely here, and it was one of *his* men who told me what little we know about what has happened at Malwood."

"What else do you know, Father? And where, oh where, have I seen you before?"

"Not nearly enough, Alicia, about anything," he said, patting her shoulder gently. "And as for the other…you will just have to work that out for yourself! But what I do know is that if we are to reach Malwood before lunchtime we cannot linger here one moment longer!"

"Do you think Gui could still be alive, Father?" She asked him in a small voice, looking up at him beseechingly, tears in her eyes again.

"I cannot tell you that, my dearest child," he answered her softly. "But it must be possible. We know that his parents have perished in the fire...but of their son we have heard nothing, and in this case no news could very well be good news. So...it is possible. But to be certain we must first *get* there! Come now, my little Lady Bright Eyes," he said with the warmth of Spain in his voice. "Tears will not serve us now. There will be a time for grief later." And so saying he pulled her to him again and gently kissed her forehead, while he made the sign of the cross over her in a simple act of blessing.

"Now!" he said briskly, smiling down into her upturned face and dropping his arm to her shoulder. "Come and meet your saviour while I and

Brothers James and William see to poor Saffron. James is a wonder with horses, and assures me that our dear old lady will be fine in just a moment." And turning he swept her towards the man now approaching them from across the clearing, his horse nodding behind him, ears pricked in interest, and his giant hound loping along beside him, his master's hand resting on his grey and brindled back.

"This is Allan," Father Matthew said, his dark eyes sparkling in the early pre-dawn light, now turning the sky from grey to faintest, palest primrose. "Allan-i-the-Wood, Under Sheriff to Sir Joscelyn. And this somewhat tattered fairy Queen," he went on, presenting her to him, "is the Lady Alicia de Burley, of Castle Malwood. Now, I'll just leave the two of you together for a moment while James, William and I get Saffron and the tilt-cart organised. Look!" He pointed eagerly to the rapidly brightening sky, rubbing his hands together gleefully. "The sun is up at last. Oh, what a difference that makes!

Come now, we still have a fair few miles to go, and I want to be gone from here within the hour, so don't linger with your conversation!" And with a fresh bounce to his step, the tall Benedictine left them to greet his two companions, cowl thrown back from his fine head, his long black robe swirling over the rain-soaked grasses of the clearing.

Chapter 35... The White Rose of Malwood meets Allan-i-the-Wood.

Alicia turned then and studied the man before her, his face, beneath a wild, russet mop of unruly curls, was weather-beaten and cragged, a fine white scar running down one side of it. But he had merry eyes and a wide mouth for smiling and Alicia liked him immediately.

"Quite a man, our noble priest," Alan said in his deep voice, the richness of his Devon burr making Alicia smile. "He has more knowledge in his little finger than I have in my whole body. I have never met such a man before."

"Yes!" She said simply, shaking her head. "He truly is the most amazing person I have ever met too. He knew my parents better than I ever did myself, and is close both to the King and to my Guardian, God rest his Soul." She added, crossing herself. "A man of deep understanding and knowledge, as you say, and full of more surprises than a bag full of wild cats!"

Then, with a smile and a shake of her head at the thought of a bag full of wild cats actually being opened!...she went on: "So! You are the one whom I must thank for my life tonight?" and she dropped him a slow and gracious curtsy. "And I am so sorry that you have lost three good men in the process," she said sadly, as he took her hand and raised her up again. "And that others have been badly hurt. Please be assured that I will do all I can to help their families. The King also will surely do his part. I am his Ward, and Richard is a gracious man as well as our King."

"I thank you for that, my Lady," he said, his eyes darkening with sadness. "My men will appreciate that greatly, and those left behind will thank you also." And both paused in their talking, their thoughts clouded by all that had happened that night just passed. Then, with a shake of his shoulders he looked up, and turning to her he said: "But come now, to brighter things. What of you, My Lady?" he queried, his eyes crinkling into a smile. "*You* are the one who jumped that tree! That was rare horsemanship indeed. I would not have believed it had I not been there to see it with my own eyes!"

241

"You saw me?" She gasped in surprise.

"Certainly! We had been following you for some time, not knowing who you were..."

"But I was mounted on Rose's mare!" She snapped at him. "You *must* have known it wasn't Rose...so it *must* have been me!"

"No, my Lady! We had none of us seen you before this night. It could have been the Baron's daughter on Rose's mare, stolen from her stable for all we knew!"

"Hmmm...I suppose so," she answered slowly, mollified. "So was it you then I heard in the Forest? I knew something was out there. I could 'feel' it. Scared me half to death! Why didn't you call out?"

"We were curious..."

"...*Curious?*" She interrupted him indignantly, turning away and then back again.

"Yes, my lady," he went on, with a grin. "It is not often that we find a maiden riding hell-for-leather through the Forest, especially one mounted on a mare I know well! Then, when we saw that gurt big tree in your way, we were sure we would have you in a moment. But you jumped it! Amazing!" And he clapped her softly.

"You, Allan-i-the-Wood, are a shameless flatterer...and a ragamuffin!" she said with a broad smile and a slight incline of the head to acknowledge his applause. "However...I was pleased with myself, a bit! And with Sunburst of course," she added swiftly. "She was simply magnificent. But I surely wouldn't want to try that again in daylight! The man who trained that horse is worthy of a golden chain, whenever I catch up with him!"

And Allan smiled then and bowed his head.

"*You?*" She gasped then, her eyebrows flying up. "But..but how? I..I mean, Father Matthew told me you were new here. Brought in specially."

" That's true, My Lady," The craggy Verderer said, his eyes twinkling as he spoke. "But Edward is a cousin on my mother's side, so I have always popped in to the 'Head' from time to time. That is partly why I was chosen for this job. I already know the Forest. Anyway, Edward asked me to school this mare he was wanting for his Rose...so I did. And a rare joy it was too, as

Sunburst loves to jump."

"Well, Master Under Sherriff," Alicia said, giving him an even deeper curtsey, with a brilliant smile to go with it. "You both saved my life this past night, for without your training Sunburst could never have leaped that tree! So…a real gold chain it shall be, and not just gilded brass I promise you!"

And she laughed and dropped him a deep curtsey, as he thanked her warmly with a bow of his own taking her hand to lifted her up at the same time, her eyes taking him in more closely as he did so to look him over carefully: thinking how much Agnes would like to meet so bold and handsome a man as Allan-i-the-Wood, the King's Under Sheriff of the New Forest. He was *exactly* what she had been looking for…Agnes's 'King of France' at last… and a far, far better man than Jules Lagrasse any day! And she smiled at the thought of something good coming out of all this madness after all!

"A silver penny for them, my Lady?" he asked her quietly, amused by her silent study of himself and his horse and hound.

"Oh…nothing of any matter," she replied easily. "I may tell you one day, if I get the chance. So," she continued, looking into his pale blue eyes. "You finally bagged me and brought me here," she said, bringing her thoughts back to the business in hand. "It seems you and Father Matthew are well matched! I am King Richard's Ward, you know. And I am sure the King will be delighted to know of your loyalty and your leadership. You are not married, Master Allan?" she asked quietly, her head on one side, her eyes shadowed.

"No! I have never yet met with the right lady. I love what I do, and there are not many lasses who will put up with my hours and my absences without griping so much that they make one's life unbearable. But I live in hope, my Lady, for I do not wish to spend the rest of my life alone. And I want little ones too!"

"Then be sure to come to Malwood soon, Master Allan," she replied brightly, her eyes alight with mischief. "For I know someone with whom you would just love to meet…and whom, I know, would just love to meet with you too!"

"My Lady?" He questioned her, eyes raised in surprise.

"She is the sweetest and loveliest maiden in the Forest…"

"Who is this secret beauty?" He interrupted her, laughing.

243

"I will not say," she ended mysteriously, her eyes sparkling with amusement at his confusion. "You will just have to come to Castle Malwood and discover that for yourself!"

"Father Matthew said you were 'special', my Lady, and now I can see why. Wit, beauty, mischief…and a caring heart," he said slowly, looking down at her with a warm smile. "Your man, Sir Gui, must be formidable indeed to have won your heart so completely. You can be certain that I will be calling at the castle before long, as much to meet with your man, of whom I have heard so much…and whom I am certain you will find alive and well," he added firmly, seeing her sudden distress. "As to meet with this mysterious and beautiful maiden you were speaking of."

"You will not be disappointed, Master Allan, I assure you," she said with a broad smile. "I shall tell her to expect you!"

"Does she like Hounds?" He asked her cautiously. "I mean large hounds, My Lady. Most girls don't!"

"Loves them, Master Allan," she said with laugh. "Especially when they look like shaggy rugs on four legs! What's he called?"

"Bouncer!"

" *'Bouncer'?*" She exclaimed, startled. "That's brave for a Wolfhound! He should be called something high and grand in Celtic…like..well, like, 'Cuchulainn' or 'Sceolan' though I can see why not!" she added with a laugh, as she watched his hound leap about on his great shaggy paws. "And he's only a baby, too," she added, ruffling his great hairy head with her hand. "He's big now, but he'll be huge when he is full grown. And who is this bold fellow?" she asked, smiling, as her elbow was butted by a pair of enormous nostrils, followed by a hopeful *'Brrrrough!*' from a large set of whiskery lips.

"This is Caesar," the Under Sheriff replied with a grin, giving his huge chestnut a hearty bang on his withers. "Hoofs like dinner plates, but can go for miles at pace, even with two up. Saved my life more than once…and always looking for titbits, the rogue!

"So I can see," she said with a dazzling smile. "Truly you are an original, Master Allan. Your secret lady will love you for it," And she laughed delightedly. "Just make sure you come soon! For your gold chain from me, as much as for another set of golden chains as well for all you know."

"Thank you, my Lady, I will do my best to do so. But come on now," he continued briskly, seeing that one of his men had brought Sunburst up for her to mount. "I see Father Matthew is ready at last. All is done here now, and it is time to leave!" And with a warm smile on his scarred and craggy face, he threw her up onto Sunburst's back as lightly as he had brought her down in the first place, before springing up on to his own great chestnut gelding.

With a click of his tongue he kicked Caesar forward, Alicia bringing Sunburst round to join him, as with many creakings and groanings of the old tilt-cart, Father Matthew, the reins firmly between his fingers, brought Saffron, with her leg still neatly bound, plodding up beside them. The two other Benedictine Brothers, James and William, their cowls thrown back off their heads, striding along on either side to help with the wheels should that be needed as they moved off across the rain-soaked clearing.

Overhead the sky was just turning a delicate blush-pink as the sun nudged gently up from below the far horizon, banishing the pale primrose and duck-egg green of the early dawn to bathe the rain-spangled clearing in a blush of golden warmth. Each droplet suffused with sparkling glory to welcome the newborn day. All across the leaf-strewn grass were draped a vast mist of spiders' webs that flew apart as the men and horses began to shamble forwards. Above them the last vestiges of the great storm had been swept away to leave a clear, fresh, rain-washed sky already turning from pink to softest, brightest blue.

All around them the Conqueror's great forest breathed and sighed. The trees steaming in the early morning heat from the new-born sun, creating a drifting mist that hung upon the ground and shrouded the trackway up ahead. Boar rooted amongst the great trunks for tubers and acorns while pigeons crooned in the trees above, the sudden clap of their wings as they dipped and swooped across the clearing loud in the soft silence of the morning, making the men look up and smile. It was time to go. And, with a bow of his head, and a silent signal to his men to spread out through the trees, Allan kicked Caesar forward, his great hound keeping easy pace beside him as he led the little party out of the clearing and onto the narrow track that led to Castle Malwood.

In moments the early morning mist, shot through with broad, opaque shafts of sunlight, had swallowed them up, leaving only crumbs of fresh bread for the questing fox that slipped out into the clearing to nose them over. Head up, with ears pricked and brush down, he searched the air for the tantalising scent of warm rabbit, and with barely a glance at the still smouldering fires and the piles of warm dung still steaming in the early morning air, he trotted swiftly across the empty clearing and was gone.

245

Chapter 36...How the Lord Baron was forced to flee the Forest.

From the moment of arriving at the Saracen's Head that wild night of the fire, everything that could go wrong suddenly seemed to have done so! There had been a violent row at the entrance because the Innkeeper, the Aubergist Edward Sergeant, was away from home on some kind of errand and the idiot left behind had known nothing and had had to be threatened just to let them in! The horses he had ordered to be ready weren't...they were up in some corral and running loose; and then, and almost beyond comprehension, while all were relaxing in the wide hall below...Rochine had let the bloody girl slip through her fingers! Left the girl's room unlocked and unguarded...and before anyone had known any more about it the damned Innkeeper's wife, Rose, had helped the little bitch escape into the Forest!

His fury had known no bounds and he had ordered the woman, Rose, to be seized and the Inn razed to the ground in an effort to discover where the wretched girl had fled to? Obviously back to Malwood...but by which trackway had she fled? And in the midst of all that, and before he could set his men into the kind of violent action they so enjoyed...he had been halted in his tracks by the seizure of his daughter! The Lady Rochine had somehow allowed herself to be captured, and by the man Forrester, the very same *ignorant fucking pig!* who had sought to deny them access to the Saracen's Head in the first place!

The man had somehow seized Rochine, pinioned her arms behind her back, and with his sword at her throat come down the stairs threatening to slay her if he, The Lord Baron Sir Roger de Brocas, Lord of Narbonne and Gruissan, did not instantly leave with all his men! That alone was insupportable; worse still the man had raised the Inn against him too, just as the Innkeeper, Edward Sergeant, had returned, a giant of a man with a club in his hand the size of a ship's timber! And now with a dozen armed men at his back, it was not worth fighting over. A case of *Force Majeur* against his small command which had enraged him even further. As if it was not humiliating enough that they had lost their prize, they had now been driven off by a parcel of English peasants! And so they had left, vowing vengeance and taking that idiot Georges Routier with them, whose face had been raked open from chin to scalp by that bloody girl's boot. Gore everywhere and a mess of torn flesh and muscle. He had been minded to finish the fool off there and then, rather than hinder their pursuit of the Lady Alicia de Burley who had burst through de Vere's men as if they had been a pack of noisy children playing soldiers with wooden swords!

And so, once ready and mounted, with shouts of rage and spurs jabbed into their horses' sides, they had thundered out of the Inn yard in a spray of stones and muddy water and taken off after their quarry without a moment's pause. Not back the way they had come, Sir Roger was certain their prey would not have done that, taking a different route back to the castle so, at the edge of the town, he had pulled them all up and ordered de Vere to take two men and track Westwards, while he took the rest, including the injured Routier, and went North West in a circle to see if he could cut across her trail that way; and had not gone far when he found the torn tracks left by her mare as she had raced away from the Inn. And giving a loud '*Halloo!*' to de Vere to follow him close, Sir Roger led his men off along the mired trackway that Alicia had taken some thirty minutes earlier, waiting for de Vere, his Guard Commander to catch up with him before once more digging in their heels and hurtling after her.

Above them the storm was swiftly clearing away, the great cloud wrack that had been so dense and black before now broken up and blown away by the wind, still gusting fiercely through the trees, so that the moon's harsh silver light bathed everything in flickering, fleeting shadows as the clouds raced across its face. One moment all would be bright and clear, with trees and men in sharp silhouette against the waterlogged ground…the next plunged into utter blackness as its light was suddenly extinguished. And when that happened, Lord Roger would fling up a hand, give a mighty shout, and bring them down to a steady amble and not continue at a wild gallop for fear of missing something vital or thundering into a fallen tree of which there were many all around them. And it was during one of these sudden slow downs that de Vere's expert trackers found her trail.

"My Lord!…My Lord Baron, to me, quickly. There is something strange here!" And leaping off his sweating horse's back the man had crouched down beside where a tree had almost fallen slantwise across a narrow diverging bridle-path leading further North West from the main trackway they had been following.

"See here, My Lord Baron," the man said, pointing down to the smatter of spoor on the ground, while de Brocas leaned down over him from the back of Charlemagne. "See, how this tree has disguised this narrow trackway? Well, there are clear signs here, M'Lord, where a cart has gone through, a tilt cart with spoked wheels by its track. Heavily laden from the depth of its passage and accompanied by men, from the size of their spoor. Two, maybe three. Not more. Their tracks overlie the cart's. See? This big rut, My Lord? It must have got stuck here. You can see where two men in studded shoes must have pushed it. Now, My Lord, see this?" the tracker went on, pointing to where a fresh hoof appeared to have imprinted itself on top of the others. "That is a completely fresh track, and smaller than the other hoof marks. And see, too, My Lord," he went on turning around. "See? Here are another, smaller set of shoe prints, where someone got down to look at this fallen tree, before leading a horse beneath it."

"How do you read all this, soldier?" De Brocas asked him in his dark voice.

"Gervaise Houlier, My Lord Baron," the man said, looking up briefly before squatting down with a wand off a torn tree branch to point his way. "See, M'Lord. Three men and a cart came through here much earlier. Perhaps before the storm reached its peak. This passage is narrow, as is the track, so they had difficulty in making the turn – and then the cart stuck and had to be pushed out. See? Deeper marks here from their toes, and these are sandaled feet, My Lord Baron; and heavily studded, such as monks wear. So, a parcel of monks with a laden tilt cart and horse came this way, and took this turn. Then the tree fell partway across the track, and later another rider came by and stopped just here. See?" he went on pointing to the smaller indent in the mired trackway. "A child? or a girl, by the size of her feet? A girl, I think, My Lord Baron . The Lady we are chasing. See, where she got off her horse and examined the trackway? Her marks are all on top of those already there. Then she led her horse under the fallen tree. Look! There are a few strands of hair here amidst its twigs and broken branches, very fine. And some darker, coarser ones from her horse's mane. No doubts about it, My Lord. This is where our quarry went!"

"Excellent, Houlier. Well done! I am seeking a monk as well as our escaped Lady who seems to have been following him, according to some varlets at the Inn. You are a credit to my forces, and I will not forget you. De Vere, double wine rations for this trooper and a handful of silver for his skills when we are back on board the *Christopher.* Now, lads. Lets shift this bloody tree

248

and get after her. She cannot be far ahead of us now!" And calling his men forward, he watched while they forced the tree right to the ground, before remounting and hopping their horses over it. Then, once all were clear he gave a great shout and hallooed them forward once again, urging their horses once more into a further wild gallop, the moon's brilliant silver-white light shining down on them like a giant lantern showing them the way.

Round the bends and sharper twists and turns of the forest path they galloped that night. Hooves pounding, water and mud splashing, harness jingling and chiming, both that on their backs and that on their horses also. It was a wild ride, with their hearts in their mouths every time they had to jump a fallen tree for all were wearing armour as well as carrying weapons, so jumping anything could cause a problem. So it was with a great roar of "**HALT!**" that Lord Roger brought his whole command to a sudden plunging, sliding stop in a spray of torn turf and muddy water as, hurtling round a shallow bend, they were confronted by a huge tree that had fallen right across the trackway, its branches shattered in all directions, one huge limb torn off from the very centre of the tree to leave a giant gap, over which no horse in his command, weighed down with arms and armour could possible have leaped. Nor was there any swift way around it either as its root bed was one vast tilted ruin, with a huge pit behind it from where it had been ripped out of the ground by the fury of the storm; and its immense crown stretched deep into the forest in an impenetrable hedge of smashed branches, twigs and torn greenery.

And at that very moment they were attacked.

With wild shouts and howls of rage all around them, armed men seemed to rise up from the very ground and with one great shout leapt at them from every side. Some were armoured, with sharp weapons of steel; many were not, and attacked them with staves and clubs. Some had bows, and in moments a violent sleet of arrows had been unleashed amongst the Frenchmen, two of whom were struck down almost immediately, the arrows ripping through their armour to tear out their throats in a vile spray of blood that coated everything, the shouted '*He! He! He!*' of the successful longbow archer ringing out across the clearing.

But after that it was a vicious, brutal skirmish, as Lord Roger's men fought the foresters with all their skill, driving their horses at them and flensing down at their enemies with sword and battle axe, de Brocas using the great flanged mace he always carried in its special bucket holder close to his right hand. And with that he killed his first Englishman, roaring: "*A Brocas! A Brocas!*" as he swayed Charlemagne sideways with his body weight and reins, swiftly shuffling the huge horse sideways across one man's leaping attack to force him off balance and then smashing him down with a terrifying blow that crushed his head and battered him to the ground, his brains scattering all over Charlemagne's bardings, his blood drenching the great horse's fetlocks.

And all around him de Vere's men fought their way free of their attackers, cutting, thrusting and parrying the wild blows of their unexpected enemies, teeth gritted and faces twisted with rage as they slashed down at heads and arms, backing and turning their horses...not trained for war and squealing in terror from all the shouting, crashing, screaming of close quarter battle...the sickly scent of blood covering many of them on that desperate wind-filled night.

Rochine, completely unarmoured and with no weapon to her hand, was Lord Roger's principal concern and he roared out across the brawling mêlée: "De Vere! Get The Lady out of here! Get her out and I will follow you. We must break clear. Go! *Go!*" And swinging Charlemagne round he fought to clear himself a space in which to fight, bringing the remains of his command close about him, to mask de Vere's escape with his daughter and small escort of two men, leaving himself and four others to hold the line until he could get clear.

And as he saw de Vere break free, so he dug in his spurs and drove his great destrier forward, itself screaming with rage and lashing out with his armoured fore feet as he had been taught to do, his mouth open and his nostrils wide. For Charlemagne was a true war horse, trained to fight as well as his master. To bite and neigh and scream out his rage as did his master, and stamp and trample and paw the air with his enormous feet, iron shod; ferocious weapons in any close fought fight. And where Charlemagne led the others followed, and with a great shout Sir Roger de Brocas and his men fell upon the foresters with renewed fury, cutting their way through them, trampling them underfoot: *Left! Right! Left! Right!* Lord Roger and his men struck out across their horses withers, taking blows on their shields and dealing them out as well. *Left! Right! Left!* Again, the screams and howls of the wounded ringing out across the forest, along with the violent clash of weapons and the brazen neighing of horses.

Even so did Lord Roger's men kill again, and so did he. His second Englishman, this time with his long sword, a balanced, slicing blow that hewed through the man's neck and shoulder in a violent sheet of blood that fountained up from his body as he screamed out in mortal agony, and fell senseless to the ground. And with that scream the way ahead opened for the Frenchman and his vanquished escort, and with shouts and cries of their own they took off into the wind-brushed night as if all the Hounds of Hell were at their tails, pursued by arrows and the roaring jeers of their triumphant enemies.

★

An hour later and Lord Roger had to admit they were hopelessly lost; flailing around in the rushing darkness of the forest, not knowing in which direction they should go, nor which way was south to where he knew their ship was waiting. Even though the sky had largely cleared, the storm wrack was still sleeting across the moon's silver face and nowhere could he get a clear sight of the stars to determine which was the North Star...and dawn was still too far away to show him East from West.

Fleeing the way they had come, they were soon back at the small tree that had blocked their way off the main trackway that Lord Roger knew led back to Lyndhurst, but with the countryside now raised against him for certain, both there and around Malwood, and with more than one injured man to care for, it was imperative they got off that trackway and distance themselves from any present danger. So turning away from Lyndhurst he led his troop further along the original track until they came to a small crossroads and turning left, they all plunged back into the forest intent on putting as much distance as possible between them and any force that might have been sent to hunt them down.

Like the great wild boar he so represented, The Lord Baron led his sounder into the deepest parts of the forest, where the great trees were the oldest: huge gnarled trunks with branches drooping almost to the ground and twisted roots reaching out in all directions. And on every side dense thickets of hazel, holly, black alder and dogwood, crammed in one upon another to make an impenetrable barrier, with occasional clearings ringed by huge clumps of brambles that reached above their horses' withers and numerous small streams and runnels crowded with silver birch and hawthorn, now overflowing with the rain that had cascaded down upon them as the storm had lashed the forest.

251

Dawn found them all wet and weary, horses and men both, with wounds and bruises stiffening and a real sense of lassitude amongst some of the men who had expected by now to be safely at sea, with England rapidly disappearing behind them and their prize quivering amongst them. Instead here they were, in a vast unknown forest, with everything gone wrong and trapped in a country filled with enemies, where every man's hand was likely to be turned against them for what they had done.

Only the Baron, The Lady and his Guard Commander, Gaston de Vere, were unmoved and as determined as ever, convinced of their ability to break free as they had always intended and take ship as planned.

And as the light grew so did their spirits, for as the sun rose behind them in the East with a pink blush that swiftly spread across the rain-washed sky, they could see that the track they were on led right to the very Western edge of the forest, beyond which was real open country at last, and as they reached the very tree line itself, Lord Roger could see a tiny settlement below them, brushed golden by the new day, not far from a narrow winding river that disappeared into the blue distance far to the north of where he was sitting Charlemagne.

Still upright in his saddle and still fresh despite all that had gone before, Lord Roger leaned forward and crossing his arms on the tall pommel of his saddle, looked down on what he could see and smiled, for the hamlet was tiny but ideally placed. The river and fields beyond it were shrouded in early morning mist, pale and opaque, through which the light flowed in shafts of writhing primrose as the sun pushed the grey light of early dawn aside to bring forth the new-born day.

Just a mean handful of cruck houses and turfed bothies clustered round a couple of good barns, the little settlement lay absolutely at peace that lovely morning. There was also one larger thatched building that stood to one side of the tiny hamlet, and fronted a narrow trackway that ran from left to right and out of sight. Close by was a small forge from which the smoke was already rising, a horse tethered outside waiting to be shoed, the distant dink of a heavy hammer coming up to them clearly; with a covered well and a wide drinking trough beside it.

A short distance below the tiny settlement was a further trackway leading westward across a ford in the river.

The larger building had a corral behind it in which a few horses could be seen drinking from another water trough. A sturdy building it was, steeply pitched, its thatch dark with age, an outside stair case up one side of it. And from its highest ridge a long column of white smoke was gently spiralling upwards into a clear sky, now washed with blue and blushed with pink, shot through with gold and crimson streamers as the sun finally rode up over the horizon. All quiet and peaceful, two people winding water from the well, their laughter clearly coming up to them in the still morning air, and nothing else moving as far as the eye could see.

"That looks a likely place, My Lord?" de Vere said, sidling his horse up beside the Baron, now standing in his stirrups and looking down at the river sparkling in the early morning sunshine, the mist still rising off it as the sun rose higher. "Looks like an Inn," he said, pointing to the largest building. "We need to rest the men, and the horses. And get our wounded seen to. A good meal all round will do us all wonders. And there's a blacksmith's down there too," he added, pleased. "He can check these horses over before we have to leave again."

"Gaston's right, father." His daughter's musical voice broke in on his reverie. "And you need a change of clothes! Those leathers are beyond all care. Burned, singed and bloodied; they are fit only for the fire. And this place is both tiny and isolated. There can be little chance of their knowing anything, and this is the only trackway to it that I can see."

Turning, Baron Roger looked at his daughter as if she were not there. As if she had not spoken. His eyes dark, black and without pity, his face hard as iron and even she quailed, only too well aware that it had been her actions that had brought them all to the very brink of disaster.

"Houlier!" he called then, looking over his shoulder. "To me! How do you read this trackway?"

Swinging off his horse, and thrusting his reins into a fellow trooper's hands, Gervaise Houlier made his way past the Baron, with a pat on the withers

253

for Charlemagne as he passed the great horse by, and moved off down the trackway ahead of him looking intently at every mark and dimple as he walked. Squatting down several times, sometimes turning over stray leaves he saw lying there, sometimes picking things up to smell them or rub them between his fingers, he spent several minutes in his careful search before turning to stride back towards where Lord Roger sat impassively waiting for his principal tracker to report in, while the bulk of his command sat their horses like sacks of meal.

"Clear, My Lord. All clear! Nothing has come this way save the beasts of the forest. A stag not long before us…you can clearly see his slots still filling with water and his fewmets are warm. A fox too, even earlier. I can smell his rank scent, and his prints are overset by the stag's. But no horse has passed by, My Lord, nor any foot traveller either. There has been no human traffic along here my Lord for some days."

"Good Man, Gervaise. Good Man! Right, Gaston. Get down there with two of your lads, and make the people down there known to you. I will follow shortly with The Lady and all the remainder. Bespeak us the best room they have, and ask the woman of the house if she can find spare clothes for the Lady Rochine. I have spare leathers behind my saddle bag. And, Gaston. Go easy? I have no wish for another such *contretemps* with an Innkeeper as that we had last night! So, curb the men!

Chapter 37... Tyrrell's Ford !

Tyrrell's Ford.

A small wayside Inn made famous by Sir Walter Tyrrell, a powerful Norman Baron, who had fled that way ninety years before, while escaping from the Forest after the sudden death at his hands of the Red King, William Rufus, second son of the Conqueror.

Staying at Castle Malwood, the royal party had set out on a planned hunting trip, Sir Walter especially accompanying the the King who had hunted fiercely all day, as had his father the Old Conqueror in his time. But towards the end of the day, with the sun setting before him, he had given the deer he was aiming at too much lead with his bow, and in the difficult light he had shot Rufus down instead, the King falling forward onto his arrow driving it into his heart. Some say the arrow glanced off an oak tree first, others it was a planned and brutal murder.

Accident or otherwise, Sir Walter fled.

Riding *ventre á terre...like the wind across the ground...*Sir Walter galloped for one of only two fords across the River Avon beyond the Forest that existed, and for the Inn that marked its place, where he could find immediate shelter, food and a fresh horse from the Inn Keeper's daughter who was his Mie. There he famously had the blacksmith reverse his horse's shoes before crossing the river, from where he fled to Poole and then back to his extensive estates in Normandy. Many claimed that the new King, the first King Henry, the Red King's younger brother, had paid him in gold and favours to shoot his brother down: certainly Tyrrell was never punished and his family in England were showered with gifts and favours by the new King!

Now Tyrrell's Ford was host to another murderer, for minutes after de Vere had made himself known at the Inn, the Keeper and his wife and daughters, Lynn and Poppy, swiftly ran out to bow before their so unexpected and exalted guests, the Lord Baron Sir Roger de Brocas and his daughter the Lady Rochine when they arrived with the remainder of their escort.

★

Two days the Baron and his party stayed at Tyrrell's Ford.

Two days while they rested and licked their wounds and told their story of being attacked in the Forest by wild brigands: outlaws and violent marauders who had killed two of his men and injured others, two very badly, for they were slashed and hacked about, more dead than alive when they had arrived. But the Innkeeper's wife, Mistress Linnet, had proven herself to be good with a needle and had stitched up his men and poulticed and cosseted them also, and her good man, Peter Oldsmith, had fed and watered them well.

Two days while the news of what had happened at Castle Malwood swept out through the Forest and round about, but not to Tyrrell's Ford, where de Vere and his men guarded the trackways and disrupted the Earl of Southampton's messengers with silent death and kept the Inn ignorant of what had happened, just astonished that no-one wanted to come by, as Tyrrell's was one of only two crossing points into the Forest on that western side of the Hampshire Avon.

Then, on the third day, just as morning was creeping in, darkness turning into light, they paid their shot in silver and left.

The night before Lord Roger gathered de Vere and his daughter to him and walked with them down to where the western trackway disappeared into the rushing waters of the Avon, crossing over the narrow cart-way that led from Christchurch in the South to Ringwood and Fordingbridge in the North, one trooper from his command on the road above the river's crossing, another below, and it was while they were walking down towards the ford itself that one of De Vere's men, on a sweating rouncey, rushed up to him and thrust a fragment of torn parchment into his hand, which he swiftly scanned, his face changing as he did so, the colour draining out of him as he read.

"What is it, de Vere?" The Baron growled at him, his brows rising in concern.

"That bastard has survived!" De Vere said tersely, handing the blood streaked parchment to the Baron as he spoke. "His parents are crisped sure enough and half the castle with them...but the bloody Lion of Malwood has survived!" He ended, turning to where the Lady Rochine was standing shocked beside him, her hand to her face in disbelief.

"*God's Blood!*" De Brocas swore violently, snatching the parchment out of de Vere's hands. "*Impossible!* I left him shot through beneath a huge timber and a great pile of rubble with the fire just feet away from him and roaring. I only just got out alive myself."

"The Earl's message is quite clear, My Lord," de Vere said quietly while de Brocas scanned the bloodied message with fury, not wanting to incur his Lord's wrath, while his daughter laughed. "Sir Gui de Malwood is alive!"

"You railed at me for losing the girl, My *so* clever Papa," She said bitterly with every bit of distain in her husky voice. "But you? You have allowed the Lion himself to escape. Scathed maybe, my dear Lord Baron," she sniped at her father, sarcasm dripping from every syllable. "But alive! They have humiliated you…all of us! Now what?"

"*Nothing!* Nothing has changed!" de Brocas snarled in his dark, gravelly voice, ripping the message parchment apart with his bare hands and hurling the pieces into the river. "We leave tomorrow at first light, as planned yesterday. I now know exactly where we are and where we are going. This trackway here runs alongside the river right down to the coast to a place called Christchurch, beyond the Forest boundaries. From there we turn East along the coast road to the little port of Lymington, cross the river there and then we are just a mile or so from where the *Christopher*, and Master Giles Walter will be waiting for us at Pitt's Deep. Then off and away back to Bordeaux."

"But…but what about Sir Gui, father?"

"What about that English *bastard?* He will come by his just deserts, my little Lady, I assure you. I planned for just this situation!" he added grimly. "You know that. We planned it all at home before we left; now we will see if the men I have chosen can carry out their tasks."

"The Cousins, My Lord?" De Vere asked, looking at de Brocas's face, mouth like a trap, eyes on fire.

"Yes, Gaston. It is precisely why we put them there. A back-up in case our primary strike failed, remember? Those two are both clearly established in the castle without a hint of doubt, and as we have seen, *trusted!*" He exclaimed softly, with a wicked sneer. "No other way would they have been put in such a sensitive place on guard that night were that not so. So at least you got that bit right, Rochine," he growled at her, his anger towards her dying down at last. "Now, if they do what they have been told…and Fabrizan worries me more than Jules; his mouth is too foul for my liking and his temper too fiery. But…if they do what we discussed at home, and as long as Jules can control his cousin,

257

they will do well."

"And the other part, Father? The message part that you have also worked so hard to perfect?"

"Hmmmm, my little Mercuries?" He said to his daughter with a sudden grin, as he rubbed his hands together and chuckled. "Feather-weight, not feather-brained! They are the very best part of it all. Of those two boys whom al Moukhtara had under his care at home, the boy Robin is a true natural, Raheel was hugely impressed with him, and that is no mean feat I assure you. The other one, that Henri Duchesne, is no more than a hewer of wood and a drawer of water, but good with a knife! . Those two are charged with getting into the castle alongside all the other riff-raff who will want to join this ridiculous Crusade. Once they know when those bastards are to set out, Robin will send a bird to de Courcy at Nantes who will send a boat out to tell El Nazir when to expect them. Then, when they arrive his son, Siraj, will pounce on them from behind the Île de Hoedic..."

"...And once they are thoroughly engaged with fighting them both off," de Vere said, banging his hands together in sudden glee. "El Nazir will sweep up from behind the Belle Île and attack that fat Red Cog of theirs, batter it in pieces, snaffle the girl on board...and leave that bastard to the bloody crabs and fishes!" And both men laughed.

"But how do you know they will use a red cog?" The Lady Rochine asked, puzzled.

"Because the Malwood family are creatures of habit, my so dear daughter," the Baron replied chucking her under her chin with a smile, suddenly returned to good humour. "They have been using that same ship for many years now, the *Mary*, and its giant Shipmaster, Master Thomas Blackwood. He brought the wine up from Bordeaux for that wretched party three nights ago and is still at Beaulieu. It is to him that that-that *Boy*, will go for help!" he snarled viciously. "He will want to chase us and chase us hard. Well, let him. No matter what he does, El Nazir will put him and his fat Red Cog down for good...and then deliver the fair Lady Alicia to us as planned. We cannot fail! Now, come on. We have a lot to do, and I want to be away from here before cock crow. The *Christopher* awaits us at Pitt's Deep. God knows, that bloody man, Walters, has been paid enough to be there; we only have to reach him and we will be away on the first tide.

So..." he said then, turning towards his daughter and slipping his arm around her pretty waist. "Those two might have won the first hand. And it is true that I feel humiliated by what they have done…a feeling to which I am not used!" he exclaimed with cold, biting anger. "But they do not know what they have taken on, My Bird! They do not know yet to what depths of misery and despair I will drag them. Sir Gui will still have the Emerald and she the bracelet you gave her?" he said to Rochine, giving her squeeze as he spoke. "Yes?"

"Yes, My Lord," she replied, looking up at her father meltingly.

"But I have the Crystal which binds them both to us my lovely," he said with a wicked smile, dropping a kiss onto Rochine's forehead as he turned back toward the Inn, de Vere following. "I have the Crystal that binds them. They can do nothing we will not know about…and therein lies their doom!" And throwing back his head he laughed, the sudden noise startling a pair of woodies from the trees that shot out with a frantic burst of wings and leaves.

"Those two turtle doves may croon together for now," he snarled, watching the two wood pigeons soar and sink down into a further clump of trees with a distant clap of wings. "But soon they will cry a different tune I promise you," and he laughed again.

"They do not know it yet, but we have them trapped. Between us, My Lady, we are invincible!"

Chapter 38... The Lion of Malwood comes into his own.

By the time Gui was compos mentis again the fire was over, though the ruins still smoked and steamed abominably and great stones, cracked and heated beyond endurance, continued to fall amidst tall spires of sparks and ashy debris. Everywhere were signs of both the fire and the storm: burned and shattered buildings, dead sheep and cattle, carts hurled over, roofs without tiles and fallen trees all over the place. The village too had suffered badly: whole buildings torn apart, others utterly demolished and crops flattened, completely ruined by the wind and rain together. It would take weeks to sort it all out.

Lying on a narrow pallet in the cool of the castle Chapel, the morning sunlight bursting through the coloured windows, Gui finally awoke to find the gentle face of old Father Gerome bent over him, Agnes kneeling by his side chaffing his hands, the apron over her blue kirtle smirched with blood and Sir Richard L'Eveque, the Guard Commander of Castle Malwood, standing looking down at him.

He felt light headed and his whole body, from top to toe, was one giant ache. His head was bandaged where it had been jagged open against the beam as L'Eveque and his men had hauled him out, his chest and loins were bruised from de Brocas's feet and there were lacerations all over his face and body as well, as much from his rescue as from breaking out of his room. All in all he was not a pretty sight. But it was his shoulder, where De Brocas' bolt had struck him that gave him the most pain and was causing everyone the most worry so deeply embedded in the joint was it, right up to its fletchings, that the muscle pad that surrounded it had seized solid around it. And looking at it Sir Richard decided that any attempt to pull it out might well cause an even more dreadful injury.

A broad head it was for certain, because a bodkin armed quarrel at that range would have gone right through him. But single barbed, or double, he had no idea? And he was loathe even to touch the thing! But cutting his jacket free from it was essential if Gui was to be moved, so with infinite care and the very sharpest of skinning knives, he sliced the leather away from it as close to the shaft as he dared.

With the flesh around it purple-coloured and swollen it looked ghastly, making him wince as his hand brushed it. Pray God it was not poisoned! He was also aware that leaving the bolt in place would cause less bleeding than trying to remove it, so all that could be done was to bind the wound in such a way that as little pressure as possible was placed on it. Nevertheless, whatever they did now all knew that the arrow would have to come out, the frightening thing being that, while they knew what was needed, no-one had the skill or knowledge to remove it! So vile a barbed weapon would surely take greater expertise than the castle doctor could command! Yet if it was not drawn, and speedily, then the wound would surely fester and Gui would die!

More than anything else, however, was the very fact of the arrow itself, where no arrow should be, that had shocked them all so soundly.

★

It was bad enough that the men whom Fitzurse had put on guard there had all been killed, but up until dragging Gui out of the passage and into the Chapel, they had simply assumed that he had been injured by the falling roof while trying to reach his parents' room. Now they all knew better, for when Sir Richard and his men had cleared the altar and laid Sir Gui down on it, there the thing had been, sticking obscenely out of his shoulder like some evil, feathered growth. Clearly foul play of the very basest kind had been loose in the castle that dreadful night, and Sir Richard had a very clear idea indeed of who lay at the bottom of it all! A supposition horrifyingly confirmed by those of his men whom he sent to seek out Alicia, for when they returned they brought with them not just two apparently very confused and bedraggled French guards, but also the appalling news that, without doubt, the Lady Alicia de Burley had been forcibly abducted!

Not only were the two men whom he had put at the base of her tower found drugged and senseless at their posts, but the other two...two of his very best men, chosen for their good sense as much as for their fighting ability, and whom Fitzurse had personally placed outside her door...had both been foully slain.

The one stabbed through the neck and stomach, and dragged onto the wall walk beyond her door, the other stabbed through the brain and left on the tower head. There was blood everywhere, along with smashed glasses and broken platters. Alicia's jewellery box had been rifled of its contents, there were clothes scattered round the room, and some of her great cedar wood kists had been left open. And the portcullises that separated the tower from the wall-head on either side of it had also been dropped!

He and John Fitzurse had questioned the two Frenchmen, Lagrasse and Fabrizan, very thoroughly...but they had been unable to throw any light on what had happened: The Lady Rochine had come to her room for some sort of shoulder wrap during the latter part of the evening, while they had been drinking the hot, spiced wine that had been sent round to all the guards for whom it had been ordered. They had chatted, as was expected of them if spoken to by a guest. She had stayed some five or ten minutes, during which time Jules had gone up to the room to get her wrap and Lucas had popped out to sort out some problem or other for de Vere, the Baron's Guard Commander.

Then The Lady had gone back to the party.

It had been some time after the two girls had returned that the two men had begun to feel drowsy and wobble-headed...and then swiftly unable to stand or speak. And the next thing they knew was that they were being dragged before the Castle's Guard Commander and ordered to give an account of their actions.

Sir Richard L'Eveque had been very tough with them.

But their statements had been borne out, not just because he himself had seen the Lady Rochine both leave and return to the Great Hall....but also because he had seen Lucas' meeting with de Vere, and when the lees from their wine had been given to one of the many mongrel curs that wandered the castle grounds it had very soon shown all the symptoms of which the Cousins had spoken, and was still asleep under a table! Not only that but there was not a drop of blood on either of them, and on the floor above and on the roof there were pools of it everywhere!

He sighed with frustration and concern.

So that must have been when they were drugged; when she had gone across from the party to get her wrap. That was the only time that both men had left their posts. While they had been out either doing her bidding or sorting out a problem, both 'things' that the men were supposed to do, she must have slipped something into their beakers! He sighed with bitter frustration, as much for the fact that they had carried out their instructions...as for not seeing through the wretched woman's stratagems. And that was just plain unfair!

Now, *all* had disappeared: the Baron, his daughter, their men...and Lady Alicia, were no-where to be found. It was as if they had just vanished into thin air! Sir Richard rubbed his forehead with his large hands in concern and groaned, cursing the Baron's wickedness and Sir Yvo's determination to invite the bloody man and his daughter here to Castle Malwood. For she was plainly *'in it'* right up to her elegant neck!

Whatever had Sir Yvo been thinking of? He must have been mad!

Sir Richard drew his hand across his forehead again and frowned in anxiety as he looked at the arrow now buried up to its thick fletchings in Gui's shoulder. Arrows were nasty things at best! You couldn't just pull them out, because of the barbs; if you tried that the whole shoulder could come apart, he had seen it happen. *Dreadful!* Sometimes, if you were lucky, you could cut off the fletchings, hammer the thing right through, and then pull it out with a pair of pliers. Especially if it was an armour piercing bodkin! And those sometimes you could just wrench out. Otherwise they had to be cut out, and that was a horribly painful and bloody business, with fat gobbets of flesh and oceans of blood everywhere and, as often as not, useless, as such wounds often mortified, going yellow, green and black, followed by delirium and a dreadful death!

Sir Richard looked down at his young Lord and shuddered! God forbid!

Either way it was a dangerous procedure, needing both skill and knowledge...neither of which they had in the castle at the time. Indeed not many people did at *any* time! They had a doctor of course, old John Tuckwell,

263

but he had little knowledge of battle wounds. He would as soon ask Johnny Tuckwell to take an arrow from Gui's shoulder as he would Wulfric the dog-boy to clip a tiger's claws! The very thought of the old fellow having a go at Gui's shoulder almost made him blench. No! He must send out for better help: to the Earl of Southampton perhaps? Or even to distant Beaulieu Abbey?

He looked down at Gui's shoulder and the foul bolt sticking out of the bandages that surrounded it. Just how much time *did* they have before they would have to attempt something themselves? Or stand by while the wound began to go sour on them and stink of rot and blackness?

He wiped his head again. Dear God that this should happen now, with half the castle gone up in smoke and flames; Sir Yvo and his Lady dead; an armed maniac on the loose somewhere, plotting God knows what; the Lady Alicia disappeared, probably kidnapped; and the son and heir injured beyond his ability to do anything more to help than had already been done! And Sir Richard groaned again both in heart and spirit as he looked down at where Gui lay, white-faced and drawn, lips pursed in pain as he tossed this way and that to try and find some comfort for his tormented shoulder.

And…*God's Wounds! Where was Alicia?*

At this moment there was so much going on that Gui hadn't actually noticed that she had not yet been to see him. Or…even if she had, he wouldn't have noticed because he was still drifting in and out of consciousness. So, in *his* mind her absence by his side was not yet critical

, but that could not last, and then what? On the one hand he must organise search parties immediately. On the other…Pray God that somehow she turned up! And preferably before Gui had to be told that she had gone, probably with the Baron and certainly unwillingly! Otherwise why deal with the guards in the manner that they had been? And not just her guards either! He groaned and rubbed his head again. Not good! Actually *bloody awful!*

Looking down at his friend, now the new Lord and Master of Castle Malwood, he smiled as recognition flitted across Gui's face at last. And, having made certain that he was as comfortable as possible, he left Father Gerome and

Agnes to it, striding firmly out into the rapidly lightening sky as the new dawn of palest green and blue blushed upwards from the East, intent on doing all he could to sort out the mess around him before Gui should choose to call for a report…and to do his best to find Alicia!

★

Some hours later, now propped up on pillows and swathed in tight bandages, Gui's whole shoulder throbbed mightily and felt it was on fire. No matter how he lay it still hurt abominably, and his temper was none the better for having to swallow the most disgusting infusion of herbs you could imagine, which made him retch every time he was forced to swallow it.

"God's Wounds, but I feel as if the castle guard has been using me as a hacking post!" He exclaimed, lightly touching his hand against his wound, and twisting sharply in pain as it brushed against the arrow's heel. "However did they manage to get me out?" He groaned. "I thought my end had come early!"

"Sir Richard and Big Nick broke in through the side door that Sir Yvo had specially built," Father Gerome replied, wringing his hands together as he spoke. "Then they dashed in, followed by about half a dozen of the men. They reached you just before the floor burned through. He and his men looked like grizzled scarecrows by the time they got you back, my Lord, singed all over, lost their eyebrows and burned in some other places as well. They dragged you out between them more dead than alive. How they managed it is a miracle!"

"What's the state of the castle?" He asked groggily, struggling to focus his eyes. "And the village? We must do all we can to help our people, Richard. And the crops will have taken a frightful battering too. But perhaps with harvest still some months away, they might recover?"

"The Great Keep is blackened but untouched," the old priest said, rubbing his hands together nervously. "But the New Hall and the whole South Wing is a gutted ruin, my Lord; completely destroyed, along with all the thatched buildings nearby. The village has taken a pounding; many crops are flattened, but might recover, and there are trees down everywhere. Even the soldiers quarters went up in smoke and flames. What's left is still too hot to touch, and the main curtain wall behind the Hall is cracked through from top to bottom!"

"*Sweet Jesus*, Father. That's unbelievable!" Gui exclaimed, screwing up his face as he jagged his shoulder. "It's over ten feet thick there. Dear God, but it must have been some blaze to have weakened the mortar so badly. No matter, Father. It can be repaired…even if we have to take the whole lot down and start again. The old thatched buildings the same, though we will have to do something quickly for the men and their families! What about the rest?"

"Almost untouched my Lord. Oh, singed and smouldering I grant you, and the smoke damage is extensive, but your father's insistence on not having the buildings too close together and all the important ones given slate roofs, like the stables and the forge…"

"…And the Chapel, Father," Gui added with a smile. "That has a stone roof for even greater protection!"

"Well, my Lord," the little priest said, bobbing his head and smiling down at him. "Sir Yvo, God rest his soul, always had a kindness for his chapel. And all those other buildings are safe too. Sir Yvo saw to that at least…" And his voice trailed away as he realised what he had just said

"*Splendour of God!* Gui exclaimed then, crying out in sudden anguish. "My parents, Father! Sir Yvo and Lady Margaret! They died in the fire! He did for them both, the black-hearted, murdering swine!" And his eyes blazed with anger, making the old priest shiver at his young Lord's rage and despair.

"*Where's that fucking bastard, de Brocas?*" he roared out then, ignoring Agnes's squeak of shock at his language. "It was he who set fire to the castle! It was he who locked me in my room and used what passes as Greek Fire to murder my family. He hoped to murder me also!" Gui went on. "That's what this arrow is doing in my shoulder! And if I ever lay my hands on him again, I'll slit him from chin to navel. I swear it on my Knightly Oath!"

"*Holy Mary, Mother of God!*" Agnes whispered, horror struck. Her eyes like saucers, her hand to her mouth in shocked surprise.

"Agnes, my sweet girl," He said then, somewhat exasperated. "For pity's sake, how else do you think I got this bolt in my shoulder? For certain it wasn't St Michael, though I wish he had been there to see me fight the bastard! That Man-of-Blood had locked my door from the outside and jammed something into the lock so I couldn't get my key into it," Gui told her, his eyes fever bright. "I was trapped, but young Simon had left my axe in there and I used it to smash my way out. He was there, Father, the bloody swine!" He exclaimed, turning to look up at the old priest, whose kindly face was white with strain and shock.

"Right there! Outside my parents' room capering like a madman and boasting of what he had done. I confronted him. Fought him; but he shot me with a small crossbow he had hidden across his back. But it did not stop me," he rushed on, almost incoherent. "And I would have had him *even then*," he cried out, anguished, "had I not slipped in my own blood...and the next moment the...whole...world...came...crashing down on me!" And he slumped back exhausted, his voice just draining away as he spoke the last few words, eyes closed and sweat pouring down his face.

"So, y' young scamp!" said a fresh, brisk voice as Gui lay there panting from his wild outbreak, Agnes chafing his hands and dabbing his forehead with a cool compress of mixed herbs.

"Greek Fire, eh, My Boy? Very, very nasty! Not surprising the New Hall went up like a tinder-box so swiftly! Now, I wonder from where the good Baron got that?" And Sir James Bolderwood, his father's stately, white haired Seneschal, and now of course his own, came slowly into the Chapel, Argos closely at his heels.

"Oh, Sir James," the old priest said, his face lighting up the moment he saw him. "We have been so waiting for you to arrive back safely."

"Me too, James," Gui said a moment later looking up at him with a rather crooked smile. "But I don't think it was real Greek Fire. Had it been it would have burst into flame the moment that bastard threw it out of its gourds and would have consumed him as well! And anyway, there is no way the Knights would have given even a flagon of it to anybody. As I understand it they only make it when they need it, and the whole recipe is not known to anyone except the Emperor. Nor is its method of delivery. All of that is guarded by their lives. No. James. I think this was what is called 'Arab' fire.

More oily and resinous, takes longer to combust and needs to be fired for it to go. Nevertheless, it is filthy stuff and in the confines of the New Hall was explosively deadly! My parents never had a chance. And if it hadn't been for Sir Richard and his lads, neither would I!"

"Well, Gui," Sir James said quietly, coming to stand over where the new Lord of Malwood now lay, white faced and scrunched with pain. "I am here now. I came the moment Peter Rudyard reached me, not knowing what to expect when I got here. Nor knowing who was living and who was dead." And, dragging up the Bishop's great carved chair from beside the little pulpit, he sat himself down. "The New Hall has gone, Gui," he said then, gently reaching for Gui's hands. "And with it, very sadly, Dearest Boy, your belovèd parents.

I know! *I know!*" he said gently, firmly pressing Gui's shoulders back down as he struggled to sit up. "I know just how terrible you feel...and how angry you are, too. But you, Dear Boy are very definitely alive and kicking, even if it is rather feebly just now!" He added with a smile. Then, more seriously, in his clear, clipped speech he said: "And remember, Gui, you are now also, *de facto et in veritas*...in very fact and truth...the rightful Lord and Master of all the Malwood-Burley estates, *and* our Liege Lord's Royal representative for the whole Forest.

Truly you have come into your own, Dear Boy," he said with simple definition. Not as any would have planned or wished it. But you are now '*Sir Gui*', in every possible way, like your father before you. And, '*Lord of Malwood*', and whatever actions you take must be done with careful thought...not on impulse! Be prudent with your anger and your determination. There are many who wish you well, Dear Boy, *and* wish to help you. So the time to kick-back, and kick-back hard, will soon be with us, I promise you.

"What about the Village, James. And all our people?" He asked then, reaching up a hand to the older man, sitting beside him.

"The village has been torn apart, Gui, and there have been some deaths. It is all very sad, but I have spoken with our Bailiff, John Beeman and with the Reeve, David Hedger and have pledged them whatever help they need. Certainly there will be no shortage of timber, both for repairs and for firewood this winter…and they can take what they need without fear of any dues. Truly, My Lord," he added with wry humour. "There are more trees down than you can shake a stick at!" And they all laughed.

"And the crops, James?" Gui asked then. "What of them? It was so looking like a good harvest."

"Well. That is not so good, Gui," Sir James replied with a sigh. "Much looks flattened and rain sodden. But the wheat and barley are still two months from harvest so much may recover. We will just have to see. If necessary we will have to buy in the flour our people will need this winter. But it is all in hand I promise you. I am not My Lord's Steward and Seneschal for these estates for nothing," he said with a slow smile and a stately bow of his head towards his new Lord and Master, lying before him like Death warmed up!

"And we care for our own at Malwood! Your father established that years ago, and his father, Sir Alun, before him. First however, we have to get that arrow out of you, Dear Boy," he said calmly, putting his hand on Gui's forehead as he spoke. "And get you better. Then there are certain things you must be told. Things that I urged your Dear Father, my greatest friend, to share with you…as did your mother also, but which Sir Yvo, for every good reason, would not! All that has changed now, and I have a duty to tell you everything, but not until you are stronger. No! Dear Boy," he said quietly, holding up his hand to prevent the new Lord of Malwood from interrupting. "Assuredly I *will* answer all your questions. But, truly, now is not the time.

Your father was awaiting the arrival of a very special friend and guest to your betrothal whom, if I can just find him, is probably the only man in the whole Kingdom who has the skill and knowledge we need to sort you out. So! Forgive me, my friends, but him I *must* find, and fast too! I will be back soonest. In the meantime I leave you in the capable hands of Sir Richard L'Eveque…your Guard Commander now, My Lord!" he said, giving Gui another gentle bow as he used his new title again. "Who will be with you any moment." And with his usual quiet smile he stood up, pushing back his chair as he did so, before pausing briefly to ruffle Gui's head then walking swiftly away.

269

Chapter 39…Agnes Fitzwalter tells all she knows.

Still wearing his smoke-blackened and singed leathers, and looking grim in the extreme, Sir Richard filled the doorway as he entered.

Though not as big a man as Gui, Sir Richard was still impressively large, with a square face and jaw and deep blue eyes set well apart. They gave him a pleasant, open look that sat well with his temperament and his cool, lazy air of competence; and he moved with surprising grace. In all the years he had known him Gui had never seen him flustered or confused and his laid back attitude and manner of speech only served to add to his reputation, for in fact he never missed a thing, was highly organised, and a tough, experienced fighter. And when he dropped his laconic style was really the time to sit up and take note! Gui's father had always trusted him implicitly, and his men adored him. Gui had no intention of doing otherwise and the two men had been good friends for years.

"Trust Sir James, Gui!" Sir Richard said in his lazy drawl, sitting down with a sigh in Sir James' empty chair. "He knows what he is about. Pray God he finds this mysterious stranger whom your father hinted at last night. Otherwise…"

"…Otherwise," Gui broke in, wincing at a sudden stab of pain in his shoulder. "I will just have to pull the wretched thing out myself! "

"Maybe not such a good plan, Dear Boy," Sir Richard said with a slow grin. "Those barbs are so firmly lodged in your shoulder that they *cannot* just be pulled out without wrecking everything else! We must wait and see what must be done. You know that is right!"

"*God's Bones!*" he exclaimed, frustrated, as Agnes fluttered round him anxiously before settling beside him on a stool. "I know! *I know!* It's just it *hurts* so much!"

Then, looking round at them all, surprise making him raise his eyebrows, he said: "Where's Alicia? I haven't seen her, I am sure of it. Is she alright? Why is she not here? You must send for her, Richard," he went on, turning to his tall Guard Commander. "I swear de Brocas was after her when he left me for dead! By God and the Pheasant! Just wait 'til I get my hands on that man, there will be a bloody reckoning then, I promise you!"

And he paused then to look at them at all:

At Agnes - pretty, flustered, anxious; Father Gerome, standing beside his altar, devastated by the murder of Sir Yvo and Lady Margaret, but seeming almost to be haunted by some *other* awfulness that he could not bring himself to name. And, finally, at Sir Richard, leaning back in his chair, lackadaisical as ever, seeming smooth and unflustered...yet-yet uncertain about..something? Almost as if he was trying to keep him from some as yet hidden truth maybe?

He looked at them all then and knew that something was not right! He sighed, and, turning to speak directly to the one person there whom he knew would be unable to control their emotions...he cruelly knocked his wounded shoulder, and crying out in sudden agony he put his right hand up instinctively to support it.

"Good heavens, Gui!" Sir Richard exclaimed, ignoring his request concerning Alicia. "What is that huge chunk of jewellery doing on your hand? I swear I have never seen it before!"

"Nor have you, my friend," Gui replied with a sudden grin, despite the pain in his shoulder. "Nor has anyone for more than a generation. That, my good and simple Knight," he went on, holding out his hand and turning it to show off the huge gem stone more clearly. "Is *the* Malwood Emerald!"

"*No!*" They all gasped, almost in unison.

"*Yes!*" Gui exclaimed with enormous satisfaction. "It *is!* The famous Malwood Emerald, gifted to Phillipa de Brocas by my Grandfather for her lifetime on the day his greatest friend got married. It was the family's most precious heirloom, found by old Sir Gui de Valance, my Great Grandfather

271

when the land for this castle was first being cleared. It is believed to be Roman, and vanished the day Grandmother Phillipa died, and has never been seen since...until last night, when Baron Roger gave it to me as a betrothal gift..."

"...My God," Sir Richard interrupted. "That's almost unbelievable! Why?"

"Richard, I have absolutely no idea!" Gui replied, as astonished as any of the others around him. "And why he didn't take it back off me when he left me for dead, I don't understand either!" And he extended his finger, so that everyone could look at the way the great stone winked and gleamed at them in the growing sunlight, awed into silence by its beauty.

"It really is lovely, my Lord," Agnes Fitzwalter said quietly a few moments later, breaking the spell. "You must be very proud to have got it back again after so much time. Whatever did the family say?"

"Agnes, I never got to tell them! De Brocas gave it to me last thing before turning in. My parents had already gone to bed, and Alicia..."

And he paused then to look around at them again from underneath his eyebrows, before shaking his head at them: "No! Sorry, people!" He exclaimed suddenly, looking around at their faces, all trying to be bland, and none of them succeeding. "But this just will not *do!*" He said firmly, looking at them from beneath raised eyebrows. "You are keeping something from me. I can *feel* it! And you have yet to answer my earlier question, my so good friends...which I have *not* forgotten, despite diversions over jewellery! So come on now, where is Alicia? Enough is enough! Richard? Father? Agnes? Where is my future wife...and now Chatelaine of this castle? *Where is Alicia?*"

There was a sudden, desperate silence at that, and a strange air of still, watchfulness stole over all of them.

"*Splendour of God,*" he growled, getting suddenly angry. "Are you all deaf? Or stupid? Come on! *Tell me!* For I swear I'll choke it out of one of you miserable wretches in a moment, arrow, or no arrow! Please. I ask you again! *Where is Alicia?*"

For a moment, no-one spoke, until the silence became almost oppressive.

Then, in his usual slow, drawly voice, his tall Guard Commander said: "The thing is Gui, and Sir James did not want you to know this yet, but, the truth is, Dear Boy, we don't know!"

"*What?*"

"We don't know!"

"What do you mean, '*You don't know!*'? He snarled. "*God's Blood!* Richard, this is not London! The castle is not so large that you cannot find one small girl in it!"

"Well, actually, My Lord," Father Gerome said quietly, putting his hand up with a smile. "Not so small now! Don't you think?"

"Oh, Father! *Really!*" Gui exclaimed exasperated. "You know very well what I mean!"

"Gui, calm down! *Calm down*, before you do yourself an injury!" Sir Richard broke in on him. "Gerome means no harm, he's only funning, but, in very truth, we have searched high and low; everywhere. But she has just disappeared...completely! Her rooms have been ransacked, all her jewellery is missing, and the men I put there either drugged or murdered..."

"...*Explain!*" Gui interrupted urgently. "'Drugged or murdered'? What do you mean, Richard?"

"The two at the bottom of the tower were found drugged. The two outside her door were both killed. Very nasty!"

"And Alicia?"

273

"Gone! Along with the Baron, his daughter and all their men."

"*De Brocas!*" Gui cried out violently, hissing the man's name through clenched teeth. "De Brocas! The black-hearted, bloody *bastard!*" And struggling upright, before anyone could stop him, he turned and swooped on poor Agnes, where she was sitting on her stool by his side, seizing her wrists in an iron grasp as he did so, ignoring the fierce pain in his shoulder as he dragged the terrified girl towards him.

"Agnes, *where's your mistress?*" he seethed through gritted teeth as the girl cried out and began to weep. "I left her in your charge last night, *Mistress Fitzwalter*," he sneered bitterly. "After the party broke up, and before I went to see the Baron. God rot the swine! So what has happened to her? Tell me, you *wretched* girl," he roared at her, shaking her like a tree in a violent storm. "*Where is Alicia?*"

"*GUI!*" Sir Richard shouted out, leaping up and seizing his friend's hands, ignoring his wild shout of pain as he did so. "*Put that girl down this instant!* How *dare* you treat her so! She is as distraught as you are, as we all are! How *dare* you manhandle so faithful and special a retainer and friend as Agnes Fitzwalter in so violent a manner? She is *not* to blame, and is as appalled by Alicia's disappearance as you are...*as are any of us here!* I have sent armed men in all directions to search for her, and Sir James has sent to the Earl in Southampton to have all the ports along the coast searched and watched as well. We are all doing what we can. Agnes loves her *too*, you know. Remember, she was her 'darling' ever before she was yours, *you great bully!*" He seethed at him, as angry as anyone had ever seen him, as he moved to lead the sobbing girl aside.

"Come now, Agnes, my dear," Richard went on, gentling the terrified woman whom Gui had instantly released. "Sit here, quietly now, beside me," he said softly, fetching a lovely carved stool for her to sit on, giving the young Lord of Malwood a furious glare as he did so. "And, calmly and quietly tell us all you know."

"I d-don't know much, Sir Richard. R-Really I don't" she stuttered, wiping her teary face with her blood stained apron. "When the fire started I was w-with the other girls in the Lower Hall and we all r-rushed to save what we c-c-could," she said, gulping for breath. "Before the flames drove us out. Then when you and y-your m-men began to organise things I ran across to find her…"

"Then…?" Sir Richard asked, gently.

"Oh, Sir R-Richard," she went on, turning her tear streaked face towards him, wringing her hands as she spoke. "You know what an independent little p-puss she is, and her tower rooms were set well away from the fire, so I wasn't im-mediately worried. But, my Lord," she said then to Gui. "When I finally went to find her, surprised by then that she had not c-come out to help…she'd gone! Jules and Lucas were un-unc-conscious downstairs," she stammered at him, her face streaked with tears. "There was b-blood everywhere upstairs, and…and they'd all gone! The room was empty, My Lord. There were signs of frantic packing," she went on then more strongly, as she took hold of herself. "Clothes strewn all over the place, two of her big kists left wide open, and her jewellery box empty. But there was no-one there…Just a great pool of blood by the door."

"What about the guards, Agnes?" Gui asked her calmly. Anxious now not to upset her further. "Not the Cousins, I already know about them. They were downstairs unconscious. I mean the other two, whom Fitzurse put outside Alicia's door. What of them, Agnes?"

"Slain, Gui!" Sir Richard broke in. "The one stabbed in his neck and belly, then dragged onto the wall-walk just beyond the tower entrance. The other, killed on the roof, throat stabbed up into the brain. Left where he fell. Then both portcullises were dropped."

"*What?*"

"Yes! Both of them, to cut the tower off from any help that might have come to her along the curtain wall I suppose."

"Whom did they slay?"

"David Oats and Johnny Foxglove!"

"The *Bastards*. Good men both. Loyal and well liked. Does Jane know?"

"Yes, and Rachel Tyler. Her man was killed outside your door, along with Tom Redmane."

"I know. I found their bodies when I broke out. How are the girls?"

"Much as you would expect, pretty devastated. Distraught at their loss."

"*God's Throat!* Richard, how dreadful is that? And without doubt the two outside my parent's door as well. Bastards! *Bastards!* How I wish Alicia were here now. She would know *exactly* what to say...*and* what to do for their families! As would my mother too! God rest her soul, poor love."

And he turned away then, his eyes full of tears, both of rage and distress.

"No matter, Gui," his friend said softly. "Sir James and I will see them right, I promise you. They will not go without!"

"God's Bones, Richard," Gui said quietly, dashing the tears from his face as he looked up at his friend. "But they planned this well! A huge diversionary fire, and the main prize snaffled from beneath our very noses!" He turned then again to Agnes, sitting disconsolately on the carved stool beside where they had laid him, her head in her hands, weeping quietly.

"Agnes...Look at me. *Please*," he asked her softly, reaching out then to touch her gently on her arm. "*Please*, Agnes. I am so *very* sorry, my dear. I *never* meant to hurt you...Please forgive me."

"I k-know, my Lord," she said brokenly, looking at him through tear filled eyes.

"It was just that I was so-so, *very* angry about Alicia disappearing. I just lashed out at the first object that I could lay hands to, and that happened to be you! I'm truly sorry."

"Oh, Sir Gui! M-my L-Lord," Agnes stuttered through her tears. "Please-*p-lease* don't be angry with me any more. I'm *so* s-sorry! So *v-.very* sorry!" And crouching forward on her stool by Gui's side, she covered her face with her arms, rocking herself on her heels in her grief, keening for her little one, for her nursery companion...for her friend, for whose sudden disappearance she felt so utterly responsible.

"Come now, Agnes," Gui urged her gently, ruffling her head as he spoke. "No more tears. I'm the one to say 'sorry', my dear, not you. I had no right to lose my temper in such a dreadful way, it is not your fault that those murderous swine forced Alicia to go with them. I expect they told her I'd been killed along with my parents; God knows...I should be dead!

"Oh my Lord. I f-feel so awful!" Agnes cried out through a flood of tears. "I k-keep thinking that if only I'd stayed with her, or thought of her sooner after the fire started...then n-n-none of this would have happened!" And she buried her face in her hands and sobbed.

"Yes it would, Agnes," Gui answered her softly, putting his good arm over her shoulders and rocking her gently. "Oh, yes it would! I believe they intended to take her no matter what. If you had stayed with her, I am sure they would have killed you too! Keeping one girl silent is one thing; keeping two has never been known to work yet! Just be grateful, my little lady, or you could have ended up like poor David Oats and Johnny Foxglove! So stop blaming yourself, Agnes. Just *please* forgive me? Or I'll be in *such* trouble when she finds out. She will give me *such* a scold!"

"Oh, my Lord," Agnes exclaimed then, rubbing her eyes, her gulps turning into giggles. "We will *both* be scolded! She will call us both 'a big pair of sillies' for worrying so, and box our ears" she ended, laughter breaking through the sorrow at last.

277

"Come now, that's better," Gui said, relieved. "Weeping over spilled milk never solved anything!" Then, after a moment's pause for thought, he asked her: "Did you see anything, or anyone doing anything..strange? Or..or unusual that night?"

"You mean, when I went to the tower to find her?"

"Yes, Agnes. Anyone scurrying about, or trying to hide things?

"No, my Lord. Just a small a party of guests leaving on their horses. It was raining fit to burst just then, with the wind driving it in my face..."

"...I saw those people too!" Richard L'Eveque broke in. "Maybe seven or eight men or so, with the one in front riding pillion. Holding someone in front of him. But no-one rushing or hurrying in particular..." he trailed off, looking down at Gui with ever widening eyes: "No! You don't think? Surely not?"

"Yes, Richard I *do* think!" Gui replied darkly, quirking his left eyebrow. "After all, why not? Everyone rushing madly about, flames leaping and roaring into the night; pouring with rain; just one more string of party guests leaving the burning castle? What could be more innocent looking? Move steadily and keep moving..."

"...And the guards on the gate would see what they would *expect* to see. What Agnes saw. And anyway, with the New Hall going up like the Devil and Hell-Fire had broken loose, how many of them were watching anything else that night?"

"My Lord," Father Gerome said, his voice almost a whisper as he struggled to make sense of what Gui was saying. "You don't mean to tell us that group they saw was the Baron and his party leaving? Surely not!"

"By God's Bones, Father!" Gui exclaimed then exasperated. "Of course it was the bloody Baron! How else do you think he left the castle, with Alicia in his clutches? Fly over the walls, like some bloody great bird? And all his men and horses with him?" Then, in an utter fury and agony of spirit, he cried out: "*Hell Fire and Damnation*, de Brocas. I will kill you! *I Will Kill You!*"

Chapter 40...Father Matthew saves the day!

"*Enough*! My Lord Gui de Malwood." Exclaimed a cool, clipped voice from the open door of the chapel, accompanied by a sharp *Clap! Clap!* of hands that startled everyone. "Enough!" The words with a rich Spanish lilt both short and hard that instantly silenced all other conversations: "This really won't do! If you don't stop all this wholly unnecessary movement and bestial shouting you may yet do your shoulder irreparable damage. Beyond even my skill to put right! And abusing a loyal and ancient Clerk in Holy Orders will not help your cause with me!"

And on that crisp note in walked a tall, ascetic looking man of later middle years, dressed in the black garb of the Benedictine Order, his hands clasped within the confines of his long-sleeved habit, his cowl lying back against his shoulders.

"Come along, now, all of you!" He went on firmly, his voice musical with the sounds of Spain and the south Circle Sea. "This noble Lord needs that arrow removing," he said, pointing to the broad green fletchings still protruding obscenely from Gui's shoulder. "Then quiet and, above all, sleep! And, Sir Richard L'Eveque," he said turning to where the castle's Guard Commander was lounging astonished in the Bishop's chair. "Sir Gui needs to be carried to his own chamber...immediately! Now, move, my children," he added flipping his hands at them, scattering the small coterie of followers clustered round Gui's simple pallet as though he were shooing chickens. "And let me see what I can do!"

And without another word he bent over Gui's prostrate form to examine his reluctant patient.

"Hmmm," he said laying a cool hand on Gui's brow. "No fever yet then. That's good. Very good. So, Sir Richard," he said, clapping his hands together again and turning to give his orders as if he had been doing so in Castle Malwood for years. "Bring in your men and get him moved. The sooner we can get those steel barbs out of him the better, there really is not a moment to lose! And this place," he said looking round him with a smile, "is the House of God, and a very beautiful place too, Father Gerome." He added inclining his head gravely to the ancient little priest, standing open mouthed at the casual use of his name.

"However, it is *not* a hospital...nor yet a mortuary! The only people who should be lying here are the buried dead...and this young man is very clearly *not* dead, not yet at least! Nor, with God's Will is it my intention that he should be so either...for many, many years to come. So, please, can we have him moved...*now?*"

"Who, in all that's Holy, are you...Father?...Brother?" Gui questioned him weakly, gazing around at the astonished group of figures clustered round his pallet like frozen statues. "I am confused. And, what's more," he added warming to his theme. "By what right do you come here and tell my people what to do?"

"*I*, my Lord," the tall monk replied with a smile, ignoring Gui's other question entirely. "Am, *de facto*, 'Brother' Matthew, the Master Herbalist from Ellingham Priory. But, as I am also a consecrated priest, you, my Lord, may also call me 'Father'!"

"From Ellingham?" Sir Richard broke in, amazed. "But that is twenty miles away! What in the name of God and the Pheasant are you doing here?"

"I am the man whom your Sir James is seeking..."

"Oh!" Sir Gui exclaimed, the light slowly dawning: "You're the man whom Sir James is seeking..."

"...The only man in the whole Kingdom who can sort out your arrow!" Sir Richard cut in with a smile, before adding: "But that still doesn't explain what he is doing here in the Forest?"

"*He's here because Sir Yvo asked him to be, you idle hound!*" Came a warm, familiar and much loved voice that stunned them all into petrified

281

immobility, as into the frozen circle around Gui's bed, now goggle eyed and completely stunned…swept Alicia!

Eyes alight with mischief and tears in her eyes she lifted her skirt wide where Rose had split it, and with a shriek of excitement, bare legs flashing in the smoky sunlight, Alicia rushed across to where Gui was lying, mouth agape like a stranded fish, and, ignoring everyone else in the little building she gave a whoop of joy and flung herself into his arms.

"Oh Gui, my Gui, *my Gui!*" She cried out in ecstasy, as he struggled to keep her away from his injured shoulder, while burying his face in her hair. "My Love, *My Love!* Hold me, my darling. Hold me to your heart. I have missed you so, my darling, *darling man!* I thought I would *never* see you again! *Never!*" And she covered his face with kisses until with a squeak of dismay, she realised what she was doing and slipped away to kneel by his side, her fingers fluttering over the arrow's feathered stump, her eyes suddenly wide with shock and dismay.

And with that, movement returned as well as reason, and she was surrounded by her friends, hugged to deatgh, kissed and exclaimed over; and bombarded with questions as everyone sought to find out where she had been? What had happened?…and how she had escaped? Not just from the Baron's murderous party of armed guards, but from the Baron himself and from his daughter.

★

"O h, you big pair of sillies!"

She said to Gui and Agnes after many questions and answers. "Weeping over me? I could box your ears, the both of you!" And suddenly everyone laughed at that, much to Alicia's surprise until it was explained to her, and then she hugged everyone again in the wildest joy and release of tension, until their boisterous good humour was interrupted by a loud, dry cough, and all turned to look at the tall, dark Benedictine, his eyes fiercely bent upon them.

"Ahem! In case you hadn't realised it, all of you," he said to their startled faces. "This young man still has dangerous barbs of cold steel stuck in his shoulder that must come out, and swiftly too, if there is to be no lasting damage. Of course I hate to break up your revelries in quite so churlish a manner," he continued dryly, his eyes sweeping over them all as he spoke in his warm Spanish lilt "But could we move him please? *NOW!*" He ended, his voice as calm as before, simply more sharply clear.

"As yet your noble Lord has no fever, which is remarkable in itself, so his wound has not yet started to fester, and I would rather deal with it before that happens than afterwards," he added darkly, "when it may then be too late to save him!"

"Yes Father, of course!" Sir Richard replied swiftly, his face a picture of both consternation and remorse, and he left the chapel instantly to call up a handful of his men to pick Gui up, pallet and all, and move him to warmer and more secure quarters.

Meanwhile Sir James had returned, coming in closely behind Father Matthew and Alicia, himself absolutely delighted to have found both the man whom Sir Yvo had been so desperately seeking the night before, and himself that morning and, of course, to have discovered Alicia with him. That had been a complete shock, leaving him almost as goggle eyed as the rest of them!

"However, Gui cannot go to his own rooms of course," he said, as half a dozen of Sir Richard's men rushed into the chapel at their commander's urging. "They have been completely destroyed in the fire. You are to take him to his parent's old chamber in the Great Keep. And all Alicia's belongings are to be moved there also. Agnes Fitzwalter, go you ahead now and organise it, and have John Fitzurse report to me immediately. And as for me? There is lots of space in that rackety great building for an old body such as mine is now. And you will be *right* next to Gui I assure you...so I doubt he will lack for nothing." he added archly, with a sly grin: "For I am *sure* that you will see the poor boy has *all* that he could *possibly* require!"

"*Sir James!*" She exclaimed, looking sideways at him with a wicked smile. "I don't know *what* you could *possibly* mean." And they both laughed.

Behind them came another dry cough.

"Ahem! If you have finished with your jollifications, could we get on, please?" Father Matthew asked, raising an eyebrow. "It is lunchtime now – and it would be so nice to have that arrow out of him by suppertime…don't you think?"

"*Sorry Father!*" They all chorused together, and while Sir James and Agnes hurried off to complete their arrangements, Sir Richard returned with a dozen of his men to lift the new Lord of Malwood safely to the Great Keep.

So, with Sir Richard striding ahead with four of his men to clear the way; Alicia walking beside Gui holding his hand, while four of the Malwood Lions carried his pallet, they all set out for the great Forework that led up to the Great Keep: Father Matthew's tall and somewhat austere figure striding behind them with Brothers William and James, now caught up with him, falling in behind, and four more of the Malwood Lions bringing up the rear. Looking back as they all moved off across the castle garth, Alicia thought with a smile that it only needed the Village Crier with his bell at head of the procession to complete the picture!

Chapter 41... Father Matthew prepares Sir Gui for surgery.

However the operation to remove the arrow that de Brocas had fired into Gui's shoulder was infinitely more intricate and ghastly than anything that Alicia had ever experienced.

Once L'Eveque's men had carried Gui up the great open Forework and into the Keep itself they then had to get him off the pallet on which they had carried him, and walk him up the narrow winding staircase that led up to Sir Yvo's old apartments on the floor above the Great Hall, that being the only way they could get him there. And once arrived it was clear, as Sir James had said, that the apartments had been much altered and extended.

The main chamber was huge, with a vast bed against one wall with a large overhead canopy from which heavy white damask curtains covered with scarlet Lions-Rampant hung in elegant festoons. There was a beautifully carved stone fireplace of stags and hounds against another wall and, because they were so high up in the huge building, two pairs of large double windows with beautifully rounded arches had been let into three of the walls with deep cut chevrons carved into them, all painted in bright, cheerful colours. And, beneath each window, broad seats had been built and the stonework boxed-in with polished cherry wood; deeply padded seats had been added and prettily embroidered cushions that Alicia recognised as some of the Lady Margaret's finest work.

The oak flooring was polished and covered, not with woolfells as her room was, but with a great thick carpet that Sir Yvo had brought back from distant Persia, which had cost the rents of the whole estate for nearly a year! Rich and soft, with amazing colours of deep red and black, orange, green and blue the whole thing glowed with warmth, and was as lovely to walk on as it was to look at. Indeed, just as Sir James had said, it was a much lighter and brighter room than Alicia had remembered, made even more so when the varlets who had accompanied them, under James' instructions, removed the boxed window frames with their pretty coloured glass to let the warm June sunlight flood in.

Meanwhile, with Father Matthew's help Gui was placed carefully on the bed, the great criss-cross of broad leather straps that supported the horse-hair filled mattress giving gently to his weight.

Stripping him to his skin and propping him up against a number of heavy linen bolsters, the tall Benedictine, with infinite gentleness, palpated the flesh over his ribs, now a ghastly mixture of black and blue tinged with purple and crimson edged where the Baron's boots had struck home, and Alicia gasped when she saw what he had done to her man, and covered her face with hands in shock.

"Well, my dear," the tall Herbalist said with a smile. "You'd better get used to this! And be assured, this looks far worse than it truly is, and is no different from any number of Tournament injuries that I have seen over the years...or battle injuries either. Mind you, he was not wearing a gambeson, or any other form of armoured protection..."

"...Nor were the Baron's feet armoured either, Father," Gui said, wincing as the tall monk continued to explore his bruises. "Otherwise..."

"...Otherwise," Alicia chipped in. "You'd look even worse! Yes, I know that my darling. I have seen it before with Sir Yvo, and you after that Christmas Tournament last year so I am not that worried about this," she said with a sweep of her hand. "You will surely live to fight another day."

"True, my lady," Father Matthew said, straightening his back. "And there is nothing cracked or broken that I can find. He may look rather multi coloured for a while, but that is all. And I have a magic ointment that will bring all that bruising out in next to no time. One that really works, I assure you!"

"What's that?" Alicia asked, interested. "Lady Margaret used Witch Hazel."

"Arnica! A simple mountain herb that has amazing curative qualities, especially when turned into an ointment. I always carry some with me and I will give you some to put on for him later. Now, my Lady, let's have a look at this arrow!"

"Don't mind me, you two," came a plaintive voice from the top of the bed. "You may find all this very interesting...but it's *my* shoulder you're about to prod, and a little bit of loving care would not go amiss!"

"Oh, darling," Alicia said, turning with a chuckle to drop him a kiss. "I'm only doing my bit to help Father Matthew get you better. Now, Sweetheart, hold my hand, because I think this might hurt!"

And, no matter how hard he tried to be gentle, the tall Benedictine Herbalist hurt his patient a lot. First he gently unbound the wound itself, the sight of which made Alicia blench and grip Gui's hand hard herself, for it was not a pretty sight.

Firmly embedded in flesh now gone from red to almost purple, from which dark blood oozed every time it was touched, the arrow thrust out of his shoulder, the blood still sluggishly welling out from beneath the green fletchings in fat, gouts of thick looking fluid. And every time Father Matthew tweaked the shaft it made Gui gasp in pain and clench his teeth and hands, as the agony ripped into him, and sweat ran freely down his face.

"Who are you, Father?" Gui asked him again when the tall monk stood up at last and turned to look at him, wincing as he settled back against the mound of pillows and bolsters that supported him. "And what did Alicia mean when she said that Sir Yvo had invited you?"

"That is too long a tale for now, my Lord," the man replied with quiet firmness, turning back his long sleeves. "Your Lady knows much...but not all. And Sir James much more still! All you need to be certain of, Dear Boy, is that I really *do* know what I am doing...and, My Lord of Malwood," he added enigmatically, looking at the young man before him from beneath his eyebrows. "As your Lady so rightly said...I am *not* here by accident! Now," he went on briskly, stretching his long arms. "Let the dog see the rabbit!..." And with great care he now examined the wound again, tapping the heel of the bolt where it protruded from Gui's body, observing where the flesh was particularly swollen and inflamed and where small strands of cloth seemed to have been drawn down into the wound by the arrow when it had struck, and had been left behind by Sir Richard when he had cut Gui's jacket away from him.

The shaft itself was solidly gripped, both by the joint into which it had been fired as well as by the tightly contracted muscles that had clamped themselves around it. Almost like being in a vice on a blacksmith's table! Finally, very gently placing his hand around the feathered heel of the bolt itself, he gently pulled at the arrow, infinitesimally twisting it as he did so.

The result was spectacular!

With a sudden agonised cry, Gui's whole body leaped against the bed, and the sweat poured out across his forehead in a fine salty dew of utmost torment. His eyes rolled in his head as he thrashed from side to side, showing more white than colour, and his whole body and spirit groaned. Alicia also drew in her breath sharply, hissing it over tightly clenched teeth as Gui gripped her hand as fiercely as any hawk had just thrust in her pounces on first sight of her quarry. It may have been only for a moment, but it left Gui ashen faced and panting for breath, and Alicia feeling somewhat sick and light-headed.

"Hmmm, *very* nasty!" The tall Herbalist proclaimed gently, standing back again at last, pausing to press his cool dry hand against Gui's sweating forehead.

"I am sorry to have hurt you so cruelly, my Lord," he said in his calm manner. "But there was a chance that it might have been bodkin tipped, for piercing chain-mail armour. Sadly it is not! It is barbed, as I feared it would be, but only single barbed I think, thank God! You were quite right to leave it," he said, turning to Sir Richard. "If you had pulled it out, as many would have done, you could easily have dismounted the whole joint along with it, and ripped out all the tendons.

Nor can it be driven through, for the same reasons. I shall have to cut down to the barbs, force the joint open and then ease the whole head out with special forceps. It will not be without much pain, my Lord," he said quietly, looking down at Gui's white strained face. "But it can be done. Are you ready for this?"

"Yes, Father!" He exclaimed, closing his eyes momentarily. "As ready as I ever will be. Just get on with it, please. The sooner it is out, the sooner I can get after my quarry. Do your worst, Father…"

"No, My Child," the tall Benedictine doctor replied with a smile. "I shall do my very *best*, otherwise your Lady will roast me, and our beloved King, whose trust I hold, will want my head on a charger! And I would *infinitely* prefer it to remain where it is, don't you think?" And he smiled.

"What do you want from us?" Sir Richard asked, gesturing round the room.

"Four of your best men to help hold our young warrior down so that I can do my work well; oceans of freshly boiled water; clean and freshly pressed linen and cotton strips for swabs and bandages…and the prayers of Father Gerome that God gives me a steady hand, a bold heart and a sharp eye!"

"No more than that, Father?" Gui asked him, sardonically.

"Well, that will do for a start anyway, you young rascal," Sir James said, walking into the room to see how things were going, and gently ruffling Gui's hair as he spoke. "You just make sure you come through all this in one piece, Dear Boy. We need you, remember? You are the Lord of Malwood now," he added in his clear, quiet manner. "And all men will look to you for leadership now that Sir Yvo has gone, me included! You cannot slip your responsibilities by being so selfish as to die on us over so small a thing as an arrow!" He ended dryly, his eyebrows lifting in unspoken query as he turned back towards the tall Benedictine doctor. "What next, Father?"

"Plenty, Sir James," Father Matthew said, rubbing his hands together briskly as he turned to his two companions, Brothers James and William, who had come in behind them all. "First we need to re-arrange the furniture slightly.

Bring me those two chests over there, put them together and cover them with clean linen, which Agnes can arrange before she leaves us. William, James, go down to the cart and bring me my herbs and my instruments, you know the ones I mean, and the leather case with all my phials. I especially want the Frankincense and the flask of poppy juice I prepared before we left Normandy..."

"Normandy?" Alicia exclaimed, astonished. "What were you doing in Normandy, Father?"

"Being very busy about our Liege Lord's business, my Lady!" he answered her dryly. "Which would have been infinitely better served without childish illnesses and violent storms...and, right now, without unnecessary interruptions!"

"*Sorry!*" She whispered, making a swift grimace at Sir Richard.

"Quite so, young Alicia," the tall monk said to her, with a lift of his brow. "God Willing, there will be plenty of time for questions later. Now," he went on, turning back to Brother William, "This operation will require special measures, so bring me the case with my new forceps, and my new scalpels. I will also need more light to work by. So, everybody, bustle about now. The sooner we can make a start the better.

The rest of you, save Sir Richard...out! You too, please, Sir James," he said with a warm smile, bowing to the elderly knight as he ushered him with all due deference to the door. "You have much to do elsewhere, I know. And, truly, there is nothing more that you can do here now, save get in my way. Sir Gui is in the very best of hands, I promise you!"

"I never doubted it, Father," the old knight replied in his quiet, precise way. "You come recommended on the *very* highest authority. I know!"

"Indeed?" Father Matthew queried, holding Sir James' gaze with a piercing look from his shrewd brown eyes.

"Indeed, Father!" Sir James replied, with a stately bow of his head, his own eyes steely in their sharp regard, adding very quietly: "We will talk later." And with a final nod of recognition he left the room.

"Father," Alicia said then, taking him determinedly towards the nearest window. "The others must go, for certain. But this is my man who lies here in his nakedness and his pain and I will not leave him now!"

The tall Benedictine stood looking down at her for a moment, a warm look in his deep-set, brown eyes: "It will not be pretty, my Lady," he said softly, the richness of his speech, with its Spanish lilt in it seeming so out of place in this deep English heartland. "The pain will be great. Greater than you saw just now… and I saw how pale you went, my Lady! There will be much blood also, and his bowels may loosen…and he will cry out for it will seem like torture…and will sound like it. Are you ready for that, my child?"

"What use would I be to him, Father," she said firmly, looking him in the face. "If at the first challenge I was to fall by the wayside? I am no china miss," she went on, taking his fine hands with their long, delicate fingers in hers, looking up at him as she did so. "I do not break easily, Father, and my love for this man is infinite! If I cannot care for him now when he needs me most, where would my Honour be? What would my love be worth, both to him and to myself? No, my place is here…no matter how awful it may be." She said, her wide blue eyes locked on his deep brown ones, his hawk-shaped nose so clearly defining them, his smile serene.

And with that single deep look the scales fell from her eyes and she gasped, realising in that one single moment of intensity *exactly* where she had seen him before after all! For *his* was the face that had saved her from the Baron's grasp the night of the fire; it was *his* eyes that had beaten the Baron down and defeated him, and recognising that she smiled up at him with dazzling effect, the words: "It was you, Father!" softly on her lips as she did so.

Indeed it was all that she could do not actually to cry out and throw her arms around him. But her smile alone was enough to tell the tall Benedictine Father that she had indeed worked 'it' out at last, as he had told her to. He smiled back at her then and gently inclined his head towards her in recognition of her discovery, his eyes as full of love and care as she had seen them when she had been so terrifyingly racked by the Baron's power the night Gui's parents had been murdered.

"*It was you!*" She said again, tears springing to her eyes. "I knew I had seen you before when we met in the Forest. I just couldn't work our where, or how. Now I know." And she bowed her head and brought his fingers up to her lips in a simple gesture of love and thanks.

"Just so, my Dearest Alicia," he said, allowing her to kiss his fingers. "Just so. I told you that you had your father's sharpness," he added, gently releasing his hands from her grasp to lay them in blessing on her forehead. "I knew you would get there in the end. But now is not the time to discuss such matters," he went on, holding his hand up to forestall more questions. "It is enough that you know. The rest can wait for better times than this. Are you sure, my dear, that staying here is truly what you wish to do?"

"Father, my love for this man is as deep as the ocean and as wide as the sky. 'To the moon and back' as my Rose was used to say to me when I was little. He needs me now more than ever he has done before. He may be too proud to say so, but I know that he needs me. And I, Dear God in Heaven," she added crossing herself. "I need him too. More than ever after yesterday! Trust me, Father," she implored him. "I am no china miss…I will not fail you!"

Outside the sun blazed down as it had the day before, but now there was a cool breeze gently flowing round them that moved the soft drapes about the bed, and fluttered the flowers that Agnes had brought in with her. Beyond the walls the lake shimmered in the sunshine, while from a distant tower top a thrush with fine speckled breast of cream and black sang out his heart. Father Matthew heard the thrilling music and sighed: "So be it, my Lady Alicia…my little Lady Bright eyes," he said, bowing to her gently with a warm, approving smile. "So be it. Now, go and hold his hand, and be prepared. Hold it firmly, my child, right up against his palm or, in his extreme torment, he yet may break your fingers!"

Chapter 42... *Father Matthew sets out his stall*...

With Sir James gone and Father Matthew's acceptance of Alicia's presence by Gui's side, all was immediate bustle and organisation as the men whom Sir Richard had sent in rolled up the carpet to leave just the polished oak floor beneath their feet and moved the chests around to Father Matthew's directions. Meanwhile his two Brother monks, James and William, laid out the white linen sheets he had asked for, and a further chest was brought round and similarly covered so that the instruments he might need could be laid out upon them for swift ease of sight and usage, just as Hippocrates had ordained.

Alicia, fascinated by such detailed preparations, having never seen anything like them before, was full of questions: "What is all this, Brother James?" she asked amazed. "No doctor I know of would do anything so...so specific!"

"No, my Lady," he replied with a shake of his head. "No other man would! But Father Matthew has some strange ideas that he has picked up on his travels, and he insists on it all!"

"He also believes in making sure that everything he uses is clean as well," Brother William added, hanging a large blackened kettle from a hook that could be swung back over the fire. "Hands, instruments, bandages...*everything!* I cannot see the point myself. What's wrong with good honest dirt?"

"Because it is just that, Brother...dirt!" came the Father Matthew's crisp reply. "In Aesculapius's treatise on wounds..."

"Greek!" Was Brother William's whispered response to Alicia's sudden raised eyebrows and unspoken query.

"...he insisted on clean water, clean bandages and clean instruments. Hippocrates the same! So, 'dirt' is out and 'clean' is in!"

"Hippocrates, Father?"

"Another '*Greek*'," he replied with emphasis, giving Brother William an amused glare. "The father of all modern medicine. He took what Aesculapius had started and then refined it. Compared to what our so called 'doctors' do here, the Greeks and Romans were in another world! I have seen what their methods can do in the East, and in my small way have done my best to copy them; because they work! Now, my Brothers," he said briskly, turning to where they were now standing before the fire. "Where's my poppy juice?"

"Here, Father," Brother William said, handing him a finely wrought chalice of gilded silver.

"Give it to the Lady Alicia, William. She can give it to our patient."

"What is this, Brother William?" She asked, looking rather uncertainly at the dark coloured liquid within.

"This is poppy juice, my Lady. For the pain. It is one of Father Matthew's most special Eastern potions, from the souks of Constantinople and far away India, a land of which few have even heard. He makes it with his own hand and it will help keep Sir Gui still while Father Matthew…"

"…Cuts into me!" Gui finished for him sardonically. "Thanks a lot! Here, Alicia. Give it to me. I know it will taste like gall, but I have heard of it. It takes away the spirit so they say, leaving the flesh strong enough to take the knife." And he tossed the dark coloured fluid down his throat with a frightful grimace of disgust. "*Gheugh!* Ye gods and little fishes, but that was *truly* vile!"

Nevertheless, within minutes it was visibly having an effect, for Gui's eyes started to roll in his head and then, seemingly moments later, his speech slurred into a meaningless jumble of broken words and phrases and his body slumped sideways on the bed. Father Matthew, who had been watching him keenly, rubbed his hands together then and swiftly ordered Sir Richard's men to bring Gui over to the improvised operating table, now placed in the brightest part of the room with extra candles in their iron brackets at its head, and lay him down on it.

Beside him, on a separate table, lay a row of strange instruments, the like of which no-one from Malwood had ever seen before. And, while Father Matthew stood over his patient, Brother William came and stood nearby, ready to hand him whatever he asked for.

Laid out before him were two strangely shaped knives with ivory handles, one larger than the other, with short rounded blades of sharpest steel; forceps, with long and short handles, all with tiny criss-crossed teeth for better gripping, and, finally, an instrument with blunt, curved blades and handles that cunningly opened outwards to make a large open oval in the centre.

Then there were more homely objects: a pair of heavy pliers, a large pile of cleanly cut linen and cotton cloths, and two large bottles of some sort of clear liquid that looked like water, but clearly wasn't. Finally, in a small silver dish was a strange curved needle with a reel of fine clear, sinewy thread, beside which lay a pair of small shiny, steel scissors.

"What is all of this, Father?" Sir Richard asked a little darkly, his brows drawn anxiously together.

"The tools of my trade, Sir Richard, some of which I have bought and some I have had made, and all in the best traditions of Aesculapius and Hippocrates…whom the Romans knew all about, and the Arabs have tried to follow…and, sadly, we have all forgotten. *Any* doctor in the Roman army worth his salt would have known all these instruments…and how to use them too! They spent years in training, and went to specialist schools to do so. Why do you think I have spent so much time on my travels? St Luke, my favourite of the great Apostles, was a Greek doctor. Did you not know that?"

"Yes, Father, I did, actually," Alicia replied with a grin, feeling inordinately proud of herself. "Father Gerome told me. He has also told me much about the Greeks and Romans too. He is far more knowledgeable than many think. Sir Yvo chose him especially because of it."

"Did he now?" The tall Benedictine said, looking down at his almost unconscious patient, a wry smile on his open face. "The boy's father always was a man of surprises, he must have listened to me after all. Eh…but I shall miss him!" And he stood a moment in silent contemplation.

"Did you know him then?" Sir Richard asked, surprised.

"Better than you can possibly imagine. Have you not spoken with

Alicia yet?"

"No, Father," Alicia, chipped in swiftly. "He hasn't had the chance to. We've all been too busy with Gui."

"Well, Sir Richard," the tall monk said with a slight incline of his head. "You should do. There is much she can tell you, though not all. Not yet. Is that not so, my Lady? Even though we are now both safely at the castle!" And they both laughed.

Sir Richard, looking at the tall man before him, at his open face and solid air of confidence and experience sighed, suddenly unnerved by all the strange things the tall Spanish monk had brought with him that he did not understand; and thought of the odd comments he had made about his being here to order...and orders from those higher up the chain of command than just Sir Yvo! And he shook his head. And looking down at the young Lord of Malwood, almost naked before him, defenceless, the foul obscenity of de Brocas's arrow thrusting its feathered shaft out of his body, and he sighed again.

Father Matthew looked at the tall knight and smiled.

He was so out of his depth with all this ancient learning! Give him a castle to attack or a raw body of men to train and he would be in his element, or put him in the battle-line with sword and shield and destrier...and he would be formidable. He had seen so many good men just like him, great on practical solutions, but shy of unexpected innovations. And yet clearly Sir Richard loved his Lord and was not without understanding. He smiled again. Give him time and he would win him to his side, but right now he needed his willing support and that at least he was certain of receiving. Sir Richard sighed once more and shook his head, and grinned back at Father Matthew's unspoken query: "About your travels, Father?" Sir Richard asked him then. "Have you travelled far?"

"Oh...my travels?" he asked after a second's confusion at the swift change of direction in the tall knight's thinking.

"Yes. I have been to many places. Even beyond Constantinople and Jerusalem; to Persia and the edge of India; a strange, wonderful land of elephants and tigers, and a thousand different temples. And I have learned many things, some of which even I do not understand…only that they work. This liquid," he said, picking up one of the bottles of clear fluid, "is called 'Arrack'. It comes from far way in the East, almost at the end of the world, like my poppy juice. It is a powerful spirit made from rice that can cleanse wounds of evil, though I still don't know why. It can also cleanse minds of reason just as easily! I added some of this to the poppy juice I gave Gui, that is why it worked so quickly. It will not take *all* pain away, but it does help to deaden the senses most strongly.

"Can you not…'put him out' more than this, Father?" Alicia asked pleadingly. "Even as he is you will hurt him cruelly, I know!"

"There are other herbs I could have used that *do* bring true unconsciousness," he said, looking down at her with great compassion. "Like Mandragora, which you call Mandrake, or a combination of Henbane and Hemlock. But the latter two are very dangerous, and as for Mandrake, I do not have it with me.

"I have heard of Mandrake, Father," Alicia said quietly. "They say that it has human shape and screams horribly when it is pulled from the earth. Like a tortured child. It can only be pulled at the full moon by a black dog. The very scream can kill you…and the dog!"

"More wisdom from Father Gerome?" He asked piercingly.

"Yes, Father. He does his best, you know. Do not sound so disparaging!"

"I did not mean to, my child. The Roman surgeon and herbalist, Dioscorides wrote a whole treatise on it and he does not mention *anywhere* a single *thing* about screaming plants, black dogs or moonlight! I read a copy of it in the great library of Constantinople. The Romans were amazingly practical people, and their army doctors hard headed professionals, they would never have had truck with such nonsense. So what do *you* think? Truth or fiction?"

"I do not know, Father," she said after a moment's thought. "The Church's teaching is supposed to be divine."

"You shouldn't believe everything you hear, my Lady, especially from country priests with only a little learning!" the tall Benedictine said then with a soft smile. "Sometimes a little learning is a dangerous thing, don't you think?"

"So…I must not believe everything I hear from a priest?" She asked, looking at him with her head on one side.

"Only if it comes from me!" He replied with a chuckle, appreciating the wit in her swift riposte.

"So no Mandragora then, Father?"

"No, Alicia. I am afraid not. I have used it a lot in the past; boiling the roots and mixing the infusion with wine to induce unconsciousness. But the required ritual today, of using a black dog tied to the plant with cords and under a full moon, is just too much nonsense for me to bother with. God alone knows from where people get such strange ideas! So I have used Poppy Juice, known as 'Opium' instead. It is the very best that I can do, my Child."

"Then I thank you for that, Father," she replied solemnly. "You said you would do your best, and I believe you."

"What about these special knives of yours, Father?" Sir Richard asked, changing the subject.

"These sharp knives are called 'Scalpels', and are made from the finest Damascus steel," he said, picking one up. "They are the sharpest blades known to man; it is said you could cut a sunbeam with one of them," he added with a grin. "And these," he went on, pointing to a few pairs of strange scissors with crinkly like teeth at each end, "are 'Forceps', for picking things out of wounds. And this instrument with the long, curved, blunt jaws is a 'Retractor' for keeping wounds open, so you can operate more easily. We may not need that, but it is good to have it to hand just in case. Right!" he exclaimed, briskly putting down the strange new forceps.

"Lecture over, people! It is time we made a start," he continued, looking closely at Gui and moving his hands over his face and body. "The boy is as 'out' now as he is ever likely to be. Alicia," he said, handing her a cool bowl of lavender water and a pile of large cotton cloths. "Stay by his side and keep his head bathed with this tincture. You others," he added sharply, picking up the first of his Damascus scalpels. "You hold him down, hard. Even though I have warmed the blade, and his mind may be far away, his body will still leap at the first touch of steel. Let me just put this strap of leather between his teeth, then we can start. I have known a man almost bite his tongue off in his torment. Another broke his teeth and cracked his jaw. I do not want that to happen here! Now, My Lady Bright-Eyes...let's to it!"

Chapter 43......And cuts out the Baron's steel.

In the event, the next hour was every bit as awful as the tall Benedictine had suggested, if not worse!

Having first washed his hands, another strange custom he had picked up from the Arabs amongst whom he had travelled widely, Matthew first dipped the blade he had chosen in a bowl of boiled water, then ran some of the Arrack over it as well, and then over the wound itself, making Gui's body twitch and heave as the fiery liquid bit into the swollen wound.

Then, with infinite care he stripped the feathers off the quarrel so that they could not obscure his vision of the wound. Each soiled fletching he handed to Brother William as it came clear, leaving a cleaned stick end for his pliers to grip onto when the time came to free it from Gui's shoulder joint.

Next he asked for the larger of the two scalpels from Brother William. This he cleaned in the same way as the first and warming the blade before placing his left hand firmly on Gui's upper chest and laying the glittering steel against his flesh. Then, taking a deep breath, and with great care and strong, steady pressure, he cut solidly into the injured shoulder. Despite his drugged state, Gui's eyes flew open and his whole body jumped and bucked with the agony of it, while the men holding him strained their own muscles to hold him still.

And he cried out horribly.

A dreadful howl of agony as Matthew cut into him, displacing the leather strap, and he bore down on Alicia's hand until she could hardly feel her fingers. Sweat poured down his face and he looked ashen, tossing his head from side to side and crying out again as the tall Benedictine surgeon cut deeply into the wound once more to slice away fat gobbets of flesh which he plucked out with a small pair of forceps, dipping into his shoulder as a heron would for minnows in a stream.

And with that came the blood.

It came in fat, scarlet gouts 'til the monk's hands and fingers were red with it, and it ran down in streams over Gui's chest and onto the linen cover on which he lay. And every time it flowed Brother William mopped at it with a soft linen swab from his pile on the end of another pair of forceps. Each used swab tossed to one side until the polished floor was littered with them, like scarlet flower heads after a violent storm.

"Hmmmm. It is as deep into the joint as I feared," Father Matthew said quietly. "But no matter. I can get it out. You, William, hold his arm back against the joint. Brother James, you will need to hold his body outwards. Sir Richard, do your best to keep his legs steady. It will need great pressure when I call for it as we must almost dislocate his arm from his shoulder. But with God's Grace, and a little twist and a jerk, this thing will come free of the joint, and I should then be able to lift it out.

My Lord," he said, looking down at Gui's ashen face, eyes rolling in their sockets. "Be brave and bite down *hard* on the strap I am putting back between your teeth. The worst is yet to come. But, I do assure you, you *will* be alright when it is over. Ready James? William? Everybody? Good! Then we will do it on my mark...*now!*"

So saying, as Brother William pulled back on Gui's arm and James pushed his shoulder forward, Father Matthew probed with his right hand into the joint to feel when it had opened sufficiently for him to grasp and twist the arrow-head free at last.

Alicia, watching from the top of the improvised operating table, was appalled by the amount of tension the men were putting on Gui's shoulder, and her eyes flooded with tears as he screwed his shut, his teeth clamped on the thick leather strap Matthew had slipped between them. Grunting and crying out in agony through its thickness, sweat poured off his face and body in salty streams that Alicia, herself as white as a sheet, kept mopping off him with her cool lavender soaked cloths, while the three men worked on him relentlessly and Sir Richard and his burly troopers held his legs and body down to prevent him from lashing out. And all the while she gripped his hand and told him of her love and how brave he was, the tears running down her face as she

301

witnessed his dreadful torment.

Finally satisfied, Father Matthew picked up the pliers and, with great care, placed them round the arrow's shaft, below where earlier he had cut off the fletchings, and as close to the barbs as he could get. Then, checking that his little team were ready, while pressing once more on Gui's upper chest, he grasped the pliers strongly in his right hand and gave the bolt a firm twist and pull with his wrist.

Giving a single terrible cry Gui's whole body leaped and shuddered. There was a frightful gush of bright blood from his shoulder, and with an awful groan he slumped into unconsciousness at last.

"Done it!" the hawk-nosed monk shouted and, then, a moment later: "Got it!" And, very slowly, he drew his hand back until, with a gasp of triumph, he held up the bloodied steel on its mangled shaft for all to see. "Now, hold him still why I just check through here for any stray bits of cloth that the arrow might have taken in with it. Good! Good!" he said a moment later, as he drew out several fragments of cloth and leather on the end of his smallest forceps.

"Now...William, I'll just wash it through with a little more of this Arrack and then you can gently release his arm and push the shoulder back into place. James, you hold the wound open with this retractor," he said, handing him the strange implement he had explained earlier with its curved, blunt metal jaws. "And I will pour in some more of this Arrack to wash out anything that may have been left in there. Excellent! Now I will put in a neat row of stitches with my little curved needle. More Roman magic this," he added a few minutes later, as he mopped at the white spirit, now running pink over Gui's chest, with a soft cotton swab. "The Romans were excellent doctors. They used finest animal gut, as I do," he said as he deftly worked on Gui's shoulder. "From the cat, which will not of itself fester, nor infect the wound as long as it is properly cleansed before hand.

Now we will put a fat pad of this fine, soft cotton against the wound, with a little of this salve underneath it. Frankincense, this, people," he said, looking round at them. "And frighteningly expensive, but the Greeks swore by its good effects on trauma after surgery...and so do I. Now a little of this too," he went on, smearing a foul-looking, green webby mixture over the stitches."

"What on earthy is that, Father?" Alicia asked with a grimace. "It looks just disgusting!"

"This is a paste made from Yarrow, which many call 'Knight's Milfoil'," he said with a grin at her twisted face. "It is said that Achilles himself used this to treat his soldiers' wounds, and is a speciality of mine. It is under the virtue of Venus. An ointment of which cures wounds, and is most fit for such inflammations as we are hoping to prevent. It can also be used against the bloody flux. And is not only good for green wounds, like this one, but also for ulcers and fistulas, especially those that are full of moisture.

Greek, of course!" He added with a raised eyebrow at Brother William. "Horrid isn't it?" he asked, grinning at his appalled, yet fascinated audience. "Works every time. Mixed in with Agrimony and Shepherd's Purse...and common nettles!! All sounds pretty shocking, I know, but it really works, I have used it often!

Now, Brother James, we must lay these bandages across and round the wound, but not too tightly, Hippocrates was very clear about that. 'Neatly and cleanly', were the very words he used, so that movement will still be possible, though severely restricted. I don't want him moving his arm and ruining all my handiwork! Right, all that's left to do now is to move him back to his bed, prop him upright and support his shoulder with one of those bolsters...and leave him to rest.

And a few moments later, when all had been completed, he said softly: "He will come round shortly, so be ready with a bowl, Alicia, for he will be horribly sick after all we have done to him, and he will feel as weak as a kitten. Send that lovely lady of yours...Agnes?...for some restorative broth from the kitchens. Not too rich to start with. Brother William is our expert. He can go with her and help your cook prepare it. And no wine for a while, that will only inflame the wound, not calm it, so lots of that wonderful spring water I hear you have so much of, and some of this poppy juice for the pain!

Well, God Willing," he said, looking down at the white faced young man before him, his left shoulder now swathed in soft bandages. "The worst is over, and we will soon have him as right as rain and fighting fit again in no time!"

B ut it was not to be as easy as all had hoped.

Not that Father Matthew's confidence was ill placed…but despite all that could be done fever set in, and by the evening Gui was hot and shivering by turns, his face flushed and his lips and mouth dry as dust. Soon his mind became unclear and his speech broken.

When uncovered to renew the dressing the wound was red and swollen, and the area around it grown hard and yellow. Called at once by Alicia, who had stayed by Gui's bedside almost all the time, Father Matthew sucked in his mouth and palpated the wound gently, making Gui moan and toss his head.

"Hmmmm!" He said gravely, looking down at Gui's shoulder. This is not so good. I thought I had cleaned the wound better than this. The Arab doctors hold that wounds can mortify if they are not cleaned properly, or if some bit of cloth or other stuff gets in with it. There must still be something in there that the Arrack did not flush out."

"Why the spirit, Father?" Alicia asked him, anxiously. "I was surprised you used it earlier."

"It is purer than water, even when it has been boiled."

"Why boil the water anyway? I saw you do that too."

"Because the Greeks held that boiled water was somehow cleaner. Better when dealing with wounds. The Arabs do the same, and certainly fewer of their patients die as a result of it. I don't know why, but if it works…why not?"

"The same with the alcohol?"

"Yes, my Child; Greeks again I am afraid. Aesculapius and Hippocrates...and the Roman army doctors. They held it cleansed things. Like this," he said pointing to the hard yellow mass that was pushing against the edges of the wound. "That is called 'pus'. It is a kind of poison and we *must* remove it as soon as possible or his whole shoulder may go bad! Once that happens there is very little hope! So we *must* clean the wound again immediately, and re-stitch it and drain it so he will get better. Truly, my little one, it must be done now! In the meantime he must drink as much water as possible...and boil it first!"

"I know," she said with a smile and a soft sigh of resignation. "The Arabs say it is better that way!"

★

R e-opened with his smallest scalpel, the foul gush of thick, stinking pus that burst from Gui's shoulder made Alicia feel quite sick. And with it came a sliver of bright metal and several pieces of dark cloth that Father Matthew removed instantly on a large pad of clean linen.

Clucking over his patient, Father Matthew, again with William and James' help while Sir Richard and his men came up once more to assist, probed and washed out the wound with Arrack a second time, plucking out two more pieces of with his forceps as he did so after which he cleansed the wound again, putting a short length of bulrush tube into the wound as a simple drain packed around with more Frankincense, and then left unstitched to heal from the bottom up, but bound firmly with clean cotton bandage and his own poultice.

"Now, we really have done all we can. And look," he said holding up the arrow head for all to see, "that sliver of metal came from here. See, the very point is missing. It must have broken off when it hit Sir Gui's shoulder. It is a perfect fit. And these are more fragments of leather from his jacket. That is good!" And he sighed, putting his arm around Alicia's shoulders as he came and stood beside her, looking down at Gui's flushed face.

"Well, my child, he is truly in God's hands now. All we can do is keep him cool and the wound washed with lavender water, and cleansed with Arrack, and we must do our best to get as much fluid down him as possible...and wait and pray."

★

All through that night, the day following and the next, Gui's fever mounted and delirium set in. Groaning and swearing, he tossed and turned in his bed, crying out for his mother and for Alicia...and cursing de Brocas's name. And all the time Alicia stayed by his bedside and administered to his every need, cleaning him when he soiled himself; washing his body with cool lavender water; laving his shoulder with it every time the dressings were changed and then cleansing his wound with Arrack. The fierce spirit making Gui groan and cry out until his shoulder was soothed with boiled lavender water, brought up chilled in a sealed flask from the deep water of the castle well. Helped by Agnes and Father Matthew they lifted him to help him drink and change him; and twice a day she checked his shoulder, helping the tall Benedictine to wash, cleanse and re-bind it.

Outside, the castle and the little village it protected struggled to come to terms with its losses, both the loss of their Lord and their own losses from the storm; and there were many burials.

Of Sir Yvo and his wife, there was pitifully little left from the fire. Indeed it was hard to find anything of them amongst the shattered ruins of the New Hall, now only a blackened, empty shell. No more than a few shards of long bone, their skulls and their wedding rings, untouched even by the extreme heat. And they found Sir Yvo's great fighting sword, its handle twisted and burned, but its shimmering blade of finest Damascus steel undamaged, and they brought it and laid it on the altar of the old chapel beside their golden wedding rings.

The rest, what little there was of them, was reverently gathered up and put in a beautiful little casket which Alicia wept over bitterly, for she had loved them greatly and, apart from Gui, they were all the family she had left in the world whom she cared about. Nor was she the only one to show such grief, for both had been well loved by all who knew them and the whole countryside was shocked at the news of their awful deaths.

Meanwhile the roads and byways were scoured for news of de Brocas and his party as knowledge of what had happened at Castle Malwood became more widely known. North, South, East and West the Earl of Southampton and Sir Jocelyn, the Sheriff of the New Forest, sent out search parties. All knew that Sir Yvo stood close to the King's Grace and that the Lady Alicia was the King's Ward, and the husband-to-be of one of his favourite young knights. It would bode ill for anyone to hinder the Sheriff's search...and much good for those who helped it. Yet search as they did through Beaulieu, Lyndhurst and especially Southampton where their enemies had first landed, even Poole and Christchurch, there was still no news of the Baron and his daughter, and all the time Gui's fever mounted.

Great candles were brought in to his room and incense burned.

One of either Father Matthew or Alicia was constantly in attendance with balms and salves and herbal infusions that they urged Gui to drink. And James Bolderwood, his Seneschal and Richard L'Eveque, his Guard Commander, were never far from call, deep concern etched in every line of their faces, and on the fourth day, with hope fading and his fever still mounting, poor Father Gerome came in tears and said Mass over him, and everyone walked around hushed and silent.

That Sunday the little church in the village was packed, as all who could do came to offer prayers for their Lord's recovery, and leave little gifts of food or other comforts to temp his appetite. He was Sir Yvo's son, and well known to all of them, and he was a good Master, as his father had been before him, understanding of their needs, and kindly. He was firm and fair in his judgements in the monthly Courts he had shared with his father, Sir Yvo, since his knighting, and they loved him for it.

That night, as his fever increased still further, Father Matthew became ever more anxious, especially as his surgery and aftercare had worked well; the wound now dry and pink with health, the drain removed and the flesh soft with no taint of death. No pus, no stink of rot and no black and mortifying flesh. As he and Alicia bathed and washed the wound yet again, and put fresh bandages on his shoulder, he bowed his dark head over the young Lord of Malwood and

307

prayed for his deliverance.

"Last Rights, Father?" Sir James asked in his quiet way, coming softly up beside him, where he stood with Alicia.

"*No!*" Alicia broke in fervently. "No! He is *not* going to die. I will not *let* him die. I will *not* let the fever take him as it did Agnes's family, and my mother in her childbed and her babe. Not now! Not now that his wound is healing and I am here beside him. I won't *allow* him to die. I positively *forbid* him to do so!" she said firmly, wiping Gui's hot brow while he continued to moan and fling himself about in his distress, the soft linen cloth steeped in cool water drawn from the deepest well, and scented with lavender. "The Angel of Death will not take him from me now. By God, I swear it!" And she flung herself into Father Matthew's arms and wept.

"My Child," he said then gently, taking her hands in his and turning her to face him. "You must be prepared for the worst. I know how much you love him," he went on, putting his arms around her again as her body was suddenly racked with sobs. "I know, *I know!* But your love alone, Alicia, will not be enough.

Tonight's the night, I *feel* it," he said, laying his cool hand on Gui's flushed and burning forehead. "The crisis is very near. His fever will either break...or God will claim him from us. Salvation...or Death? It is all in His Hands now. I have done all I can..."

"...*But I have not!*" Alicia interrupted him fiercely, dashing the tears from her face. You may have finished with him, Father. But I have not even *started!*" And turning to them all she said: "Go from here now. All of you!" she implored them.

"I am his betrothed before God, the closest to being his wife that he will ever have without me actually being so. You have done all you can," she added, looking around at the men with tears in her eyes, and at Agnes standing opposite her. "All of you. You too, dearest Agnes," she said, gathering her friend up in her arms and giving her a huge squeeze. "And I thank you all for it. But now it is up to me and my maker. Pray for us Father?" She begged him as she pushed them all out of the door. "Pray for us. That you *can* do. I will not surrender him to the Angel of Death without a fight! You have all done the best you can...the rest is up to me!"

And she firmly closed the door behind them.

Chapter 45......*But is defeated by a pure and loving Heart.*

The Lady Alicia de Burley turned to where Gui lay on the bed, panting for breath, his head bathed in sweat even as his body shivered, though the fire still flamed up the great chimney, while outside the moon rose to throw its silver light across the room. "My wonderful, *wonderful* man," she said softly, looking down on him. "Father Matthew has done all he can. Now, my most precious darling; we will see what a little real loving can do for you as well. My love brought you to safety last time. Let us see what more it can do for you now?"

And without another word she slipped off her dress and then her undershift 'til she was standing naked in the moonlight, her firm breasts tip-tilted in her hands, her loins a delicious shadow of desire as she walked towards him, her beauty ethereal, unsullied and pure, like a marble goddess, in the harsh silver-white light that bathed the countryside.

Lifting the bed covers off him, so that the heat of his tormented body rushed over her, she leaned forward, letting her breasts brush against him, again and again, chest to chest until he moaned in his throat, she also, her nipples aching to be touched, on fire from the heat that was consuming his body.

Closed though his eyes were, yet did his body 'see' and 'feel' all that he could not fully cling to with a sentient mind. And as she teased and kissed his chest...so she felt and saw his loins stir. A first loving caress, as she reached for his silken manhood, intent on turning his fevered brow into such a fever of loving that the fire now so engorging him would burn the fever out and leave him cool and sated in her arms.

She kissed him then.

Her cool wet lips on his hot dry ones, her questing tongue flicking his to hungry life, while with her hand she felt him grow and thicken, pulsate with hot life, the blood filling his manhood as she caressed him with both her body and her mind. And, taking him between her breasts, grown taut with her own

310

desire, she felt him grow still harder, and with a smile she took him slowly, slowly into the soft warmth of her mouth. Caressing him, suckling him, 'til he was so strong and hot that she could feel him almost bursting in his eagerness, straining to reach her, wanting her, needing to fill her, to make himself one with her as she knew he longed to do.

But not yet!

Turning she reached for the lavender soaked cloths with which she had bathed his head before, and this time she used them to bathe his whole body, sweeping hand motions across his upper chest and over his belly. Down his thighs and between his legs, caressing his testicles, holding each fat, oval ball gently in her hands, before lowering her mouth to kiss and savour each one in her mouth in turn. While she washed the great flag that was his manly strength, cooling it, cleansing it as it waved above her, beckoning her on, begging her for conquest, for her to take it deep into herself as she had done so many times before.

Now at last he was indeed panting and moaning and crying out.

But not from the fever of his illness that had so taxed his body and suborned his mind…but from the fever in his blood that she had raised in him, from his red hot desire that always turned her from demure maidenhood to wanton harlot, that made her hold out her breasts for him to love and mould and fondle, to suckle 'til her teats were thick and swollen, her areolas puckered and her loins soaking with the need to feel him inside her, filling her, piercing her, so deeply penetrated that he could almost touch her heart.

"Listen to me, Gui," she said, her voice husked with loving lust, darkened with desire. "Some say that you may die! That now, tonight, this instant may be your last. But I say, *No!* Not *yet*, my love, my darling, my *most* precious man. Not yet until I have *so* sated you that heaven itself will not allow you entrance 'til my love for you has grown cold. And that, my *precious* heart, my Life, shall *never* be!

I am so ready for you, Gui!" She cried out then, raising herself up to receive him, her knees on either side of his legs, his manhood tall and swollen in

311

her hand. "So wet, so open and yet so hard and strong that life, or death, may come my love, but I will claim you *still!*" And with one fluid movement she thrust herself down onto him until he was buried in her to the very hilt and she could take his hands and put them on her breasts and suck his fingers, while she rode him to destruction.

She cried out then in ecstasy and threw back her head, her eyes closed as she savoured every moment, for she knew him so well. Knew just when to stop and rock herself on him, squeezing him with her muscles, and when to rise…drawing her body away from him until she could feel the very tip of him approach its freedom, only to have her grip him with her loins and sink back down again in rapture.

Knew when to move her hips sinuously around him as she sank down upon his shaft, slowly, slowly, slow - ly, until once more she was impaled upon him more deeply even than before…and she knew when to ride him as hard as she was able; drawing her feet up and placing them beside his body, and bending forward as a jockey would a horse, driving her self down upon him with all her energy, making him buck her up as thrust met thrust, so she could fall and rise upon him harder and harder 'til her breasts were bouncing, swaying, swinging like the gorgeous fruits they were, and she was crying out for joy and utmost pleasure.

Just so with love and laughter she took him to the very edge of life itself, to that whirling, maelstrom of passion from which no freedom can be found, nor ever sought, and where desire brooks no escape. A spinning, glittering rush, boiling in its intensity that roars through your body before exploding with the mighty *crash!* of boiling surf upon a rock bound coast. And with one, final, shouted drive of lust and loving power she hurled them both into the very heart of it, sending their spirits spiralling, singing, soaring into space where stars are born and suns explode in bursts of brilliant coruscating light that flood the universe with wonder, and reach out to touch the edge of time itself.

And as she felt him burst within her…so she felt his fever break. Felt the heat rush out of him, like hot air from an oven; the sweat dry out, and his body grow ever cooler to her touch. Heard him sigh and whisper her name at last: "Alicia! Alicia!" Felt his arms go round her as best they could as she slid from his loins to hold him close against her heart.

312

And so she held him in her arms all night, lying along his uninjured side, covered with just the finest of fine cotton sheets, the soft night breeze blowing across them; her breast against his mouth so he could savour her sweetness; her legs wrapped round him so he would not feel the cold; her lips in his hair and on his forehead, so he could always feel her love reach out to him and stifle all his fears.

★

As the dawn broke, the grey half-light turning to softest colour, she left his side at last, slipping out of the great bed to leave him sleeping, breathing softly, gently, as the sun rose to bathe the new day in its rosy light.

Pulling on her undershift, and carrying her dress over her arm, she tiptoed to the window and looked out onto a world touched with beauty: Venus still shining down upon her, Diana's silver moon still a faint orb as Aurora turned the new day from faintest green to blush-pink, shot through with gold and crimson even as she watched, the fields and hills around her still milky in the distance. Everywhere was softly shrouded in an early morning mist that covered the lake and writhed off the moat that surrounded the castle. Only the very hilltops could be seen, lushly green and sharp against the vast blue arch that sprang up overhead as Venus finally winked out and Apollo drove his blazing chariot over the land's dark rim.

From the pastures by the lake she could hear the ewes calling to their lambs and the cattle lowing as the men called them in for milking. While overhead the first of the day's swifts screamed on scimitar wings as they hurtled over the roofs and parapets of the castle in the sheer joy and excitement of being alive, dipping their beaks in the moat beyond the walls, mist shrouded and still in the early morning light.

And looking, Alicia sighed with pleasure, and a deep, deep sense of utter relief, stretching her arms out to the morning as she did so, before stepping into her dress and pulling the bodice up over her breasts, still tight from his lips where he had suckled her all night. Turned then she paused and looked down at Gui, loving him almost as a mother would her child, knowing how much he needed her and sleeping now so peacefully you never would have known that

313

just that evening past he'd been as close to death as any man could be.

She sighed and smiled: how heavy the empty heart, how light the one that's full.

And, even as she looked, her own heart turned over with a rushing sense of joyousness and love that *so* filled her that her eyes flooded with tears and she just *had* to go to him, sink down beside him, touch him, hold him, kiss him. Not with lust or hot desire, but with loving gentleness and care, smoothing his tousled hair from his brow and stroking his cheek with the fine fingers of her hand. For this was her man, and she loved him more than words could ever tell. Then, kissing him softly once more on his lips she stood beside him and smiled, her eyes and face lighting up 'til anyone seeing her would have been dazzled by her beauty.

Without Father Matthew he could never have survived to fight again. Without her he surely would have died. Together they made a powerful team. She had done her part. Now, indeed, it was up to God to do the rest!

And with a last glance around Gui's chamber, a place so filled with agony and blood just hours before, and now so peaceful and so filled with love and joy and by the rising sun's warm light...and at her man still sleeping gently like the big babe he often was...she shook her head and smiled in wonder, lifting the latch as she did so, and with a gentle shush of her skirts she softly left the room.

Chapter 46...*In which we learn more about Father Matthew; and Sir James brings good news.*

I t was the sun that roused him, bursting all over him through the open shutters in shafts of brilliant light that cast the distant corners of the room into deep shadow. Long fingers of warmth ran over his skin like molten wax, making his eyes crinkle from so brilliant a July morning. The sky, blue as a Jay bird's wing, arched overhead without a single cloud upon it, the gentle coolness of an early morning breeze fluffing over his sun-warmed shoulders, the distant sound of sheep bells and the bark of dogs all combining to bring his senses rushing back to life.

He stretched then, luxuriating in the warmth and lack of constant pain in his shoulder at last.

Four days since he had woken to Alicia and Agnes bending over him; to Father Matthew's cool hand on his forehead and the solicitations of Richard L'Eveque and Sir James when they had come to see how he was, that first morning after Alicia had broken his fever.

Long days of lying in bed recovering from his ordeal: having his wound dressed and re-dressed, gently examined and palpated since when he had gathered strength after his operation, and in that time listened to how Matthew and his father had met all those years ago in the Italian mountains, when Father Matthew had saved Sir Yvo and Sir Henry from wild Italian banditti with his amazing 'Dance-of-Death' that had slain five men in as many minutes...when Sir Yvo had been gravely wounded and close to death and how amazed they had all been when Father Matthew had revealed to them who he really was. And how, in the end, it had been Sir James, of all people, who had forced the tall Benedictine to show his hand at last and then give them his real name...

★

" Y ou will just have to show them, Matthew!"

Sir James said, with a shrug of his elegant shoulders. "They will never believe you else. And I still don't know how you do it!"

"I don't know that I do either, old friend. It is many years now! Still," the tall monk said going across to Sir Richard who was watching and listening in blank

315

bewilderment. "We will see if my wrists still have their cunning. May I?" And without another word, while everyone except Sir James looked on in absolute astonishment, Father Matthew stooped to Sir Richard's side and with a single smooth movement, drew his long tapering sword from its scabbard.

"A fine piece of steel, Sir Richard," he said, pausing to flex its fine blade between his hands, before shaking the whole weapon to test its balance. "And Damascus steel, too," he added, admiring the fine blue wavy lines that were all along its blade. "A rare weapon indeed!" He exclaimed, bowing in deference to its owner. "A blade of the very finest, like Sir Yvo's, and of the new pattern, tapering to a point, not heavy and broad bladed. I congratulate you," and he inclined his head again to the astonished knight. "This is a beautiful weapon indeed and, if driven well, will burst through chain mail like a knife through butter. Finesse, not just brute strength, Sir Gui," he added with a smile. "Now, let us see what I can do with it?"

Feet slightly apart but weight well forward on his toes, his habit tucked up in his belt, its long sleeves thrown well back, he began twisting and turning his wrist in the most dexterous manner, twirling the beautifully tapered sword first one way and then the other, the long blade flashing in the morning sunlight while Gui and Sir Richard, no mean swordsmen themselves, watched him in utter amazement...and Sir James sat back in his heavy chair with arms crossed, and grinned.

Backwards and forwards Father Matthew moved his feet as he swung and twizzled the shimmering blade, throwing it from one hand to another as if it were a small knife, not a four foot length of razor-sharp steel. It was a stunning display of bravura that held them spellbound, until finally, bringing the whirling blade to a sudden halt he threw the sword spinning up into the air, catching it by its hilt as it fell, then twizzling it dexterously to lie across his arm, hilt first towards Sir Richard's right hand. And everyone gasped and clapped, an instinctive reaction to a truly remarkable display.

"Who...Who are you?" Gui almost stuttered, he was so shocked, as he lay propped up on his good shoulder while Sir Richard thoughtfully sheathed his sword again by his side. "How-how do you do that...that amazing 'dance' with a sword?" He ended breathlessly.

"More to the point," Sir Richard asked. "Where did you learn such a skill? I have *never* seen the like before. Though I have heard of it," he added, puzzled. "But...where? Where have I heard tell of such a thing before?"

"Now you are coming to it," Sir James butted in, brightly. "You too, Gui. Think, Boy! *Think!* Where have you heard of such brilliant swordsmanship? Aye...and many times, too!"

"From Sir Yvo!" Richard exclaimed suddenly. Quietly at first, then more urgently: "From Sir Yvo! Yes?...*Yes!* I remember now!" he rushed on, almost falling over his words. "He told me of a knight whom he had met in his salad days, when he was travelling in Italy with Sir Henry, oh, thirty years ago or more. A Frenchman," he said vaguely. "No, Italian? Oh, come on Gui," he urged his young companion, still looking puzzled.

Then a moment later the mists cleared, and Gui shouted: "No, Richard! Not Italian...*A Spaniard!* From the Kingdom of Navarre, who saved father's life from some brutal fracas with wild bandits in the Italian mountains, and who had a way with a sword that had to be seen to be believed!"

"*The Dance of Death!*" The two men called out together, with a great shout of laughter.

"Yes...Sir James," Gui said when they had all calmed down again. "*The Dance of Death!* Actually with two swords, if my father is to be believed, not just one. Each whirling on top of the other. We have heard him tell that tale many times. We all have."

"Of course we have," Richard said, suddenly, looking at Alicia sitting smugly silent a few feet away, looking as if butter wouldn't melt in her mouth. "And each time more outrageously than before. Indeed, and Yvo said who the man was too. One of those impossibly long Spanish names: Don? Don?..." he snapped her fingers in frustration.

"...*Don Mateo de Silva de Pampalona!*" The tall, black-habited monk finished off for him with a deep flourish and a huge smile, and both he and Sir James laughed out loudly at the looks of utter astonishment on the faces of all the others in the room...save Alicia who had laughed and clapped the loudest

"*You!*" Sir Richard and Gui shouted out together again, stunned by this sudden revelation.

"*Yes!* My friends. *Me!*" Father Matthew said, turning round to face Gui, holding his arms out wide and bowing deeply.

"And you, you old rogue," Gui said, turning to where Sir James was

317

still sitting, a grin like a slice of melon stretched across his usually severe features. "You knew? And you, you little Lynx!" he exclaimed at Alicia, sitting there and laughing.

"Yes, Dear Boy. I knew," the stately Seneschal said with a smile, holding his hands up in mock surrender. "I have *always* known, and Matthew told Alicia when they were in the Forest, but abjured her to silence until you were better. But, after 'Don Mateo' became 'Father Matthew', and after Sir Henry, your father, died my dear," he said, turning towards Alicia, "Matthew started travelling all over those bits of the world we know of...and then some bits we don't...and so we saw him less and less."

★

Lying there in the sunshine, Gui grinned to himself. What an amazing skill! And one he would have to copy, he thought ruefully, rubbing his injured shoulder. That was the target the man had set for him to prove himself fit for battle again! To turn and twist and throw Sir Richard's sword around as Father Matthew had that sunny morning. How had his father kept quiet about him all those years? And his lovely, chatty mother? He gritted his teeth. Both of them viciously ripped out of his life by the wickedness and greed of one *Bastard* Frenchman who'd then managed, somehow, to skip free of all of them!

But not for long! They knew now to where the Baron had fled, and how. Sir James had told them all that when he had walked into his room that fourth morning after, Argos by his side, when they had all been laughing over Father Matthew's joke about St Peter...

★

"Quite a throng," the old Seneschal had observed dryly, breaking into their revelry as Sir Richard brought him a chair to sit on. "I thought I was about to quell a riot. I am surprised, I had thought this to be a sick room, not a tap room?"

"Not quite, Sir James," Father Matthew replied, with a grin, looking at Gui, Alicia, Agnes and Sir Richard still chuckling over his silly joke. "The young people were just relaxing a little. Don't you just love to watch the children having fun?"

Sir James cocked his eyebrow at that raillery and smiled. Then, turning to the young Lord of Malwood, he said in his rather heavy way, leaning forward in his chair and patting Gui's arm at the same time: "Gui, Dear Boy, I am so delighted to learn of your growing recovery, and to hear that boisterous laugh of yours once more." Then turning to face the black-habited surgeon, he added: "You have brought us all back from the edge of despair, Father. To have lost Sir Yvo was bad enough, God knows, but to have lost the heir as well would have been a disaster from which Castle Malwood would never have recovered. We all owe you greatly. However, it's time to decide what we must do next," he went on before anyone could say a word, steepling his hands and tapping his long fingers together as he spoke. "Not least because I have news, at last, of the wicked Baron and his not so merry men!"

"James!" Sir Richard said excitedly. "You're better than the Archangel Gabriel himself!"

"Well, we shall see," the Seneschal said smiling. "Though how true all of this news really is I just don't know. We are still checking the details. But, never mind, this is what I have heard: there is a young journeyman carpenter attached to the Abbey at Beaulieu named Jared, with a new wife, Lynn, whose parents, as I understand it, run a small inn on the very western edge of the Forest, Tyrrell's Ford I think it is called..."

"But that's miles away!" Gui interrupted, surprised. "In fact so far West of us here as actually to be outside the Forest where the Hampshire Avon runs down to Christchurch. Tyrrell's must be miles from the Saracen's Head - from where they chased you, my darling!" He said to Alicia with a smile.

"But not far from my own castle at Burley!" Alicia answered swiftly. "Perhaps they thought that's where I was going to? Nothing would surprise me about that awful man."

"And not that far from Ellingham Priory as well," Father Matthew added, in his firm voice. "My home when I am not junketing about the world on the King's business!" He exclaimed. "I wonder if he knew that I was in the Forest as well that night? And I was so careful not to let him see me when I was down at Gruissan that time," he added enigmatically, turning to look out of the window. "Anyone could have told him about my visit to the 'Head' that night had he cared to ask."

"Ask what, Father?" Gui asked sharply. "You worry me. There is just too much secrecy going on around me for comfort."

"Nothing that cannot be explained, Gui," Sir James said quietly. "And nothing for you to be concerned about right now, I assure you," he added very firmly in his 'Not-to-be-Questioned' voice. "And I don't think de Brocas had any idea he was close to Burley castle," he said to Alicia. "Nor to Ellingham either, Matthew. He'd just had a brutal dust-up with Allan-i-the-Wood's men and been driven off into the darkness, two of his men dead and many others injured. I am certain all he wanted was to get safely away and lick his wounds. Don't seek for more troubles than we already have, people. They are not worth the candle, I assure you!"

"Well," Gui said, giving the tall Benedictine the benefit of the doubt with a quiet smile. "They must have crashed about hopelessly to have ended up there, in the middle of pretty well nowhere, and miles from the sea as well, their only source of security after what they had done that night. Lost isn't the word for it. They must have been wetting themselves! No wonder we could find no word of the Baron's movements."

"Yes," Sir James agreed. "Allan-i-the-Wood did his job better than he realised; those Frenchies must have been very lost indeed! Anyway, according to Lynn, who was over to see her mother three days ago, everyone was full of it. Tyrrell's Ford had not had so much excitement since the death of William Rufus...and that was ninety years ago!"

"Oh! Even I know about that," Alicia chipped in with a laugh. "When Sir Walter Tyrrell shot the red King, William Rufus, by accident while hunting deer in the Forest. Some say the arrow glanced off a tree first. A great gnarled and knotted oak. It's only a mile or so away from Castle Malwood, where he was staying at the time. Sir Yvo told me all about it, and I have seen the tree!"

"Murder, you mean!" Sir James said darkly. "His brother, King Henry I paid Tyrrell to do it, of that all men are certain now. The Red King was a bad lot! Eyes of two different colours and guilty of every vice you can imagine, so the records show. And surely the King's brother, Henry, became the next King very quickly...not least because all the chief men of England just happened to be at Winchester, where Henry was too...and where the Royal Treasure is kept as well! Surprise! Surprise!

Anyway, that's where Tyrrell fled to, the ford that now bears his name. He paused there to snatch a bed for the night, a meal and a fresh horse, even though the King's men were likely to be hot on his heels. Cunningly he had the local blacksmith reverse his horse's shoes before crossing the river. When all

320

the king's horses and all the king's men rushed up the next morning, not only were they confused by the trail he had left but were further led astray by the innkeeper's daughter with whom Tyrrell had been amusing himself, so the King's probable murderer escaped, fled to Poole and then back to France."

"What happened to Sir Walter?" Alicia asked. "Afterwards, I mean? I never did know."

"Oh – nothing!" Sir James said briskly. "He stayed happily in Normandy, while his family in England were showered with good things by the new King, Henry I."

"What happened to the Girl?" Agnes asked quickly, her eyes alight with the romance of the story.

"Oh, the men came back and killed her!" Sir James replied with a shrug. "Hanged her from a tree over the river for aiding and abetting a murderer. They say her ghost still haunts the water where Tyrrell crossed over; waiting for her splendid lover to come back and rescue her."

"Poor lady," Agnes sighed. "But how brave. I would never have had such courage...nor a 'splendid lover' either. At least not until you two are off my hands!"

"No, Sweetheart," Alicia teased her. "Not until you find the 'King of France' to marry!" And they all laughed.

"Well," Sir James went on, after everyone had settled down again. "According to Lynn, Tyrrell's had a parcel of violent strangers arrive four nights past, well, early morning actually. French, she said they were by their speech: a dark haired young woman and an older man, together with six of the greatest ruffians her mother had ever set eyes on...two of them badly wounded, and all of them the worse for wear. Claimed they had been attacked by bandits and outlaws" he said pointedly to Alicia.

"The one I kicked in the face?"

"Maybe? Remember they'd also had a bloody skirmish near that tree you leaped over! Anyway, they arrived at Tyrell's soaked through, battered and needing shelter for the night, and for the next two days. Jared's wife, the girl Lynn, says that her mother was asked to find some fresh, dry clothes for them to wear, and that her sister, Poppy, was asked to take hot broth to both the woman and her father upstairs. Lynn said that the clothes she took off the man were so badly singed that they were not fit even for a beggar!

"Where did they leave after that, James?" Sir Richard questioned him eagerly. "Did the girl - Lynn?...know that?"

"Yes - they left two mornings later for Christchurch on their way to Lymington."

"Then where, James? Did she know that?"

"Yes! Some little place near Lymington called Pitt's Deep..."

"...I know that place, Sir James," Father Matthew interrupted quietly. "Hmmm. Very clever. There is a small quay there, in its own deep basin...where there is sufficient depth of water to hold a big ship safely. Hence its name!"

"Well, Father," Sir James said in his precise voice. "That's why it was chosen I expect. Away from Southampton where the search would be fiercest, yet close enough to reach easily from Lyndhurst had things gone the way they expected - and not difficult for a good local Ship-Master to find his way there from Southampton where they had originally landed to come to Malwood the day of the fire. And very private. Anyway, people. That's where they left their horses to be collected, all except the big Frenchman's destrier which they took with them. Coal black and a lovely beast I gather...so de Brocas without a doubt. And from there they sailed on the great cog *Christopher*, that was all tied up neatly and awaiting them. So...What do you think of that?" And he sat back, well pleased with himself, putting his hand out for a goblet of wine that Sir Richard poured for him from a silver-gilt decanter of Burgundy that he had near by.

"*Sweet Wine of Christ*, James! I think you are a bloody marvel." Sir Richard replied brightly, putting down the tall pitcher and rubbing his hands briskly together. "By God's Bones, but that has to be the Baron's party surely! Arrived wounded? Clothes singed by fire, all French and a coal-black charger? Too many coincidences to be anything else!"

"I agree," Gui added quietly, gritting his teeth at a sudden twinge from his shoulder, his eyes watering with the effort. "Clearly he had a ship waiting for him, and a place to leave his horses. So...now that double-dyed French Bastard has whisked himself away to the fair land of the Franks! But, more to the point which part, my friends?" He asked, looking round at them all. "Where to now?"

"He could have gone anywhere!" Sir Richard responded thoughtfully, going over to the fire and kicking the pile of logs smouldering sulkily into flaring life. "Cherbourg, Brest...Le Havre? Anywhere, even Spain, knowing his Moorish connections!"

"No! Richard," James broke in, with his clear, precise voice. "I think not. He is not welcome everywhere, and certainly not by our own King, at least not after that nasty business with Prince John. Remember the Aquitaine rebels whom Richard wanted so badly? Didn't de Brocas give them shelter in his castle at Grise?

"Yes! That's right. He did," Sir Richard said, turning from the fire, now a mass of leaping flames. "The King was furious. More so when Philip wouldn't make his vassal hand them over to Richard's Justice. Probably knew just what kind of 'Justice' Richard had in mind! Our King was incandescent! The Court rang with the famous Royal Plantagenet temper for weeks!"

"So the good Baron would not want to linger anywhere Richard might get wind of him and try and seize him." Gui replied eagerly. "The King has a long memory I assure you, so you can rule out anywhere in the Empire, certainly in the North. No! I reckon our man has gone South."

"*Narbonne!*" Sir Richard and Sir James exclaimed together.

"No...Château Gruissan." Father Matthew said in his firm Spanish lilt. "That is where he will have gone. That is his ultimate refuge. The Château is enormously powerful, sits like the top tier of a giant wedding cake on a circular promontory that sticks out into a vast bay, what people there call an 'Étang' and closely joined to the Circle Sea itself; the Mediterranean. The Lord Baron is allied to the Count of Toulouse and to King Philip of France and it would take an army to break in. So, my friends," he said, his quiet words falling with deadly intent into their silence: "Not Narbonne...but Gruissan."

"I agree, Father! And this business is not over yet, I am sure of it. The man has the cunning of a fox and the morals of a cur, especially after a defeat like that which he has just suffered. And I guarantee he still wants Alicia!"

Chapter 47... Reflections and shocking Revelations.

A powerful enemy the *so* worthy Lord Baron Sir Roger de Brocas of Narbonne and Gruissan, Gui thought bitterly, leaning back against his pillows, as he looked out at the blue sky through his open windows on that perfect, sun drenched morning. But after what Father Matthew had revealed to them yesterday it might just be that this noble scion of the House of Brocas was not quite as untouchable as he liked to think he was?

Splendour of God! How could Richard stomach his brother, Prince John, in the way he did? If it was me I would have had him locked up for good and thrown away the keys, the little *shit!* What a devilish plot they had hatched between them, Philip, John and Roger, and how frightening! The Assassins? Enough to make anyone shudder, they must all be mad to involve such dangerous men in their foul schemes. Certainly, what Father Matthew had told them all had been a truly shocking revelation!...

★

"Very well," he had finally agreed, albeit reluctantly. "I had hoped to keep all this back until Sir Gui was truly fit and firmly back on his feet again," he added quietly in his rich Spanish voice, moving over towards the window to sit in its wide embrasure, looking back at them all with the light behind him. "Of course, this was all discussed with Sir Yvo, and Sir James...and the Lady Margaret...and would have been made clear to you all had it not been for the truly awful events that have since swept over us. But as it is, you are all right and I cannot hold off any longer."

And with a sigh, putting his hand into the deep scrip that lay at his feet, he drew out a fine leather covered case, capped and closed at one end with scarlet seals on a broad ribbon of equally regal colour, which had several other seals hanging from it. There were also a number of other papers he laid out beside him on the broad window seat, all clearly of equal importance.

While everyone watched, Matthew broke the case open with his strong fingers and from within drew out a tightly rolled parchment, ribbon-tied and stamped with more seals in several places, and while most waited to see what it truly was the tall Benedictine held in his hand, Gui at least drew his breath in sharply, recognising it for what it was, his eyes narrowing as Father Matthew moved away from the window to show them all more clearly what he held so firmly in his hands..

"How far back does all this go, Father?" Gui asked suddenly.

"To the coronation in September, and the meeting that the King had with your father the day following your return to Malwood; and again at the Christmas Tournament."

"Sooo," he said thoughtfully. "Father *did* have a further meeting with Richard about de Brocas after all, as Sir James suggested to me the day of the fire. But when I asked him, the old buzzard wouldn't say what it was about!"

"No, Gui," Sir James chipped in. "Your father insisted we all agree that neither you, nor Sir Richard were to be told anything. Not least because Richard didn't want you to be any more involved than was necessary..."

"The King?" Gui asked. "Not L'Eveque?"

"Of course '*The King*', Sir Gui!" The tall Benedictine replied sharply. "Stop interrupting and listen! We couldn't tell you, not just because the King didn't want you involved more than was necessary for your Honour's sake, but also for fear that you might, inadvertently, alert the 'Man-Eating Tiger' we were so trying to catch. And we couldn't tell Sir Richard without telling you, that would have been unthinkable..."

"So you didn't tell either of us! Yes I can see that, now," Gui said, breaking in again. "But when was all this decided? It couldn't have been in London, Sir James wasn't there."

"No, Dear Boy," the tall Seneschal said quietly, getting up from his chair, and walking to where Father Matthew was standing with the King's sealed document in his hand. "It was decided long before you went to London, at the time that your father wrote to de Brocas about your Betrothal, the King and he having already agreed that de Brocas should be invited."

"Agreed to invite him?" Gui gasped out, looking bemusedly from Sir James to Father Matthew and back again. "Richard? King Richard? Why?"

"Because, for reasons I will explain, he wished it! And whom your Father might choose to invite to so august an occasion as the Betrothal of a

325

King's Royal Ward, especially in his absence, was very much in his interest. The Lady Alicia is his Ward, remember? And is fully deserving of the King's protection, especially with regard to Prince John...or anyone else for that matter!"

"The Prince, Sir James?" Alicia asked, appalled, her eyes large with dismay.

"Certainly, Alicia," he said calmly, looking down at her horrified gaze. "You have been very much on the Prince's mind since he met you last year at his brother's coronation. He would have laid his hands on you then, too, if he could have done, despite being newly married to the wealthiest woman in England! Why do you think your Guardian had you whisked away so swiftly from the Court?

But Richard no more trusts his baby brother than you do, or any of us here for that matter, and he had no desire to leave so valuable a marriage prize unclaimed before travelling Outremer. He knew that John was beholden to de Brocas after the last rebellion before King Henry died at Chinon, and that the Lord Baron was close to King Philip, despite his refusal to join in with the Crusade. But it suited Philip to leave de Brocas where he is, and the last thing Richard wanted was for one of John's creatures to walk off with one of the wealthiest heiresses in England!"

"Is that all I meant to the King?" Alicia sneered hotly. "A marriageable pawn on the Royal Chessboard, to be bargained for and sold off to the highest bidder?" She exclaimed bitterly. "I am surprised he did not offer me to one of Philip's people in exchange for peace in the Vexin!"

"*Alicia!*" Gui exclaimed, reaching for her hand, only for her to snatch it away angrily. "How can you think so?"

"Well? What *else* can I believe?" she snapped back, jumping up from beside him and whisking herself across the room, her eyes sparkling with anger. "That has *always* been the lot of girls like me. We have no say *what* happens to us...to our lives, especially when the safety of the realm may be at stake. We get sent to the marriage bed, along with our knights and our castles, with downcast eyes and are told to hope for the best!"

"Well in this case, Alicia," Sir James said quietly. "You couldn't be more wrong! The King loves you enough to name Gui as your husband, in the face of his brother's spite...*and* against the advice of some of his senior Barons,

326

jealous of Gui's preferment and the great wealth and prestige, that marriage to you will bring him.

Of course he could have 'bargained' you off, you silly girl!

That is his unalienable 'Right', as the Lord King of this realm. After the civil war that devastated England during the reign of King Stephen...which *I* fought in, God Help me!...the King needs to be certain of whom his friends are, and advantageous marriages are one way to ensure that, and no-one would have blamed Richard if he had decided to do exactly that, not even Sir Yvo himself!

Instead Richard has agreed to your marriage to the man you love, with his blessing, *and* the gift of rich vineyards from his mother's inheritance near Bordeaux on the day of your marriage. All that in a bid to redress the losses your family took, years ago, from the predations of the very de Brocas family with whom your two Houses have been at feud since the time of the Conqueror! The papers for which Royal gift, Father Matthew has in his scrip, along with others he was also charged with bringing to this castle. Yes, a surprise indeed, young lady!" He added severely, in his dry, precise voice, looking across first into Alicia's shocked face, then into Gui's. "I would say you have *both* been extremely well cared for, wouldn't you?"

"I...I am sorry, Sir James," Alicia stammered, dropping a deep curtsey to the old Seneschal as she spoke, abashed by her outburst. "I should have known my Lord the King better. But what of de Brocas and his patron, Prince John?"

"Yes," Gui asked, quietly, himself astonished by the richness of the King's gift to the pair of them. "What indeed?"

"I think Father Matthew can best answer those questions," the elderly Seneschal replied in his stately manner, sitting himself down again. "He stands closer to King Richard than maybe any of you realise."

"Father Matthew?" Sir Richard queried, amazed.

"Even so," the tall monk replied, coming forward with his still rolled-up parchment. "This was all to have been made clear to you, Sir Gui, the day after your betrothal, for reasons I will make clear shortly. Your father would not allow you to be told sooner, despite advice from Sir James and your mother for him to do so. He said that you were too guileless, too straightforward in your approach. Not enough of a dissembler for his and the King's plan to work should you know of it beforehand. And now that I have met you, and seen you 'at work' I think your Father was probably right."

"What plan, Father?"

"To invite that 'Man-of-Blood' to your betrothal party, *with* his daughter, and then, after the knot had been duly tied and safely sealed, as it were, to have them *both* arrested for High Treason against the Realm. That was what your father stayed to discuss with King Richard after the coronation, and again at Christmas. About de Brocas. He was the 'Man-Eating Tiger' I spoke of a few minutes ago...and for whom *this* Royal Warrant has been specially prepared!" And with a flourish he broke the seals at last and pulled an immaculate scroll of creamy parchment open for all to see.

And there, almost at the bottom, deeply embossed with a King crowned and enthroned in splendour, with drawn sword and orb in either hand, was a huge scarlet seal from which broad ribbons with more seals on them now hung down.

" *That is King Richard's Great Seal!*" Gui breathed out huskily. "I have never seen it so close. It is only ever given to those whom he trusts absolutely." There was a moment's stunned silence then, for with the King's Great Seal came the very *essence* of the King in person. It was as if King Richard himself was standing there amongst them all, in full Royal Majesty and power, and they were both humbled and amazed. And while all the men present briefly knelt and bowed their heads, both Agnes and Alicia dropped deep curtseys as if the King himself had stood amongst them.

"Correct, Sir Gui," the tall Benedictine replied a moment later, with a slight bow of his head. "The King gave it into my own hands a few weeks ago, in Normandy, before journeying to Vézalez to meet with King Philip, with orders to seek out your father and break de Brocas once and for all.

"For High Treason?"

" *Yes!*" Father Matthew answered fiercely. "*And of the very vilest kind!* De Brocas has been plotting to have Richard murdered by the Assassins in the Holy Land. The blood stained followers of Sheik Rashid ed din Sinan..."

"...*Murder!*" Alicia gasped, clutching Gui's hand fiercely. "Our King? He would not dare!"

"Yes he would. And aided and abetted by those far greater than he!"

"Who, Father?" Sir James asked quietly.

"I will tell you shortly."

"So," Sir Richard breathed out in a hushed voice. "The Old Man of The Mountains is still alive and kicking!"

"Very much so," the tall Benedictine confirmed slowly, turning to look at Gui's tall Guard Commander, his brown eyes at their sharpest. "You know of him then, Sir Richard?" he questioned, dangerously. "I am impressed!"

"Only what I have heard, Father," he replied cautiously. "I have never been beyond the Circle Sea, so do not bend those sharp eyes on me and seek to find an enemy!"

"I am very pleased to hear it...but I was not thinking anything so dark, I promise you!"

"Well, that's alright then," the tall knight answered with his slow smile. "I know that he lives in Castle Masyaf, somewhere between Tripoli and the Kingdom of Jerusalem, and has a band of fanatical followers called 'The Assassins', supposedly named after the drug, Hashish, that the young men he wishes to train are given first, so that he can persuade them that only by carrying out his orders can they ever hope to reach Paradise..."

"...Oh, the seventy beautiful virgins and all the good food they can eat in the wonderful gardens!" Gui growled. "Just in case they get skewered in the process of their murderous activities!"

"So, Sir Gui. You know something of these people too?" Father Matthew asked quietly.

"Like Sir Richard, father. Only what I have heard, and that alone is enough to chill anyone's blood!"

"And rightly so, My Son. The Assassins are trained to the highest degree to move swiftly and silently in any environment; day or night, but more often at night. They are expertly skilled murderers with the knife. Long blades especially made for the purpose, and they are faithful to their Grandmaster unto death, and, no matter how well defended or guarded a place or a person may be, they *never* fail!

Their hands are soaked in blood. Muslim, Christian it matters not, providing the price is right. For him it is a matter of politics not religion, and the politics in Outremer are complex and often murderous as well: treachery is just a game out there it seems!"

Alicia shuddered as she heard that, and gripped Gui's hand more tightly. 'Assassins', 'Murder', 'Treachery'! The very words sounded frightening. What were they all getting into?

"You have heard well, Sir Richard," the dark faced monk said, with a slight incline of his head towards him. "I commend you. The Assassins are every bit as frightening, and as powerful, as you have been told. Their followers are fanatics who indeed take a drug called 'Hashish', at the start of their training, a drug which makes them impervious to the fear of death, and convinces them of their true place in Paradise. It is why they are so successful...they have absolutely no fear of death.

Some say they were named at the beginning, in Persia by their founder, Hassan-i-Sabbah, as the 'Asasiyun', the Founders of 'Asas'...the Faith! No matter, they are indeed terrifying killers to whom de Brocas has already paid over the ten thousand marks necessary for the King's death through contacts of his daughter's, all slavers operating out of Cyprus with the connivance of Isaac Comnenus, the so called 'Emperor' of that island."

"From whom has the money come?" Gui asked, his face drawn and grim. "Who could afford such a monstrous sum? Who are the other plotters, Father?"

"Philip of France and Prince John!" Matthew replied bleakly, and everyone gasped in horror at his words.

"*Splendour of God!*" Sir James exclaimed. "Does the King know?"

"Yes! He knows...and is doing all he can to conceal that knowledge in order to make the best possible use of it! Such knowledge is power, especially on the eve of war with the Infidel in the Holy Land, and even more so with King Philip as a somewhat reluctant partner!"

"*How do you know all this, Father?*" Gui questioned him shocked and appalled by what he had been hearing, as indeed they all were,

"The king already had his suspicions about John and Philip, and he had long known of de Brocas's desires with regards to the Lady Alicia, and his deep hatred of both your families. John is not always discreet in his plottings. He has a young man's arrogance, and was not aware of his Royal brother's scrutiny, believing Richard's muscles to be in his arms and legs and not his brain…and has no regard to the quality of those whom the King has gathered around him either!

The man is a born fool, both a liar and a deceiver. He shows all the worst traits of his parents, and none of the good…and his father indulged him beyond all reason, making him ever more dangerous. Pray God, Richard has a long and successful life! Left to himself, John would wreck this country in a twelve month…and the Empire in not much longer! Philip will eat him for breakfast, and grind the remains into the mire! He is a subtle and dangerous man, Philip of France!

As for de Brocas?" Matthew went on, disgust in his every word. "He has long been suspected of a variety of wickedness and interference, especially after he sheltered those rebels the last time, refusing to hand them over to the King's Justice. And John's interest in Alicia, on de Brocas's part did not go unnoticed either, I can assure you. Why else do you think the King was so determined that you should both be safely betrothed before Gui left England for the Holy Land?" he added, turning to where Alicia was sitting, shocked, beside her fiancé.

"Richard was concerned that John might try and seize the throne in his absence with the aid of French troops, paid for by Philip and led by de Brocas. John has never been secure in the lands he was given. His Father did not call him 'Lackland' for nothing! And it was his name at the head of the list of principal rebels of that final rebellion against him in '89, that finally broke King Henry's heart. De Brocas has been a crony of John's since long before then, and all men know that Philip would give the *earth* to have Richard dead, and little brother Johnny in his pocket!

But the King lacked proof…so he sent me to find out what I could.

I journeyed right down to Narbonne, and from there to Gruissan, and a long and tiresome journey it was too. I even went into the Château Grise itself, right into the 'Tiger's' lair. And it is no mean lair I can assure you! An immensely powerful fortress, and stuffed with armed men of every hue at that! I had many useful conversations and discussions there with people who are closer to the Baron than he may realise, and was able to bring back hard

331

evidence of John's foul plans, and of the Baron's deep involvement that Richard had been so desperately seeking.

Papers that I was to bring with me here to show the Baron that his evil treachery was not a figment of the imagination...but as real and inescapable as his own death!

"What was the pay-off, Matthew?" Sir James quietly asked him.

The Spanish Herbalist snorted with disgust then, and turning to where Alicia was sitting, her mouth almost hanging open in amazement, as he said in his rich baritone:

"You were, my Lady! You were the Baron's 'pay-off!' De Brocas's prize for bringing all this about, you and all the Malwood-Burley lands, both here in the Forest and elsewhere. *Everything!* Worth playing for, wouldn't you say? Philip was to get the Vexin off John, which has been a bone of contention between the Frankish and the Anglo-Norman Kings since the Conqueror's day! John would gain the throne of England, very much as Philip's pensioner, but with the promise of peace between them. As for his Royal brother, our own King Richard of England?...Seven feet of dusty, desert soil!"

"*No!*" Gui and the others exclaimed, horrified by Father Matthew's litany of wickedness.

"*Yes!* Sir Gui! *Yes!* All of you! I have *seen* the papers.

After all I got them and put them in the King's hands myself. But, rage as Richard might...and he can rage pretty well I can assure you! He is in a very difficult situation. Not only does he need Philip's support for his Crusade, he just doesn't have enough men, nor the money to 'go it' alone, but, also, de Brocas is one of Philip's people, and his lands are under Philip's protection! They may be near our borders in South Aquitaine, they may nominally be Richard's after his father's war in Toulouse in '59. The war in which De Brocas' father was killed by Sir Henry. But they are still disputed...not Richard's by right, even though they should be. So, while *of* his lands...they still are not truly *within* them!"

"So, Richard could not move against him as he would have liked." Sir James commented tersely.

"Correct! This 'Tiger' of ours had to be lured out of his lair, safely away from lands controlled by the French King into lands ruled over by Richard, and without any interference from John who has his spies everywhere. Indeed that was where Allan-i-the-Wood fitted into the picture. There were questions about John de Grey's loyalty to the King, he is seen as being more in favour of John than of King Richard, so Richard had him replaced by someone known to be rock solid, rather than have anything go wrong with de Brocas' proposed arrest. And someone who knew the Forest of old.

For Baron Roger had to be openly accused and arrested, by formal Royal Warrant *and* with the evidence attached, brought with me as proof positive of the Baron's vile schemes in order to avoid a huge upset with Philip! These!" And, to their amazement, he pulled out a clutch of parchments from his scrip as he spoke, and waved them in his hand.

"If that could be arranged, and John's interest excluded...then Philip would *have* to support the Baron's arrest or be seen by the whole of Europe, and by the Pope, as an aider and abetter of wickedness on an unbelievable scale," he went on.

"Just *imagine* the row that would ensue if Philip's involvement with the Assassins was to become common knowledge! No ruler would feel safe in his bed again for fear that one of the Assassin's long knives might not 'get' him next! And Philip would lose his throne, quite literally, to a Crusade against him...*in his own country!*...for siding with Infidel murderers against Europe's foremost Crusader next to old Barbarossa of Germany!"

★

G ui looked out of his windows and growled.

Infidel Murderers and wicked Frenchmen indeed! *God's Blood,* but he was desperate to be up and doing! What he needed now was action. He'd had enough of 'bed rest' to last him a lifetime, and if he didn't get off it soon he would go mad!

He grunted, and banged himself against his pillows.

Who would have believed that the King's own brother, let alone Philip of France, should have hatched such an evil plan? Yet the proof was there for all to see, as Father Matthew had shown them. However, with Prince John and Lord Roger involved, perhaps he shouldn't be that surprised after all. He

333

grunted again and sat up. He just couldn't bear it one moment longer! It was time to move, preferably on his own without the girls to flutter round him.

And, swinging his feet to the floor he tottered across his room on slightly wobbly legs to the broad window seat, and plumping himself down he looked out across the castle's massive limestone walls, beyond the lake, and beyond the Forest, to the furthest hills, faintly blue in the distance.

It all seemed so unbelievable! How could God let such evil happen?

Take my parents, he thought. They didn't deserve to have their lives stolen from them in so brutal a fashion, nor did anyone else who had lost their lives that dreadful night! And now, just when I need my strength the most...I can barely move, and feel completely useless! And he smiled then, thinking of Alicia, for that was what he had said to her two days ago, and her response had been both swift and timely:

"Not completely useless, my darling!" She had said softly, giving his hand a squeeze. "To me you are everything, whether whole or not. And there is certainly *nothing* wrong with your imagination...nor your loins!" She added with a wicked grin. "So stop beating yourself up with a stick. There are enough problems for us to face as it is without you covering yourself in sackcloth and ashes!"

"The Lady Alicia is right, Dear Boy," Father Matthew had said then, reaching out to touch his arm. "The fire took your parents, and other good men too, and that is a terrible thing. But we are not here to judge God, My Son. He has His own plan for us all...even though we may not see it now. But neither does He mean for us to sit around doing nothing!

Sadly Evil is very much alive and kicking in this world of ours, Dear Boy, but *so is Good.* If Evil did not exist...then Good would mean nothing. Like food without salt, or herbs and spices. It would have no flavour. It is Man's lot in life to strive, and in this world in which we live we must strive mightily to succeed. That is one of God's most precious gifts, that He has given all of us an indomitable spirit with which to achieve that. And when we are faced by Evil, we are able to use that other Godly gift, the gift of the Holy Spirit to defeat it. Remember, Gui, all it needs for Evil to flourish is that Good men do nothing! And for you, for all of us here, that is just *not* an option!"

Chapter 48...Sir Gui passes Father Matthew's Test.

However in the end it was late July before Gui and his companions were finally ready to set out; almost a month to the day of the fire.

A week after he had fully recovered from his fever Father Matthew came and took the drain out, satisfied that the wound had healed without any mortification of the flesh and was clean and firm, though the scar itself was still a dark purple colour and the muscles slightly wasted. But nothing that exercise and patience would not recover, and constant massage with chosen unguents to ensure that the scar did not become so hard the skin would not stretch.

Indeed, every day thereafter Matthew came and massaged Gui's damaged shoulder with aromatic oils and creamy lotions, his strong fingers working away at his muscles until Gui could bear it no longer...until the next time, and the next time after that. Each day being able to bear more of the Benedictine physician's hard searching fingers; and every day he could he exercised beside his men with a wooden stick at the tall hacking posts set up in the bailey for the soldiers to work at, wielding a heavier stick weighted with lead each couple of days until by the end of the month he could cut and thrust with his sword almost as well as before the Baron had shot him.

But it was not easy, and often there were difficult, 'Black Dog' days as well.

Days that he thought his shoulder was truly on the mend when something small would cause a setback, like reaching for a full pitcher of water off the table, only to find his arm wouldn't lift it. Or days out with the men in the Bailey helping to shift rubble or war gear, when suddenly his shoulder would give way and he would have to drop whatever he was carrying back onto the ground, his whole arm and shoulder seared with pain. Then it would take the combined efforts of both Alicia and Father Matthew to make him cheer up, slow down, and take greater care before he did himself an injury from which he would not so easily recover!

335

But if his strength of body was still in question, not so his mind.

For Gui was a born planner and a good chooser of men. He knew what kind of warriors he wanted to fight by his side: sharp eyed and strong of body and limb; men who would trust his judgement, not question it; Men who could march thirty miles in a day and fight a battle at the end of it with courage and determination, not flee howling in fear.

And there were such men to choose from.

Men well practised in war, with battered byrnies of plate, ring-mail and leather with sword slung at their waists, fighting axe and baggage over one shoulder and their shields across their backs. And men who were not: sometimes plain woodsmen, with wood-axe and billhook, sometimes just peasants from the fields with only the tools of their trade to recommend them, who had used the King's proclamation to take the cross and escape the everyday dullness of their lives in exchange for the hope of excitement and adventure in a far off land! And sometimes there were whole families, with hand carts and animals in tow, and always a host of camp followers and ladies of the night! Gui and Sir Richard watched them coming in, sometimes with relief and pleasure at their obvious expertise, and sometimes with dismay and even amusement at their ignorance and foolishness.

"Just look at those two," Gui pointed out to Alicia one morning as she came up with Father Matthew to join the two men looking down on the bailey from the battlements above the gatehouse. "What on God's earth do they think they are doing here?"

"Who?"

"Those two down there with that donkey," Gui went on, laughing as he pointed over the battlements. "Down there with a box on its back and some kind of birds in it. The smaller one leading it has a pot on his head. Look, just going past the well head. His friend has a sickle tied to a long stick and a goose on a string!"

"Those two have to be the sorriest pair I have seen yet!" Sir Richard exclaimed, with a broad grin. "The pot I can understand, but the pigeons and the goose?"

"How can you tell they're pigeons?" Gui interrupted, astonished.

"By the way they are bobbing their heads in and out between the slats of that box, Silly," Alicia said, looking over his shoulders and giving them a shake. "Apart from chickens, only pigeons do that, and their heads are too smooth to be anything else. Hens have wattles!"

"But what on earth would anyone want with pigeons and a goose?" Gui persisted.

"Forget the pigeons. It is the goose that matters," Father Matthew's amused voice broke richly in on them.

"Why?" Sir Richard asked. "Because it's too tough to eat and the pigeons aren't?"

"Oh, it's probably tough alright, poor thing, scrawny too. But that old goose isn't for the pot on his friend's head. It's to tell them the right way to go to find the Holy Land!"

"Oh, come on Father," Alicia chided the tall monk with a laugh. "No-one could be *that* simple. Not even in the Forest!"

"No, I promise you, My Lady," he went on earnestly with a grin. "Father Gerome has assured me that geese have been especially touched by God as heavenly direction finders. That is how they know when to leave us in the summer time and when to return as the first blasts of Winter's horn are heard across the land. I heard him say so, not an hour since. Those two clowns down there are simply following in a proud tradition! Just as thousands of German

337

peasants did when Peter the Hermit's army set out on the first crusade a hundred years ago."

"What!" Alicia exclaimed, with a shout of laughter. "They followed geese? To find the Holy Land? Were they mad?"

"No, just hopeless."

"Witless, if you ask me. Like that pair with the donkey."

"And look what happened to them all," Sir Richard commented laconically. "They were wiped out almost to a man, and woman, by the Seljuks in Anatolia. Properly dished-up…"

"And stuffed, no less, for good measure?" Gui added with a grin.

"Like that poor old goose will be down there," Alicia said, as she watched the two lads making their way across the bailey. "Following geese to the Holy Land indeed! That's just the sort of simple thing Father Gerome *would* believe in, poor old boy. Thank God he's staying here when we all set out. Otherwise there's no knowing where we would all end up!"

There was a pause then, as they looked out across the warm, summer countryside around them, so lush and green and fat with life. So safe. So *known* to them all, and so different from the parched, sun-baked desert lands to which they were going, where no-one spoke their language and a deadly foe, whether Seljuk Turk or dark Assassin, lurked in the blue, shimmering distance just waiting to pounce and slay.

"Father," Gui said, after a while, turning back to where the tall Benedictine was leaning against the battlements. "Do you know Richard's movements? When Sir Yvo and I were with him last there was still much to be arranged."

338

"Well," Matthew said carefully, counting out the points on his fingers as he spoke: "One: Richard and Phillip left Vezalez on the 4th July. That we know, because our messenger with all the news of de Brocas missed him by a day. Two: the two Kings are expected to journey to Lyons together, where they will separate. Three: Philip then goes to Genoa where he will take ship with his army to Messina, while Richard is bound for Marseilles to join *his* fleet who have been ordered to assemble there by the end of August. So...Four: God Willing and barring any disasters...which there are bound to be, as something almost always goes wrong!...Richard should reach Sicily by September. Messina to be exact."

"Right!" Gui said, straightening his back and banging his hands together. "Then if we are to smoke this evil wolf from his lair, which will not be easy, *and* then join Richard before the winter storms close the Circle Sea, we need to be gone from here as soon as possible!"

"What are we doing about shipping?" Sir Richard asked, turning to look at Gui. "I know your father had made plans before the fire, but that was for ships from Southampton to Normandy for the journey down to Lyons and Marseilles. They will be long gone now, and we will need more men than we had originally intended to take with us."

"Ah!" came a fresh voice from behind them. "There I may just be able to help you," and with a small grunt of effort the trim figure of Sir James Bolderwood hauled itself onto the wide fighting platform behind the gatehouse battlements.

"I wondered where everyone had got to," he said, looking round him with a smile. "But Fitzurse told me you were all up here, surveying the 'circus' that this castle has become over the past few weeks!" he said derisively, looking down between two of the merlons and gesturing in despair at the mayhem going on below. "And, as I was in dire need of a break from all my labours, before I go completely mad," he continued, turning to face them, leaning backwards against the battlements with a sigh.

"And seeing as no-one *else* was doing any work!" he added dryly with raised eyebrows, "I thought I'd come up and make your unhappy lives more miserable by joining you for a breath of fresh air, and a glass or two of the finest Burgundy to go with it. I at least deserve it," he ended with a grin at their discomfiture. "While you idle hounds have done nothing but sit around all day and gossip!"

"Ho!" Gui replied giving a laugh. "Gossip, is it? And that from someone with the longest ears I know. You, Dear Sir James, live by it!"

"Well. There is something in what you say, Gui." His Seneschal continued, watching as three of the castle servants who had followed him onto the tower-head began opening a small folding table. "How else can I keep up with all that is going on in the County?" he added, watching carefully as they laid a white tablecloth and then put a large silver flagon of Burgundy down on it, with simple goblets to match, alongside two plates of sweetmeats.

"Now hush up Gui, Dear Boy," he said, holding his hand up to stop him from speaking, "and try this! If there was one thing your dear father could do, God Bless him, it was choose a good wine. Now, serve the others, you fellows, and then away with you back to Suchard and tell him we will all be down shortly for the midday meal."

"You're right, James," Gui continued brightly a moment later, after first savouring his drink. "Father was good with wine! Now, what's this about ships you were going to tell us?"

"Mmm, yes," his Seneschal responded, with a smile, raising his goblet as he spoke. "That was just what I needed, I can tell you. That mob down there needs sorting out in some order!" he went on, looking down again over the battlements, picking up a sweetmeat fastidiously in his long fingers as he did so: "We are running out of everything…and I want my castle back…"

"Which I will be delighted to give you, just as soon as I can find transport for France. So…James, tell me about Ships!"

"Thomas Blackwood. Shipmaster of the *Mary!*" Sir James replied blandly, looking up at the sky as if that was enough, his eyes closed as he savoured his wine and basked in the sunshine.

"Yes?...More, *please*, James!" Gui said, tapping his hands on the battlements.

"And the *Pride of Beaulieu*," his tormentor went on blandly, while sucking his fingers as if discussing cabbages or beans.

"James!" Gui said again, rising frustration in his voice. "We all know who he is, and what he owns. But not where he is!"

"Well," the tall Seneschal said, opening his eyes and smiling. "He is at Beaulieu!"

"Now, that," Sir Richard chipped in with a broad grin, "is smooth and welcome news indeed! If Tommy Blackwood is at the Abbey with the *Mary*, then he can take all of us."

"All of us?" Alicia questioned. "Our own Malwood lions, as well as the extra men Gui wishes to take with him, *and* the horses? That is some load for a single ship!"

"All the men, certainly." Sir Richard said, his face a mask of concentration. "The *Mary* is the largest cog operating between England and France. But probably not all the horses. Some, along with some of the gear on those carts, will have to travel in his second ship, The *Pride of Beaulieu*. The thing is, James," he went on, turning back, "is he there?"

"Well, he should be! If he has stuck by what he told your father after delivering those fat hogsheads we all enjoyed so much the night of your betrothal."

"He is *exactly* the man we need," Gui said, excitedly. "And his crews are first class as well! We must send a message to him at once to say so!"

"What do you think I have been doing all this time?" His tall Seneschal asked, turning to look into his young Lord's eyes with a quirk of his lips as he refilled his and Alicia's goblet. "Drinking wine? That has already been done, Gui! I wrote to Abbot Hugh weeks ago, with a letter to give Thomas telling him that you would need him!" And looking round at their startled faces he laughed.

"You sly old hound!" Gui exclaimed with a laugh, giving the older man a shake. "You *are* a one for surprises. 'Long headed', we would say in Yorkshire!"

"Just so, My Lord." His Seneschal replied with a grin and a slight bow of his head. "Just so. One does one's best!" And they all laughed.

"Father," Sir Richard drawled, as the others joined in the laughter, indicating Gui and turning to where the tall monk was standing, rolling his goblet between his shapely hands. "Is this young fighting cock of ours ready to travel now…and to fight?"

"Hmmm," the tall monk said, looking intently at Gui for a while, before adding: "I seem to remember telling this young Perseus of ours what he would need to do before I would pass him as ready for the fray once more, yes?" he questioned, looking round at the others, who all nodded in silent response. "So, Sir Richard, give him your sword and let's see what he can do with it?"

"So be it!" Gui exclaimed, staring back at Father Matthew, their eyes briefly locked together, while holding out his hand to his tall guard commander. "Give it to me, Richard. I am ready!" And, with a soft swish of steel on leather, Sir Richard drew his long sword and handed it over.

As Gui had learned and practised with Father Matthew over the weeks, so did he likewise, twisting his wrists and his shoulders as he twirled the fine blade up, down and over again, tossing the sword from hand to hand as he moved so that to those watching him, the space in front seemed always to be filled with shimmering steel. Finally, with a shout of triumph, he threw the sword upwards in a glittering, twisting throw that delivered it back into his open hand, and everyone burst into applause.

"Well, Father?" Gui queried, breathing quickly as he turned with raised eyebrows to his dark-habited mentor.

"Well indeed, Dear Boy!" The monk replied with a laugh and a brief incline of the head as he clapped Gui on his shoulders. "Though your own sword is much heavier and broader than Sir Richard's, remember, so you mustn't think that your training is completed. But I said when you could do what I did that day you would be fit to return to active service, and that stands. So, Sir Gui," he went on formally, making a small bow to the young man standing, still panting a little before him. "I pass you fit for purpose at last. Go forth and do your best!"

And with a shout of concerted joy, they all raised their goblets high and drank their fill with laughter, before turning and leaving the Gatehouse battlements to complete the planning and all the arrangements necessary for them to leave.

Chapter 49...The Cousins' plans within the castle walls revealed.

Down in the bailey two of the men who had been helping with the piles of equipment paused as they heard the shout, and looked up from their meal of coarse bread and cheese, with a hunk of bacon, on which they were chewing.

Born fighters, with powerful shoulders and strong upper arms and calves, they had strong hands too, with broad palms and thick fingers to match them. Their slightly swarthy looks, dark eyes and black hair proclaimed them to be South French at least, if not Spanish or Italian, and their eyes were sharp and hard. They looked what they were; tough men not to be taken lightly.

"Well, someone's got something to fucking crow about, Cousin," the smaller of the two growled, his thick brows drawn down as he spoke. "How much longer will we have to wait before something else happens?" And he spat into the ground at his cousin's feet.

"Lucas Fabrizan," the taller man replied, straightening his back. "You always *did* want everything 'yesterday'! Be patient, do as we have been told, and it will all work out fine...yes?"

"Yes...I know: keep our fucking heads down, do as we are bid with a smile, and generally make ourselves bloody indispensable. Yes, Jules. I *know* that. But I don't have to fucking like it do I?"

"Listen to me, Coz," his cousin replied softly, looking round as he did so. "We were put here for a purpose by Lord Roger in case something went wrong with his plans."

"But his plans..."

"Never go wrong!" His cousin finished for him. "I know. But this time they did, as we know only too well, and despite everything we did that night, the girl still got away!"

"I was never more fucking shocked than when she turned up again with that bloody monk! It was bad enough being grilled by that bastard, Fitzurse. But when that sodding bitch turned up as well...I thought our days were well and truly numbered."

"And Fitzurse was nothing compared to Sir Richard!" His cousin added, idly scratching his chin. "He may seem lazy, and sound like a dozy bumble bee, but that man's eyes can see right through you, and he's hard as steel. And Sir Gui, as well. By all accounts the Baron was lucky to escape with his skin that night, so he must be formidable indeed."

"God's Blood, Jules! He's supposed to be fucking dead!"

"But that's just it, Lucas. Every plan ever made carries the seeds of disaster in it somewhere! It only needs one thing to go wrong and the whole plan can fail. Well, this plan failed," he snarled. "Not completely, as we can all see for ourselves...look at this place: fire blackened and half burned out as it is, its Lord and Lady dead and everything in turmoil..."

"...But the bloody son and heir escaped death," Lucas broke in. "And his fucking lady escaped the Baron too! How could he *not* have known that the couple running that bloody inn were well known to the sodding family? And to that stupid little bitch especially? Well, now the fucking hunt is up in earnest, and we, poor sods, are caught in the middle. Not good, Jules!"

"As you say, Lucas, not good...but not impossible either. So, the plan's gone wrong and we are now his only support! But that's why the Baron sent us off here back in April. To get taken on by this Gui fellow," he sneered, gesturing obscenely with his hand towards the Keep. "Just in case!"

345

"And just as well!" his cousin growled, stretching out his legs as he spoke. "*And* clever too! They *need* men like us, Jules. Proven fighters, with a smart appearance and all our weapons well cared for. Just the thing that men like Fitzurse, God rot the fucking bastard, look for. We were also supposed to get close to that little bitch as well…and that hasn't happened!"

"Yes it has, you idiot. Because of our skills we were chosen to be guards at the very foot of her bloody tower, and survived a bitter grilling from Fitzurse and Sir Richard. So far we are nicely in the clear and wholly unsuspected," his cousin hissed at him. "So, *Coz*, Keep your temper under control, or we will be undone! *And watch your language!* you swear too easily! Remember, we are being well paid for this, and not just in gold either, Coz. So hush it, before someone hears you. Anyway I am now closer to the little Lady than the Baron realises!

"You mean that pretty piece I've seen you with from time to time these past few weeks?"

"Yeah. Agnes Fitzwalter."

"She's close to our quarry, isn't she?"

"She is indeed, Coz. And, God Willing…and my clever hands and wicked mouth," he added with a leer. "She will be the key that will unlock the little Lady whom Baron Roger has left us behind to keep an eye on."

"The Lady Alicia?"

"Who else, you idiot!" His cousin snapped back. "Agnes Fitzwalter is her closest friend, abigail and confidante. If I can win her to my side then her fine 'Lady Alicia' will learn to trust us too," he sneered. "I am not from the warm south for nothing, Lucas," he added, with oil in his voice. "If I can't woo her I'm not the man I think I am!"

"Jesus, you fancy yourself, don't you?" his cousin snarled, before adding: "Now that the Baron has shogged off, how are we to let that fucking corsair, El Nazir, know how the land lies?"

"*Hush up, you fool!*" Jules hissed furiously at him. "Watch your mouth! Do you want all the world to know what we are about? I'll tell you when it's time, now, come on," he said as they heard a long whistle-blast ring out round the bailey. "Let's get this stuff shifted; Fitzurse is looking our way, God rot him. He's the *last* person we need to interest himself in us too much, so, look lively and let's get on with it! And keep your eyes open for two lads with a box of pigeons on a donkey and a goose on a string…"

"*What?*" His cousin exclaimed, throwing the remainder of his water on the ground in disgust. "Fucking pigeons and a goose on a string?"

"Yes! It's another part of Lord Roger's plan."

"What do you mean another part of his fucking plan? I thought *we* were the plan!"

"And just how did you think we were going to let anyone know what's going on?" his cousin asked him, pityingly. "Us on one side of the bloody channel and he on the other?"

"I hadn't thought of that!"

"Well I had, but I didn't know either, until the Baron told me," Jules said with a grin at his cousin's blank face. "In fact I still don't really know how it all works. But he tells me that pigeons can be trained…"

"Pigeons?" His cousin hissed, appalled. "*Fucking pigeons?*"

"Yes, pigeons! You write a message on the finest of paper, tie it to a leg or behind a wing, and let them go, and then they fly all the way back to the person who needs the message."

"*Fly all the way back?*" Lucas asked, outraged. "What kind of a bloody fool do you take me for? Fly all the way back indeed! And pigeons, too? He's mad, that bloody Baron, who ever heard of such a thing?"

"Look, you mazeling!" Jules snarled at him, giving him a sharp buffet on his shoulder. "The Baron knows more things than you or I could think up in a lifetime! He told me the Romans used pigeons for carrying messages, just as the Arabs do today. And so does he. How else do you imagine he has managed to keep himself always one step ahead of so many of his enemies? He knows things, see?" He added, tapping his nose as he spoke. "So keep a sharp look out, Coz: Robin of Oxford and his older friend, Henri Duchesne. By the way, do you speak English?"

"English?" Lucas exclaimed, startled. "Fucking *English?* No...not more than a few words or so: 'Mine's a large one', and, 'Give us a kiss!' Enough to get by in any foreign land," he laughed. "Why?"

"Because of the two we seek one is English...and the other a Frenchman. They are the Prince's men."

"*God's Bones!* Jules," he exclaimed, shocked. "Prince John? Sweet Jesus, what have you got us into this time?"

"Lots of money, I hope! The Prince and the Baron have been doing business for a while now. So, providing you keep your head down and your mouth closed...and don't do anything rash without consulting me, then we may yet come out of all this as bloody heroes. Yes?"

"Yes, Coz. I know," his cousin replied with a rueful smile. "You have the brains and I have the muscle!"

Chapter 50...*Many are called but few are chosen...*

(Matthew 22:14).

By sun-down the men were exhausted, and more than ready for their evening meal at the long trestles set up in the Great Hall where there was a special buzz amongst them as John Fitzurse, Sir Gui's giant Master-at-Arms, had made it clear to everyone that the names of all those going 'Outremer' would be read out afterwards. Meanwhile food came and went as the evening progressed: fresh bread and thick meat pottage with onions, beans and carrots on big trenchers of stale bread; followed by giant apple pies with fresh cream from the castle dairies and simple platters of rich local cheese and fat, sticky dates from the castle stores; while the big leather jacks of ale and cider were heartily replenished by the castle varlets as the men relaxed. And all round the hall was a rising feeling of excitement and anticipation.

However, one tranche of men had already left, tramping off after the fire to join the many groups of soldiers and adventurers setting sail from Southampton as Sir Yvo had planned for before his death. Not willing to wait until Sir Gui was fit to travel they had already gone, leaving only the hardiest behind from whom Gui, Sir Richard and Fitzurse would choose only the very best. And then there were those who would have to be left behind to keep guard over Castle Malwood itself, for to strip the great fortress of all its fighting men would be an act of supreme folly. With King Richard journeying to Outremer, his mother following, Prince John would be free to do his worst...and no-one believed so deceitful a Prince would keep his foul sticky fingers to himself for long!

So, now was the time to tell all who was going and whom would have to stay and at the top of the great room on the raised dais, Gui sat at table in his father's great chair with his Guard Commander and his Master-at-Arms on either side of him in urgent discussion. Opposite sat Father Matthew, two sheets of parchment in front of him with quill pens, and a fat pot of ink close to his hand, with Sir James Bolderwood close beside him.

"Well Gui," Sir Richard said at last, flicking one of the parchment sheets with his fingers and leaning back in his chair as he did so. "That's it then. With one or two exceptions we take only those men who do not have wives and children to care for, making up the numbers with those men whom we have watched over the past month or so, who have not left along with all those others last month…and whom have decided to be fit for purpose."

"But that must be half the castle's complement left out, My Lord!" Fitzurse exclaimed in dismay, pointing at the list of names that had been written down, some ticked and others crossed through. "What about Ralf Longsword and John of Hordle? Two of the best swordsmen we have. And Dickon Fletcher? There isn't a man can match him for a well sighted shaft. Not in the whole county!"

"I know, John, I know!" his young Lord replied, gesturing with his hands as he spoke. "But we really need youngsters, while some have *got* to stay behind to keep guard over the castle for all the reasons we have gone over before. But I will make some exceptions…Dickon Fletcher for one, because without him there will be no-one to lead our bowmen, and they will be essential to all our plans. Though his wife, for one will not thank me for it."

"What about Ralf and Hordle John, My Lord?" His big Sergeant queried a moment later, tapping the parchment before them.

"We will take big John of Hordle," Gui said after a moment's pause. "He will be a tower of strength on this expedition and his wife will probably thank you for it…as will he! Sadly there is not much love lost between them just now, and a break might be the saving of them both. But not Ralf Longsword. For one, we *must* leave someone who knows what he's about, and whom the men will follow; and for another his lady is about to drop her fourth. She has not been well and I know he worries about her, because you told me so. We will make him up to Sergeant, he is due the promotion anyway, and is richly deserved."

"A good move, Gui," Sir James chipped in. "And one that will take the sting out of not going with you. The man is not fool, so it will give me someone to work with also, and the men will follow him."

"Thank you, James. Always delighted to please my good Seneschal wherever possible." And he reached across with a smile and shook the man's arm warmly.

"What about the horses, Gui?" Sir Richard asked, leaning forward for his goblet. "We'll need someone good for them, and there are only two I can think of who really know how to physic a sick horse, and they're both well married!"

"Pity we couldn't have taken your two Brothers with us, Father." Gui said.

"No," Matthew replied with a sigh. "They would have been ideal in many ways, Brother James especially, but they have gone on to Ellingham with Saffron. They are needed there, even more so as I will not be joining them.

"Well, that means Paul of Bartley and William Fisher!" Sir Richard grimaced. "I know they are both married but we can't take the one without the other, as they always work together. It would be like having roast pork without the apple sauce! But there aren't two better horse-doctors that I know of in all the Forest, and we will need them for certain if we wish to get from here to Narbonne in one piece…let alone the Holy Land!"

John Fitzurse, Sir Gui's huge Master-at-Arms sat back with a groan, and stretched his arms above his head: "The Holy Land! Outremer! Sweet Wine of Christ, My Lord, but that is a far step. Narbonne? Well I have been near there in my time, Sir Gui, with your father when I was just a lad and Edward Sergeant held my post, before he married young Rose. So I know how far that is. But Jerusalem, Sir Gui? That seems to me like it is a whole lifetime away!"

"Well, not quite a lifetime," Father Matthew said quietly, pushing the parchment sheets away from him and looking at the three men over the top of his glass, through the light from the sconces flaring nearby. "But a fair step for certain! Duke Robert was gone four years on the First Crusade! Marched all the way from Normandy, through Italy to Greece, over the Taurus Mountains beyond Turkey and then down to Antioch. It was a horrendous journey…and

351

then from Antioch to Jerusalem! They were seldom out of armour and there was fighting almost all the way, sometimes even amongst themselves! Men died like flies. Dust, heat, thirst, rotten food, disease…and that without Seljuk arrows zipping past their heads from every bush and rock! Grim almost beyond belief, and half never even got there!"

"Even taking ship, you will still have a distance to go," Sir James added in his dry, precise voice. "And shall be gone for two years at least. Sir Gui is right, John. This is a young man's game," he smiled wryly, "and preferably for the unmarried. That way they will concentrate better on the job in hand."

"Well, John Fitzurse," Gui said turning to meet his big Master-at-Arms' eyes. "I know you're not thrilled by it, but that's one decision made at least. So, I make that forty Malwood Lions all told from the Castle, if you count Fletcher and the others. Now, John," he went on, pulling the parchment sheet towards him. "Whom do we take with us from the rest?"

"Right!" The big man replied slowly, taking a pull at his own mug of ale and fingering the list as he did so. "If that's the away it is, I fancy the Burgundians who came in to us as a group two months ago, two dozen proven fighters. They work really well together under their leader, Jean de Beaune. I rate him highly, plus their equipment is in great condition and they know what they are about."

"That handful from the forest, they look useful, Peter of Minstead and his five fellow verderers, brilliant scouts and expert trackers. Those bills they have make fearsome weapons when well used. We might try them mounted on a tough ash shaft as a new kind of weapon. You can hook a man out of the saddle, and then turn and cut down with the axe blade on the reverse side almost in one movement. Very nasty!"

"The French call that a 'Gisarme'," Father Matthew said in his rich Spanish voice. "It is a fearsome weapon. They practice in threes: two to hook and one to hack down."

"How come Allan-i-the-Wood let them go?" Gui queried.

"He didn't have much of a choice, Gui," His tall Seneschal replied with a chuckle. "They've taken the cross! They're off on this Crusade no matter what, and mighty fed up about it Allan is too; they are six of his best."

"What about those two from South Aquitaine?" Gui queried. "I've watched them, they work hard and know their weapons. They're well equipped, their war gear is in excellent condition and they seem to know what to do with it."

"Jules Lagrasse and Lucas Fabrizan," Fitzurse replied, steadily. "The 'Cousins'. Yes, they work well. They're toughened fighters, and know how to handle themselves. Arrived in the Spring, with a recommendation from Mercardier. They've never refused a task and are always neat in the barracks."

"Those are the two who were found drugged at the foot of Alicia's tower," Gui said thoughtfully. "On the night of the fire."

"Yes. Fitzurse and I gave them a tough going over, but finished up satisfied they had no case to answer. The Baron's wicked daughter fooled them as much she fooled us. You interviewed them as well, remember?"

"Yes, I did, as much for my own and Alicia's as for Agnes Fitzwalter, as she seems to be sweet on one of them."

"Jules Lagrasse," Sir Richard drawled. "He's the sharper, and larger, of the two. A bit 'oily' if you ask me. What might be described back home as 'being as slippery as a basket of eels'!"

"Don't you trust 'em then?" Gui asked with a laugh, looking across at his Guard Commander lounging nonchalantly in his chair.

"No...just a little wary perhaps? Especially after the fire," Sir Richard replied carefully. "But, they are not robbers, nor wanted men. They were recommended by Mercardier, no notice concerning them has arrived from anywhere, and they behave with quiet confidence, like many fighting men looking for a place after all the troubles in France. They came looking for work, we were looking for good men, and they seemed to fit the bill."

"Keep themselves to themselves rather," Fitzurse said. "But they seem pleasant enough. Youngish, but steady. The taller one is the nicer of the two. The other has a mouth like a sewer. But, they work hard and are damned good with their weapons...but they are South French! I'm not entirely sure I'd trust 'em with the crown jewels, so I've still got my eye on them. But they'll do!"

"Thus speaks a Norman!" Gui laughed, banging his big sergeant on his shoulder. "So...that makes us over seventy bonny lads, not counting de Beaune, ourselves, our Squires and the girls!"

"Eighty then, all told, My Lord," Fitzurse said, leaning back in his chair, a great jack of ale in his meaty hand. "A goodly number indeed; but I would have preferred a hundred...still, you never know in this game who may yet come out of the woodwork to join us?"

"That's true, John," Gui said, stretching his arms out with a smile. "And since Agnes is so thick with Lagrasse, we'd better make the Cousins the girls' close bodyguards. That way we please everyone!"

"Have you quite finished, My Lord?" Sir James' dry voice broke in. "The men have eaten their fill and are getting restless. They have been watching us all evening, and know that you have been making your choices. Now is the time to tell them, don't you think? Then we can leave them to it. No doubt many will get odiously drunk, and Sir Richard and I will have to sort them all out in the morning1"

"You are right, James," Gui said with a laugh. "We have talked long enough. Give me that list, Matthew, and let's get it over with. There will be losers and winners tonight, as many wish to go whose names are not here...and one or two who don't, are! Still that is life, as they say, and we must all do the best we can with it! Then I will go up and tell the girls!"

Chapter 51... *The Lion of Malwood makes his vow.*

That had all been a week ago. Today they were ready to set out for Bordeaux, and from there to Narbonne, Gruissan and the Baron's lair at the Château Grise at last.

Early that morning, almost before anyone else was stirring, Gui had risen from beside Alicia to look out across the countryside to find it smirched with rain. The whole forest misted with it, and the bailey swept with fine curtains that drifted in weeping veils across walls and towers before a warm South wind. The lake too was brushed by it, its cool surface spreckled with raindrops as the breeze gusted each soft, grey swathe across it; and where the fish rose to snatch prey the rings spread out with every sudden splash. And everything was closed up: lilies, irises, water plantains and milk weed; even his mother's roses had dropped their heads and closed their petals against the rain. Only the ducks were enjoying the wetness, standing up and flapping their wings, their quacking voices sounding out loudly as they did so, before dipping down beneath the ruffled surface of the lake, their feathered bottoms and yellow feet waggling as they dabbled for food around its tangled reedy edges.

Silently Gui dressed and pausing briefly to look down at Alicia still sleeping softly, he slipped out of their room, cloaked and booted against the weather. Past the guards at the Forework entrance, huddled in their cloaks against the swirling mizzle, he went with a swift salute as he crossed the sodden bailey on his way to the old chapel, threading his way amongst the carts and waggons standing there, their loads covered with oiled canvas, all waiting for the off. Overhead the clouds were low, dark and grey, yet tinged with white as the wind gently blustered round him.

Entering the little building quietly, the scent of lavender and white roses came sweetly from the altar, softly aglow from its own great candles of beeswax, the scent of honey incense subtle on the air within the little chapel that his father had so adorned. Lighting a small candle from the huge one in its sheltered niche beside the door, always kept burning throughout the night, Gui turned then and looked up the still darkened nave towards the altar.

There his parents' golden marriage rings, and his father's great fighting sword, had been reverently laid before the jewelled cross that always stood upon it. And pausing beside the pale flame of the great niche candle, Father Gerome's symbol of God's Eternal Light in the dark and dangerous world in which they all lived, and from which he had just lit his own in its gilded holder, Gui breathed deeply before stepping forward. Then, with soft tread and the swish of his long cloak above the stone paved floor, Gui walked towards the altar below the great East window of the chapel, the painted glass for which had been so beautifully wrought by skilled artisans brought specially from France.

And there, in all humility, he bowed his head, and drawing his own fine blade from its sheath, he stepped back and stooping and laid it across the long top rectangle of freshly cut stone in the centre of the nave, before the altar rail that marked his parents' grave. Beautifully incised with the family Lion Rampant and his parents' names, he reverently placed his little candle carefully beside the naked steel, and plucking a small embroidered cushion off the Bishop's tall chair nearby, he then knelt down and prayed.

Remembering all that had happened the night of the great fire and since: the searing heat, the despair, the rage...and the desperate agony of loss...along with the wild joy when Alicia had miraculously been returned to him from the Forest, bringing with her so joyous and unexpected a man as Father Matthew...he bowed his head and in his spirit groaned.

"How could such things happen, Lord?" He cried out, his heart and soul racked with pain. "How can you take such good people, whom I need and love so much, yet let such wickedness remain alive? I do not understand! Your plan is hidden from me, and yet I thank you, Lord, for my deliverance and for returning Alicia to me, and for Father Matthew...for all his skills and brightness. And most of all, Dear Lord, I thank you for my parents, whose love and care for me were infinite."

And putting his hands on either side of the stone he bent forward over his parents' grave and wept; his body rocking as he sobbed, the anger in his soul making him cry out aloud, like an animal in torment: "Oh, my God, *my God!* Help me! *Help me!*" His hot tears falling on the cold stone and on the hard steel he had laid there. And in his sorrow he remembered his parents' funeral, how their simple remains had been buried, here, before the altar of the little chapel they both had loved, laid in a small wooden casket wrought with gold and wrapped in white satin lovingly embroidered with the Malwood Lion; then placed within a leaden box and sealed with stone.

It had been a moving service, with the whole castle present, and half the countryside as well, including many of their friends, together with the great and the good of the area, for Sir Yvo and Lady Margaret had been much loved by all. Sir Jocelyn and Allan-i-the-Wood for the Forest, the Earl of Southampton for the King; Abbot Hugh of Beaulieu for the Church, all in their full regalia, with the Bishop of Winchester to pronounce the final blessing. And the little chapel full of flowers - all his mother's favourites: lilies, roses, lavender and honey suckle, their scent filling the air and mingling with the incense from the great silver burner that Father Gerome had swung as the casket had been brought in.

Poor little man, he had done his best to lead the service, helped by Father Matthew, but had finally been overcome with grief as he'd struggled to complete the simple ritual of internment: '…Earth to earth, ashes to ashes, dust to dust; in sure and certain hope of the resurrection to eternal life…'

Gui clad in shining steel, his cyclas of finest white damask, instead of linen, covering him from head to foot and bearing the leaping blazon of his house, a sweeping cloak of vermilion pinned to his shoulder with great ouches of gold and rubies, itself covered with gold orphrey of outstanding beauty that mirrored the leaping lion of Malwood in thick gold and silver thread. Standing there with Alicia beside him, heads also bowed in reverence and grief, were Sir James Bolderwood, his father's Seneschal, and Sir Richard L'Eveque, his Guard Commander, fully armed in shimmering mail like himself, but wearing his own colours for a change, his great black lion rampant and gardant, leaping off his chest with scarlet claws and great mouth agape, teeth and tongue both scarlet too, upon its field of ermine.

But poor Gerome had been unable to go any further, collapsing into a little heap beside the grave, tears coursing down his gentle face.

So it had been that Father Matthew, his father's oldest living friend, had completed the service, his cool, steady voice with its rich Spanish lilt washing over them: '...who shall change our vile body, that it may be like unto his glorious body, according to the mighty working, whereby he is able to subdue all things to himself...' Well, by God and the Pheasant, He had better, that was all he could say, for if any people deserved 'glorious bodies' in Heaven...they were his parents, who had not stinted in their love for him in any way, nor for Alicia, whom they had adored and cared for as if she had been their own.

And now he was here again, alone, to pay his respects and make obeisance before his God and across his parents' grave. Here to seek solace as he prepared to leave, together with his men and many whom he cared for most, not least Alicia herself, to deliver the King's Justice upon the Lord Baron Sir Roger de Brocas, and upon his daughter, the Lady Rochine, for all that they had done to his home and family.

Here to find peace and comfort in the lovely place where he had worshipped all his life, and beg the Blessing and Forgiveness of the King of Heaven, as even now his troops, his Malwood Lions, were gathering in the Great Hall of the Keep behind him. And here also to exchange his own sword for his father's, now fully restored to its former glory, its fabulous Damascus blade, the wavy blue steel shimmering within it, glistening with oil in the candle light.

Standing now, his own sword still where he had placed it above his parent's grave stone, Gui lifted the great weapon off the altar and held it up before him. Nearly four feet of beautifully crafted steel, the blade broad at the hilt and tapering towards its end, was made of especially crafted steel, a fabulous meld of different metals marked by the fine, wavy blue lines that ran from hilt to tip that told this blade had come from Damascus, giving the owner outstanding strength and flexibility, and a cutting edge that could slice silk just dropped upon it...as easily as it could hew through bone and armour as if they were paper. The quillons gilded and chased with silver, its firm oval handle of English oak re-bound in scarlet leather strengthened with wire of twisted gold, it was a weapon such as any great hero of the ancient past might well have owned with pride; and in its great pommel of gilded steel was set a huge cabochon ruby, the colour of his house.

This had been his father's sword, and his father's before him, old Sir Gui de Valance before he had changed his name to Malwood, and for whom

Gui himself had been named. A mighty weapon from their family's Viking past...and now it was his, and stepping back he kneeled down again and turning the great blade to point downwards to the ground, he lifted up the hilt, the great gilded pommel and silver chased quillons making the very symbol of the crucifix, of the murdered Christ himself upon the cross, and with a solemn reverence he kissed it.

Then he made his vow:

"Oh God of Battles," he breathed, his eyes closed and head raised to the altar above him. "Let me be the instrument of thy Justice and thy wrath! Lord, let thy mighty power flow through me. Vengeance is mine sayeth the Lord...Then, by the Torch of the Gospels, make it so and put thy hand on me that when I wield this blade I do it in thy Holy name. Dear Lord, by God's Blood, and by all I hold most dear, I vow that I will not rest until my family is cleansed of the great evil that has been done them; so I can return home safely with my belovèd Alicia to live by my side as thou hast intended. This I swear, By Death and St Michael, on my parents' grave, and in Thy Holy name...Amen!" And he bowed his head once more in reverence.

Rising then, knees slightly stiff, he reversed his sword, bringing the blade to his lips once more before sliding it into his scabbard with a soft swoosh of steel on leather. Then, facing the altar, he bowed his head and leaving the candle burning where he had placed it above his parents' headstone and beside the sword that had been his until that very morning, he walked back down the nave to the heavy door that led out onto the wide bailey and the whole of Castle Malwood beyond.

Opening it he paused for the last time, his hand on the great iron ring that made up both latch and handle, and turning he smiled and bowed his head to the long line of his ancestors, whose plaques and banners lined the walls...and to his parents whose love for him and for Alicia had been unstinted. And with a final silent prayer in his heart for the safe return of himself, his men, and all those whom he loved, he dropped the heavy latch with a sharp '*Sneck!*' and shrugging his shoulders in the grey, dawn light, he walked swiftly back through the gentle smirr, his heart full, his head bowed in thought.

Chapter 52...How they all set out from Castle Malwood.

Four hours later they left under gently weeping skies; the whole countryside smoored with rain that purred in wide curtains across it, misting the castle courtyard as the men busily assembled.

In soft, grey swathes that pock-marked the lake and moat, it swept over them all making the horses snort and shake their heads against it. Sumpters, with their panniers packed and covered with oiled canvas, and chargers alike, flicked their ears and stamped their feet, iron shoes ringing on the cobbles that paved the bailey courtyard...chafing, restless and eager to be off, the long line of carts with all the gear they would need for their journey safely in the middle of the waiting commando, and all ready to depart.

Gui, Sir Richard, Father Matthew, Alicia, Agnes Fitzwalter and the two squires, Simon Varter and Phillip Carslake, alongside Burgundians, Verderers, South French and forty of the Malwood Lions, the very best the castle could provide, all under their formidable Master-at-Arms, John Fitzurse...all mounted and awaiting their Lord's signal to kick-on.

Every piece of armour had been shined and polished, every weapon tested. New strings for the bows: those for the longbows in the archers' scrips, and also loosely on their great bows all finely cased in oiled leather across their backs. Those for the crossbows firmly fixed and safe in their oiled linen covers, all freshly greased, all securely fastened. They, together with spare bows, and the barrels full of the countless sheaves of bolts and clothyard shafts with which to arm them were safely on the carts; along with hard rations, spare weapons, armour, clothes and tenting equipment.

For the knights their full suits of burnished mail along with their great helms of slitted steel, new padded with packed straw and new fleece linings, had all been wrapped in oiled linen and placed in new panniers on their sumpters, along with fresh suits of clothes and their personal belongings. Their shields, newly refurbished and painted, strapped on top in oiled canvas covers. Likewise all the clothes and requirements of Lady Alicia and Agnes Fitzwalter.

So Gui and Richard rode unarmoured in pleated bliauts of fine linen, in green and scarlet, over long sleeved saffron chemises of finest Egyptian cotton, each with long woollen cloaks to match bearing their own blazons, hooded liripipes against the rain and gauntlets of yellow leather. Both ladies were similarly dressed, but in softest suede, fleece lined for greater warmth, with hooded cloaks of fine russet wool over their simple wimples, lined with sarcenet in blue and amber to match their eyes, and soft gauntlets of similar coloured leather on their hands.

Father Matthew, in fine black woollen habit lined with white cotton came next. Mounted on Jupiter, his favourite piebald with feet like dinner-plates, he carried his deep leather scrip across his shoulder, his head covered with his cowl, similarly lined; his herbs and tinctures, medical instruments, bandages, salves and special potions all carefully packed likewise on his own sumpter, along with his chalice, the carved box that always carried the Host safely within it and his phials of holy water and anointing oil. Simon Varter and Philip Carslake, the two young squires came last on their bay rounceys, similarly unarmoured as their knights in long leather chausses, chemise, tunics and woollen cloaks, their own armour and equipment on sumpters behind them.

Two fully fledged Knights, two squires, over seventy men-at-arms archers, all armed to the teeth, and their own chaplain and surgeon. They would be a formidable force.

Certainly they looked a brave company under the Household Standard proudly carried by Thomas Ringwood, the giant figure of John Fitzurse by his side. Sir Richard's personal standard also there beside him, carried by Ned Bashley supported by Wat his equally huge twin; and every soldier wore a new surcoat with the leaping scarlet Malwood Lion-Rampant on back and chest, and everyone was there to see them off: Sir James Bolderwood, on whose capable shoulders would lie the full burden of caring for the estates while they was away; Suchard the cook who had made certain the food they left with was the best he could provide: freshly baked bread, pasties fat with meat and vegetables, cinnamon cakes and sweet biscuits, and huge wheels of mature cheese brought up from the stores; Big Nick in his leather apron, a great hammer in his knotted hands; dear Father Gerome to give them all a final blessing with all the castle folk who knew and cared for them so well...and Ralf Longsword with a detachment of the Castle Guard as escort for Sir James.

Sitting astride Beauregarde, his great destrier, fetlocks sleeked with rain, Gui stretched himself in his saddle and looking round at Alicia he smiled, receiving a dazzling response that simply made his heart skip.

That very night she had come to him, slipping softly through his door in the Great Keep and into his open arms, luxuriating in the strength of him as they closed about her. And they had loved one another greatly, deep penetrating love both given and received with joyous passion and abandon: a night of hot and furious loving, lithe bodies searingly entwined...and also one of great gentleness and caring, and of softly holding, touching, and caressing; of butterfly kisses and the warmest, most loving words in the velvet darkness of the night.

At dawn he had awoken, and gone to the wide open windows of his great chamber and looked out at the sweeping curtains of rain that swirled across the bailey, and at the enormous mist-shrouded Forest that stretched from the castle as far as he could see, with all its glades and heaths; tilled fields, pasture and vast stands of leafy timber.

So beautiful, even in the rain...and with a sigh he had returned softly to her side, listening to the gentle breathing of the lovely woman lying naked before him, sleeping; the urge to touch her hair and caress her face and cover her with kisses almost unbearable in its intensity. And looking down at the lush curves and softly shaded hollows of her body, and the beauty of her face, her long eyelashes and the sweet softness of her mouth, he was suddenly overwhelmed with love...with the awesome wonder that sweeps over you, with one great rush of the heart, when you look at the woman beside you, or in your arms, and know she is only there because she truly loves you...as you so deeply love her too.

Such thoughts were truly humbling. Surely his Alicia was the loveliest woman in all England. She could have chosen anyone...yet she had chosen him, and he was still astonished by it, and it had been in just that frame of mind that he had slipped out to pray over his parents' grave.

Now here she was, just a short horses' length behind, mounted on Sunburst, now a permanent loving gift from Rose and Edward Sergeant, with Agnes Fitzwalter beside her on her own mare Gillygate, while Judith, Maude

362

and Annie stood in the summer rain, tears running down their faces, clutching clean hankies to wave as the men departed. Judith especially, because young Thomas Ringwood, who'd help save him from the fire, and to whom he'd given a goodly purse of silver and the promise of a home when they returned, was her betrothed man and he was leaving with them as his Standard bearer.

Leaning back against the high cantle of his saddle Gui looked around him for the last time. Then, bringing to his lips the enamelled gold and bejewelled St Christopher that Alicia had given him on their betrothal day, he stood up in his saddle and raising his arm into the air he gave a great shout.

Instantly his trumpeters, William Bell and Roman Tinsley, blew a fierce *'Tan!-Tan!-Tara!-Tantaraa!'* and with a rattle of hooves he wheeled Beau round, Sir Richard beside him on his great bay charger, Merlin, and led off; their two standard bearers immediately behind, Father Matthew following; then the girls, the two young squires, Fitzurse, the carts and all their men in pairs behind him, while Castle Malwood rang with the cheers and well wishes of its people for all those so bravely setting out.

Across the cobbled courtyard they went without another backward glance, across the bailey and up to the tall Gatehouse, the iron points of the first portcullis high above them and running with fine streams of water. Past the great double-leafed valves, iron plated on twelve inches of solid Hampshire oak, swung back on their massive pintles, they clattered...and finally onto the great bridge itself, the hollow thunder of their hooves and the rumble of the carts' heavy wheels startling a lone heron, happily hunting for frogs amongst the tall bull rushes into sudden, clumsy flight. Before them lay the long open causeway, swirling with misty wetness, and beyond that the King's Royal Forest and the long road to Lyndhurst, Beaulieu and the sea.

Above the Gatehouse ramparts the castle's great flags fluttered in the gusty rain, and the trumpeters high on the battlements blew them a final bright and lusty *'Tan! Tan! Tara! Tantara!'* as with hoofs plashing through the puddles, the whole long cavalcade broke into a steady canter; and bouncing and joggling along the broad track that lay before them, the heavy carts rattling as they swayed and bustled along, Sir Gui de Malwood's whole commando swiftly disappeared from sight.

Chapter 53...Sir Gui meets with Tommy Blackwood and The Mary.

L eaving Castle Malwood shrouded in fine misty rain, the young Lord of Malwood led his forces through Minstead and then onto the long Forest road that linked Lyndhurst with Southampton, startling the deer they encountered on their way and scattering a small sounder of boar still out upon the sodden track. With wild squeals of terror, the stripy shoats fled off in all directions amongst the tall ferns and thick coppice of hawthorn, hazel and alder as they cantered by, their fat dams, grey and bristled, scuttling and grunting after them back into the deep cover that lined the road.

Laughing to see young wild boar behaving so like the piglets around the demesne, Agnes and Alicia pointed at their great dark, grizzled mothers as they chased their striped little ones so swiftly off the track, excited by all they saw around them as much as by the whole prospect of the adventure they were setting out on. And everywhere dripped with water: trees, trackway and themselves as the fine mizzle blew in their faces, penetrating even the most tightly wound cloak and travel pack, the breeze blowing wetly at them all the time with gentle, warm persistence.

Nor were they the only travellers about that morning, passing many of the borel folk as they trudged their way backwards and forwards between their villages, hoods and liripipes on the heads, old sacking across their shoulders along with the tools and their bait, or drove their slow, solid wheeled ox carts laden with fallen timber from the great storm, hunched over against the rain, and quick to draw out of the way of so many determined, armed men...yet happy to wave and call a greeting or a blessing as they recognised the rampant Lions of Malwood on the men's surcoats as Gui and his command splashed by.

Amongst those they bustled past were two seemingly familiar figures whom Father Matthew in particular took keen note of as he passed them by that dank, grey morning: two young men with a goose on a string and a donkey with a box of pigeons on its back, the taller of the two managing the goose; and both with capes of rough sacking and green woollen hoods with long liripipes to wrap round their necks like scarves to keep out the rain.

The minute they had heard the sullen thunder of hooves they had desperately pressed themselves back against the forest edge. Dashing forwards the young man with the goose swooped down to pick it up out of the road, struggling to hold it in his arms, all grey flapping wings, flying feathers and long cackling neck, his liripipe uncurling with his efforts and his hood falling off his blond shock of hair as he did so. While the donkey kicked and brayed in sudden alarm as the long cavalcade of men, wagons and led sumpters barrelled past it in a spray of mud, water, and torn clods of earth, its holder desperate to drop his face as the long armoured commando of horses, carts and men rode by.

Even so, Father Matthew was certain he knew them both, his eye noting the taller man's pale, straw coloured hair and shocked face, and the other's twisted sneer as he struggled with the braying ass he was leading. Then in moments they were passed them and gone. Indeed so fleeting had sight of them been on that rain-smirred morning that for many hours he was still unsure of what he had seen. But the confusion between the two young men, and the anxious, almost terrified look of the goose-boy, with his wild shock of yellow hair stayed with him for many weeks.

★

At Lyndhurst, with the rain easing, they paused by the swinging sign of the Saracen's Head, just long enough to rest their horses, and for Rose and Edward and all their people to come rushing out with hands full of beakers of mulled wine and great leather jacks filled with ale, trays of fresh baked bread, newly pressed cheese and thick slices of sizzling fat bacon. Rose and the children, cloaked and hooded, clustered round Alicia, patting and admiring Sunburst, while Edward and the others made general conversation. Then, to brave shouts and a frenzy of waving hands they were away again, taking the turning for Beaulieu just past the little town to travel beneath the tall elms, oaks and beech trees of the forest, the trackway mired and thick with fallen leaves and standing water.

But the Forest was not only a huge mass of trees. There were also wide tracts of open country in between the heavy stands of timber; great areas of heath where huge elms and oaks stood sentinel, great spreading chestnuts thrust in amongst them ringed with hazel bushes heavy with green nuts amidst small coppices of beech, silver birch and holly; and everywhere white and purple heather carpeted the landscape and gorse grew in great profusion amidst huge swards of grass, thick with scarlet poppies, pink campion, and brilliant yellow corn marigolds.

Here, in the dawn and even time, the deer came out to eat, treading delicately on slotted hooves from beneath the trees, heads up, ears wide and alert for danger, often to mingle with the sheep and cattle of the great Cistercian monastery; just then grazing peaceably, undisturbed by the large party of armed men who hustled past them in a muffled thunder of flying hooves and thick clumps of tufted grass.

So at last they came to the tall gated entrance of the great monastery, and while the Abbot was summoned, the monks came running out with sustenance for the two knights, Alicia, Agnes and the whole of their commando just them arrived panting at their doors: fresh white bread and the fat meat pasties for which the Abbey was famous; crisp lettuce and neat fat, white headed scallions, and bowls of wild strawberries and cherries from the orchards, Abbey woods and gardens…as well as fodder for their beasts.

"Alicia," Gui said, turning round in his saddle. "You and Agnes must stay here and wait for Abbot Hugh while Father Matthew goes off and speaks with their Herbalist. Richard and I will go and find Master Thomas. He will be down by The Hard I expect, a few miles further on. You two," he said to the young Squires, Simon and Phillip, "stay here and make certain the men all get fed and then take their horses to water, and give every care to my Lady and to Mistress Fitzwalter. Do you two young scallywags understand me?"

"Yes, My Lord!" Came the swift reply.

"Alicia?"

"Yes, *My Lord!*" She barked back with a laugh and a mock salute. "We *will* be here, Oh our Lord and Master!"

"That's alright then!" he replied with a mock bow and a wide grin. "Just be nice to Abbot Hugh," he added, leaning towards her. "He is not used to having two such pert and insolent young ladies in his care! He is used to subservience and order! So, if you're not careful he will have you both on bread and water! Now, Richard," he said with another grin at the girls' mock-rueful faces. "Come on! We don't have all day!"

By then the skies had cleared at last, and Gui and Sir Richard took off their hooded liripipes, and kicking-on they ambled their horses down towards the distant harbour beneath a hot afternoon sun that sparkled on the myriad raindrops that hung, like fat crystal tears, from every frond and twig and made the wet earth steam.   And as they rode down from the Abbey the signs of the great storm that had so recently struck the area, were still strongly in evidence: smashed and damaged buildings, ships in every state of repair, wagons laden with fresh and seasoned timber and everywhere the constant bang and tap of adze and hammer and the rasp of saws from shipside and saw pit. Gui, who had been there often on his father's business, had never seen it so busy.

"Well I hope we find Thomas soon, Dear Boy," Sir Richard said lazily, pulling Merlin aside to let a huge wain of oak beams rumble by him. "Because the day is already well advanced and there is much yet to do before we can set sail. I just hope Sir James is not mistaken. It is weeks now since the storm, and Thomas will not want to linger once his ships have both been fixed."

"We use Thomas for everything, Richard, as you know," Gui replied riding easily with one hand on his hip, swaying to Beau's lazy clopping movement. "Have done for years, and always at the most amazing prices! Furthermore, James has sent especially for him to meet us here. He will not let us down I promise you. If something had gone wrong he would have sent to say so. Just keep a sharp lookout for the *Mary*, which is painted red all over, or the yellow of the *Pride of Beaulieu*."

"Red and Yellow? That's a bit startling, isn't it?"

"Hmmm," Gui said, grinning.   "Maybe, but Thomas likes bright colours. It's his way of saying; 'Here I am, choose me!'"

And a few minutes later, while rounding a bend in the sea inlet they were following, they saw the *Mary* at last, tied up to a wide wooden quay with men crawling all over her, while supervising the work was a huge square shaped man with a wild bushy beard and arms like the great boughs of a chestnut tree, gnarled and knotted with muscle. He was standing with his legs apart, his hands thrust on his hips, and swearing non-stop at the sweating gang he had working for him. His deep voice coming easily across to them where they sat their horses, and Gui and Richard stretched back in their saddles and laughed.

"Well?" Sir Gui asked, rounding on his friend and poking him in the ribs. "I told you he'd be here, O ye of little Faith! There's no mistaking Tommy Blackwood anywhere. He has the loudest voice and the greatest number of oaths of any man I know, and his legs are a byword on these coasts, for they're as bent as the roof-trees of a cruck-house. Couldn't catch a pig in a passage, him. But his heart's in the right place and he's here for certain to give us the sail we so badly need. Come on; let's see what he has to say for himself."

And kicking their horses forward the two men rode down the track and presently drew rein within easy calling distance.

★

The *Mary*, like the *Pride of Beaulieu* being warped up beside her, was a Great Cog. A fat, deep-hulled merchant ship, with high, wooden battlemented castles that made up the bow and stern.

The stern castle considerably bigger than the forecastle, the fo'c'sle, was built out on great wooden stilts beneath which was the tiller, with the Master's cabin to one side and his Mate's on the other. And she carried a single main mast, like a whole tree, that soared out of her deep waist and was held in place as much by a massive wooden 'step' with huge shaped chocks all round it, as by a web of thick shrouds that ran up from each side of the ship, and were crossed by other ropes all the way up them, the ratlines, up which the crew could scamper every time a change of sail was ordered. They ended just below the massive yard arm...more like a crossed tree...that carried the huge rectangular mains'l.

This swung from a great iron collar, with ropes running beneath its whole length on which the men could balance on their feet to pull up the sail if it needed reefing due to bad weather...or to let it out again. Above that was the crow's nest, almost at the very top of the main mast from where the look outs

368

could keep a weather eye open for storms, rocks and any ship that might heave itself up over the horizon.

Jutting out from the bow was a long wooden spar, the bowsprit, from which the sprits'l, a much smaller sail, could be hung on its own cross tree to help the *Mary*'s steerage and for greater speed. Right at the stern, instead of the old fashioned side steering board, was a fine rudder that hung off the sternpost and could be moved from side to side on mighty iron pintles by a thick steering bar. She was also quarter decked fore and aft above the main open cargo deck, with sufficient room right at the stern below the quarter deck, for two or three small cabins, with useful storage space as well, and steep ladders leading down to the cargo hold beneath and up to the fighting castles fore and aft above.

The very bottom of the *Mary*, the hold, where the ribs were themselves planked across, was decked right from stem to stern to give firm footage for horses and for men, but was also provided with broad slats around the edges, where they butted up against the sides of the ship, so that any water that came on board would go straight into the bilges from where it could be pumped out when necessary. This decking also formed a sound base on which all the cargo could safely be stored and lashed down tightly, for which there were great ring bolts along the sides and across the deck itself.

Her great, fat hull was painted red all over, and on her vast mainsail of thick linen, strengthened with broad leather strappings at every corner, was a huge scarlet rising sun in splendour, with rays of gold, crimson and orange that spread out in all directions when it was raised. And right then her crew were swarmed all over her as they rushed to get her ready for sailing.

"Hey, Master Thomas!" Gui shouted out. "Leave those poor buggers alone for a while, and give me a moment of your time."

Turning with surprise and a joyous roar of recognition the giant Ship Master gave a final shout of abuse at the work gang busily stowing fresh cordage and checking the tarred rigging that ran up on either side of the thick mast; and seizing a nearby halliard he swung himself neatly onto the quayside for such a large man and walked towards them with the rocking, rolling gait of a sailor more used to the unsteady deck of a heaving ship than the firmness of dry land.

And truly Thomas Blackwood was a big man in every way! Not just in height and breadth but in width of shoulders and the size of his upper arms, thick with corded muscles, and hands like shovels from hauling on the great sheets and halliards that moved the *Mary's* sails, and shifting a myriad cargos of huge bales of wool or greasy woolfells, and the great hogsheads of wine and barrels of ale and oil with which he traded all round France and Spain, and even into the wide Circle Sea itself, the beautiful Mediterranean. His face was a great square of ruddy cheeks and battered features and his eyes, deep blue as the seas he sailed, were edged with crows feet from wind, sea and rain and reaching for the far horizon, as much as from laughter which spilled out of him in boisterous waves along with a voice of thunder that could burst through the fiercest storm wrack or the wildest screaming tempest of sword and battleaxe.

"Well if it isn't young Gui de Malwood!" He boomed at him, thrusting a huge ham of a hand up at him, his fine, blue eyes twinkling merrily. "I have been expecting you all day. You and your men," he added with a smile at Gui's look of surprise. "And your Lady, what was took by that French villain, de Brocas. Had a message from Sir James a few days back to expect you. The *Mary* is ready now, and the *Pride* is already being warped alongside as you can see. Then, my Lords," he added, pausing briefly to roar an order to some of his men in a voice that made Sir Richard wince. "We can begin loading straight away,"

"Well, Master Blackwood, you have confirmed my faith in you...and delighted me also!" Gui said, throwing back his head and laughing. "Here was Sir Richard, a 'doubting Thomas' indeed," he said, laughing at his wit. "Wondering whether you would still be here or not...and now not only are you here as promised, but also ready to load and set sail. I am humbled, Master Thomas, and more pleased to see you than you can possibly know!"

"Well, My Lord, when I received Sir James' first message I was horribly shocked. We all were. My crews have served your good father for many years, he helped me get started, did you know that, Sir Gui?"

"No! I did not. But then there are many things I have discovered about Sir Yvo since his death that I did not know before. I couldn't be more pleased, it has clearly been a great thing for the both of you."

370

"Aye, Sir Gui, that it has. And we shared in the business too, as is only right and proper. And what started with one ship, the old *Mary*, is now two, *The Pride of Beaulieu*, under her Master, Robert of Christchurch, but bound to me by oath and contract. Both deep cogs, with plenty of space for cargo…be that wool or wine, or soldiers and horses for the wars! We can take both as easily. Their sides drop down for ease of loading, Sir Yvo and I made sure of that! We could see that there would be a ready market for war transport…ever since the Old King set up the Cinque Ports a few years back. And they're both painted in bright colours, so everyone will know they are mine!"

"Yes," Gui said slowly with a grin, blinking slightly at the sight of them, bright red and canary yellow, both side-by-side. "There's certainly no mistaking them, Master Thomas. Well! The sly old fox! He surely was 'Long headed' indeed, my dear Papa! No wonder there always seemed to be money available for things, even when the harvest was bad, or the cattle got a murrain!"

"Aye. That was the way of it. He didn't always let the left hand know what the right hand was doing, did Sir Yvo! But that was a *bad* business with the fire, Sir Gui," he said sadly, shaking his head. "Downright *wicked!* I'm only sorry I couldn't make the funeral, my Lord, despite wanting to. That storm created havoc with both my ships, for all they were both at anchor. Tossed us about something terrible. Still, all fixed now. So, what of the Baron, my Lord? What of the bastard Frenchman who did all this to your family?"

Chapter 54...How Gui was surprised and Master Thomas proved his worth.

That Man-of-Blood has fled the country, Master Thomas!" Gui said, sitting relaxed on Beauregard's massive back while he leaned down towards the huge bearded shipmaster. "Along with his bitch of a daughter, the Lady Rochine, and six of their men: skipped safely away some few days after that storm. Left from the shore-side at Pitt's Deep – opposite Lymington."

"I knows of Pitt's Deep, Sir Gui," he said darkly. "A rare place for skulking...and I knows which ship likes to lurk there too! Was it the *Christopher* that bastard sailed in?" he asked then, his head thrust forward, his black beard positively bristling, deep voice full of menace.

"You know of her?" Gui asked sharply, as he watched Thomas suddenly bang his hands together, his big face cragged with hard feeling.

"Aye, My Lord. I know of her...and her Master, Giles Walter; and a more weasely, rapscallion piece of human shite you couldn't hope to meet. A bad man, Giles Walter, Sir Gui! Suspected of piracy, but never caught at it. I wouldn't trust him with a barge pole, let alone a whole ship's company. He'd sell his grandmother if the price was right. Aye and cut her throat if it wasn't!"

"Do you know where we can find him?" Sir Richard asked.

"He sails between here and Cherbourg regular, even in the winter months, but right now he'll be in Bordeaux for the wine mart. If you were to ask me, my Lords," he went on, hands on hips and looking up from one to the other as he spoke. "I'd wager all I own that if he was involved in that piece of skulduggery, then it will be to Bordeaux that he will have gone. I swear it!"

"By God, Thomas," Gui replied with a shout. "That is all we needed!

That is the last bit of the puzzle! Now, my large and fearsome friend, I need a fast passage there for myself, and all who are travelling with us; our chargers and our sumpters, eighty of my men, four good cartloads of assorted gear and supplies...the Lady Alicia and Mistress Agnes Fitzwalter..."

"...And Allan-i-the-Wood, as well," a deep voice chipped in from behind them. "If you'll have me that is?" And with a broad grin on his face, the burly under-sheriff kicked Caesar forward, his huge hound, Bouncer, at his side, and held up his hand.

"*Splendour of God!*" Gui exclaimed astonished, reaching across Beauregard's broad back to take it. "What are you doing here, so far from home?"

"Well, seeing as you have got a quarter of my men with you already, my Lord," he replied with a laugh. "And the Baron has fled, I've got the others now all striving to go too, and Sir Joscelyn thought it might be best if I came along to lead them...bringing the other eighteen with me for good measure! So...here I am, and the rest of my lads are up with your Lady and the good Abbot awaiting your decision."

Gui looked at him, both astonished and delighted, not just because he had met him at his parents' funeral, and liked him immediately, as Alicia had done...but because he felt he needed another strong English commander as a balance between Jean de Beaune and his Burgundians and Sir Richard and their own Malwood Lions. His men were known to be good, and the added extra was another unexpected joy, for it would give him over a score of expert longbows for his command, who could also become useful gisarmiers as well, as Father Matthew had suggested a few days before.

Then he looked at Sir Richard, who was sitting his horse laughing.

"Did you know of this?" He asked, looking at him quizzically with eyebrows raised, his head on one side.

"No, not really," his tall Guard Commander laughed. "Though I knew that Alicia was hoping that Allan would come and join us, for she spoke with him at the funeral, and with Sir Joscelyn and the Earl as well. She was very impressed with him when she was in the Forest the night of the fire, at how cunning his men were and how brave. And she thought Allan would make an infinitely better consort for our Agnes Fitzwalter than Jules Lagrasse!"

"You mean my Lady planned this?"

"Nooo," Sir Richard said slowly, with a lopsided grin. "Not exactly planned it...so much as simply executed it! For here the man is, with leave to be here from his Lord, and the Earl himself, so who are we to countermand it? *Force majeur*, Dear Boy," he drawled lazily, with a smile. "*Force Majeur!*"

"Well, Master Allan," Gui said, turning back towards him with a wry look, shrugging his shoulders in acceptance. "It seems as if I have been neatly out-marched and had my whole battle turned! Though this will be no picnic Master Under-Sherriff, I assure you," he went on, his face growing sterner as he spoke. "We journey first to Bordeaux and then down to Narbonne and Gruissan beyond to smoke that rabid wolf from his lair and put him down once and for all. Then we travel Outremer to join the King on his Crusade to re-take Jerusalem. Are your lads prepared for that?"

"We have discussed all this, my Lord," Allan-i-the-Wood said, looking Gui steadily in the eyes. "Every man of them will journey with you to deal with the Baron, that they are determined on. Beyond that, we shall have to see. Some I know will journey Outremer, others may not. It will be their decision to make as free Englishmen. But I, my Lord, am with you to the end!"

"Bravely said, Master Allan," Gui replied, giving him his hand again. "I too have heard much about you, and you are welcome to join our merry band. So, Master Thomas," he said, turning back to where the bearded Ship Master still stood looking up at them. "Can you take us? Mine and Sir Richard's chargers must travel with us, Father Matthew's piebald and Lady Alicia and Agnes's mares...and, now, Master Allan's mighty chestnut as well. Also the sumpters, for they carry all our armour and our personal needs, and have been carefully packed and accounted for.

Everything else we and the men need is on the carts. We had word that

374

pirates may be active here abouts, which is not unusual these days Sir James informs me. Sometimes out of Jersey I am told, sometimes out of coves along the Savage Coast down towards Nantes, so we will break out sufficient weapons to beat off the most determined attack, just in case. It seems best to be prepared. I know it's a lot, Master Thomas, but can you do it?"

"By these finger bones I'll want to know the reason else!" he boomed at them, holding up his hands with a huge grin. "Of course I can take you. It is what you have commissioned me to do, and what the *Mary* was built for. But we'll need both ships, as I surmised from Sir James' letters. And he is right about the pirates, especially just now with the wine mart being held in Bordeaux.

Rich pickings if they have a mind to it. But with all your jolly lads on board it would be a foolish pirate indeed to attempt us. And we are known to be tough customers, anyway, Master Robert and me. So, fuck all pirates I say, My Lord! You just wait, we have wine and ale on board sufficient for all our needs and stout hearts to crew her. You will be in Bordeaux before you know it.

We have wooden stalls stowed in their fat waists that we can swiftly bang into place, and space to spare for the fodder you will need, and all your gear. It'll not be the most comfortable journey you've ever had, but by God I'll get you there! What will you do about the rest of your men's horses?"

"We'll leave them with the good Abbot Hugh of Beaulieu. He can turn them out to pasture with the Abbey's horses or leave them to roam the Commons in the Forest. Either way they will be quite safe until Sir James can arrange to have them rounded up and taken back to Malwood. Abbot Hugh can choose four of the best of them as payment for all his trouble.

"What of your men, My Lord? Do they have all they need with them?"

"All the men will carry their own personal weapons and shields along with their saddles and assorted tack, and hard rations for three days. We will buy remounts in Bordeaux when we get there, for there are always any number of excellent beasts for sale in that city. Sir Yvo deposited a tun of treasure with the main Templar House in London and I carry their Letter of Mark with me, so my credit is good the world over. And we have stout chests of specie with us also for the men's pay and any immediate needs. It will not be a problem."

"Right!" the enormous Shipmaster replied, banging his hands together again with a great *crack!* "That's settled then. We can make up enough stalls for those beasts you need to take with you, and between the two ships there will be room for all the rest of your men and their gear. It will be tight, mind you. But the old *Mary*'s used to that, aren't you old girl?" He said affectionately, banging his hands on the red ship's tough sides.

Gui and Richard grinned at one another like a couple of schoolboys and gave a spontaneous whoop of relief: "God's Wounds, Master Thomas," Sir Richard replied. "You make all difficult things sound easy! If all men were as strong in heart as you there'd be no problems to solve! I know that we're behind de Brocas and his gang by several weeks now, but at least we know where they're going, and with God's grace we'll be able to press the bastards hard. I give you my deepest thanks!"

"Me too, Thomas; and here's my hand on it," Gui added, bending down to shake the shipmaster's massive paw. "Now if you'll excuse us we must bring up our men and make sure that they have eaten, and those horses that are going too. How are you for provender, if any?"

"For horses? Absolutely none. For men, some, as I said. I know the Abbey will do what it can, but we will have to put into Brest for fresh water and extra provisions before making the final jump to Bordeaux, otherwise you will have very unhappy horses, and men, on your hands. And that will never do!"

"Well, as you say, I'm sure Abbot Hugh will help us there, and will tell Brother Wilfred, who sees to the Monastery stables, to let us have what we need. When do you mean to sail?"

"On the next tide if I can, otherwise it'll be tomorrow, and no-one wants that, I take it? So, you've not got long if you wish to get away today! And I, My Lords, must get these idle black-legged sons of Southampton whores back to work, or we'll never be done. I'll look for you before the sun falls below the Abbey tower. There is much to do, especially with so many horses to get safely onboard. 'Til then farewell." And with a roar to his men he rolled away from them back towards the gangplank that had now been swung into place, waving his giant arms like a windmill and gesturing violently at the idle younkers who were even now hurrying back to work.

"I wouldn't want to be one of those men if they got the wrong side of him!" Allan exclaimed, laughing, as he watched them all at work. "I've not met the redoubtable Master Thomas before today, 'though I have heard of him. Dear God, has he got a voice!"

With that they all jabbed in their heels and cantered back towards the Abbey Gatehouse, while behind them Thomas Blackwood's men rushed to re-arrange the *Mary's* waist, dragging out large wooden partitions to make crude stalls, and getting ready to drop her broad sides and put the horse ramps in place while their Captain, from his vantage point on the stern castle, bellowed at them through a metal voice trumpet, and stamped his feet on the deck in frustration. The *Pride's* crew bustling under their Master as well, in order to be ready for the Lord of Malwood's men to embark that evening.

★

Up at the Abbey Gui and Sir Richard found their men standing by their horses' heads having had their meal washed down by quantities of the nut-brown ale for which the Abbey was as famous as its pasties, while Gui's big Master-at-Arms and the two Squires, together with Lady Alicia and Mistress Agnes Fitzwalter, conversed easily with the Abbot, who had arrived to greet them.

As soon as Gui, Sir Richard and Allan-i-the-Wood came up he bustled over to offer them whatever help he could, for the Abbey owed the Malwood-Burley families much goodwill over the years, having been well endowed with valuable lands at the death of Gui's grandfather, Sir Alun de Malwood, and again when Alicia's father had died. In his turn, Abbot Hugh had been a good friend to Sir Yvo over the years also, and was eager to do all he could to assist his son, the new Lord of Malwood. Swinging off their horses, pleased to give their bodies some rest at last, for they had all been in the saddle since early morning, the three men came round to meet him, and knelt briefly to receive his blessing.

Abbot Hugh was a tall ascetic man of Norman stock, dark haired still, with sharp blue-grey eyes, and he ran the great Monastery with a firm hand.

"My Lord, I cannot tell you how distressed I was to hear the news of your parents' death. It was a privilege to attend their funeral. And now I see you are set out to track the villains who murdered them to their lair?"

"Yes, Father Abbot," Gui replied grimly, as Sir Richard left them to bring Allan to meet once more with Alicia, while she, delighted to see how well her little plan had really worked, rushed across with Agnes to introduce her and to make a fuss of him and his enormous bouncing friend.

"They have the best part of a month's start on us," Gui said, smiling at the ladies making up to their newest recruit. "So we are desperate to get on our way. Thomas says he knows that Master Giles will be in Bordeaux..."

"Oh...they sailed on the *Christopher* then?"

"You know the ship too?"

"Oh Yes, Sir Gui. I know of the *Christopher* and her Master, Giles Walter!"

"Not a good man, I hear?"

"No, my Lord. Just about as bad as they come. We lost a whole cargo of wine to him, a year back. I swear he pirated it from us, but could not find the proof to have his vessel seized and him and his villainous crew hanged at Southampton. There is nothing he will not do for money!"

"So, I have heard. But perhaps we will be fortunate and come up with him at Bordeaux?"

"Yes!" The Abbot interrupted, "He will have gone there for the wine festival. All the best wines from last season's harvest come up for sale about now; and many merchants go there. Well!" he went on, after a brief pause, rubbing his hands briskly together. "There is no time to waste. Come in Sir Gui, Sir Richard, and you, my Lady, of course," he added, turning to where Alicia was teasing the enormous wolfhound. "And your friend, Mistress Fitzwalter, and you too, Master Allan. It is not often we have such exalted company. Sir Gui, let me know precisely what it is you require, and the Abbey will do all in its power to help you!"

And, with a quick glance round to see that all was well, they disappeared through the great doors to the Abbot's private house within the Abbey walls.

★

They left just as the sun was beginning to Wester, the sky free of clouds and the river a dancing mass of bright white horses, the wind ruffling its surface just as the tide paused before the turn; everyone anxious to get on board so that their ships could catch it

Journeying down to the Hard, loaded with the forage on a great Abbey wain: ale, wine and all the other provisions necessary for their immediate journey, they were led by Gui and his commanders, in company with Alicia, Agnes and the two squires, together with the four waggons they had brought with them from Malwood. Escorted by all their men, their armour flashing in the evening sunshine and with flags and surcoats flying, they made a thrilling sight; and minutes later Father Matthew followed them, his great leather scrip over his shoulder, filled to bursting with all the herbs, ointments and bandages that he had not been able to bring with him from Malwood. Now that they had all the necessary food for themselves and their horses to make a start, all were keyed up and anxious to be about their business. All they needed now was a fair wind off the land to see them safely on their way at last.

Chapter 55...It was young Wulfric the Dogboy who found it!

I t was young Wulfric, the Dog Boy, who found it!

Tightly jammed into a gap between Bellman's teeth, Sir Yvo's old boarhound, who had not stopped grieving since his master's fearsome death. Lying with his nose on his great paws most days, eyes dull and sharp ears flat, he seemed to be slowly pining away. Now Wulfric, with tear stained face, his back still smarting from the Huntsman's belt and his legs and side from his booted feet, had come to share his misery with his old friend, and sit and pull the hound's silky ears through his fingers and roll around with him in the straw of the dog house, in the hope of stirring the great hound back to life.

For Wulfric was Master Nathan's Hair Shirt, and he did not wear him kindly!

Nathan Picket, the Master of Hounds, and Sir Yvo's chief huntsman, was jealous of the boy's natural way with animals, and with Sir Yvo's favourite hound in particular. To Master Nathan the boy was an affront to his status. Now, with Sir Yvo and his Lady dead, at last he had been able to take swift action and dismiss the brat with a final beating. Yet he could not just sit by and let the great hound die, for that would count against him greatly. So having beaten and turned the boy out of his post the moment Sir Gui had left the castle, he had then ordered him to see what might be done with Bellman before he joined the common castle varlets...or take another vicious beating, concerned that the huge beast was not eating properly, but frightened to handle the giant hound himself.

Knowing that Wulfric had a particular relationship with old Bellman that he would never have, as the boy was the only one, apart from Sir Yvo, whom the great beast would allow anywhere near him, he had dragged Wulfric away by the ear from his lunch in the lower kitchens which he shared with the castle drudges, and brutally kicked him on his way with the threat to throat-cut the old hound if Wulfric could not sort him out!

For Bellman and Wulfric were old friends.

The boy, tall now and skinny, with a wild mop of russet hair, large grey eyes and a friendly mouth, had arrived at Malwood with his mother from near Gloucester, just after Bellman had been born, and never lost his Gloucester burr. And after his mother's death a year later, the boy had spent many a night in the hound box, his eyes streaked with tears, cuddled into the beast's huge body, and had growled and struggled for scraps amongst them all: Wolf hound, Lymer, Rache, and Boarhound, even Sir James' great Talbot, Argos. 'Til the Lady Margaret, horrified by the state into which the boy had fallen, and the raw treatment he was being given, finally rescued him. Sir Yvo gave him the job of 'Dog Boy', and Nathan had been seriously advised to mend his ways as far as Wulfric was concerned. And it was during those times afterwards that he and Bellman had really become friends, Puppy to Puppy, and, ever after, if the great hound, who was Sir Yvo's favourite, had a problem, it was to Wulfric Sir Yvo would turn for help, much to Nathan's disgust and bitter jealousy.

Now, with his beloved master gone, Bellman had seemed to turn his face to the wall, not eating or playing as he used to do. Instead just lying there in the sunshine feeling as lost and miserable as ever he had been when he was a puppy, and newly taken from his dam. Wulfric had been a friend then, just as he was now, and the sound of the boy's voice and the touch of his hand, made the great hound open his eyes and bang his tail hopefully on the ground.

"So, what's wrong with yew, yew gurt big lump?" Wulfric said, shaking the rain from his hair, before flinging himself down beside him and putting his arms round Bellman's great neck. "Why bain't yew eating the meat they've given yew? It's good meat, too. I had some for my dinner, until that bastard dragged me off it! Look, I've brought it yew to taste," he went on, getting up and going over to a large wooden pail he had brought with him. "Good and chewy, Bells," he said, using his favourite expression for the huge animal. "And I've mixed it with oats just as I knows yew like it," he chattered on as he poured the rich meaty porridge onto a great battered tin dish he had also brought with him. "Look, Boy. Just yewm get a taste o' that!"

But though the hound sniffed it and licked it and gurrrrffffed at it...he wouldn't eat it, pawing at the side of his face instead and growling deep in his throat, the deep rumbling, gurrrfffing sound enough to raise the hackles on anyone's unprotected neck.

"Now...What's this then?" Wulfric asked, looking intently at the giant hound's long jaw line. "I wonder what's really wrong with yew, Bells? Eh? What's with your face, boy? Let's have a look inside, shall we?" the boy went on in his soothing sing-song voice, as he grabbed Bellman's huge jaws in his neat hands and prised them apart so that he could look over his enormous teeth.

And there it was!

A small brass cylinder, with a piece of cork at each end covered with wax, and jammed like a thick stick between Bellman's shiny back molars. And the more he had worried at it and gnashed his jaws together...the tighter it had become. No wonder he couldn't eat and was so thoroughly out of sorts with himself! Poor old boy. Now...how to get it out?

Wulfric stood up and scratched his head for a while, his mind full of ideas. Then, with a smile he called Bellman to him and trudged off through the rain from the castle kennels to the Forge, with its mighty bellows and blazing fires, the old hound trailing miserably after him.

The Forge was where Big Nick was bound to be, and there he would ask the huge Smith for a nail. Not an ordinary rounded iron nail, but a horse-shoe nail, with its wedge shaped sloping edges, that he thought might be just right to prize out the tough metal 'stick' that Bellman had so successfully jammed between his great back teeth.

Nick smiled when he saw the lad, for he was quite a favourite, and listened open eyed at his request, before shaking his head in amazement.

"What? Poke that bloody great hound with a nail?" he rumbled. "Youm mad, young Wulfric! I'd sooner poke a hornet's nest with a broom stick! At least I'd get to run orf! You'll have your hand right in amongst all they fangs. One scrunch and he'll 'ave your wrist orf!"

"No, he won't, Nick. He knows I, does Bells. Him and I are great together, I've knowed he since a pup, and he, I. He's just moped 'cause his master's dead and no-one's been fussing he enough, nor I now, since that bliddy Nathan turned I out this morning. Now Bell's got some sort of metal pipe jammed a'tween his teeth and it has to come out. Nathan won't touch he, 'cos he's afeared o' our Bells. Ever since he gave me a whippin' and Bells went for he! But not I. I'm not afeared o' that great hound. Nor never wull be neither. He and I have been friends since we was pups together. You give I that gurt nail, Nick, and I'll have he fixed proper in no time!"

"That Nathan turned you out of your post, Wulfric?" Nick asked the boy, concerned.

"Yes...Had me in the moment Sir Gui had left. Said I was no bliddy good to man nor beast, gave me a proper belting and told me to clear my stuff and get out! Next thing, he gives me a good kicking as well and tells me to sort out Bellman first, or he'll cut the old dog's throat! I don't care about me, Nick. But I'll *not* stand by and see Sir Yvo's favourite gurt hound throat-cut without I do something to help he first! So, give I that nail and let's see what I can do. Bliddy Nathan Picket! What does he know?"

"Well, young'n, rather you than I!" Nick replied with a grin, as he handed Wulfric what he had asked for, ruffling the youngster's wild mop of hair with his enormous, calloused hand. "And as for that Nathan," he added grimly. "We'll see about him later. Seems to me that he's acted beyond his measure, young Wulfric, and Sir James will never stand for it. He knows what Sir Yvo thought o' thee, so don't yew worry! In the meantime, don't go blamin' me if Bellman bites thee, yew young rascal! I know I would if someone came pokin' and pryin' into my mouth with a nasty piece o' sharp pointy iron!"

"Youm as bad as that Nathan, Big Nick! All a hound needs to be good is firm handlin' and a kindly heart. Too much use o' the whip and in the end they'll turn and rend yew. One o' these days, that bliddy Nathan'll find that out for hiself! Bliddy arsehole! Some Master of Hounds he be, I don't think!"

And sitting down on a large box, Wulfric made the great hound sit, and, taking Bellman's great head between his hands, he looked into the huge animal's brown and gold flecked eyes. The boy on his box, the massive hound on his haunches, and he blew gently into Bellman's nostrils til the great beast shook his head and wruffled at him from his throat, while Big Nick looked on in amazement.

"Now, youm be a good boy, Bells," the young lad said, looking deep into the hound's eyes, til he blinked and closed them. "Open up that great maw of yourn, and let I see what's what!" And putting his hands on top and bottom of the giant hound's mouth he pulled the jaws open, while Nick stood transfixed at the boy's bravery, and Bellman's good nature with him, for with his mouth wide open, the hounds great teeth truly were an awesome sight.

They made even the giant smith feel nervous!

A moment later the boy whistled through his teeth in surprise: "There it is, you gurt lummox," Wulfric said, continuing to talk, the gentle sound of his voice making Bellman whine plaintively and thump his tail. "No wonder you can't eat! However did that'n get in there, then?" he went on, running his fingers over the hound's enormous back teeth and across the brass cylinder sticking out between them. "Just you give I a moment more of your time and I'll have this out of your gob afore yew knows it!"

With that the boy inserted the nail behind the small brass object and levered it against the jaw, making Bellman growl deep in his throat, softly at first and then louder, making Nick draw his own hand back sharply as if it was about to be snapped off! Wulfric stopped then, and looked the enormous black and tan animal sternly in his eyes once more.

"Youm be peaceable now, you hear!" He said firmly. "Yew gurt big lummox! None of that nonsense I tell ye! Now, Bells," he said calmly. "One more go and it'll be gone, I promise!" And putting his left hand back on the broad lower jaw he slipped his right hand back inside Bellman's mouth and once more he pushed the wedge shaped nail behind the hound's great back teeth and levered the brass container upwards against his bottom jaw.

Again the huge animal began to growl deep in his throat when, suddenly, with a ringing '*Ping!*', the small cylinder flew out of Bellman's mouth and bounced on the flagged floor of Big Nick's forge, skittering across it like a tiny golden lizard, before fetching up with a clatter against a pile of newly made horseshoes, gleaming in the firelight where Bellman's teeth had scored it.

"Now...what have we here?" The big smith queried slowly as he bent down to pick the tiny thing up, rolling the narrow brass cylinder across the great horny palm of his hand with an enormous forefinger. Meanwhile Bellman shook his great head, making his jowls shake and Grrrrufffed deeply, putting his huge paws up on Wulfric's chest, almost knocking the young lad over as he Wrrrrufffled at him with obvious good will, gave a single great baying bark and licked his face.

"This has been very cleverly made, young Wulfric," Nick said carefully after a while, lifting his head. "And not from round here neither; this is foreign work. And what are these a–doing here?" he questioned further, as he looked at the two pieces of cork neatly fitted into each end of the cylinder. "And what about these two feathers?" he added, picking them delicately off the underside of the little brass tube with his big fingers. "Now, where did they come from I wonder?" And he peered at the two tiny scraps of grey, feathery fluff, and scratched his head.

"You know what this is, Boy?" he said a moment later.

"No, Nick!" The boy said wonderingly, his hands ruffling Bellman's head and shoulders.

"This, young Wulfric," the giant smith rumbled, holding the tiny device up between his great sausage fingers. "This is a mystery. And there's only one place for a mystery like this, young Wulfric, with Sir Gui just gone on his travels...and that's Sir James! He knows more in his little finger than any man I know. So youngun," he went on heartily. "Yew and I are going to find Sir James and leave this little puzzle with he. Now come on, he won't eat yew. And I'll be with yew too. So let's be at it!"

385

And without further discussion, he gently took Wulfric by the scruff of his very grubby neck, and marched him off, first to the kennels to leave Bellman, and then to Sir James Bolderwood's Office in the Great Keep, heedless of the rain that was still falling all around them.

Chapter 56...Sir James and Father Gerome read the message.

Sir James' Office, just off the Great Hall, was well lit with both lamps and candles and the elderly Seneschal was sitting at his table, Argos, his great white Talbot by his side, when Nick brought Wulfric in to see him, the boy trembling with fear at being before so important a man as the Seneschal of Castle Malwood. Even though he knew he had done no wrong, he was still desperately anxious, and was almost beyond speech by the time Big Nick had finished explaining what they were there for.

"So...young Wulfric," the tall Seneschal said in his calm, stately manner, sitting back to look at the boy over his steepled fingers. "You have been sorting out Bellman's problems again, have you? Sir Yvo would have been very proud of you, young man. He is a fearsome beast, our Bellman. I have seen him tear the throat out of the biggest boar we ever had in the Forest. It took four men to haul him off that day. Yet you opened his mouth with just your two bare hands. Well done, young Wulfric! Well done! Sir Yvo was quite right to speak so well of you. Now, lad, before you tell me anything else...and I know all about Master Nathan," he said with a grim look. "So have no fear on that score, I assure you!...Now, Wulfric, Show me what you found there."

And, without further ado Nick took the delicate brass cylinder and put it in Wulfric's hand so that the lad could give it to Sir James himself, who laid it with great care on a wide flat sheet of unused white parchment that he took from a proper document chest behind him, so that it lay there gleaming in the bright lamp light. And it was very unusual. About an inch long and the width of a large bulrush stalk, with a tiny sliver of cork at either end, each sealed in place with red wax. And it was very light, with a fine groove in the metal all around it at top and bottom.

All three looked at it in silent amazement while Sir James rolled it backwards and forwards across the white parchment surface with his fine, long fingers, before picking it up to examine it more thoroughly.

"Wherever did the hound get it from?" Sir James asked after a while.

"Don't know, m' Lord." Wulfric replied. "But he's been off his food since shortly after Sir Yvo was killed. Master Nathan thought it was because he were pining. Said Bells would get over it and to leave he be. But the hound continued to lose ground. Then, this morning he told I to see what I could do. H..He said if I couldn't sort he out he would have Bellman throat-cut! And I couldn't let that happen, Sir James. Not our Bells! So..so I took he to Big Nick's. And when I ope'd his great maw, I found that...that 'thing' stuck between his large back teeth, so he couldn't chew properly. Perhaps he picked it up somewhere in the forest while rootling about? Anyway, m' Lord. I went to Big Nick, got a horseshoe nail off he, opened Bells' mouth and dug that brass thing out wi' it, together wi' a couple of feathers that were stuck to the bottom of it against Bells' jaw."

"It were right bravely done, Sir James!" The giant smith said, but the elderly Seneschal's mind was not concentrating on young boys with horse-shoe nails, but on something else entirely, for he turned away then for a few moments before swinging back to ask sharply: "Feathers? What feathers, Boy?"

"These, Sir James," Big Nick said quietly, putting the two grey bits of fluff and feather together on the parchment. "I found they stuck underneath it when I picked it up."

Sir James bent his head forward then, and studied the two tiny grey-blue scraps of feather intently, picking them up and blowing on them, while Nick and Wulfric watched him open eyed with bated breath.

"Have you had any birds in your Forge lately, Master Nicholas?" The Seneschal asked him quietly, his eyes cool and hard. "Careful how you answer now. For what you say may be very important."

"No, my Lord," the big smith said after a moment's thought. "No birds and no odd grey-blue feathers either. Why, Sir James?"

"Because, unless I am very much mistaken," he replied slowly, holding the feathers up to the nearest light. "These are pigeon feathers. And if they were found together with this little fellow," he went on, rolling the brass tube with his finely chiselled fingers. "Then it is reasonable to assume that the two, in some way, must be connected! Perhaps Bellman found a downed bird...our pigeon?...and ate it! It is just the sort of thing he would do. And in doing so, this little canister got trapped between his teeth." And he stood up then and urgently called for his guard, who came in immediately.

"Jason...go find Father Gerome, and ask him to come to my Office immediately. I don't care *what* the dear man is doing, do you hear? He is to come to me *at once!* If he argues, bring him anyway, *no matter what!* Now, you two, find a chair each, or a stool, or something, and come and be seated. It is time we opened this little Pandora's Box, and discovered what is in it. Because no-one takes so much trouble to seal a thing so carefully, if all it contains is God's good fresh air!"

And with infinite care, beneath the goggle eyed gaze of the Castle Smith and the Dog Boy, the Seneschal of Malwood Castle, Sir James Bolderwood, broke the twin scarlet wax seals and pulled out the tiny cork stoppers. Then, picking up a long steel pin he had to hand, he held the tube up to the light and, with great care and a soft sigh of success, he teased out a tiny roll of the thinnest papyrus paper.

"Hmmm," he said as Nick and Wulfric gasped in amazement. "As I thought. A message! Now...what does it say I wonder? And where's that blasted priest?"

At which point the door was first banged and then flung open, and Father Gerome, horribly flustered and somewhat irate, was almost thrown into the room by two of Sir James' burly guards, who promptly turned on their heels without a word and shut the door again behind them.

"Ah...Father, thank you so much for coming," Sir James said smoothly, without giving the little priest a chance even to open his mouth. "We have developments here that require your expert advice. Tell me, Gerome. What do you make of that?" And he stepped to one side of his wide table so that his thoroughly jangled visitor could see what lay there.

"*Sir James!*" He exclaimed, angrily. "I *must* protest! Your men interrupted me at my prayers, and…"

"…I know, Gerome. I know," he said, breaking in on the little priest's diatribe, holding up his hands. "Protest away, Dear Boy, by all means. You may even complain to the Bishop himself when next he comes here. That is not the issue. The issue is *that*," he said, pointing with a quivering finger. "That '*thing*' on my table! Tell me, Father, now, what do you think that is?"

Father Gerome, stopped gesticulating then and stooped to look at the small brass cylinder. Then, with a gasp, looking startled, and with much greater care, the old priest studied it again, picking the small tube up and examining it carefully, particularly fingering the two little grooves at either end.

"Well, Gerome?" Sir James asked him quietly. "What do you think?"

"Well, God Bless my Soul!" He exclaimed astonished. "Goodness me, James," he said, looking first at the brass canister on the parchment and then up into the quizzical face of the tall Seneschal. "I have not seen one of these in twenty years. But there is no mistaking it, goodness me, no! It is a message casket from a carrier pigeon! The idea came out of Cathay I believe. The Romans used them, and so do the Emperors in Constantinople still, and the Arabs in Outremer. This is a common design out there. Sealed with cork and wax, and then tied with fine silken cord in these little grooves under the wing, or round the leg.

My Dear Sir James," he asked astonished. "However did you come by such an…an *Eastern* thing here in the Forest?"

"The Dog-Boy found it, Father. Young Wulfric! Stuck between Bellman's back teeth. The message is here, Gerome," he went on urgently, pointing to the flimsy message roll. "I want you to read it with me to be certain of there being no mistakes. Come now, old friend. We must take heart. I thought that was what it was the moment I saw it. Clearly a spy has been at work within our midst, more than one I suspect, and I think I know who as well. But, no matter about that. Let us see now that which they would die for us not to!" And so saying he unrolled the small rectangle of wafer-thin papyrus.

Four pairs of eyes stared down closely at just six tiny spidery words and two numbers as Gerome read them out: Red. Hoedic. Jules. Lucas. Green. 4/5. Bordeaux.

For a moment no-one moved or spoke a word. All too shocked to do more than breathe, and even that none too easily, as the full enormity of what they had before them finally struck home. Because, though much of what was there did not mean a great deal to all clustered into the Seneschal's Office that rainy July morning…the names 'Jules' and 'Lucas', meant everything!

"*By God's Throat*, Gerome!" Sir James spat out, standing upright with a jerk. "Not just spies, but *murderous* spies! And two lots of them too, if I am not mistaken!" Then, with a groan, almost of despair, he banged his forehead and said: "*Sweet Wine of Christ*! Old friend, how did I not see it before? Jules Lagrasse and Lucas Fabrizan! Those *bastards*. I thought at the time those names seemed familiar somehow! Lagrasse and Fabrizan are two villages close to Narbonne! I went through them, years ago, when I was fighting down there in King Henry's Aquitaine campaign. That is *all* De Brocas land. And I will wager my life that those were two of the Baron's men.

Splendour of God!" He exclaimed a moment later. "They are the very two whom Fitzurse put at the foot of Alicia's tower the night of the fire…and, *God help us all*!" He shouted out, horrified. "They are in Sir Gui's expeditionary force to seize de Brocas! *Jason*!" he roared then, striding swiftly to open the door just as a startled face looked round. "Send me Peter Latchmere and James Appleyard, and tell Ralf Longsword to meet me in the lower courtyard as soon as possible. Quickly! *Quickly* man! And ring the alarum bell, *we do not have a moment to spare!*

"What about the rest, Sir James?" Father Gerome asked anxiously. "What does it all mean?"

"Well," the tall Seneschal said slowly, taking the tiny message in his hands and walking away from the table, deep in thought. 'Red', I'm sure, will be the *Mary*, which we all know is going to Bordeaux. 4/5 must be days, I think. The names we all know about, God curse them! Green is the colour of Islam and, if I remember the charts I have looked at with Thomas Blackwood in the past for this stretch of water, Hoedic is one of a small group of islands near the mouth of the Loire. That is all pirate waters and pretty deserted countryside. They call it the *Côte Sauvage*...the Savage Coast, and rightly.

I fear that Sir Gui and all his people are sailing straight into a trap!" He said then, grimly, turning to look directly at them all, his eyes diamond bright in the lamp light. "Father, how stands the time?" he snapped out, as the little priest looked on in stunned amazement while the urgent tocsin of the alarum bell began to ring out across the castle yard, the bailey and the whole sleepy countryside.

"Well after midday, Sir James," he said after a strangled pause. "The sun is well over the church now. They will have to ride like the wind if they are to catch them before sunset."

"Well they will just have to ride like the bloody wind, sped on by your prayers, don't you think? Now bustle about. Nick? Wulfric? Away with you both...but be sure to come back and see me later, there are matters yet to sort out for you both. Right now we have two things to do: Get Peter, James and Ralf off to Beaulieu immediately with a message from me...and then organise a thorough search for two young men with a donkey and a goose on a string!

Great God in Heaven! How could I have been so blind?"

Chapter 57...The Mary and the Pride of Beaulieu set sail for France.

By the time the last horse to be going had been brought on board both ships, the last bundle of hay and straw had been safely stowed, and the sides closed up and made secure against the sea with good pitch and oakum, the sun was sinking towards the horizon in great gold and scarlet streamers, the clouds edged with dark purple, and the tide had turned.

Roared on by their Captain, the *Mary's* shipmen raced up the ratlines and edging out onto the massive boom they loosed her great sail; and casting off from the wooden bollards on the quayside she idled away from the shore, assisted by her sailors with long quants to pole her further into the estuary until at last she caught the wind. The *Pride of Beaulieu* following shortly after, with the sumpters, Caesar, Sunburst and Gillygate...and a goodly share of their provisions and stores of war...the two destriers and Jupiter sailing on the *Mary* with the bulk of the men.

So Sir James' desperate messengers were just too late!

Even as they reached the Abbey on almost foundering horses, Sir Gui and all his men were already boarding their transports. And by the time the Abbot had arrived to tell them where they all were, and they had raced the last few miles down to the harbour...the *Mary* and the *Pride* had sailed. And though the men stood up in their saddles and waved and hallooed to them in the gathering dusk with all their might, their words and shouts were lost in the rush and crumble of the waves along the shore, and in the wild mewing of the gulls above their heads.

All they could do was sit, exhausted, with drooping hearts, and watch them sail away.

★

With the wind keen on her port side the *Mary* heeled her fat bottom round and bore steadily away from the shore followed by the *Pride*, both ships tilting to the pressure of wind as the tide helped to carry them out, their great sails brailed round to catch the breeze now blowing stiffly away from the land, the *Mary* with the Sun in Splendour radiating out from her mainsail on every side; the *Pride of Beaulieu* with a vast golden Ram's Head with huge curling horns filling the centre of her mainsail too. Well armed and provisioned, they were both fast ships with freshly careened bottoms and carried experienced crews of their own. They were a match for any but the most determined foe, and with the Malwood Lions on board, any enemy tempted to attack them would have a rare job on his hands!

Despite the rumours of French pirates in the Channel, Thomas Blackwood was keen to press on. And while the last dying gleams of the day slowly faded from the western horizon, the tall stern lanterns dwindled into distant stars as the two great ships disappeared into the breezy darkness of the night.

★

Gui and Alicia stood on the *Mary's* stern castle leaning on the wooden battlements that ran round them and watched the shore slide away, waving to the people standing there getting gradually smaller and smaller, and to a small group of horsemen who came clattering down to the shore side to stand in their saddles and wave at them too, their voices thin with distance, mingling with those of the gulls who flew screaming and swooping around their heads.

They smiled and waved and shouted back: "Thank you! Thank you! Farewell! Wish us God Speed!" Then, with their arms around each other they turned to watch the sun go down in crimson splendour.

Dipping like a fiery ball below the far horizon it left the sky washed with palest green that blended with subtle beauty into the blue and purple of the coming night, paving the way for the first bright star of evening to light the night. The sea now turned black and barely ruffled with white horses, bubbled beneath the *Mary's* bows as they bowled along, the mewling gulls still following them hopefully in a crowd of swooping grey and white.

Behind them England slowly faded out of sight as the dusk fell gently into darkness around them while below, in the waist of the ship, the men gathered quietly in groups to watch their homeland pass from view.

"So, my darling," she said snuggling into his shoulder, his cape drawn round her. "We are away at last. How lovely of the Abbot to send some people to wave us good bye, and what a pity we had not the time to be married before we left, as your parents had so wanted."

"Was that what my Father had planned for then?" he asked her, holding her close.

"It was supposed to be a surprise, sweetheart. But your mother never was one for keeping a 'surprise' like that quiet. And anyway, we girls, we need to plan such things with care. Imagine what would have happened if it had all been left to your father?"

"Hmmmm. Bit of a disaster I expect, my darling," he said with a wry smile, nuzzling her hair. "Still," he added, sighing deeply as he looked out with unfocused eyes across the darkening sea. "It is difficult somehow to accept they have both gone from our lives for good. And that all of this," he went on, sweeping his hands across the crowded deck below and at the *Pride of Beaulieu* behind them, barrelling through the waves with her fat bows, her sails filled and spray bursting over her bowsprit, "is all on account of one man's wickedness, and not some magical fairytale."

"Don't worry, my darling, '*Quos Dei delere cupiunt insania afficiunt!*'" She said quietly, turning to kiss him.

"What's that, Alicia?" He asked startled.

"Well, Really, I had thought that *something* of Father Gerome's teaching might have stuck in that great head of yours!" she said, laughing up at him. "'Those whom the Gods wish to destroy, they first send mad!' So bear up sweetheart, you still have a long way to go before *that* happens! We will get there all in good time Gui, and at least we are together. And there's no way the wicked Baron can get to us from here, so there's no point in worrying yourself silly over something you can do nothing about. Come on down with me now and have something to eat.

Matthew has got some sort of tasty pottage cooking on Master Thomas's brick galley that smells really good, and we all need a proper rest after our ride today. We are all pledged to serve you, dearest of men...including me. Some from need, some from desire, all from loyalty and respect.

And though you and I may not be formally married, Oh my most *noble* Lord and Master," she added, smiling wickedly up at him, shamelessly fluttering her lashes. "We *are* formally betrothed and *no-one*, my darling, darling man. *No-one*, is going to prevent me from being as good and proper a wife to you now as ever I would be had we been formally married...as your parents so wanted us to be! Tomorrow is another day, and who knows what it will bring? Just look to the present and let the future take care of itself!"

She smiled then at his quizzical, almost downcast look and kissed him again.

"Now come on, Honeyone...I've had enough of these megrims, and so have you. We need you fit and well, not sunk in reverie and suffering from a permanent fit of the dismals! What's done is done, my darling, and there is nothing you or I can do about it. All we can do now is to look to the future and trust in God to help us find the right way forward.

And right now that's to go down there, join in with our friends and have something to eat! Personally, I am starving and I just can't *wait* to find out what Agnes thinks of Allan Wood. I think he's perfect for her. All I need to do then is to find someone equally lovely for Richard!" And they both laughed...and with her arm across Gui's shoulders she drew him away from the stern towards the warmth and candle light of Thomas Blackwood's cabin and Matthew's cooking.

Behind them the *Mary* and the *Pride*'s broad tracks spread away into the darkness as they sailed on into the night, great lanterns shining out from both sterns, broad sails reaching to catch the wind and fat prows driving steadily towards France.

★

In the bows of the *Mary*, while the other men grouped together after their evening meal in the waist of the ship and talked amongst themselves or stood leaning out against the thick bulwarks watching the waves, the Cousins sat and cleaned their armour. Their heads close together and their voices soft, their words masked by the thump and chuckle of the *Mary*'s bluff bows as she shouldered her way through the sea.

"Did those two idiots get that message off then?" Lucas asked softly as he and Jules sat on two large sacks of oats, checking over their chain mail hauberks. "I thought they'd never get those bloody birds sorted! Did you see them this morning as we went by on the road?"

"Yes. Pressed into the wayside as far as they could go, trying to keep their heads down and hoping nobody saw them for long enough to be certain who they were."

"Stupid, bloody birds too!" his cousin sneered. "Who would have thought a man as intelligent as Baron Roger would put his name to such a ridiculous bundle of fucking feathers? No wonder those two arseholes had such problems!"

"The problem wasn't so much with the birds, Lucas," Jules explained patiently. "They were fine. The difficulty was to get it done without being spotted! The Prince's choice of two such seeming numbskulls is very clever, though why he chose those particular two for his scheme I have no idea!"

"A love of fucking pigeons, I expect," Lucas growled in response. "Sodding, bloody pigeons! Messier birds you couldn't hope to find. Better for eating than flying bloody messages! Did you see how tiny those message rolls were? No wonder Robin had so much trouble getting them into their stupid little canisters. He kept dropping the bastard things. All fingers and fucking thumbs him!"

"Still, once it was clear where we were leaving from, and our immediate destination, he and Henri got them away in the end, three days ago. Took Sir Jasper off with them for a wander in the forest, along with that ridiculous goose, with both pigeons in little bags under Robin's cloak, and slipped them in some clearing or other, once they were well out of sight"

"Pigeons, a goose on a string and a fucking donkey called 'Sir Jasper'! Those two are quite bloody mad! Let's hope they really did get clean away."

"Oh yes, Lucas. I'm sure they did. Lost in the stews of Southampton by now and writing up a neat report for Prince John, before setting out to return to Gruissan. They may even get back before we do. And those two lads are not mad...just very clever, well that Robin of Oxford is for certain. Henri Duchesne is quicker with a knife than he is with a pigeon, and looks like a mazeling: sneering face and twisted smile. By seeming so stupid and harmless no-one's going to seek to search or question them. They'll just see what they expect to see, two silly youngsters out for a lark. Never guessing that so simple an appearance could hide so terrible a reality! So...yes. The message has gone out. Twice actually, in case a hawk should take one, or one should get lost along the way. All we have to do now is be prepared."

"How long, Coz?"

"Four days. Five maybe, as I hear that we're putting in to Brest first for fresh water and more fodder for those horses. So, plenty of time. Then, when we are just passing Belle Île, it should happen, unless something goes wrong."

"Then?"

"Then, as soon as real danger is spotted...in this case El Nazir's galleys...we know that the plan is for the girls to be put into the Master's cabin for safety, and guarded. Four men. Might even be us doing it if I can get enough words with that Agnes. Anyway, once the attack proper has started and is going full blast, we knock off their guards, no matter who or where, and as soon as El Nazir's boat comes up on our stern, we get out fast, taking both girls with us for good measure. Right?

"Right!"

"Good! Now take this," he said, handing his own mailed hauberk to his cousin. "And stow it carefully, along with yours, and put these arm bands safe behind your shield grip," he added, handing them to him swiftly, "just in case. I'm going to slip away now and see if I can have a swift word or two with Mistress Fitzwalter. *Ware Hawk!* Cousin," he hissed urgently. "Fitzurse on the prowl!"

With that he stood up and handed Lucas his mailed coat with a bright laugh, and a bang on his shoulder, almost bumping into the massive figure of Sir Gui's Master–at–Arms as he did so, who stood looking at him for a moment with a curious half smile on his face.

"Now then, lads," he said in his thick Norman-French. "What mischief are you two cooking up, eh? Tucked away down here where no-one can see or hear you?" And he looked at them both, his keen eyes noting their sudden confused nervousness and uncertainty. "Anyone would think you boys were plotting?" He said casually, with a laugh, his look as calm and empty as a beehive from which the queen has swarmed.

Lucas almost jumped, and his hand stole to where his long knife lay close against his side. Then he relaxed. The big bastard knew nothing, or else they would both have been fucking arrested long since. But it was a nasty moment. He shrugged, and grinned to himself. Fine end to everything if he really had tried to stick a knife into him, the bloody sod! For a moment Jules froze, his mind racing as he tried to think of anything they could have done or said that might have given them away. He saw his cousin's hand slide towards his knife, and closed his eyes. That really would put the cat among the pigeons! And he almost laughed at the irony.

John Fitzurse looked at both men and, despite his smile, was concerned, noting the way that Lucas had started...almost guiltily at his jokey mention of 'plotting'...and then let his hand drift towards the long knife he always carried. And the man, Jules, had also reacted strangely. Nervous? Uncertain? Didn't seem likely, given what he had seen of the two of them since they had first arrived back in the Spring.

399

Intriguing though!

And what were those two green armbands that he had seen? And why was Lagrasse so quick to cover them over? He shrugged. He never had liked the South French! Perhaps that was what was bothering him about these two: they weren't Normans!

And then there had been that business with the drugging the night of the fire, and the killing of David Oats and Jonny Foxglove! Was that all too smooth? Too easily explained? Certainly there'd been no blood on them, and God knows there'd been enough of that everywhere! He shrugged again, instinctively not trusting them. Well, he hadn't been able to shake either of them over anything about that night, but they were up to something, he would stake his life on it. So, he would watch them! Oh yes, he would surely watch them! And he gave a lopsided grin, keeping his eyes empty and his whole manner bland.

"Of course we're plotting," Jules replied with another laugh, opening his eyes to find Fitzurse looking at him strangely. "How to persuade that lump of a Burgundian mercenary, Loic de Martinville, to do my watch tonight, so I can get some quality time with Mistress Fitzwalter. There's nothing like a boat trip to aid a romance. Kisses stolen under the stars are always sweeter than wine!"

"Ho! So that's what's on your mind, is it?" The big sergeant said, looking down at them from his considerable height. "Well not tonight, my lucky lad. Firstly, the lady concerned is dining…if you can call it that on this miserable tub!...with Sir Gui and his party, to which the Under Sheriff has been invited and, secondly, I've got you marked for a stint in the crow's nest at dawn, along with one of Master Blackwood's best men. You've got sharp eyes, and I am told there may be corsairs as well as pirates about in these waters…and we wouldn't want to bump into any of those, my lovely lads, would we?"

"No, Sergeant!" Jules said smartly, cursing the big man's nearness and his so startling closeness to the truth. The big bastard had actually made him sweat.

" 'No Sergeant's' right, soldier! Corsairs are filthy stinking scum! Nasty, brutish, evil sons of bitch-whores who ought to have been killed at birth! I hate 'em bad…and Master Blackwood hates 'em even badder, since they took his daughter! So get some shut-eye. I'll tell de Beaune to put de Martinville on instead of you, and I'll tell Mistress Fitzwalter you were thinking of her!"

And with a great laugh John Fitzurse went on his way. A word here, a word there, a joke somewhere else as he moved amongst his men, before turning and making his way up the ladder to the Master's cabin to report 'All's Well!' to Sir Gui, while adding that the two South Frenchmen needed watching. Certain that they were up to something…but not knowing, yet, just *what* that certain 'something' was!

While all the time the *Mary* and her saffron yellow consort, under reduced canvas for the night, pushed steadily on across the starlit, empty darkness of the Channel.

Chapter 58...How they all set out together from Brest.

D awn that first day found them well up the Channel with a fair sea running, and by midday they had cleared the north west tip of Brittany and were slipping through the 'Throat' into Brest for fresh water and fodder for the horses, as well as fresh bread, meat and wine for the men.

Once safely moored up together, they mucked out the boxes in the waists of both ships where the horses were stabled, and took this break in their journey as a first opportunity for the leaders to put their heads together and discuss what they should do if pirates really did attack...or the rumours about Corsairs should be true!

So they met in the Master's cabin on the *Mary* with several jugs of ale and wine and a fistful of beakers, and a platter of warm pasties and sweet tarts, while the two squires stood outside to ensure their privacy.

"So," Robert of Christchurch, the *Pride*'s Master said, after some heated discussion. "I want to be quite clear about all this: If you are attacked, I am to clear my yard arm and make for shore, leaving you lot behind to shift for yourselves. But if *I* am attacked, you will come to my aid in the *Mary*! That seems to me an unacceptable situation, and one wholly without honour..."

"And I agree!" Gui said, to their amazement. " Forgive me. But I was just testing you."

Then, looking at the Under Sherriff and his attendant Ship Master, ignoring the ripple of resentment following his last statement, he asked with quiet reasoning, like a man throwing a stone into a mill-pond: "Would you feel the same if you were carrying the Lady Alicia and Mistress Fitzwalter?"

There was a concerted gasp at that, as almost everyone in the cramped cabin seemed to start forward at once, all wanting to express their dismay, anger, horror...and agreement at the same time; and for a while Gui and Father Matthew allowed them to do exactly that until the young Lord of Malwood banged his hand on a nearby chest and said: "*Enough!*" Sounding so like his late father that he made his tall Guard Commander jump, and his fiancée smile!

"Enough of all this row and discord! There are very good reasons for my suggestion. But I am going to ask Father Matthew to explain it to you, for he can do it far more eloquently than I!" And turning, he offered the tall Benedictine a somewhat caustic and very discontented audience.

The dark habited monk rose then, and looking at all the expectant faces around him he smiled.

"You must forgive Sir Gui, my friends, because this is very much my idea, not his. And he wasn't testing your courage, or your determination, just your imagination, so please do not be offended. But we feel that it has real merit, and he has asked me to explain it to you. Quite simply…I do not trust the Baron not to make a further attempt to seize Lady Alicia! No, wait," he said calmly, holding up his hands for quiet as everyone tried once more to break into speech, "and hear me out first. Listen! This is a man used, always, to having his own way, and, moreover, not one given to failure either.

We have all heard it often enough; that his plans never fail? Well, at Malwood they did. They came seriously unglued! Oh yes, he damaged you, and damaged you badly, but he failed to knock you out for good, as he intended. The castle fire was a diversion, but though his parents died in it…Gui did not and, most important of all, the Baron didn't get Alicia either. She escaped him! Not only that, but he lost two of his men in the process, courtesy of Master Allan," he added, with his customary gentle incline of the head. "And, into the bargain, he got driven off and forced to flee! In short…he was humiliated!

Now, I ask you. How would any one of you feel, if you were the so 'good' Baron today?" And he paused there for his words to sink in before adding: "Wouldn't you be absolutely *burning* to be revenged? Consumed by it? That a parcel of numpties, to use one of Gui's Yorkshire expressions, should make such…such a monkey out of you! And get away with it? Surely you would want to be revenged as soon as possible, wouldn't you?

And how better to achieve that than by re-capturing the most valuable piece on the chess board, the one that you lost in the first place…the Queen herself! Lady Alicia. And, believe me, de Brocas has the resources and contacts to achieve exactly that, if he so chooses!

We know that Pirates are abroad in the Channel. Thomas knew that weeks ago, and they are nothing new. But," and here he turned with an apologetic look towards Gui, who responded with a typically resigned shrug. "There is still more disquieting news, I am afraid," he added, lowering his voice as almost everyone's face fell. "News that Gui, Richard, the two Masters and I have kept to ourselves so far; but can do so no longer. There are strong indications that Barbary Corsairs may also be busy in our area. They have been active off Ireland, and can cover great distances more quickly than you may easily imagine.

No…I cannot be more specific," he said, in answer to the horrified looks and cries of dismay that came from Alicia and Agnes, who clutched at each other's hands. "This is not the first time that Corsairs will have taken slaves from the Irish coastline, and they may have nothing to do with us at all. But right now? After all that happened at Malwood a month ago?…And Baron Roger is known to have connections with these people!…I think it is all too much of a coincidence for us to discard the idea that he may have a hand in this somewhere."

"Hence the outrageous suggestion that I should flee from any impending action, if something dreadful should be spotted heading our way." The Master of the *Pride* said quietly from the corner of the room, where he was sitting with Allan-i-the-Wood and Jean de Beaune, whittling with his broad bladed knife at a thick stick of beechwood.

"Exactly, Master Robert," Gui replied, turning towards him. "We need a decoy, the *Mary*, like a partridge trailing a broken wing before the fox to lead him away from her chicks, you in the *Pride*…"

"…Until she has drawn him far enough astray for her to flap her 'broken' wing and rocket away to safety!" The big Verderer broke in excitedly. "Yes…My Lord. I can see that, and it just might work. Only our 'partridge' will turn into a tiger and tear the Corsairs limb from bloody limb!"

"Well - that's the plan anyway," Gui said quietly, leaning back against the cabin walls.

"But how will this-this ghastly plan *work*?" Alicia cried out at Gui, distraught at the thought of being separated once again from the man she loved so much. "How do you intend to lure your Fox sufficiently for us to escape its terrible embrace?"

"We will get two of our men to dress up like you," Sir Richard said, "And then let the dog see the rabbit! Believe me, my Lady," Sir Richard replied calmly to her snort of disgust. "They will see exactly what they expect to see, as we did the night of the fire. What they will have been told to look out for is - two girls! They don't know what they look like, just that they are 'girls. Nor will they know which of the two ships those girls are on either, until we show them off. Then we leap off like a deer before the chase!"

"And girls wear dresses in bright and pretty colours!" Master Robert said slowly, suddenly chipping in. "So, if our 'girls' show themselves boldly enough - the enemy, Corsairs or not, will see them and follow the *Mary* hotly, ignoring the *Pride* as she slips further and further away because their prey is on the red ship, not the yellow! By God's Bones, Father," he said with growing confidence. "This crazy plan may not be as crazy as I first thought!"

"And we will weaken the appearance of the *Mary* to encourage them to pounce on us, by hiding the majority of our men until the last possible moment," Sir Richard continued in his lazy drawl, adding with a smile. "We might even get some of them to fall as if killed, to encourage them to come in against us more quickly.

Then we will unleash Hell upon them in such a manner that they will never have experienced before!" Gui said, banging his hands together with a sudden clap. "Though I doubt that our *so* noble Baron will be on board, more's the pity. But we will bring such total war to his allies that they will not hurry again to his support, if at all. The infidel are brave - but they are far from being foolish!"

After that the meeting rather lost its cohesion, as everyone wanted to talk and ask questions of each other, Alicia and Agnes most of all as the thought of being separated from the bulk of their defence in the face of such horrifying enemies was truly frightening for both of them. Nevertheless Father Matthew restored order after a while, simply by banging a loose iron ringbolt he had found on the wooden table and shouting: "*Quiet!*" in so loud a voice that the babel of sound around the room was instantly quelled.

Then, with that achieved, he significantly dropped his voice as he continued: "Be careful now, all of you. We do not want to advertise abroad what we are thinking, ports like this one have eyes and ears everywhere, indeed, who's to say we are not already being watched?

So my friends," he added in his quietest voice. "What is it to be? I will give you five minutes to make up your minds. We will go outside. When you are ready, come and join us." And stepping away from the table, he opened the door that led onto the quarterdeck and left the cabin, swiftly followed by Alicia and Agnes, and finally by Gui and Sir Richard.

"They don't like it much, Father," Gui said moments later, listening to Thomas and Robert of Christchurch arguing in the cabin behind them, interspersed with Allan-i-the-Wood and Jean de Beaune's scattered comments.

"And I don't like it much either, darling." Alicia said sharply. "The very idea of the Corsairs terrifies me, let alone the prospect of actually meeting up with them! And not to have you by my side is simply appalling! Who will look after us if nearly all our men are in the *Mary*?"

"Sweetheart, you will be in a safer place on board the *Pride* than you think. She is a stout ship, and newly built. At the first sign of trouble she will shorten sail and bear away for the shore…which we will have held in sight all the time…and take herself amongst the rocks where no galley can follow. Anyway, Honeyone, you will have Allan Wood, and all his men to guard you, many of whom are longbow archers. Rare men with a shaft, my darling. And I will give you a half a dozen of our own Lions as well, with Big John of Hordle to lead them, together with the Cousins. That should please you, Mistress Fitzwalter," he added, mock formally, with a smile. "I hear Jules Lagrasse is quite a favourite of yours!"

"Well, so he is, Sir Gui," she said with a grin. "But then so is the Under Sherriff! There is something about that man that I really do like. With two such ready swains on hand a girl *must* feel safe!"

"Well, you may Agnes. But this girl," Alicia said pointing to herself, "needs her own true man by her side - not a parcel of gamekeepers, be they never so lusty or ready for a fight. Oh, Gui," she cried, clutching his hand to her heart. "Can't Agnes and I stay with you in the *Mary*? I so don't want to be separated from you again!"

But before he could reply there was swift movement behind them, the door to the cabin opened, and the four men stepped out, with Tommy Blackwood in the lead.

"All done and dusted, Sir Gui," The large Ship Master said gruffly. "We agree. Unanimous decision. And we put ourselves under your command, for any fighting that is! Anything to do with ship handling is our department, for I'd as soon give the sailing of my *Mary* to you as you would the mounting of a siege to me!" And he spat on his palm and held it out.

"Well done, Thomas!" The young Lord of Malwood replied with a huge grin, spitting on his own palm and smacking his hand into Master Blackwood's as he spoke. "I never doubted you! Now, we have much to do before we sail again tomorrow, so talking's over. Let's get this play on the cart!"

★

That night Gui and Alicia lay entwined in the Master's cabin, bodies and hearts together. Slicked with passion and elated with their love, which transcended all other feelings, lifting them to such peaks of emotion, of pleasure and of rapture, that they wished never to return to the hot, dusty plains of everyday life. Spent and sated they lay like warm spoons curled in together, his hands around her breasts, face pressed into the hollow of her neck; her rounded haunches soft against his loins, both fast asleep, safely guarded throughout the night by men they had known for years and whom Fitzurse had put there to watch over them.

★

Beneath the foredeck the Cousins brooded over the sudden change to their plans, after Fitzurse had dropped in on them just after they had seen their leaders meeting on the deck above.

"Fucking *Bastard!*" Lucas growled at his cousin, after the big Master-at-Arms had told them they were to transfer to the *Pride* before first light. "Now what do we do?"

"Do as we have been told, Coz. With a smile! Remember? And keep our noses clean! Look, we will still be within slitting distance of those two bits of skirt...and of those who will be guarding them..."

"But El Nazir's men will attack the wrong ship, you fucking *idiot!*" Lucas replied furiously, hurling his knife to stand quivering in the deck. "While we sail for safety. What fucking good is that to us?"

"Have you still got the rest of that material we used to make those green arm bands?" his cousin replied quietly.

"Yes, Jules, behind the hand guard on my shield, together with the armbands themselves. Huge piece of fucking of silk," he said, bemused by the sudden change of subject. "For shit's sake. What sodding good is that to us now? The armbands were to identify us when Nazir attacked the *Mary* in person. We won't be on the fucking *Mary* now, cou-sin!" He concluded with a pitying sneer, slowing his speech to decline each separate syllable with stunning contempt.

"Oh, *God's Blood*, Lucas!" His cousin replied, exasperated with him. "*Use your brain, numbskull!* All we need to do when Nazir shows his hand at last is to stand at the back of the *Pride*...for she will be sailing away from him as fast as her sails will carry her...below the stern castle, and hang what's left of that green material over the rudder, and he's bound to see it! El Nazir is no fool, Coz. He will see that and know *at once* where the girls are! In fact we can create our own merry hell on board the *Pride* by attacking the steersman when he least expects it! And we will have our own armbands as well to protect us from Nazir's crazy boys, for I swear some of them are so hopped up they would attack trees if he told them to!"

"You're bloody mad, you are!" His cousin replied disgustedly. "That will get us both fucking killed for certain!"

407

"Well if we fail in this the Baron will kill us anyway, so what have we got to lose? And, if this succeeds, we will be heroes! All is not lost, Lucas. In fact this way may yet turn out to be better!"

★

Just before first light Sir Richard called Gui and together they helped arm Alicia and Agnes, slipping the smallest suits of chain and leather armour they could find amongst their men over their shifts, leaving their dresses behind in exchange. Luckily both girls were taller than many of their friends, so fitting them out was less of a problem than it might have been. Nevertheless, even with shields across their backs and with their helmets on, they still seemed two very weedy soldiers to any who might be looking at them with a critical eye.

But in the pre-dawn darkness, as they moved off alongside those others who were also transferring to the *Pride* that morning under Gui and Sir Richard's watchful eyes, they did not appear exceptional. Just two more down-at-heel spearmen off to join the crusade! The occasional sailors from other ships, out to empty their slop buckets into the harbour, did not give them a second look.

And at dawn, with the sun's rosy light just breaking over the little port, the two ships sailed.

Taking the earliest possible tide, before anyone else was really about, they slipped their moorings and, with sails still furled, they silently quanted themselves out of the harbour and into the Rade de Brest where the men raced up the ratlines and broke the sails out at last. There they caught the wind and made a clean passage back down the 'Throat' before turning South for Bordeaux in brilliant sailing weather, and were off and away down the long Atlantic coast in no time.

They had two more days of that as the weather stayed fair, the sun glistening brightly on the dancing shark-blue waters, lightly ruffled by a firm following wind that thrust both vessels forward 'til the water beneath their sterns was bubbling like a mountain stream and their great sails billowed out hard before them.

Days when the men lounged idly about the decks beneath an azure sky without their armour, wearing only their toughened leather breeks, delighted to give their sweaty bodies a thorough airing.

Days when the *Mary* spilled sufficient wind from her sails to allow the *Pride* to claw her way up beside her, a white bone in her teeth as she thrust through the blue-green waters so that the two could sail together, side by side,

408

and Gui could wave and shout across the narrow gap that separated him from Alicia, her track a blue-white bustle of torn sea, touched with deeper green.

Days when the two men who had been chosen to play the role of Lady Alicia and Agnes Fitzwalter amused themselves and their comrades by aping the presumed manners of the gentry, turning their Lady's fine 'breasts' into provocative pouting 'tits', by stuffing ever more woollen flocking down the front of their dresses and pushing out their chests, while swaying about the deck with their hands on their hips, 'til they had everyone falling about with laughter.

Otherwise the men on both ships spent their time checking and polishing their weapons, or in practice-fighting up and down the deck with spear and sword and battle axe under the critical eyes of their leaders and their giant Master-at-Arms, John Fitzurse.

They were now over a month behind their quarry, and even with a fast passage there was no chance of catching up with de Brocas before reaching Bordeaux! He would be long gone. But when they did, by God, but there would be a bloody reckoning!

Chapter 59...How the Corsairs pounced on the Red and Yellow Cogs.

On the second day out from Brest they came in sight of the Belle Île, off Quiberon Bay, with the huge mouth of the Loire Estuary ahead of them, just two sailing days away from reaching the Garonne River and Bordeaux at last.

Gui smiled ruefully at the recollection of all the frustrations they had been through since the night of the fire, and his own injury at the Baron's hands, and was just about to ask Master Thomas whether they would need to put in to Nantes for further supplies when a thin cry came down to them from the masthead: "Sail Ho! Fine on the starboard quarter!"

It was one of Tommy Blackwood's men high in the crow's nest who saw it first; a thin white sliver of sail on the horizon that seemed to hover there like a distant sea bird, never getting any nearer but not veering away either and had called down to the deck below, and the Master had hurried off to see for himself what was happening.

Within a few minutes he was back, with Father Matthew, concern writ large across his brows. "My Lord, I think we're being followed!" he said, shading his eyes as he looked out to sea. "But who or what she is I've no idea. She's too far off to make out any device."

"De Brocas?" Gui queried. "Out here?"

"Certainly out here, if he can manage it," Father Matthew replied quietly. "Far from prying eyes and any chance of passing help. But it will not be de Brocas who is running this pursuit. That will be left to an expert in sea craft and warfare!"

"Pirates then, do you think Master Thomas?" Gui asked quietly as they stood on the stern castle looking back the way they'd come. "We were warned they were out!"

"I can't say my Lord. It's possible, 'though they usually hunt in pairs, and it would have to be bold pirates who'd make an attempt on two ships so obviously travelling together. We are known in these parts as being well able to look after ourselves!

410

Anyway, the *Mary* and the *Pride of Beaulieu* have shallow bottoms and can go where other ships with deeper keels cannot. We can go amongst rocks closer inshore that are ideal for hiding amongst if things start looking really ugly. There aren't many who sail these waters that know their way around the rocks as we do, Master Robert and I. We'll not let you down My Lord, that I promise thee, by these finger bones!"

"I never doubted it, Master Thomas." Gui said with a smile, banging him on his broad shoulders. "But I have a mission to accomplish, and I want no bastard pirates to stand in my way. Time is most precious, and this is one case when I'd rather run than stay and fight. So crack on the sails, and let's show them a clean pair of heels. And signal Master Robert on the *Pride* to do the same. But, be careful Thomas. The *Mary* has proved herself to be the better sailor, and it would be ruinous indeed were we to lose touch with one another now."

And, leaving the captain by the huge tiller bar, he and Father Matthew swayed their way over to join their companions, looking back along the *Mary's* bubbling track and at the *Pride of Beaulieu* smashing through the waves behind them, the huge ram's head on her sails seeming determined to reach out and butt them.

"Trouble?" Richard asked, turning as they came up to him.

"Don't know," Gui replied, rubbing his hands. "Thomas thinks we are being followed."

"Followed?" He queried, throwing back his sleeves.

"Yes," Matthew said. "Master Thomas thinks that there is a ship out there on the horizon shadowing us, but with the wind behind us there is no way we can easily turn and find out. Anyway, we don't have the time for such luxuries. See, he is going to break out more sail and try to out-run it, as Sir Gui has asked him to."

With a roar to his crew Master Thomas rolled across the deck and began to loosen the heads'l sheets from the wooden cleats on the starboard bulwark, while his Mate did the same on the other side.

"Now my lads, lets shake the last reefs out of her. Let the wind fill her belly, then rope her down tight. Jump to it, you miserable whoreson brained oafs! I want to see this old tub really move. Rufus, layout the extra boom and sail across the bowsprit, and you two idlers draw up some water in the buckets and give that sail a soaking. Wet sails hold the wind better than dry! Come on, *come on!* I want to see the Loire before the sun sets, or I'll throw one of you

411

buggers over the side to lighten the ship. I carry no passengers on the *Mary*, so jump my beauties, *jump!*"

With a rush of bare feet and a great shout the crew ran to carry out their Captain's orders, so it was not long before the ship was carrying as much extra sail as there were sticks to bear it.

The difference was instantly noticeable, for instead of just one man on the great tiller bar, now two were needed to keep the *Mary* on her course as she barrelled through the waves. The pressure of wind and sea was enormous, and both helmsmen were forced to exert all their strength, their feet placed well apart on the straining deck, their arms like iron bars as they strove to hold the Mary to her course.

"Now you'll see her fly my Lords!" Thomas shouted as he moved back to re-join Gui and Sir Richard on the stern castle, alongside Father Matthew. "There isn't a vessel afloat can touch the *Mary* when she really has the wind in her apron. We'll leave that shadow far behind, you mark my words."

"Aye, providing nothing carries away. Look at the way the mast is bending, and the whole ship is quivering like a tree in a storm."

"Don't you worry about that stick, My Lord, it's weathered far more than this little breeze," Thomas said, hands on his hips, his body finely balanced on the balls of his feet as the *Mary* thrust her bluff way through the waves. "Finest Scot's pine that. I chose it myself when she was a-building in Southampton. By Our Lady, I'd be the laughing stock of the Cinque Ports if that went ...Hey Jamie Codling, Johnnie Peterson!" he roared down at his two helmsmen on the main deck, struggling with the tiller bar. "Keep her head up! If you veer a single point we'll be on the rocks off Hoedic island before I can crack my fingers. Master Adam!" He bellowed at his Mate. "Two more on the tiller, lad! Yarely my boys, *yarely!*"

In truth they really were creaming along, the waves hissing and boiling past the Red Cog's sides with the shore line of the Belle Île just coming up on their starboard side, as they took the inside channel between the Island and the mainland off their port side not more than a few miles or so away, and before long not even the masthead lookout could see the sail that had dogged them for so long.

★

412

Having made so much good ground Master Thomas continued to push the *Mary* hard, and with the wind in her coattails she and the *Pride* behind her burst through the waves in fine style, creaming through the blue water with the sun on their backs and the coastline of the Belle Île now beginning to slide by them in all its verdant lustre. But in the joy of their passage lay a danger that none had really expected, for as they passed between the Belle Île and the Île de Hoedic, the entrance to Quiberon Bay, with the Île de Houac and the Cardinals just beyond them on their port side, two long sleek galleys, with single banks of oars and a tall mast each with lateen sails, pounced on them.

Surging out to meet the *Mary* from behind the Isle of Hoedic, now lying fine off their port bow, they came head-on under full power, their oars flashing in the bright sunlight as they drove towards them. Their decks crammed black with men they looked exactly what they were; grim sea wolves whose only intent was pillage, rape and murder.

"Corsairs! My God, *Corsairs!*" Thomas shouted out, gesturing furiously with his hand. "It is as you suspected, Father! This whole thing's been nothing but a bloody trap! They'll be up with us sooner than you realise, my Lord, those bastards can really move, and if they once get on either side of us, as they will surely try to do, then we'll be in serious trouble."

"But that's just what we have planned for, Thomas!" Gui shouted at him. "Quickly now! Get those two young 'ladies' of ours up here fast. Up on the fore castle. Tell them to scream, point, wail and fling themselves about. What's the *Pride* doing, Father? Swiftly now, let me see."

Behind them the Yellow Cog was carrying all the sail she could and was less than half a cable away from them, everything billowing hard, when the galleys had sprung into sight. At once she put up her helm and began to bear away to port, towards the nearby Île de Houac and the ancient fortress that guarded it, her crew rushing up the ratlines and out across her yard arm to reef her sails and slow her down as she turned towards the shore.

For one heart stopping moment they thought the Corsairs would go for her too after all, as their swift advance seemed to stall with sudden indecision. But, no sooner had the *Pride* begun to fall away, than the two men wearing the girls' clothing appeared on the *Mary's* forecastle to caper and cry out, pointing outboard to the two sleek sea wolves that had appeared as if from no-where, and clinging on to one another in wildly affected terror.

And with that the two galley captains seemed to make up their minds as, with one accord, the two narrow-prowed vessels surged forward once more

413

towards the stout *Mary*, drums and crashing cymbals ringing out in a wild cacophony of sound…and the attack began.

★

"This is going to be very dangerous, Sir Gui," Matthew said urgently. "I've seen pirate ships like these in action before. They can turn on a silver penny, backwards or forwards, the wind means nothing to them. And see there!" He pointed, shaking his finger for emphasis. "By the look of things the leading one has a scorpion bolted and lashed to its deck. Soon she will cross our bows to come up on our starboard side; so there'll be a few pebbles about our ears presently."

"Look!" Gui shouted. "The other one is holding back. I bet they are waiting to see how well armed we are before they commit themselves. The moment they start throwing things our way have some of the men fall as if killed. We must lure them in to us if we can. If they hold off they may pound us to kindling with that catapult of theirs before we can ever get to grips with them."

"The fucking *bastards!*" Thomas called out over the crash and rattle of spray as the *Mary* thrust herself through the waves. "I've not seen their like in these waters before, so somebody must want you out of the way, and badly Sir Gui, or my name's not Thomas Blackwood! That bloody Baron has powerful friends, My Lord!"

"How long do we have before we are in range of that thing?" Sir Richard asked, watching the way the two sleek galleys moved towards them. "I have not seen one in action at sea before."

"Less time than you think, Sir Richard," Father Matthew answered him, "especially as we are carrying so much sail. They've timed it perfectly. Oh, what I wouldn't do to have my old harness on my back right now!"

Gui looked at him and smiled: "Father, you know that cannot be. But what you can do is prepare your knives and needles, for we are going to need your healing skills today more than your fighting ones, my friend. Go now and make ready your bandages and instruments, Father, and trust me to care for *you* this time!"

"Now you'll see, Sir Gui," Thomas said excitedly, looking keenly at the approaching galleys as the tall Benedictine made his way below. "See! They are splitting up, but I think I may yet be able to surprise them. We're

414

moving faster than they realise, and the *Mary* is broad and heavy. They may not have time to loose off more than two or three shots at us before we'll be amongst them, and if I can take out the leading one, the one with that oversized popper, then we have a real fighting chance."

"How will you do it?" Gui asked him.

"You leave that to me. I'm going to take the tiller myself, for this will take exact timing or we're finished. As for you, My Lords," he said, turning to the two knights with a smile. "You'd better get down amongst your men and get some harness on those broad backs of yours. I've a feeling we're going to have a very busy few minutes shortly!"

"Thank God we do not have the girls with us, Richard," Gui said darkly. "Love her as I do, Alicia is one responsibility I would not want to have right now. Agnes as well. God's Blood, but I pray that they are safe!"

"Don't worry, Gui. They have Allan-i-the-Wood, Hordle John and the Lions to care for them this day, and those two French fighters, they are in safe hands. Now, come on, it's time we dressed ourselves properly, don't you think? And this time I will wear my own colours on my back," he drawled, holding up his long cyclas. "My Sable Lion, Rampant and Guardant, with his red claws and tongue on his field of Ermine, to your Gules Rampant on his field of Silver! Very impressive don't you think? Hey, young Carslake, you idle hound," he shouted then to his squire. "Come and earn your daily crust with Simon by helping us to arm! Then arm yourselves and take station near the Master and protect the helm. With your lives if necessary!"

★

During the brief time of their conversation the two galleys had indeed separated, just as the Master had suggested they might, and there was feverish activity in the bows of the leading warship as her crew winched down the arm of their scorpion in preparation for their first shot. Suddenly they leapt back, its solid timber arm came slamming up, and the first rock was hurled on its way.

By then Gui and Richard were down among their men, feverishly drawing on their armour, helped by their squires, checking their weapons and marshalling their troops in the waist of the ship as they came to readiness, sending some to man the castles fore and aft and others up to the armoured crow's nest high above the mainsail with their crossbows. All around them the *Mary*'s crew were also busy arming themselves, drawing on thick leather and

415

iron reinforced byrnies and selecting the weapons of their choice from a great iron bound chest right abaft the main mast.

Then, with a sudden rush and whistle of compressed air, the first stone plunged into the sea with a terrific splash less than half a cable's length from her port side, to be greeted by jeers and shouts of derision from the men, some now running to take up their positions in the fighting castles, and up in the crow's nest high above the reeling deck.

But it had been no mean shot, and all knew that there would be several more before they could close the range sufficiently to take the fight directly to their nimble enemies.

Again the Scorpion's arm came swinging up, the stone it had flung turning over and over in its flight before plunging down towards its quarry. This time it was much closer, just hurtling past the mast, snapping some of the shrouds before crashing into the sea near enough to throw a tall column of spray across her sharply canted deck.

"Down you go, my boys," Gui roared at some half a dozen of his men on the stern castle, who dropped like stones about the deck. "Let the bastards think they have hurt us!"

All this time the three vessels were steadily converging on one another, with one still holding back half a cable's length behind; while the *Mary* churned through the seas, thrusting the short rollers aside with her sturdy wooden shoulders in blue-green cascades, the spume rising up to splash the men crouched down behind the timber mantlets they had thrown up around the *Mary*'s waist to raise the height of the bulwarks.

The two galleys acted likewise, their oars rising and falling faster and faster as they worked up to attacking speed, white bones in their teeth, green crescent flags rippling and snapping in the wind of their passage, their men thickly crowded along their decks as they prepared their final approach.

"Look out ahead!" Master Thomas roared to his men. "They're firing again. It'll be their last chance to hit us hard before we're down amongst them. So brace yourselves, they'll have our range now!"

Even as he spoke, there was a whistle in the air followed by an appalling crash up forward; and the *Mary* shuddered throughout her length as if she'd hit a reef. The wooden battlements and timbers of her forecastle flew up into the air like a giant's kindling; bowsprit, spar and sprits'l all disintegrating into mangled shards of wood and shreds of ravaged canvas. And as the great stone burst through her forecastle, so it hurled a handful of the *Mary*'s crew spinning to the main deck below, before smashing into the *Mary*'s stout inner

416

planking...there to bounce off, all energy spent, rolling around the Mary's deck a menace to all who struggled there. The men it had sent flying in a welter of arms and legs, thudding like rag dolls onto the main deck, their bodies shattered, their blood smearing the planking in long scarlet gashes.

"Get that bloody stone overboard!" Sir Richard bawled out. "Now, lads! Before it crushes someone's foot...get the dead overboard too, and drag the wounded to the sides!" He shouted to his Master-at-Arms. "See, boys! That other bastard is still holding back," he called out again, pointing to the other galley now less than half a cable's length behind its leader. "So down you go again, lads. Ten more should give them better heart!"

"Well done. Sir Richard," Thomas called out above the jeers and cries, as the great stone and their dead were heaved overboard, while the men fell about like shot rabbits. "That's done it. See how that other one is coming on now. Keen as mustard! Yarely done, my lads. *Yarely!*"

But in positioning herself for that final shot the leading galley had made a bad mistake. As she had backwatered furiously to give her engineers a better shot she had slowed considerably and now lay almost stationary in the sunlit waters of the narrow channel between the islands; and in doing so she'd taken no account of the real speed of her quarry, now fast bearing down on her with all the speed and agility of a runaway bull.

"*By God's Throat!*" the Master roared out, as he saw what had happened. "The silly Bastard has made a mistake! I have her! By God, *I have her!* Now my Moorish friends, let's see how you like a taste of your own black-hearted medicine?"

Throwing his weight against the tiller bar, two other of his crew helping, Master Thomas forced the *Mary* to alter course a few points, and with the wind right abaft her mainsail she bore down on the enemy vessel like an avenging Fury, as her Galley-Master desperately tried to re-start his rowers and manoeuvre his vessel out of the way.

But there was no escape, and with smashing impact the *Mary* crashed into the corsair galley, heeling her over as she struck her amidships, shivering her starboard oar banks to twiglets as she graunched along her side, bursting her bulwarks apart.

"Now, my beauties, **NOW!**" Thomas roared at his men, his eyes flashing in the bright sunlight, "Hack that anchor through and we'll send her to the bottom with a present of good English iron!"

Indeed his men had been waiting for just this moment and leaping up, two of them hewed with concentrated fury at the thick ropes that held the anchor fast to the *Mary*'s side with their axes while their comrades roared them on and howled insults at their enemies.

At the third blow the tautened hemp cracked apart and the anchor fell with a terrific *Crash!* full on the canted side of the enemy vessel, with such force that her timbers, already strained and broken, sprang apart like the rotted staves of an old barrel, bursting into fragments, and with a hissing roar the sea poured in and she fell on her side and began to sink.

With screams of terror the men who had been crowding her sides in preparation for their assault were cast headlong into the sea, and, weighted down with body armour and weapons, most went straight to the bottom. Those few who had managed to grasp onto some piece of the wreckage that now littered the water were no less fortunate; for those who were not sucked under by their vessel as she sank were swept away by the stiff current like so many corks, their despairing cries fading away to dismal whimpers of distress as they were carried farther and farther out to sea.

But the force of the collision had brought the *Mary* herself to a plunging halt, and with a wild thunder of kettle drums, a howl of trumpets and a mighty cheer, the other galley surged along her port side. Ropes and grapnels came snaking and whipping up over the *Mary*'s sides, and with that a furious battle began.

Chapter 60...How the Red Cog tore her enemies apart.

O f that desperate fight Gui had little clear recollection afterwards, for while his men in the two castles and higher up in the crow's nest made constant play with their bows, both cross and long, he and Sir Richard, with Master Thomas in their midst, his mighty body encased in thick iron plated leather, led their men against the enemy hordes that now swarmed onto the *Mary's* stout deck, howling for their blood.

Smash! Stab! Cut! Hack!

They hewed through flesh and iron as if they were parchment 'til their armour was red with blood and their blades were chipped. Gui and Sir Richard, shields in hand, bellowed encouragement to their men as back and forth across the bloodied planking they reeled, first one side and then the other giving ground. The fighting both fast and furious, the noise horrendous and screaming warriors on both sides falling in a spray of blood and bones.

Hemmed in by enemies, and hampered by the horse boxes and other piles of gear, Gui and his men took some little time to sort themselves out, and many fell, but soon they were able to present a united armoured front that the Saracens could not break. Again and again they hurled themselves at the steel line that fronted them, roaring their battle cries, faces made hideous by their rage and hatred as they fought their way onto the *Mary's* decks in an effort to swamp the defenders with sheer numbers. While most were armoured, many were not, and in minutes those were swiftly slain, bodies pierced by arrows or cut down by sword and battle axe, their blood gushing out across the deck as others rushed to fill their places, and always the fighting seemed to be centred on the two Christian leaders in their great barrel helms and snarling blazons: the Sable Lion of Richard L'Eveque and the Scarlet Lion of Gui de Malwood.

But particularly on Gui, who led from the front using his shield to force an opponent to open his body to his sword's thrusting, hacking blade: shearing arms from shoulders in a single terrifying blow, thrusting through body armour and boiled leather to skewer an enemy to the backbone, hewing through helmet and skull in a vile spray of blood and shattered brain pan.

So Sir Gui de Malwood fought until his sword had lost its edge and was thick with blood, when he changed it with his squire in favour of a flanged mace looped securely over his right wrist and gripped in his strong hand. Thus re-armed, and with his laminated shield on his other arm, he plunged back into the fray, warding off blows with the one and doing dreadful execution with the other, for wielded with all his strength his iron headed mace was a truly brutal weapon, crunching the skulls on which it fell in a splatter of brains and splintered bone; and crushing the arms and shoulders of any corsair on whom it landed.

Bigger than any other warrior from either vessel, the Lion of Malwood stood head and shoulders above the howling, bloody press like a great oak in a storm, his arm rising and falling like the hammer blows from Thor himself as he smashed and battered at his enemies. The sweat pouring off him, his shield hacked and scored, his helmet dented and his armour filled with Saracen arrows like a porcupine and running with blood, he was his enemies' worst nightmare come to real life. No Djinn could compare with the horror of Sir Gui's battle rage as he stamped and smashed his way forward through the howling ranks of his foes, the flanged head of his great mace thick with hair, torn flesh and bloodied sinews. Nothing seemed to be able to stop him, and the pile of mangled bodies grew like a wall around him 'til he was forced to clamber onto their blood-boltered remains to get at his next victims.

Thus he took the fight to the Corsairs, and in a series of short, sharp rushes the Malwood Lions began to press forward at last, roaring '*A Malwood! A Malwood!*' as they barrelled and thrust their way into the press of raging figures all around them; wielding their weapons with all the fury at their command and leaving a trail of death and human debris in their wake.

The din was horrendous: the clash of arms, the whistle and thunk of arrows, the murderous battle cries, the screams and howls of the wounded, and above all the constant thunder of the Turkish drums and cymbals and their brazen trumpets. The noise was appalling…and the stench of blood, piss and faeces hung over the stinking waist of the *Mary* like some foul miasma.

To Gui, with his great fighting helm on his head, his horizon seemed to be bounded by a sea of snarling black and brown faces twisted in their murderous rage, intent only on the slaughter of everyone on board the *Mary*. Yet the more he killed the more seemed to appear. Yelling and screaming defiance in their own cursed tongue, brandishing their weapons like flails, and urged on by the relentless pounding of the great kettle drums that the Saracens always used when going into battle, the human tide seemed endless.

But in fact their enemies were beginning to waver.

Unable to withstand the fury and shock of the constant charges against them, they were being forced steadily backwards to where their own vessel lay, still lashed to the Red Cog's bluff sides.

★

When the two galleys sprang into view, all on board the Pride of Beaulieu was sudden exhilaration or outright fear.

At once, Robert heaved on the tiller bar to turn them away towards the nearest land, the Île de Houac, and the safety of its ancient fortress and its host of little islets, while his men raced up to reef the sails as he spilled the wind out of them to slow the vessel down. Shallow bottomed or not, there were many rocks along the shoreline, and he had no desire to tear the bottom out of her if he could help it.

Swiftly Allan-i-the-Wood mustered his men in the waist, while John of Hordle led his lions up onto the wide stern castle, sending some to the forecastle above the bows and two up into the crow's nest, with a crossbow apiece and a goodly supply of heavy bolts with which to arm them.

Alicia and Agnes, still wearing their chain and leather armour, joined the men on the stern castle rather than be hustled to the Master's cabin just beneath, while the Cousins were told off to guard Robert of Christchurch's back as he handled the great tiller, with two of Allan's men on either side of him for good measure.

"*Sweet Jesus!*" Alicia exclaimed, white faced, as she looked out at the *Mary*. "Did you see how swiftly they moved? And so many men, Agnes? And all those rowers? I had no idea it would be like this!"

"Corsairs!" Agnes Fitzwalter breathed out appalled, her voice hushed with fear. "God aid us, Sweetheart," she added clutching her chest. "But my heart almost fails me! They are the worst, my Lady," she said, trembling. "The very worst!"

"No matter, Honeyone," Alicia said to her briskly. "Fearsome or not we must be brave. Our boys have enough to do without having to start worrying about us! And they are good men, Agnes. Hordle John is the best swordsman in the castle, Allan-i-the-Wood is courageous and resourceful; and the Cousins are proven fighters. Keep our heads and we will be fine! Sweet wine of Christ. Look at them go!"

★

Jules and Lucas, standing on the quarter deck before the Master's cabin door, the Master himself on the tiller bar before them, could not believe their luck! It was almost as if it was all meant to be. All they had to do when the time came was put on their green arm bands, drape the remaining large piece of green silken over the great rudder and hang on until Sheik El Nazir could reach them. Hacking down the Master and his guards just beforehand; for there was no doubt in Jules' minds that it would be El Nazir himself who would come...not some other Emir!

"Have you got that spare bit of green?" He called to his cousin above the shouts and yells all around them.

"Yes. Stuffed just inside my jacket! The armbands also. Will he come?"

"El Nazir? Without a doubt. And we will know it too, for these heathens make more noise when they attack than the whole Worshipful Company of bloody Blacksmiths! Drums, cymbals, trumpets...you have never heard the like I assure you. And his flag is green and gold."

"What then?" his cousin asked. "How can we be certain they won't fucking kill us along with all the rest? And what about the girls?"

"God's Bones, Lucas! Do you never stop worrying? Leave that to me. Of course we can't be certain. But with the prize they have come for struggling in our arms, and all that lot out there screaming bloody murder and fighting for their lives, then will not be the time for them to do so. And as for the girls? - Don't you worry about them! When it gets really hot up there they will be sent down to this cabin, you can be sure of it; specially for us to guard," and he laughed. "As I have said before, you miserable sod! Concentrate on the job in hand and we will be fine! Just take care not to insult their God with some stupid arsehole comment from your foul mouth!"

"Fucking Hell, Coz," Lucas said with a huge grin, "But I'd give a fine ruby to see that bastard Fitzurse's face when he finds out the truth about us! He will be foaming mad for certain!"

And they both laughed, standing right before the girls' cabin, legs apart and nimble on their feet, drawn swords in their hands and the scarlet Lions-Rampant of their enemies leaping off their chests.

★

On board the *Mary*, with their enemies beginning to scramble backwards and victory in their grasp, Gui and Sir Richard gathered their men together for a last final push to clear their decks.

But it was not to be!

For at that moment, whirling down on them from nowhere, a great stone crashed with horrifying impact full onto the *Mary*'s stern castle, smashed through the wooden bulwarks, hurling baulks of timber and shattered bodies high into the air in all directions before crashing into the sea with a monstrous splash.

And with a demonic howl of trumpets and a thunderous crash of drums, a third galley, unseen in all the tumult around them, swept by the *Mary's* stern from behind the Belle Île, packed with yelling, roaring, fighting men, a catapult at one end, a huge ballista at the other and great flags in green and gold with crossed scimitars in silver rippling from her mastheads.

Long hulled, with twin banks of oars, fifty aside, twin masts and lateen sails, this was a true fighting dromond from the Circle Sea. Packed with fighters and armed with a great ram of sharpened bronze that thrust out from her bows below the waterline she was a terrifying enemy, and even as she rushed past them her engineers were already preparing to fire her secondary artillery - like a giant Roman ballista rather than a scorpion, it was a low trajectory weapon, mounted on a simple turntable, and could be swung round to face in any direction.

Moments later she fired.

Flying almost horizontally from less than half a cable, the great stone whirled over the *Mary's* port quarter and crashed into her starboard side up forward, just behind her bows, with all the force of Thor's hammer, breaking Merlin's horse box into pieces as it flew by, and shaking the whole vessel to her very keel plate. Punching its way through the inner planking it bored right into the *Mary's* heavy starboard-side strakes where it lost all energy and stuck fast. Gripped by the tough oak, it thrust out of her gored starboard side like some foul stony pustule, water spurting in around its jagged edges every time the *Mary* heeled in the heavy Atlantic rollers. Gui and his men, stunned by so sudden and violent an assault, not knowing if they were to face another horde of enemies, paused for a moment in shocked dismay...and their defence wavered.

Moments later, the great warship fired again with her ballista as she swept by without stopping. Her weapon now trained astern, the stone smashed into the *Mary's* portside with devastating effect.

Whistling over the deck of the Corsair galley still grappled there, it shattered the Mary's port timbers right to the waterline so that the sea exploded all around the men fighting there, making the Red Cog leap and shudder again as it burst through into her waist. In a wild maelstrom of arms, legs and whirling planks and stanchions, the great stone ripped the *Mary's* port side open as easily as a hunter would gralloch a deer, casting down Corsair and Christian alike so that the sea, now red with their blood, quite threatened to overwhelm her.

423

Taking heart from the carnage caused by the dromond's brutal attack, the Saracen Corsairs redoubled their efforts to seize the Red Cog, fighting even more furiously than before in expectation of fresh support from their large consort, driven on again by the ceaseless pounding of their great drums. But the dromond did not stop to grapple the *Mary* and pour in the fresh troops the Corsair attackers so badly needed. With a roar of defiance, having so fiercely hammered her in passing, she swept by in pursuit of the Yellow Cog ahead of them, now flying a great flag of green silk off her fat rounded stern.

On board the *Mary*, the pause in the defenders attack was only a brief respite for their enemies.

Immediately realising their new attacker was not about to board them, Gui's men took a fresh grasp of their weapons, and, despite the damage that the *Mary* had suffered, and the shock of it…sea water now sloshing all around their feet, Sir Richard's charger free and fighting mad and yet another great stone rolling about amongst them…they assaulted their enemies again with renewed rage and valour; and unable to resist this fresh violent pressure, the Corsairs wilted - and quite suddenly the lust for battle went out of them.

Gui, fighting like a madman at the head of his men, with Sir Richard in close support, felt the difference immediately: "On them! **On them!**" He roared through the breath holes of his helmet. "Advance Lions! They Fail. **They Fail!** Now, trumpeters blow me the charge!"

And up through that screaming mêlée the brazen shout of Gui's trumpets soared into the brilliant sky above: '*Tan!-Tan!-Tara!-Tantaraaa! - Tan!-Tan!-Tara!-**Tantaraaa!***… the ringing, piercing '*Come to me! Come to me!* **Come to meee!** call that whipped-up his men's hearts to a blazing fury and brought them plunging across the *Mary's* bloodied deck to slay their enemies and hurl them back into the sea.

With that wild call still ringing in their ears Gui and his men began to fight their way down from the shattered castles fore and aft of the ship, driving the Saracens before them like cattle for the autumn slaughter as they came in at them hand and foot, yelling their war cry, '*A Malwood! A Malwood!*' And flensing at their opponents mercilessly with their swords and axes in a violent orgy of blood letting and unfettered battle-rage they thrust into their wilting enemies until suddenly, with howls of terror, the Corsair pirates turned and fled, many dropping their weapons in their desperate attempt to escape…but it was hopeless. Blocked in on every side they were cut down to the last man.

No quarter was given.

Those who were too wounded to fight further were simply cast over the side to thrash their lives away in a sea already stained red with the life-blood of the many who'd gone before them; and as the decks were cleared Gui and Sir Richard forced their way urgently through the press of wild figures to where his Ship-Captain stood bandaging his arm, using his teeth to pull the knot he was making tight against his bleeding flesh.

"Quick, Master Thomas," Gui shouted, taking off his helmet. "Fire pots! Do you have any? Oil and wicks? Anything that will burn! If we can cast some fire in amongst these fucking bastards while they are still disorganised we'll do for them completely. She'll go up like a tinder box and we won't have the problem of trying to sink her!"

"Aye Sir Gui, good thinking. I always keep some ready in a chest beside the mast, together with a tinderbox and a good supply of flints."

"*Good!* Go, now, with John Fitzurse," he said urgently. "Before it's too late! Sir Richard and I will try and get up onto our stern castle and see where that bastard dromond has got to. And will someone grab that bloody horse...and heave that other fucking stone over board!"

The next moment, while Thomas Blackwood and John Fitzurse ran across the littered deck to set about seizing the fire pots, so others closed in on Merlin, still stamping and squealing with fear and rage, and on the loose stone that had ripped the great hole in the Mary's side; Gui and Sir Richard rushed to clamber up what was left of her shattered stern castle, stepping over the dead and injured as they went.

Seizing hold of a section of timber battlements they looked out.

Off the port side the galley that had grappled them was already beginning to work clear of the *Mary*, those who had managed to escape the slaughter having hacked through the ropes that had held her fast and were now desperately poling their galley away from the Red Cog, despite the brisk fire that Gui's men had opened on them from above. But within seconds Fitzurse had raised a small flame from the tinder box, and thrusting the oil-soaked wicks of the fire pots into its bright fire, he and Thomas were already hurling them down onto the Corsair' decks in a rain of fire, where they crashed and burst into eager flames that ran in burning streams of oil across the pitch-caulked decking.

First the rigging caught and then the sails, the fire spreading rapidly around the ship while her men ran panic stricken amongst the thick smoke that began to billow out from every corner. Many, in desperation, cast themselves into the sea, their robes on fire, while from below her deck came the screams and cries of the terrified rowers.

As the fire caught hold she was soon one huge mass of leaping, towering flames, burning furiously from stem to stern, the flames roaring and hissing as the sea fought to quench them, her crew below decks howling as their bodies roasted in the flames that had engulfed them. But, beyond the scenes of devastation, of shattered timbers, smashed oars and broken bodies immediately around them, and beyond the fiercely burning galley off their port side, the *Pride* was still doing her best to clear away from the action, hotly pursued by the dromond, her oars flashing in the sunlight as they drove her forward.

The Saracen's sleek greyhound to the fat hare, drawn from the *Mary* by a great piece of green material that was waving from the canary yellow cog's stern like a distant flag.

Then...disaster!

When she was just moments from safety, the *Pride of Beaulieu* inexplicably threw up her helm, and staggering into the wind with her great sail flapping, she was instantly in irons unable to move, and lost all way immediately.

Sweeping level with the *Pride* the dromond now brought its weapons into play again and in quick succession put two great stones into her, the one smashing her forecastle apart in shower of smashed timber and falling men, the other crashing through the waist of the ship, tearing out whole sections of her sides and bulwarks above the waterline and casting them into the sea. Next...with one set of oars backing as the other drove forward, the dromond suddenly stopped and spun round in a moment, to surge back on her tracks and cross the Yellow Cog's stern, where she firmly grappled her, lying across the *Pride of Beaulieu*'s rudder, now held flat to starboard, like a huge sea anchor.

And then the enemy boarded her.

From his vantage point on the *Mary*'s shattered stern-castle, beside himself with impotent rage, Gui roared and pounded the *Mary*'s broken sides as he and Sir Richard were forced to watch, helpless, while their men fought furiously with the Saracens across the water.

"*God's Blood!*" Gui bellowed as Father Matthew rushed up to join them. "What has happened? Why didn't they board us when they had the chance? They had us cold, but she never stopped, just pulled away and leaped down on the *Pride*!"

"I don't know, Sir Gui. But what is that great piece of green she has now flying off her stern?" Matthew cried out, pointing furiously. "Green is the colour of Islam! From where has that come? Surely it is a lure, and they have stooped to it like a hunting falcon on a heron!"

"*Splendour of God*, Thomas!" Gui roared out in anguish, hammering his fists on the shattered bulwark. "That must be treachery! *God's Throat! We are betrayed!*"

"Can we not make some headway here?" Sir Richard broke in desperately to Father Matthew who had come running up to join them. "Lady Alicia and Agnes are over there. Can we do nothing to help them?"

"No, Sir Richard," the tall monk replied sharply. "We can't! The *Mary* is trailing wreckage on every side, and water is pouring on board each time she rolls or dips her bows. We are as close to sinking as makes little matter. If we try to sail her now she will surely go down like a stone!"

"*God's Blood,* Richard!" Gui called out desperately, as his guard commander climbed higher up the Mary's broken side "What is happening over there? Why is no-one in control? What are our leaders doing?"

"All they can, Gui!" Sir Richard called back to him then, pointing to where the dromond lay across the *Pride*'s broad stern. "See! Our men are still fighting, I can see their bolts flying into the enemy. Look! Look!" he called out again, excitedly. "Even now she is cutting herself free and backing away. They have driven her off. Oh, bravely done, boys! *Bravely done!*"

Chapter 61... What happened aboard the Yellow Cog.

O
n board the *Pride of Beaulieu* those gathered on the fore and stern castles had watched in awe as the whole attack had developed.

They had groaned and cried out when the *Mary* was hit by the galley's scorpion, and roared on their comrades as she had then hurled herself into the Corsair's side, shouting out and hurrahing as the shattered oars flew up into the air, followed by the crash of her great anchor plunging into its side. And they had jumped up and down with excitement as the enemy vessel had then rolled over and sunk. Then, when the second galley grappled her, they shouted and jeered afresh at their hated enemies, cheering whenever they saw a Saracen fall to the sleet of arrows that flew across at them, and crying out when one of their own men fell to the deck.

So caught-up with the action were they that no-one saw the great dromond surge out from the far point of the Belle Île, its great banks of oars flashing in the bright sunlight, until it was too late, and they shouted out, first in disbelief, as it smashed three great stones into the *Mary*'s helpless sides, then in horror when it dug in its oars and spun towards them.

But in fact the Yellow Cog was far from finished.

Expertly steered by her Master, Robert Christchurch, she dipped and turned around the rocks that even now were beginning to appear above the sea as she swiftly scuttled towards the safety of the shores of the Île de Houac, and of the small castle that defended it.

Then, minutes after the second galley had burst into raging flame off the port side of the *Mary*, and the *Pride of Beaulieu* was almost amongst the cluster of rocks and islets off the coast of Houac, there was a dreadful, piercing scream and the Yellow Cog suddenly threw up her helm, turning sharply up into the wind, her great sail flapping helplessly against her mast, as the sound of sword on sword rang through the ship, along with the shouts and cries of men and the wild screams of terrified women.

★

I
t was after the Dromond attacked the *Mary* that everything on board the Yellow Cog changed.

The moment the powerful corsair warship made her appearance, her great green and gold flags fluttering from her mastheads, Lucas Fabrizan swung into action, pulling a huge piece of green silk out from behind his shield where he had kept it hidden, along with the two armbands he had been given months earlier, he slipped one arm band up over his upper forearm, handed the other to his cousin, Jules Lagrasse, and then leaped for the stern of the ship.

With everyone intent on maintaining the *Pride's* course, or up in the fore and aft castles watching the attack on the Mary develop, no-one was watching the two men standing right back from the steersman, and it took only a moment of effort for them to tie the soft material to a couple of cleats on either side of the great tiller beneath the stern castle, so that it billowed out behind them like green smoke.

And there they remained until the dromond turned towards them when, minutes later, John of Hordle, the giant swordsman whom Gui had put in charge of his men onboard the *Pride*, brought Alicia and Agnes down to the Master's cabin and handed them over to Jules Lagrasse for their immediate protection. By then the Yellow Cog, with her Master at the helm and two of Allan Wood's men on either side of him, was within half a cable of reaching safety, when Jules and Lucas showed their true colours at last.

With their swords already drawn they stepped up behind Allan's men and without warning brutally hewed them to the deck in a spray of blood and severed sinews that splattered everyone...at the very moment that Alicia, anxious to see what was happening on deck, opened her cabin door.

Expecting to see the two men whom Allan-i-the-Wood had ordered to guard the Master, standing close by...she was in time to see the Cousins, each now with a wide green band on his right arm, hack them both to death instead!

And before she could scream or shout out a warning, even as the *Pride's* Master turned in horror at the scarlet rain that fell all over him, Lucas drew back his sword and struck Robert Christchurch down with a massive blow to the head, bursting his brain pan apart in a shower of bloodied gruel and shards of bone, before stepping forward and thrusting his sword through his body for good measure, twisting his blade as he pulled it out, spilling his intestines across the bloody deck as did so.

And as her Master fell the *Pride* threw up her helm and went out of control...and Alicia screamed.

A wild, piercing, shrieking cry that brought Agnes Fitzwalter running from the cabin, only to be caught by Jules Lagrasse with his shield arm and pulled to his side, even as Lucas struck Alicia with the pommel of his sword, felling her to the deck with a single awful blow and cutting off the frightful noise as though with a knife.

Hearing Alicia scream Allan-i-the-Wood turned, saw what was happening, and rushed with drawn sword towards them, followed immediately by the men nearest him, and by Bouncer with his fighting collar round his neck…and all hell broke out around them.

Unarmed, though still armoured, there was little Agnes Fitzwalter could do with Alicia thrust unconscious into her arms, except kick and scream which she did lustily; but without some kind of weapon she could not bring real help to Allan and his men as they struggled to get at the two Frenchmen from between the heavy wooden timbers that supported the stern castle, Bouncer leaping and snarling beside them, ready to savage any enemy he could get his huge teeth into.

Stab! Stab! Cut and Block! The two Frenchmen men fought like demons, Alicia and Agnes bundled up behind them, their swords flicking out, their shields parrying every blow made against them, as they shouted and roared their defiance of Allan-i-the-Wood and Hordle John. And with the two girls so close beside them no archer dared try a shot for fear of striking either one of them.

Then, moments later, the great Dromond attacked them.

The two stones she hurled struck the *Pride* with such force that the whole ship quivered and bucked beneath them and men fell about like toy soldiers; the forecastle was smashed into shattered fragments, and a whole section of her bulwarks ripped away as if it had been wattle and not good English oak, casting men and weapons everywhere.

Then came the arrows.

Not the thick, heavy bolts of a crossbow, but the lightly barbed arrows of the Saracens that filled the warm air with the sound of bees, but had a vicious, waspish sting that could as easily put out an eye as gouge the face and neck, forcing the fighting Lions to raise their shields and drop their heads, just as the great dromond swung against their stern, and grappling irons came winging up to bind them close.

Moments later, led by a tall Saracen in Christian mail and pointed helmet, they were boarded by a scrambling horde of yelling, screaming infidel Corsairs: Turks, Arabs, and black infidel warriors from Morocco, Algiers and Tunis, even fighting Bedu from the desert. The most brutal men from along the Barbary Coast and beyond who had joined Sheik El Nazir for the joy of fighting and taking booty, all of whom were merciless killers whose very name struck terror into all who sailed the Circle Sea.

"*To me, you Lions!*" Agnes screamed out desperately above the tumult. "*To me! To me!*"

" *A Malwood! A Malwood!*" came the deep reply as Hordle John swept his men forward to drive their enemies off the deck and rescue the girls before they could be taken. "*Advance, Lions!* **Advance!**" he roared, his sword thrusting and cutting, piercing an Arab belly here, hewing a Moroccan arm off there; blocking a Turkish scimitar with his shield, before hacking the man's head off in a fountain of blood with a vicious, swingeing blow that no man could parry.

And right in the stern Bouncer fought beside his master as fiercely as any armoured man, his jaws red with blood, his fur matted with it as he too went for his enemies with eyes aflame and mouth agape his great teeth as ready to rend and tear a Corsair's flesh as willingly as any wolf his master might have cornered in the Forest...all striving to reach Alicia and Agnes across the *Pride*'s swaying deck, already running red with the blood of the wounded and the slain.

Pressed back against the tall stern post by the leaping, twisting figures of Jules and Lucas, as they hacked and parried and fought with all their skill and energy to keep their attackers at bay, Agnes, with Alicia now groggy and drooping at her side, could do little more than shout and shove mightily, but the two men were so strong and well armoured that nothing she could do would move them.

Then suddenly, before Allan and his men could break through their guard, under harsh, urgent orders from the Saracen leader on board, suddenly there were hands all over her, and both she and Alicia, the White Rose of Malwood, were both lifted off the Yellow Cog's deck, arms pinioned to their sides, and passed like bundles of carpet over her stern and down onto the great open deck of the corsair warship followed, moments later, by the two Frenchmen, the Dromond's boarding captain, and those of his men whom the Malwood Lions had not slain.

And all the time the drums beat and the trumpets and cymbals brayed and clashed.

Within seconds the grappling lines were cut through, and men in baggy green trousers ran up with long poles to quant the dromond off the *Pride*'s stern, despite many falling to the bolts and clothyard shafts the Malwood Lions again and again fired into them.

Agnes Fitzwalter, tightly held by her captors, kicked and struggled desperately to get free, shouting and screaming all the time, until silenced by a vicious blow to her belly; the Lady Alicia, almost recovered, doing her best to follow suit.

But it was useless.

With a sudden deep **boom!** both banks of oars rose up as one out of the side of the ship where they had been laid and flashed down into the deep blue of the ocean and, with a wild surge of power, the great Galley leaped forward. Swinging round she left the *Pride*, battered but still afloat, a stream of arrows pursuing her, and sped across the sea towards where the *Mary* lay, broken and sinking, the sun high overhead, the men aboard her shouting their rage, and beckoning them to come and fight.

But that was not her intent.

★

Powerless to intervene and with the *Mary* floundering, barely still afloat, Gui was not clear at first as to what was happening.

From the moment the great galley had appeared, to her attack on the Yellow Cog, had seemed but a handful of minutes. Yet here she was already pulling away again, and turning to attack them.

"**Beware Gui!**" Father Matthew shouted out fiercely. "Pull your men back to either end of the ship. Every fighting Dromond has a great ram beneath her bowsprit. If she gets that into us we will be finished!"

But the young Lord of Malwood could not bring himself to speak, for even as the great warship came rushing in on them, a bright bone of spray in her teeth, so a huge white flag of Truce broke from her mainmast and with a sudden move of her oars she turned and came to a surging halt, not thirty yards from where the *Mary* lay wallowing in a sea of wreckage, smashed oars, dead bodies, torn sails and trailing shrouds and halliards...while Gui stood there unable even to move.

For, on the galley's broad fighting deck, Alicia was standing, Agnes by her side.

Still in her tattered armour the Lady Alicia de Burley held her head up defiantly, her face streaked with blood where Lucas had struck her, Agnes drooping beside her, both held tightly in the hands of the two Frenchmen, Jules Lagrasse and Lucas Fabrizan. They, heads back and laughing, shook their prisoners mercilessly at their friends on board the *Mary*, two huge men standing fore-square behind them, each with a great scimitar cocked over his massive shoulder, ready to cut down each prisoner in an instant should any of Gui's men deny the white flag that flew above them. While all on the *Mary* raged and shook their fists in helpless fury at those who had so wickedly betrayed them.

Close by, in a long tunic of red and gold over wide blue leggings, a turban of white silk on his head with a single massive ruby in its centre stood a man of medium height and build, with the confidant air of command in every fibre of his being. Stepping forward he threw up his hand and all around him was stilled.

"I am Sheik El Nazir," he called across in perfect Frankish. "I have a message from the Lord Baron Sir Roger de Brocas of Narbonne and Gruissan, for the Lord of Malwood."

"I am the Lord of Malwood," Gui roared back swiftly. "What does that Man-of-Blood say to me, who has murdered my parents, and uses common pirates and the wickedness of evil men to seize that which he failed to capture for himself?"

"The Lord of Narbonne bids me tell you that he has the prize he came for," the Corsair leader answered him derisively, pointing to Alicia, still standing upright despite the treatment she had suffered. "Through her he will claim all that is his by right, and from her body raise up a new line to follow him. She is yours no longer. To the victor the spoils!"

"For now, El Nazir, that may be so," Gui shouted back at him defiantly. "But not for long! Know that you have seized the Ward of King Richard of England, and my Bride-to-be. I did not know Islam made war on women? Release them both now and spare yourself much pain. No stone else will be left unturned to seek you out, I promise you!"

"You are the one who will suffer pain, Infidel, not I!" the great Corsair leader called back sharply, ignoring Gui's threat. "King Richard is *nothing* to me," he shouted. "And this Lady is my prize of war." And with a wave of dismissal he bellowed: "Take them down!" Turning without another word to leave the deck, while Gui and his companions stamped their feet and shouted out in fury.

No sooner had El Nazir disappeared than the air shook to the solid ***thump!*** of a mighty drum deep within the dromond, and immediately her oars rose up into the air as one.

"*Noooo!*" Gui cried out, the sound dragged from his very soul. "***Noooo!***"

But the next thud came, and the next, and with them the oars swept down and up and down again, each mighty thud following on as the great galley began to move, faster and faster with every stroke, the oars in perfect unison, carving great parallel whorls of blue and white water as they thrashed the ocean into foam.

"Alicia! *Alicia!*" Gui cried out in fury, as Jules Lagrasse dragged her across the deck, screaming out Gui's name her hands reaching out to him in desperate supplication; poor Agnes hauled off behind her, her feet dragging along the smooth planking as she was removed, all resistance knocked out of her.

"I love you! *I love you!*" Gui shouted out in anguish across the widening gap, leaping down and rushing across the *Mary's* bloodied deck to her shattered forecastle, the drums beating faster and faster as the dromond picked up speed: "I will come for you! *I will! I will!*"

And, finally, his sight blurred with tears, he heard her beloved voice calling out to him for the last time, like a gull's cry on the wind, clear and piercing in its agony: "I love you, my darling! I love you! *I love you! Remember me! Remember meeee!*"

And in that moment she was gone.

Historical Note

The Third Crusade is the one most associated with Richard. He did set out with Philip Augustus, King of France from Vézalez on 4th July 1190, as the book says he did, and his travel journey was exactly as described by Father Matthew and the two Kings did not get on at all. Richard was a born warrior, Philip simply wasn't...but he was cunning and subtle, where Richard was open and straightforward. It made Philip good at winning the Peace! Richard's exploits in the Holy Land were simply amazing, as good as any Blockbuster Movie today, as you will discover later in the series.

The Conqueror's great Forest *was* vast, and still covers a huge area, after all he cleared out seventy villages to create it! Lyndhurst, now a busy town, still remains the only substantial one left in it. Tyrrell's Ford is real, now a hotel, and the fords, there are actually two of them, are still there. And real also was Sir Walter Tyrrell whose name it bears, and who fled the Forest after he shot the Red King as described, and whose death stone, The Rufus Stone, is just about a mile from Malwood Castle...but did not exist until the 18th Century. William's death remains a matter of dispute: was it an accident or was it murder? The real truth will never be known. Certainly Tyrell was never pursued, and his family in England did do very well out of Henry I...the younger brother who took his place and was known in later life as 'The Lion of Justice'!

The great Cistercian Monastery at Beaulieu is now a splendid ruin and well worth a visit, as is Bucklers Hard the ship-works made famous in the eighteenth century for building fine warships for Nelson's navy. I have the monastery full of busy life at the time of this story, but in fact it wasn't founded until 1205 by King John, though its first Abbot was indeed Abbott Hugh. The Cistercians were great wool merchants, and wine producers, as well as monks, shipping their produce far and wide so Bucklers Hard was in operation long before it became famous for warships in Napoleonic times.

Malwood Castle, and Alicia's home, Burley castle, are both real…but are iron age forts. Castle Malwood still has spectacular earthen banks, but the stone castle as described in the story is based on Bodiam Castle in Sussex which sits in its own lake and is another wonderful place to visit.

Though Gui and his family and friends are strictly my invention, the events through which they move and the people, like Prince John, Eleanor of Aquitaine, Richard Lion Heart, Philip of France, Saladin, El Raschid – The Old Man of the Mountains – and the Assassins were all very real…as was the plot to have King Richard murdered while he was in Outremer, only for some reason the contract was changed and it was Conrad of Montferrat, Heir to the Kingdom of Jerusalem, whom the Assassins killed and for which Richard was blamed.

The Benedictines, the Black Monks, were every bit as influential and learned as the story makes them out to be; and Ellingham Priory was an 'Alien' House of the Benedictine Order, later suppressed by Henry V in 1414 And, of course, the Church was hugely venal in many ways as The Lady mused at the Betrothal dinner…witness the Borgia Popes! And the tales of Pope Sergio III are all too horribly true!

The Battle of Hattin in 1187 was an absolute disaster from which the Crusaders in the Holy Land never recovered, despite all that Richard could do, though they hung on to their coastal castles until Acre, seized by Richard in that Summer of 1191on July 12th, was finally re-captured after a terrible siege almost exactly a hundred years later, on May 18th 1291!

Glossary

Abigail	An 'abigail' is the generic name for a young female servant, but most 'abigails' often became highly valued close personal servants, even much loved companions, like Agnes, whose care was given for love not just to order.
Actium	Battle of Actium between Mark Anthony and Octavius...later the Emperor Augustus, first Emperor of Rome...following the murder of Julius Caesar. Major sea battle that Mark Anthony lost because Cleopatra panicked and ordered her fleet to retreat, when it should have attacked!
An 'Alien' House	For foreign monks, usually a Priory, where the 'Mother House' for those who lived there was overseas. 'Alien' Houses paid no taxes to the Crown and Henry V suppressed them all by Act of Parliament in 1414.
Apollo	The Roman and Olympian God of Light and of the Sun, who drove his flaming chariot across the sky. Synonymous with Helios, an earlier Titan God of the Sun and his brother Hyperion, the Titan God of Light; all worshipped in the same way. The Celtic equivalent was Lugh.
Ashlar	Blocks of smoothly worked stone, every face a flat perpendicular.
Aurora	The Roman Goddess of the Dawn and herald of the Sun.
Bailey (The)	This was the courtyard, sometimes huge and often down to pasture, that lay within the encircling walls and separated the Gatehouse entrance to a castle from the final defensive fortress itself, at this time often built on a great mound of earth called a 'Motte'. Moats full of water...Mottes hills of earth! By the time of this story the castle Motte was being replaced by massive stone Keeps: London, Dover, Rochester...sometimes called a Donjon and, because of the Crusades, being built round instead of square...like Windsor, Orford

437

and York. The Bailey contained all the buildings necessary for the castle: stables, forge, dovecote, storage barns etc, and was the final refuge for the local people in the event of an attack.

Bailiff

A man appointed by a Lord to work with the Steward and the Reeve to manage an estate. He comes midway between both, and had wide powers to fine and punish the Manor workers. The Bailiff, with the Steward, determined what work was to be done...the Reeve then managed it all, and the workers, supported by the Bailiff.

Baldric

The belt that carries a sword.

Ballista

Roman style stone throwing machine, could also fire a heavy iron-headed bolt, a torsion machine worked by ratcheted arms and twisted animal sinews.

Bears

There were bears in the great forests of England right up to the Conquest and beyond, but not by the time Alicia fled into the Forest! However there *are* wild brown bears still in the Pyrenees, similar to the Grizzly bear from the Rocky Mountains. Now sadly very few in numbers, which the French Government want to increase from a stock of similar bears still wild in Eastern Europe. Their farmers are not impressed!

Benedictines

Black monks...because of what they wore; and the most influential Monastic Order.

Betrothal

In the Middle Ages a 'Betrothal'...what today we call an 'Engagement' was like a marriage. Blessed by a priest and accompanied by serious promises, you could not then marry anyone else without first formally being cleansed of your vows. It was because Edward IV married Elizabeth Woodville while still betrothed to Eleanor Butler that his children were later declared illegitimate, and his brother, Richard III, took over the throne. In Victorian times a broken engagement by a man, without consent, could lead to a suit for Breach of Promise! Very serious stuff!

Bilges

The very bottom of a ship, below the lowest deck cover, where loose water from leaks, rain or sea can collect and then be pumped or bailed out.

438

Blazon	The heraldic beast, or device, worn by a knight with its heraldic background.
Bliaut	Long over gown, often pleated, worn by both men and women. Very popular for generations and made of every material known in those days.
Borel folk	Illiterate country workers
Brigandine	A tough leather coat studded with metal plates, where the plates are *underneath* the jacket, not on top like a byrnie.
Bulwarks	The sides of a ship above the deck, as opposed to 'Bulkheads' which are dividing partitions below deck.
Byrnie	A tough leather coat to which metal plates, scale armour or chain mail has been fixed. Sometimes just thick boiled leather with loose chain mail on top.
Cable	A 'cable' is taken from the length of an anchor cable in the days of sail, usually 100 fathoms. Six feet to a fathom; so, 600ft in imperial measurement, about 200 yards. Officially one tenth of a nautical mile!
Cabochon	Gemstones were not 'cut' as such in those days, they were shaped and polished. The cutting wheel was not invented until the late 1400's, and true faceted stones, as we know them today, not until after 1914.
Cambric	A light-weight material made from Egyptian cotton and used for making fine shirts, or night gowns.
Candia	Candia, the modern city of Heraklion, on Crete. The whole island was then an outpost of Venice and famed for its slave trade. Candia was seized by the Ottoman Turks in 1669 after a sixteen year siege. The longest siege in History!
Cantle	The high back to a medieval saddle
Casque	The round dome-topped helmet that came in around this time, sometimes with a nasal protector, sometimes with a perforated faceplate when it was known as a 'salt cellar'
Chausses	Trousers, usually leather, like the 'chaps' worn by cowboys, but could be any favoured material. Often

overstitched with chain mail, and covered by a long hauberk.

Chemise	An under shirt, or blouse, could be of almost any material to suit the wearer, the occasion and the purse! Worn by both sexes. Sometimes took the place of a girl's shift or nightdress.
Chain Mail	The most usual form of body defence at this time. Best chain mail was a mass of individual iron rings riveted and interlocked one around another, weighed around 80lbs and covered the wearer from head to foot. In these times the hood, and the mittens, were an integral part of the whole suit, and it took two men to help put it on and pull it off.
Christian mail	This was much thicker and heavier than Eastern mail, and Syrian arrows could not pierce it!
Cistercians	White monks, and the greatest sheep and cattle breeders of the Middle Ages
'Clack' of wine	A large swallow or good mouthful of wine.
Collops	A cut of meat, usually venison but can be beef or lamb.
Crenellations	The proper name for 'Battlements'. The Crenel is the gap between the Merlons...the upright 'teeth' that make up the battlements. Any knight wishing to turn his earth and timber castle into a stone one had first to get a 'Licence to Crenellate' from the King. Any castle built without Royal authority was illegal...Adulterine!...and could be destroyed.
Curtain wall	That stretch of battlemented wall that lies-'hangs'-like a curtain, between one tower and another around a castle.
Cyclas	A knight's long over dress, only ever worn over armour, that carried his blazon, usually of white material...but could be coloured.
Demesne	The home farm
Destrier	A trained war horse, or charger...hugely expensive. Cross between a Shire and a heavy hunter. Now an extinct breed.

440

Devil Wind	Today this is called 'La Tramontane' and blows violently from the North West down the Pyrenees towards the Mediterranean, sometimes with torrential rain. It howls and rages and can drive people mad, hence its name!
Djinns	Muslim Spirits of fire, we call them Geniis, made famous by Aladdin! Can be really evil, and always tricksy, Can assume human form, often hideous and sometimes found in bottles!
Diana	Roman Goddess of the Moon and Hunting: her twin brother, Apollo, tricked her into shooting her lover Orion in the head while escaping from a giant scorpion. Her father, Zeus/Jupiter, could not make him immortal, but put him in the sky alongside her, so she could be still be with him every night. Ahhhh! Bless!
Drudges	Menial servants, usually women, who worked in the kitchens or about the castle, doing manual labour.
Doucets	The testicles of a deer: quite a delicacy when cooked in a white wine sauce.
Doxy	A low born mistress, or woman of uncertain morals, often found in ale-houses…what today might be called a 'tart' or a 'slag'. One up from being a whore!
Ermine	The white body and black tail of a stoat in its winter colours; very exclusive and very expensive. Used for the edges of valuable clothes, even a lining, and as a decorative background for a knight's blazon: still worn today in full House of Lords regalia.
Fetlocks	The lovely long hairy bits above and around a horse's hooves
Fewmets	The droppings of any hunted game animal, but especially of deer, as in this case.
Fistula	A long, narrow pipe like ulcer that forms in a duct between different organs.
Flambeaux	Flaring beacons in an iron basket on an iron stand, very much like a giant torch.

Friars	Wandering monks, usually in brown habits. The Franciscans wore grey.
Furlong	A measurement of land, still used in horse racing today. One eighth of a mile - 220yards. A cricket pitch is one tenth of a furlong!
Gambeson	Like a thick eiderdown, a tough leather coat, split to the waist between the legs for ease of movement, stuffed with wool and stitched all over in pockets to maintain conformity. Usually worn under a knight's chainmail armour to protect him from the battering effect of weapons in combat.
Garderobe	A loo. Great things to look for when out castling
Gralloch	The gutting of a deer after a kill, usually done immediately; and in past times all the lights and offal were given to the hounds.
Great Helm	A close fitted barrel helmet made of hammered iron, or steel if you could afford it, with slits for the eyes and perforated for breathing. Padded with wool and straw and fitted almost to the shoulders. Secured by a strap under the chin and sometimes connected to the waist by a chain. Many crusaders had a cross shaped piece of iron/steel across the front and over the back of it for additional strength: could be domed or flat.
Greek Fire	Truly a horrendous weapon, and remains a real mystery even today. Modern chemists believe it was a form of napalm, probably petrol-based based, with pine resin, sulphur and maybe saltpetre added: but no-one's quite sure! Water spread it and it could only be extinguished with sand, vinegar or old urine! Only the Eastern Emperors had the recipe, and it died with the last of them at the fall of Constantinople in 1453. It could also be pumped out like a flame thrower through a great siphon from the bows of a galley...or used in grenades with a wick of some sort. The Moslems tried to replicate it but were unable to perfect it. Their's was known as 'Arab Fire' and seems not to have been nearly so explosive as true Greek fire.

Guerdon	A reward to a Knight for his courage and his chivalry, usually from a Lady as a symbol of her love, and often given before going into battle or at a Tournament, signalled by the gift of a piece of silk placed around the end of his lance…to be reclaimed afterwards.
Hauberk	A knight's jacket, or whole coat, of chain-mail or overlapping scale armour, sometimes loose and worn over a gambeson; sometimes stitched or riveted to a tough leather jacket/coat and by our times reaching to the ground if the knight could afford it.
Heater shield	Shaped like the bottom of an iron. Easier to use than the kite shaped shield of earlier years: came into fashion about this time.
Herne the Hunter	Mythical God of the Forests and of the great beasts of the forest also, probably of Celtic origin
Jack	Leather 'Jacks' were the tankards of the Middle Ages, and hugely popular everywhere…they remained in use right up to the 20th Century. Only in England were they made waterproof.
Kist	A large wooden chest, for clothes or armour, often strengthened with iron or brass. In the case of the Royal Treasury…literally filled with gold and silver coins!
Marchpane	What we call Marzipan. Name changed in the 19th century.
Meinie/meisnie	A knight's personal armed followers, his own household troops.
Mie	Your lover: could be used for a much cherished child
Mistral (Le)	Violent cold wind that blows down the Rhône valley from the Alps into the Mediterranean basin, and can cause sudden ferocious storms. Usually blows for about three days. Can combine with La Tramontane to cause even more trouble. Napoleon passed a law that excused 'Crimes of Passion' if committed when the Mistral had blown for more than three days!
Liripipe	A long tail of material attached to a hood, that acted like a scarf in foul weather.

443

Lure	An essential falconry item for recovering a bird: usually the wings of a wood pigeon, because the grey and white feathers flicker when it is swung, or some other game bird. Sometimes fixed to a small piece of wood and then to a long cord that can be whirled round and round to attract the falcon/hawk, with a tasty lump of meat tied on its back to reward the bird when it has been successfully 'lured'.
Lymer	A scent hound, like a bloodhound, but wholly different in shape from today.
Mangonel	A siege weapon, sometimes like a giant crossbow on wheels, sometimes with an upright bar against which a throwing arm could strike instead of a bow.
Mantling	What a bird of prey does to protect its kill, by drawing its shoulders...its wings, right over the prey object. Bats do the same thing.
Medium	Usually a woman through whom Spirits can be heard and even seen when in a trance.
Merlons	The upright 'teeth' that make up the battlements of a castle.
Meurtrières	Murder holes in the roof of a castle gateway passage through which boiling oil or any kind of missile could be poured or hurled upon an enemy below.
Nemesis	Traditionally the daughter of Zeus and the distributer of Fortune and Retribution, neither Good nor Bad necessarily, but each in due proportion to what was deserved. Often seen as the implacable distributer of Divine Retribution against Hubris...human arrogance before the gods!
Orphrey	Beautifully intricate embroidery, often with gold and silver thread, very expensive and very popular at this time.
Ouches	Great broaches of intricately worked gold and precious stones most used to pin a cloak to the shoulders.
Outremer	This word literally means...'Outside the Realm'...and could apply to anywhere beyond the borders of one's

444

own country; but by the time of this story had come to signify the Holy Land! No King could make his Barons go 'Outremer'...he could only persuade them to do so.

Palantir	A Seer Stone, a great crystal ball used by anyone of sufficient intellect and mental power to view things from afar, sometimes through a Medium.
Palfrey	A light riding horse, little bigger than a pony and usually ridden by a woman. Infinitely more delicate than a destrier, or even a rouncey.
Paynims	A very medieval word for a heathen, a pagan, or any kind of Moslem infidel.
Pommel	The high front of a medieval saddle, or the weighted handle end of a sword, iron or steel, sometimes with a fancy jewel set into it.
Poniard	A dagger with a fine pointed blade.
Quillons	The cross piece at the top of a sword or dagger: could be chased...incised... with gold or silver.
Rache hound	Like a modern fox hound. Hunted by scent and sight.
Reeve	A vitally important post held by an important villager who was annually elected by the village/Manor to manage the manpower on the estate. He was given the authority to beat those whose work was poor or slack and he brought wrongdoers before the monthly Manor Court if necessary.
Revetted	Lined with shaped stone
Rouncey	A breed of Spanish horse that was most popular at this time as a 'maid-of-all-work'. About fifteen hands, so not a large animal, but sturdy and strong in work.
Sabatons	Steel boots that could be worn over the foot mail.
Sarcenet	A thick silk material used for lining garments.
Sendal	The finest of silk material used as a lady's light over gown or negligée.

Sconces	Wall fittings for holding a torch, or a big candle. The torches themselves were usually made of long bundles of reeds, or strips of unseasoned soft wood, usually pine, tightly bound together and dipped in pine resin; could come in a portable metal holder.
Scorpion	Similar to a small mangonel sometimes with a sling: a torsion weapon.
Sanglier	The wild boar, big and dangerous, especially around mating in the autumn, or if cornered…or sows with shoats at heel who feel threatened and will defend their young with extreme vigour! A large male can weigh over 600lbs and have five inch tushes that are razor sharp and deadly. Usually nocturnal, but can be seen in early morning or evening.
Seneschal/Steward	A hugely important post on any great estate, or in the Kingdom; usually a member of the Knightly class, like Sir James at Malwood, often a family member on a big estate, who 'ran' everything in the absence of his Lord, or alongside his Lord if he was at home.
Sheets	In sailing, 'sheets' are ropes for handling sails or spars.
Sherbet or Sharbat	A deliciously refreshing drink made with fresh fruit and spices, very popular in the Middle East where alcohol remains forbidden: even better with ice.
Shoats	Young wild boar; prettily striped in ochre, chocolate and cream for the first six months or so.
Sounder	A group of wild boar, usually sows, young males and babies. Adult males are much more solitary except at mating time in the autumn when, like rutting stags, they are at their most dangerous.
Sumpter	A horse used especially for carrying goods in boxes or whicker panniers carried on either side on a special frame called a 'crook'. Like the rouncey, not a big horse, but strong in work. What today would be called a 'Pack Horse'
Talbot	A very large pure white scenting dog for hunting game, now extinct. The heraldic beast of the Earls of Shrewsbury: like a big Dalmatian…but with a heavier

446

jaw and without the spots. Norman, very popular with the Conqueror.

Thews	The mighty muscles in any fighting man's strong arms and thighs!
Trebuchet	The 18" cannon of the medieval world. A huge stone throwing machine that could hurl a 300lb stone, or even a dead horse, over quarter of a mile! An enormous timber construction worked by a vast counterweight, with a throwing arm the size of a tall pine tree with a sling on the end. Monstrous and accurate. The best example of a full size working trebuchet is at Warwick Castle...and they have never tested theirs to the limit!
Trencher	A large, thick piece of stale bread that served as a plate on which your meaty meal could be served. A good 'trencher man' was one who finished off his meal by also eating his 'plate' having already eaten everything else!
Trumpet sleeves	Long deep sleeves, sometimes almost to the ground and often trimmed with ermine. The sleeve hangs down from the upper arm, which itself is usually tightly sleeved by an undergarment called a chemise...what we call a shirt or blouse.
Tushes	A wild boar's fighting tusks...up to five inches long and deadly!
Vassals	In the Middle Ages a Vassal was anyone holding land from, or owing allegiance to, someone else: peasants were vassals of their Lord, Lords were vassals to Barons and Earls...and all were vassals to the King who, in turn...technically...was a vassal of the Church, which sanctified his Kingship, the Church was a vassal of the Pope and the Pope was a Vassal of God! All of which led to terrible rows between Kings and the Church as to which was the greater, and whom should pay homage to whom! A knotty problem as you can see!
Verderers	Technically they were what today would be called 'Gamekeepers', with all the skills with birds, animals and habitat that that implies, but in the Middle Ages

	they were also Officers of the Law; and given tough powers of Life or Death over poachers!
Vexin (The)	This was a small buffer 'state' between Normandy and the lands ruled directly by the King of France. Remember, France was not a wholly independent country. Very powerful Barons, like Richard - who 'owned' two thirds of France in 1190! – could do, and did, exactly as they wished. So 'The Vexin' was really hot property, and caused huge problems between the Kings of England and the Kings of France!
Wimple	This was usually a very simply made woman's headdress held in place with a fillet of precious metal, or a different piece of material. Not the hugely elaborate headgear that came into fashion in the fifteenth century!
Withers	A horse's shoulders.
Wolves	Typical European timber wolf…and were a real menace in the Middle Ages, specially if the winter was cruel, forcing them to seek food from the farms and villages….so very much a part of Gui and Alicia's life in the Forest in 1190. The last British wolf was shot in Scotland in 1680, and extinct throughout the British Isles by the late 1700's
Zeus	The Olympian King of the Gods, whom the Romans called Jupiter or Jove.

Very Simple Heraldry

Blazon	The whole coat-of-arms, including any heraldic beast on its field.
Colours	Azure: Blue; Gules: Red; Vert: Green; Purpure: Purple; Sable: Black.
Metals	Silver: Argent; Gold: Or: These also double as White and Yellow as Field backgrounds.
Fields	Background colours, metals or furs on which the principal device of each family is painted.

Furs	Ermine: White with black tails...the stoat in winter colours.
Heraldic Beasts	Too many to mention. I have used several, including dragons, stags, wild boar and lions:
	Lion Rampant...upright on his back feet, forward facing, paws up...De Malwood
	Lion Rampant and Gardant...upright on his back feet, paws up but looking at you...Richard L'Eveque
	Stag's Head Erased...just the antlered head of a stag looking at you...De Burley
	Boar's Head Erased: Just the tushed head of a wild boar looking forward and upwards...De Brocas
Heraldic Beasts Armed	Claws, teeth and tushes all coloured or metalled differently from the main beast: EG: 'armed gules'...all the 'bits' appropriate to the beast described on the blazon but coloured red. Stags are 'attired' not 'armed'.
Langued	Tongues coloured or metalled.

The Lion and the White Rose Series

The Lion and the White Rose

The White Rose and The Lady

The White Rose Betrayed (12.11)

The Lion and the White Rose Triumphant. (2012)